MW00680253

The Black Lily

The Arestea Chronicles
Book One

Mandy & G.D. Burkhead

The Black Lily
The Arestea Chronicles, Book One

Text copyright © 2017 Mandy and G.D. Burkhead
All Rights Reserved

Second Edition 2020

The characters and events in this book are fictitious.
Any resemblance to persons living or dead is strictly
coincidental and unintentional.

ISBN: 978-0-9989866-5-4 (print)
ISBN: 978-0-9989866-6-1 (ebook)

Cover designed by J. Caleb Clark
Arestean crest designed by G.D. Burkhead

Title page font: "FireFlight"
Book font: "Book Antiqua"

Burkshelf

Acknowledgements

First and most importantly, we would like to thank our parents: Angie Burkhead, Gary Burkhead, and Kim and Ron French. You all taught us the importance of following our dreams (while still keeping a day job to pay the bills). We love you.

We would like to send a huge thank you to our mentor and beta reader Jonathan French. You helped us hone our book to perfection and taught us many of the ins and outs of self-publishing. Thank you, sensei.

We would also like to thank the other wonderful people that helped us to polish our writing styles over the years: Mandy's high school writing teacher Ted Huddleston, G.D.'s gifted program teacher Debbie Hunkins, and our mutual Lindenwood University professors Spencer Hurst, Ann Canale, George Hickenlooper, Erica Blum, and the late, great Rift Fournier.

A huge thanks to our cover designer, J. Caleb Clark, who designed the incredible cover for our second edition.

One

Lord Geoffrey thrust into his whore one last time before spending himself. He rolled off her with a grunt, making his way towards the door that led to the privy.

"Leaving already, m'lord?" she asked. She reached out a hand as he skirted around the bed, but he swatted it away.

The Hidden Pearl was one of the classiest brothels in town and served only a very select clientele. The madame was a strict timekeeper, using her hourglass to determine the clients' fees. While Geoffrey appreciated that the madame kept young, nubile women like he preferred — this one couldn't be over fifteen — that didn't mean he was going to waste his money cuddling with a whore after he'd gotten what he needed.

After he finished pissing, Lord Geoffrey turned towards the water basin to clean himself up and froze. There, lying gently in the pitcher of clean water, was a flower.

It was a lily, dyed black, just like the one he had found in his home this morning, resting on his pillow.

He stormed back into the bedroom, the flower clenched in his hand. "What is the meaning of this?" he roared at the young prostitute.

She sat up, backing away from his sudden anger. "I don't know!" she squeaked. "A lover's token! I thought it was pretty, so I put it in the vase!"

Mandy & G.D. Burkhead

"Who's the lover?" he demanded. "What does he look like?"

She shook her head. "There was no name attached. It was just delivered in a box. Nothing else. I thought the color a bit odd, but—"

"Foolish whore!" he spat, reaching across the bed and backhanding her. The girl screamed and burst into tears. She scurried off of the bed and gathered up her clothes before rushing out of the room, slamming the door behind her.

The nobleman glared after her, then crushed the dyed flower in his hand before throwing it to the ground and stomping on it. Lilies were not a common flower in this region, and nobody bothered to dye them just for decorative purposes, especially not black. Except for one person—one whom nobody wished to meet. One of these lilies did not appear anywhere simply by accident or strange coincidence. His whore had to be extremely ignorant to not know of this particular flower's notoriety.

Lord Geoffrey hastily redressed before heading for the door himself. He reached for the latch but yanked back with a gasp just as a knife embedded itself into the door where his hand had been moments before.

The nobleman stared at it in shock, unmoving.

"Leaving already, m'lord?" came a feminine voice from behind him, mimicking the prostitute's accent. Upon hearing the voice, he turned around slowly, glaring at her.

A female figure stood before him, clad in black leather armor, all but her eyes shrouded from sight. He tried to count the number of sheathed weapons she carried but quickly gave up. "I could scream," he warned her.

"Oh, how manly!" she said, and her light-hearted laughter filled the room. "You're in a brothel, sir. No one will notice you scream or care if they do. But I'm guessing from that threat, your expression, and your sudden hurry to leave that you already know who I am and why I'm here."

His mouth formed a grim line and his back straightened. "I know who you are," he replied, "though I certainly didn't expect that you were a woman. As to why you're here…I have many enemies. It is only a matter of whom I upset enough this time to justify the expense of sending *you* in particular after me."

She gave a mocking bow. "I thank you for the compliment, my lord. As for the whom, you need look no further than your only surviving offspring."

"Rebeckah?" he muttered to himself in disbelief.

"When she learned that her brother, his wife, and their unborn child had been burned alive in their home, she wanted revenge on the murderer. She came to us to find out who did it, and to kill the person responsible." The woman shrugged. "Investigation isn't usually our thing, but her coin was good, so we took the job. We brought her the arsonist, but he begged for his life, offering up the name of the man who'd hired him. Imagine her shock to learn that her own father had left her an only child. After some long thought on the matter, she extended the contract."

Lord Geoffrey's lip curled. "It was one of my estates, actually, and my son should have known better than to offend me by marrying that filthy *peasant*." He spit out the last word. It left a bad taste in his mouth.

"Yes, terrible thing that, him marrying. Perfectly good reason to kill someone."

He glared at her. "Not that it is any business of yours, but I never meant for my son to die as well, just that whore he got with child and married out of guilt. He was going to sully our lineage with her blood. I had summoned him to my home; I thought he would be en route to visit me." Geoffrey felt his throat tighten in grief. "I did not expect him to disobey. His death was an accident."

"But you had no problem murdering a pregnant woman." Her eyes narrowed, becoming predatory. "I tire of our banter. Shall we get on with it then?"

He did not offer a reply, but instead spun towards the door and grabbed the hilt of the knife. It gave after a few sharp tugs, and he turned back, wielding it in front of him. Looking at the small woman that stood before him, he wasn't sure that she could really be the infamous assassin known as the Black Lily. Perhaps she was simply one of many? There had to be more with as many people as the Black Lily had taken out in the past five years. But even so, he knew he couldn't risk underestimating her. How had she even managed to reach the window of his rented room on the third floor of a brothel in a busy city without being seen? "If they would have let my guards into the brothel with me," he grumbled, "you would be dead by now."

"Oh my lord, it saddens me that you think so little of me," she taunted. "And here you were admiring the expense of my services only moments before. You

4

ought to know by now that we high-priced girls are worth every copper." By the brightening of her eyes, he guessed her to be grinning under her mask. "You came here to play, and so did I. So let us play."

And without further warning she rushed at him like a cat bounding at its prey. He responded, slashing the knife at her midsection, but she sidestepped it easily and caught his wrist as it flailed by. With a squeeze and a twist, she made him gasp in pain and drop the knife, while she spun around behind him, bringing his wrist with her. With his arm bent awkwardly behind his back and his hand still tingling, the nobleman felt her heel drive into the back of his knee and send him collapsing down to the floor, his nose pressed against the thick carpet, his assailant on top of him in nearly the same position he'd been on top of his whore not too long before.

"How shall we do it, my lord?" she whispered in his ear. "If you are nice to me, I'll make it quick and clean, and your widow will only have to gaze upon you in your coffin with a broken neck."

"Damn you to every level of hell!" he growled into the carpet fibers. "I should see you hanging from the gallows like your friend Robert!" He felt her stiffen against him at that, and despite his predicament, found it in him to sneer one last time. "Oh yes, assassin, we've all heard the tale. You're not all as untouchable as you would have us believe. I was there in Treventre right after it happened, you know. I saw the crows pecking at his body as it swung in the breeze! I'm surprised you weren't all caught and hanged, with the information they tortured out of him!"

She was quiet for a moment after that. He must have struck a nerve; a small victory, but he'd take it. Then she sighed. "Just for that, I don't think I'll go with quick and clean after all," she replied, and he didn't miss the barely contained rage in her voice as she leaned over him, her lips at his ear. "Tell me, *my lord,*" she whispered, "have you ever heard the old adage, 'Don't cut off your nose to spite your face?'"

The parlor of the Hidden Pearl brothel was a small room, made smaller by the vast number of partially and fully nude bodies occupying it. Cigar smoke mixed with the heavy scents of liquor, perfume, and sweat. Women lounged on the couches, draped over their patrons for the evening, entertaining them with stories and songs. Some had not made it upstairs to their rented rooms and had instead begun plying their trade in the midst of the revelry, sometimes in groups of three or four. Dark, heavy drapes veiled the windows, so as not to give a free show to any curious passersby too poor to pay their way inside. The only light came from the low burning candles that reflected off of the soft exposed breasts and thighs of the women and men.

The cheerful music and laughter that filled the brothel parlor was interrupted by a piercing scream. The gathered patrons didn't have long to murmur in speculation, though, before the cry faded out, replaced by a frantic crashing in the stairwell. A moment later, the stairwell door burst open and a man stumbled quickly into the parlor, his fine shirt and the hand over his face covered in dark, red blood. It ran freely out onto the floor, dripping onto the feet of those nearest him. The closest of the staff and patrons scrambled up from their couches or tables, backing away from the horrific sight as a gasp of fright ran through the crowd, an unfortunate few unable to avoid being spattered by his gushing blood.

The man lurched forward as if drunk, reaching his bloody hand out to the assembled masses, and through the torrents running down over his mouth and chin they could see a gaping, ragged hole in the center of his face where his nose should have been. He seemed as if he were trying to speak as he took his last, wobbling steps and fell to his knees. His eyes were wide but glazed as he turned his maimed face this way and that; but when he opened his mouth, there was only a small, ragged nub of meat where his tongue should have been, wriggling futilely.

No one could make out his words or do anything to help him even had they not all been rooted to the spot in shock. Within moments, the bleeding man collapsed forward to the floor, twitched once, and fell still, blood still pouring from his face and mouth and pooling under his head, staining the lush carpet. The house matron, the first person to work up the nerve to get closer to the man, found him already dead, his skin pale from blood loss, his wide eyes glossy in pain and terror.

When the town guard arrived at the scene, they found his nose and tongue tucked into his coat pocket, along with a curious flower. It was crushed and crumpled, its petals torn, what was left of its stem bent and broken. Nonetheless, the genus of the flower was unmistakable, as was its strange coloring.

By morning, the tale had spread throughout the city and was already making its way to the countryside beyond.

Two

Just outside the city of Treventre, nestled in the side of a large hill, was an old mine that had long since been abandoned by the locals and was now believed to be haunted. The rumors spread by the Guild long before Lily's time, along with fear of cave ins from the lack of upkeep, kept most of the city folk from ever going near the mines. It helped that those who did occasionally wander in never survived, their bodies sometimes found later on the mountainside — though the deaths of those unlucky or curious few were not the result of restless spirits.

It was in these mines that the headquarters of the assassin's Guild resided, and from there that their shadowy hand stretched out across the country and beyond, controlling their smaller outposts located in every major city, their fingers in every part of Arestea's politics — as well as several of its neighboring countries, including Aluvia, Beuteland, and Ovinurland. It had no name besides the Guild, though Lily had tried again and again to get them to rename it something flashier and clever, like the Guild of Silencers or the Shadow Hand or the House of Ending. Each time, Guildmaster Gavriel would gently but firmly remind her that their Guild was built around secrecy, and that it functioned best by not drawing undue attention to itself.

Lily made her way through the labyrinth of stone halls that she called home, past the kitchen and training rooms, the bathing room that was fed by an underground stream, and finally reached her own bedroom. Even though it was the only permanent home she knew, she was hardly ever there, as was the case with the ten other assassins operating out of the main Guild branch. They were almost always out on a mission—usually working out contracts, spying on the nobility and other likely marks, and, of course, ending lives.

The lantern she held before her cast long shadows on the stone floor beneath her feet. She slid back the curtain that passed for her door, glad for the welcome sight of her own room: her small but comfortable cot; her armoire filled with disguises for any occasion; her library of books and odd trinkets resting on shelves carved right into the smooth, hard granite walls; and a vase of preserved black lilies atop the small table beside her bed. There were only two left after her last job. Time for the next harvest, then.

Hanging her lantern on the hook in the ceiling, she stripped off her bloody garb and threw it in the corner of the room to wash later. Out of her armoire came the drabbest outfit she owned: a rough-spun, oversized tunic and pair of thick trousers with dirt stains so deep in the knees they were part of the fabric by now. Slipping into these and fastening a light cloak over the ensemble, she took the lantern and made her way back through the cavernous halls, heading deeper into the base before finding the corridor that headed up a slight incline.

A short walk later, she turned a corner and squeezed through a tight crevasse to emerge onto the mountainside. Here the ground evened out into a gentle slope just wide enough for a miniature meadow to take hold. No outside paths led up to this small, grassy plain, and neither did any lead further up into the rocky crags above. Here they kept a small garden to grow the food needed to sustain them while at home, as well as deadly plants and herbs used for creating poisons.

With the evening sun still hovering on the horizon, she didn't need the lantern, so she set it beside the doorway she'd just passed through. Even with her practiced eye and familiarity of the place, it could still be somewhat difficult picking out the crack in the stone that led back in from the rest of the nearly identical boulders behind her. Skirting around tomatoes and belladonna, carrots and nightshade, she came to her personal flower garden. The delicate white trumpet petals of her namesake peeked from the surrounding grass and wavered in the cool mountain breeze. She liked to imagine they were greeting her, welcoming her home after her long absence.

And in the center of the flowers was a small flat stone with a name carved into it.

Robert.

It had nothing else, no dates, no epitaph. Honestly, she didn't know when he was born, though the day of his death would always be etched into her memory. It wasn't a true grave…it housed his skull, stolen from a spike in the public square of Treventre. An outdated, barbaric tradition, one that had been mostly done away with, but the capture of a high-ranking assassin had led the Duke of that city to believe it was worth making an

11

exception. And for that, Lily was thankful, because at least it allowed her to bring part of him home to the Guild.

With a smile, the assassin sank to her knees amid the lilies and set about weeding and pruning with the only knife she kept that wasn't designated as a weapon. Tending to her plants was her favorite pastime besides the thrill of stalking and ending a mark, and it gave her time to think, to reflect on her recent successes and her upcoming assignments, and when that had run its course, to just let her mind empty. Master Gavriel touted the benefits of regular meditation, but Lily much preferred gardening to simply sitting and doing nothing. She was most relaxed when her hands were kept busy.

Her flowers trimmed and tended, she selected a half-dozen of the oldest looking blooms, carefully picking them and setting them aside. By the time she had finished, the sunset was threatening to drain away the last of the day's light, so she gathered her bundle and headed back inside. There was a special dye she kept in her room that would preserve the plants while also giving the petals the long-lasting black sheen that was her trademark. The formula had been a gift from a former lover, though the black dye had been her own touch. She rather enjoyed that young woman's company, so she'd been careful not to feed her too much information about her gardening hobby, lest her lover intuit too much and need to be put down.

She'd barely made it back to her room and set down her bouquet when she heard soft footsteps outside her room. "Lily?" a voice called, quiet and airy.

Lily brushed the curtain back to see an older woman standing there, her long, blonde- and gray-streaked hair pulled back in a tight ponytail, her face damp with sweat from recent exercise.

"Yes, Marianne?" Lily answered. Normally the woman wouldn't bother her in her room; assassins tended to keep to themselves. If they weren't training or eating together, they usually left each other alone. While there was no animosity between them, they couldn't call each other friends, so she found it curious that the woman would pay her a visit.

"Master Gavriel wanted to see you," Marianne explained. "He asked you come immediately, that he has something very important to talk to you about."

"Alright," Lily replied. "Thanks." She waited until Marianne had left, then stripped out of her gardening clothes and into a soft velvet robe to keep off the subterranean cold. Lily paused to admire the cherry blossoms decorating it, remembering when Robert had brought it back for her upon returning from a kill far across the ocean. Once she was passably presentable, she made her way to her master's chamber. It was set off by itself at the very back end of the man-made caverns, the largest of the bedrooms, and one of the few in this renovated settlement to boast a heavy oaken door rather than just a thick, muffling curtain. They all enjoyed their privacy, but Master Gavriel above all others guarded his with a care bordering on the zealous, though none of them could blame him.

Lily reached the door and stopped, not bothering to lift a hand and knock. She'd learned early in her time here that it was a wasted gesture. "Enter," her master's deep voice called through the portal nearly as soon as she'd reached it.

She did as she was bade, stepping into a room filled with priceless treasures from all over the world. Hidden behind one such treasure, a masterwork of a painting long since thought destroyed, was a crevasse in the stone. At first glance it seemed like any other crack in the wall until one slipped inside of it and discovered a hidden tunnel which led to an escape route out of the mines. It was just one of many that ran in all directions out of the mountain should they ever be discovered and attacked. Learning them all intimately was one of the first tasks any new assassin needed to accomplish; keeping them free and clear of debris, pests, and the occasional squatter in the form of a bear or a lost traveler was a bothersome but necessary chore that they were all required to perform now and again. She hoped that wasn't what this meeting was about.

Keeping her expression neutral through long practice, Lily sat in the only chair in front of Master Gavriel's desk, draping one leg lazily over the other. She didn't care that the pose made her robe fall open, revealing the milky skin of her thigh, and she knew that her master didn't either. In fact, Gavriel seemed not even to notice it, but instead looked her straight in the eyes with his storm-gray gaze.

When they had first taken her in as a child of eight, she had been afraid of him. As the years passed and her body changed, her fear transformed into curiosity, and she had dreamed that one day he might fall in love with her and marry her, making her the mistress of the

Guild. It didn't bother her then that he was more than twice her age, for he was ruggedly handsome. He still was, even in his fifties, with exotic ebony skin and long grey braids that hung down to the middle of his back. As a child, she had adored him and worshiped the ground he walked on. But he had never shown even a passing interest in her, nor in any of his assassins, as anything other than useful tools to be honed and sharpened. As she grew older, Lily realized that her affection for him was not truly love or even lust, but simply a deep respect for the incredible man that he was.

After a moment, his lips lifted in a rare smile and he tossed a sack of coins on the desk between them. "My congratulations on an excellent job, child," he said. "The nobleman killed in a crowded brothel, with none having seen the assassin enter or leave, has become the talk of the town. Some think it was political, but rumor spreads easily, and most have figured out it might have something to do with his family issues. The prostitute was questioned, of course, but they could find no connection between her and the assassination. How, then, did your calling card end up there before you even arrived?"

"It was easy enough," answered Lily with a self-satisfied smirk. "I simply sent it to the girl claiming to be a secret admirer. I asked her to light a candle and place it in her window when Lord Geoffrey arrived to have his fill of her, as was his weekly ritual, telling her that after he had gone I would whisk her away and she would never have to see or hear from him again. I'd learned that she despised him greatly, rough brute that he was. And I kept my promise. She never *will* have to see or hear from him again now, nor will anyone else."

"I hear that's not the only flower you left him. One in his home as well? On his own pillow?" Gavriel lifted an eyebrow, and Lily grinned; but when his smile suddenly vanished, so did hers. This had been a test, hadn't it? He did not return her amusement.

"You can't deny a girl a little bit of fun, can you, Master?" she asked, trying not to show her disappointment.

Gavriel's eyes narrowed. "That was very dangerous for you to do. You could have been caught had he suspected when and where you would strike at him. I have told you many times before that you need be more careful. When you put yourself at risk, you put us all at risk."

Lily rolled her eyes, decorum forgotten. "He's dead, just as the client requested. And I was not caught, and no harm is done. Well, not to us, anyway." When she saw that he still did not look pleased, Lily sighed in exasperation. "What do you expect? He was such a boringly easy target. Give me someone more exciting next time! You sent Sa'heel to the Meli islands last month after a mark. I want to go somewhere exotic!"

"Enough!" Gavriel lifted a hand to silence her, and Lily sat back in her chair, pouting. "In the sixteen years since you joined us, you've made quite a name for yourself, Lily. While I don't always agree with the…flamboyancy of your methods, I'm proud of you. But discipline has ever been one of your bigger shortcomings. Ours is a venerable, if taboo, profession;

see that you comport yourself with dignity, both on the job and here at home."

Lily sighed, then solemnly bowed her head. "I'm sorry, Master," she said. "I sometimes forget myself. I will do better."

Gavriel nodded. "That said," he continued, "you're in luck. You want a more exciting assignment, and you shall have one. In fact, what you have done up until now will seem like child's play once you receive your next mark. I have been setting it up for a number of years now, and we are finally able to take the first step. But I believe only you are worthy to fulfill this contract. It is, perhaps, the most important one you will ever receive."

Lily's eyebrows rose at that. Gavriel had never been known for his theatrics. "Alright," she said, "you have my interest. What is it, Master?"

Leaning back in his chair, Master Gavriel steepled his fingers. "You will infiltrate the imperial palace to murder King Alec and his successor."

Lily blinked in surprise, then let a lazy grin spread across her face. The king and his brother, the crown prince. Dead at her hands. Her calling card would be left—just the one this time, restrained, like her Master had chided her—and all would know who'd done it. She would take her place in the history books to be speculated about for ages. She would become the most infamous assassin in the entire nation—no, even in other nations they would fear her, all over the world. She had been waiting for a job like this her entire life.

"I shall take a coach there and have it done in a fortnight," she told her master as she rose to go, already planning the kill in her head. But he raised his hand with a shake of his head, stopping her. She sank back down into the chair in disappointment.

"You are eager as ever, I see," Gavriel said. "That is good. You will need that. But you will also need patience for this assignment. You cannot kill the king immediately." He rose from his seat and walked around to the front of his desk while Lily sat and listened. "It will be difficult for you to gain access to the castle, and a quick hit-and-run is out of the question. This is no mere murder we undertake now, but a carefully plotted political move that we have devised with the client, to be unraveled in a number of necessary steps. You will have to work your way closer to the king in stages while still avoiding the public's eye. You must remove them both at once when the time is right, but not a moment before." He sat back against the edge of his desk, arms crossed over his chest. "Also, there is the problem that removing the king and his only heir to the imperial line will cause a power vacuum that must then be filled. The result in most circumstances would be utter chaos in the kingdom."

"Unless we were the ones to fill it," Lily said thoughtfully.

"Indeed," replied her master with a nod. "We are working out the details right now with our client. The gentleman in question wishes to remain anonymous for the moment, until he is certain that you are in position to strike. Then he will make himself known. We will send messengers occasionally to check on you, but other than that, you will be completely alone in the castle. So you must act with utmost caution."

Lily nodded, excitement welling up once more despite his many warnings. "What would you have me do, Master?" she asked.

"Infiltrate the castle, as I said. Then make yourself known to the king. Given common knowledge about King Alec's tastes and behavior, I believe you already know what this will likely entail. Become present at his side at all times; shadow his every movement. Wait. Watch. Listen. Any useful information that you may be able to gather—political secrets, upcoming military maneuvers, blind spots in our knowledge of the palace layout—send it back to us. Even once our puppet is installed, it behooves us to have inside information from another source. We will send a messenger to you every other month for your report. Then, when the time is right, we will send in our puppet. You will make sure he is well situated and ready to take power, and only *then* will you eliminate the king and the prince, leaving him the throne. Do it right, and you may even be able to stay in the castle and assist our puppet as he takes the kingdom's reins."

She listened intently, taking mental notes, then bowed her head. "As you wish, Master," she said, then rose and took her leave. No sooner had his door closed behind her than she was hurrying to her room once more with a wide grin on her face, already planning what she would need to pack.

She paused to glance at herself in the looking glass, holding up a lock of chestnut colored hair. Perhaps it was time for a change. Something more eye catching.

A sheet of rain fell heavily from clouds so dark they turned the midmorning skies black. The pouring rain churned the dirt of the small, bumpy country road to mud in the farmland beyond Gemadina, the royal capital of Aluvia. Farmers brought their equipment in from their fields, ranchers herded their livestock to shelter, and children ran shouting through the rain to their homes or to their nearest neighbor.

The driver of a small, black carriage, the only one on this muddy stretch of road, could only turn up his collar against the storm and hunker further into his seat as he guided the horses slowly through the pouring rain. Inside and protected from the elements, his passengers, two young courtesans from the royal court, sat silently across from one another and stared out the window through a gap in the curtain, watching their homeland creep by. Long black hair fell in waves from their heads past their shoulders, lying gently on the dark skin of their exposed shoulders and décolletages, which bulged from tightly laced, jeweled corsets. Thick layers of silk skirts puffed out below their waists—a ridiculous and unwieldy fashion choice, they both agreed, but apparently it was the latest style in this strange country that they were headed to. And though they would not be in Arestea until the next day, and not in the royal capital Luceran until perhaps a few days after, it would not do to arrive before the king in his court and appear anything less than graceful in the noble attire of their new patron's culture. And so they suffered the excess fabric and constraining corsetry during their journey in order to become at least passingly familiar with it.

They were pulled from their tedious and silent reveries when they realized that their carriage was slowing, until it soon came to a complete stop. "What is this?" Rosalita, the elder of the two by half a year, asked her companion with a frown. "We've barely left. Why stop so soon?"

"Perhaps our driver forgot something?" her junior, Olivia, said as she stifled a yawn. "Perhaps we need to turn around."

"Gods above, I hope not," said Rosalita, tugging at her dress and adjusting her seat, trying to get more comfortable. She gave up after a few seconds and slumped back against the carriage wall. "I've already made my peace with leaving. I'd rather just get this damnable trip over with as soon as possible."

A moment later, they heard the clop of hooves and the rattle of wheels drawing closer from behind them, down the road back toward Gemadina. Olivia twitched the curtain on the door aside further and they both peered out into the rain, trying to catch a glimpse of the approaching carriage.

"Good morning," they heard the driver of the other carriage call as it rolled to a stop beside their own. "Sorry for the inconvenience. Glad I caught you before you got any further, though."

"And what's so important you were sent to chase me down in this weather?" their own driver asked. "Did the king forget something before he sent me off?" They heard him dismount from his seat and land in the mud, cursing under his breath as he walked past the window toward this new arrival. He glanced at the two and gave them a shrug as he passed, and the two women crowded the same bench to try and peer further through the window.

"Actually, yes," the other man answered, and they heard him dismount as well. "Or some*one*, anyway. One more gift for their King Alec. Only seems this one was fashionably late and missed her ride."

"Say what now?" their driver asked. They heard footsteps and a pause, then, "Oh, another one? How many courtesans does one king need, anyway? My papers only mention passage for two."

"His majesty evidently thinks it's better to seem too generous than not enough, I suppose. Here, updated papers. Add them to your pile."

"Damn bureaucracy." There was a click as a door opened, and then their driver came back to their window. "Well, in you go then, miss, more's the merrier," he said as he opened their door, and Rosalita and Olivia both slid back on their bench away from the rain as another young woman hurried over and hopped in.

She was smaller and a bit paler than the both of them, dressed in a thick cloak of forest green over a sapphire blue dress in the same style as their own, tight and fitted at the bust and waist and flaring into ruffled layers in the skirt. As she sat down across from them and pulled back her hood, long curls of dark red hair spilled out, far too vivid to be her natural color. The newcomer glanced at them both with dark hazel eyes and offered a sheepish grin.

"How was she late to an arranged carriage ride with this many kings involved, anyway?" their driver asked his fellow.

"Caught up with her hair or her makeup, I don't know," the other driver answered. "You know how high-class women can get."

"Three beauties like that just handed to another nation," they heard their own driver grumble. "You'd think Arestea was a damn dragon we had to appease with tributes of maidens to keep it from eating us."

"Isn't it?" the other man asked. There was a creak as he got back in his seat, and a soft whinny from one of his horses, impatient to get going again. "His majesty seems to think so, at least."

"Hmph. Almost makes you wish for actual dragons again," their driver grumbled as he passed their door and climbed into his own seat, sending the carriage rocking slightly. "At least that sounds like a straightforward problem. None of this political chicanery."

"If magic ever comes back, my friend, you can have your dragons," the other driver called. There was the muted snap of reins, then more shuffling hoof beats and creaking of wheels as he turned his now empty vehicle around behind them. "Me, I'll stick to paperwork and ferrying pretty women about. Safe travels."

"Same to you," their driver called back, then snapped his own reins. A moment later, the carriage was rolling slowly forward again, the washed-out landscape passing leisurely by their window once more.

Rosalita and Olivia both waited for their new companion to speak, but she did not seem interested in making conversation. "Well, they called us beauties," Olivia said, leaning against her companion, "so I suppose I'll forgive the high maintenance cracks." She pointed with her chin toward the newcomer. "But who is this one? I've never seen you in court before."

"Your patron was King Emiliano himself, yes?" the redhead asked. "Mine was Baron Obedo, who offered my service to the king when he heard of his majesty's plan to appease Arestea. In truth, I have only laid eyes on the king just the one time." She bowed her head toward them both. "I'm Camilla. Nice to meet you both."

"Rosalita, and this is Olivia," Rosalita said, then shook her head. "So you nearly made it into the palace, but now you're stuck here with us? Your luck is shit, dear."

Camilla chuckled. "Perhaps," she said, slipping off her traveling cloak. "I prefer to think of it as an adventure."

"That's one way of looking at it, anyway," said Olivia, slumping in her seat. "I'm honored to have been chosen for this, I suppose, but to be honest, I'm not looking forward to learning a whole new court. I can barely understand the language they've got there. You?" she asked, glancing sidelong at Rosalita.

"I can read a bit," her companion said with a sigh. "And I can speak a few basic words. There was never any need to be fluent in Emiliano's palace. That's what the translators were for. And besides, who would have

24

thought that King Emiliano would become so indebted to the king of Arestea in just a few short years?"

"Well, perhaps they'll provide a translator for us once we arrive, then," Olivia said.

"Perhaps I'll be able to help on that front," Camilla chimed in, smiling. "I have a passing grasp of Arestean myself. Not eloquently so, but enough to get by with, I believe."

Rosalita's brows raised. "Oh really?" she asked. "Where did you pick that up?"

Camilla shrugged. "I lived nearer the border for a time before coming into the baron's service," she explained. "We had merchants and the like passing through often enough. All of my family learned at least a little of the language just from proximity, though I don't speak it as well as some of my siblings."

"Good," said Olivia. "Then with you here, hopefully we can take our time learning ourselves. I hate studying."

"Lucky for us you didn't miss the ride after all," Rosalita chimed in. "If only just barely."

"Yes, so why *were* you so late?" Olivia asked. "Please don't say you were really doing your hair."

"I, uh…was, though," Camilla answered with a slight blush, twining a crimson lock around her finger. "After all, I wanted to stand out when we arrived. And trying to fit into this damnable dress," she added, hooking her fingers into the top of her corset and prying it slightly away from her body to take a deeper breath.

Rosalita and Olivia shared a glance, then sighed in unison. "Well, can't say we don't sympathize," said

Rosalita. "Settle into it, though. It's going to be a long trip."

Camilla only nodded and relaxed back against her seat. It had been a long trip for her already, crossing the border from Treventre and skirting Gemadina in time to intercept the courtesans' carriage, only to ride it slowly back the way she'd come. Hopefully, she thought, when she made it to King Alec's palace, she wouldn't need to see the inside of a carriage for a long while.

For now, all she could do was casually practice her alibi with these two ladies and wait.

Three

"My lord, presenting a recent gift from Emiliano I, King of Aluvia: three of the most beautiful courtesans of the Aluvian court sent to your care as a cultural exchange and as a token of friendship between his country and our own." The announcer bowed to his king and stepped aside with a flourishing wave to the three women behind him. "The misses Olivia, Rosalita, and Camilla."

In unison and with matching smiles, Olivia, Rosalita, and Lily all curtsied to the man on the dais before them.

As Lily straightened, she first glanced about to take in the opulence of the throne room. It was certainly a sight to behold, as the palace was designed with the intention to dazzle and awe those at court.

The entire palace was surrounded by a huge stone wall. As they'd ridden in the gates just minutes earlier, she had observed the usual necessary buildings: several stables, an armory, the kitchens separate from the main palace for fear of fire, and barracks for the guards to sleep in. While even these more functional buildings were architecturally beautiful, they were overshadowed by the enormous, stories-tall palace that dwarfed them. Past a large fountain and front gardens was a long staircase that led up to the front doors of the main floor, with the throne room at the end of a luxurious corridor full of paintings of previous kings and queens.

And behind two opulent double doors was the throne room itself. This was the heart of the palace, where generations of monarchs had reigned over their people, met with courtiers for official business, and hosted elegant balls. The white vaulted ceiling was intricately carved in geometric and floral patterns. Tall windows of intricate glass panes ran from the floor to the ceiling flanked by huge, thick drapes of red velvet, offering stunning views of the palace grounds bathed in sunset and sparkling with recent rain. Hanging above the gathered crowd, large crystal chandeliers sparkled from high up in the ceiling, illuminating the green and white marble floors and the golden filigree on the white marble walls.

Against the far wall from the entryway, the centerpiece of the whole court and the focus of everyone's attention, the royal throne stood out on its dais for how ancient it looked compared to the modern interior. It was made of a dark, heavy wood — mahogany, she guessed — the armrests of which were worn from generations of rulers. Except for the red cushions, it looked thoroughly uncomfortable. Carved into the end of the armrests were two lion's heads, their maws open in mid-roar. The high back reached above the king's head and depicted a dragon lifting its wings in flight.

The dragon was echoed in the royal coat of arms, which was painted on the wall above the imposing throne. The golden dragon adorned a purple shield, behind which a sword and a key were crossed in an X shape. A ribbon below held the d'Arestes name, and above the shield was a magnificent crown.

Slumped slightly in the throne, resting his goateed chin in his hand and watching the proceedings with an air of utter dispassion, sat a broad-figured and roguishly handsome man in his early thirties. Dark copper hair fell across brown eyes that appraised the women with boredom. His black and silver filigree doublet did little to hide the evidence of well-toned muscles beneath. Here was her mark: King Alec d'Arestes, current sovereign of the nation-turned-empire of Arestea, and by all accounts the most powerful man in the known world at the moment. So close, but still so far out of her reach by the standards of her mission. Lily stifled a shudder. These infiltration and deception jobs, the psychological tease of playing the game with a mark who didn't even realize what he was caught up in, it was almost like foreplay.

King Alec merely regarded the three of them through half-lidded eyes for a moment after their curtsying, then sat up a little straighter and stifled a yawn. "So this is either appeasement or tribute, and a lackluster job of it either way," he said, though whom he was addressing, if anyone, was questionable. "Three whole women. Yes, that's just as good as a hundred million acres of land and resources and a nation's worth of new tax-paying subjects, thank you heartily, Emiliano. Honestly, I don't think I've even intimated that I have any designs on conquering Aluvia, have I?"

The announcer who had introduced the women blinked and looked around, then frowned at his king. "Are you asking *me*, Sire?"

"Anyone, really," the king answered. "I forget who all I've discussed my plans with. Brother?" He turned to look up at the young man standing beside the throne. "Have I said anything about trying to take Aluvia, d'you recall?"

"Somewhat," the younger man standing beside the throne said with a sigh. "I believe your words were, 'There'd be no point in it anytime soon, the trade's good and we're decent enough allies.' I think you also called the idea 'tacky.'" He didn't look at the king as he spoke, but gazed with the same dark brown eyes out at nothing over the court's collective heads.

Lily mentally checked him off as well—Adrian d'Arestes, younger brother by seven years to the king and next in line for the throne since there was no queen and thus no royal heirs. The family resemblance was obvious, but standing beside his rakish brother, the comparatively scrawny and clean-shaven crown prince could not look any less interesting. Still, he was her secondary target, so she wouldn't have the luxury of ignoring him as the rest of the court seemed wont to do.

"Right," said the king, nodding at his brother's counsel, if such was the word. "Well then, the onus is on him for thinking the worst of me. Honestly, now I almost feel insulted." He waved a multi-ringed hand at the three women still standing in attendance at the foot of the dais. "Well, ladies, play us a song or something to brighten up this drudge of an evening," he ordered, then sat back again and gazed out over the expanse of his courtroom.

As if to accentuate his words, thunder rumbled once more, indicating that the brief lapse in rain was indeed only temporary. The rain and clouds had travelled with them from Gemadina and cast a damper over their arrival, and now tonight every noise made in the brightly lit but currently sparsely populated hall echoed from the walls and columns with each lapse into silence.

The announcer shifted his attention between the courtesans and his king, then bowed again to the latter. "M'lord, it would appear that the ladies do not yet understand our language well, being so recently immigrated. I understand they were chosen for...certain qualities of theirs beyond cultural familiarity."

"Of course," the king said with another sigh. "How silly of me to think our dear Emiliano would offer us servants who could at least understand what we say to them. That would be entirely too practical." His gaze roamed the rich outfits of the women before him, lingering longest on what they didn't cover, and his lips twitched in a smirk. "Still, I suppose there *is* undeniable value in a silent woman. It would certainly prove a refreshing change of pace from the constant empty babble of the other ladies of court I must put up with day in and day out."

A few such ladies were in attendance in this very court, Lily noticed, and yet none spoke up or showed any noticeable reaction to the king's words. It appeared the accounts she'd heard of him were true, then, if the assembled nobility was no longer shocked by or even took notice of such brusqueness.

Lily took this moment to step forward, eyes downcast in practiced meekness, and whispered gently, "If King Alec allow me, I know some of language. Us play you?" She nodded to where a harp sat in the corner of the room.

"Play me?" the king answered. "Yes, I daresay you will before too much longer." He smiled and waved a hand at the harp. "For now, though, yes, a song, why not?"

Lily curtsied once more, then made her way to the harp, motioning at her two traveling companions to follow. She gave them a quick explanation in their native tongue, inquiring as to which of the two of them was better skilled at the harp. Rosalita quickly volunteered, taking a seat at the harp, and began playing the notes of a well-known Aluvian song. Lily took the lead, allowing Olivia to supply the chorus.

As Lily sang, she glanced up at the king from under her eyelashes, hoping to catch his attention. He returned those glances without any particular show of interest. She leaned forward so that the soft light of a nearby sconce lit up her face, and her breasts heaved languidly out of the top of her tightly laced corset. King Alec only nudged the prince beside him and began to converse with his brother in hushed whispers, ignoring her but for the occasional glance.

She knew beautiful women would be one of his weaknesses — even if it weren't detailed in her dossier on him, the whole nation had by now heard of the king's habits. That said, the most powerful man in the world couldn't be expected to drool over every pretty girl that crossed his path. Was this jadedness on his part, or was his air of boredom simply sapping his attention?

She let the blood red tendrils of her hair fall into her face, half-shrouding her eyes, and licked her lips, sending him a breathless look. Laying it on a bit too strong, perhaps, she thought, but she'd met few men in her work so far that didn't at least falter in the face of outright and blatant seduction. King Alec was now completely ignoring her, though, engrossed in his conversation with his brother. She fought back a twinge of frustration and focused instead on her singing. Not like she wouldn't have plenty of time and opportunity going forward.

Then the main door to the throne room burst open suddenly, startling her and all others assembled, so that the song broke off midway on a sour note. A man stormed into the room, flanked by two royal guards who made a show of attempting to restrain him while being very careful not to actually touch him for fear of giving offense. The fact that they did not simply grab him by his very expensive clothing showed that he was powerful enough to command the respect of even palace guardsmen, whoever he was, and his entrance did not seem to surprise the king. In fact, as Lily observed, Alec's eyes finally lit up at the intrusion. Either the nobleman had been expected, or else the stir he caused was a welcome respite for the king.

"My lord," the announcer complained, turning to the newcomer, "you must be presented before you enter the royal court. It is only proper."

The nobleman glared at him and shook off the guards. When he answered, it was to the king. "I think all propriety has already been abandoned, has it not, Alec?"

33

The king raised his arms and his eyebrows in amusement, an innocent look on his face. "Why, whatever could you mean, good Duke Frederick? Tell me, to what do I owe this delightful reunion?" To the questioning looks his guards gave him, he merely waved his hand. They backed away, bowing nervously.

"You know what you've done, Alec," the nobleman growled, face contorted by poorly-contained rage as he jabbed a finger at the throne, "and this time you have simply gone too far!"

The king chuckled. "Then please, friend, enlighten your king on his own business. How might I have caused so sour a mood in such a sensible, level-headed man as yourself?"

The duke stepped forward, mounting the first step of the royal dais and lowering his voice. Rosalita decided that this would be the best time to resume the harp, perhaps to create a calmer atmosphere, and Lily tried not to roll her eyes in annoyance. Unable to overhear the conversation any longer, she read their lips instead.

"You know what you did...to my daughter," Frederick was saying. "She will never be marriageable again because of this! How dare you, Alec, after everything I've done for you! Do you know how quickly your campaigns in Beuteland would have fallen apart without the support of my duchy? And this is my thanks? How could you ruin her?"

King Alec did not bother to keep his voice down for the sake of propriety. In fact, he raised it so all in the room could here. "Oh, this is about your lovely daughter? But dear Wilhelmina raised no such argument during her stay with me." He grinned. "Quite the contrary, in fact; she simply would not *stop* voicing her gratitude. You know, at one point I had to stuff her knickers in her mouth so the servants wouldn't hear and come running, she was making such a ruckus."

Duke Frederick, losing his composure, raised his voice as well. "Only because you led her to believe you would take her as your queen if she proved the first of your *conquests* to finally be begotten with your child!"

The king scoffed. "Nonsense. I made no such promises of marriage." He leaned forward then, finally attentive for the first time Lily had seen so far. "Why, *is* she begotten with my child?"

"Thankfully no," Frederick answered, reining in his temper a bit. "But now that her purity has been ruined, and the fact so widely known thanks to your indiscretion, I will never be able to marry her off to the caliber of husband she deserves. She has been shamed, and she can no longer show her face in public without courting slander."

King Alec shrugged. "I confess, I can't see how that would be a problem for anyone," he said. "You had me worried for a moment there that my brother would have competition for the throne in the tragic event of my death. Since that's not the case, all that's left is the issue of Wilhelmina's 'purity,' as you say. Honestly, any man who turns down marriage to a woman like her on such ridiculous standards is an idiot." He raised a hand to forestall the lord's argument, then continued. "But let me console you, Frederick, since this clearly upsets you so much. In light of your complaint, I will grant your daughter a large dowry as recompense. Feel free to use it as a bargaining chip in her potential marriage suits."

The lord sputtered a moment in shock, but then his stance relaxed somewhat. "You—you will?"

"Of course. It is the least I could do. I will give her an estate—I believe there's an empty one in Hertfordshire, correct? I'm not using it. All I ask is that, in return, you refrain from these outbursts in the future in the event that I…pay her a visit every now and again." King Alec grinned once more. "She is a grown woman, after all, able to make her own decisions about the company she keeps, is she not?"

Lord Frederick's fists clenched. "My daughter is not a whore to be bought, Your Grace," he grumbled. "But…I suppose, if it will allow me to marry her off…I accept."

"Excellent." The king's grin grew wider then, and his gaze turned wistfully up toward the ceiling. "But Fred, just between you and me—and I say this with the utmost concern for you and your family, you understand—I would not be so certain, were I you, that her purity was something that I did indeed ruin. I remember having the distinct impression at the time that that was something I had missed my chance to do." He shrugged again. "Well, that or she was simply born blessed with some very interesting talents. If marrying her off doesn't pan out, she could always be a master orator with that mouth of hers."

At this last slander, any goodwill the king had bought back shattered. The nobleman flew into a rage and stormed the dais with a wordless roar of anger.

And while Duke Frederick wore no visible weapons, Lily suddenly caught sight of a brief glint of metal as he pulled his hand from his coat on his way to the still-smirking king.

Any visitors to the king's court—nobles, petitioners, courtiers, and courtesans—were first asked to remove their weapons to prevent any attempts at assassination. Even Lily and her companions had not been exempt from this caution, their ruffled skirts patted down thoroughly in case an errant dagger had found its way into the folds. Gods knew nothing else would have fit in their corsets. It would have to be a very small blade, then, only a few inches, to have escaped notice. But that was still long enough to do unacceptable damage.

Lily's instincts kicked in. In the moments it took the nobleman to mount the second stair, she glanced at the soldiers and quickly sized them up. They had yet to realize what was happening. They could stop the lord easily if they moved in time, but they wouldn't. Her eyes darted to the king, to whom the realization of the danger he was in was only just visibly dawning. If he died here and now, she failed.

The harp crashed discordantly to the ground as she pushed it out of her way, throwing herself at the would-be amateur assassin and tackling him to the floor just as he reached the throne. He certainly didn't see her coming, and it was simple enough to grab the knife from his hand and fling it across the room as they tumbled down the stairs together, spilling to the marble floor. He stared at her in shock when they'd stopped rolling, her on top of him, and as she gazed down at his frightened face, the familiar urge to finish him off almost overwhelming her. She dug her fingers into his neck, ready to twist it, anticipating the feel of his bones crunching under her hands, his windpipe crushing, his life ending beneath her. For a tense moment, as a courtier screamed in panic, the sound drowned out by her heart thudding in her ears, killer instinct almost won out.

But then the shouts of the guards froze her and brought her back to the present. She realized, as they pried her away from her intended victim, what she'd been about to do. She would have blown her cover. She would have revealed everything in a moment, a stupid moment, of amateurish, uncontained bloodlust. Lily shook her head to clear her thoughts, the guards staring at her as if she'd suddenly grown horns. But they quickly forgot about her when the downed nobleman began scrambling toward his lost dagger. One of the guards stomped on the small blade before he could reach it, while two others hefted him from the floor by his arms and subdued him at sword point.

King Alec, now on his feet, was the next to recover. He began to applaud in genuine amusement as a red-faced and sputtering Lord Frederick was dragged back out of the court by the king's men-at-arms. "Brava, my dear, brava!" he said as he stepped down off the dais. "When I demand you entertain me, you don't disappoint! What is your name, love?"

The bloodlust still pounding in her veins, Lily was caught off guard by his address. She curtsied belatedly, feeling genuinely awkward this time. "C-Camilla, lord," she muttered.

"Camilla," he repeated with a smile. "I like you. A quick mind, quick reflexes, and an obvious willingness to risk life and limb for your new king. All good things to have in a servant. If you would be so kind as to grace me with your presence tonight at dinner, I would consider myself a lucky man."

"Your wish, lord," she replied, bobbing in another curtsy. The king nodded at this, then turned and walked away behind the throne, exiting the room through a private side door. If memory served correctly, that would be the great hall, where the lords and ladies took their meals.

The meager crowd behind her erupted in a low buzz then, shock and disbelief mingling with open admiration of the new Aluvian courtesan and several declarations of intent to relay the evening's events to peers throughout the kingdom. Lily sighed in relief at the averted crisis, then walked back to the overturned harp and helped Olivia and Rosalita lift it back into its place.

Prince Adrian was behind her when she turned around again, watching her curiously. "Yes, lord?" she asked nervously. In all the commotion, she'd forgotten about him completely.

"That...was amazing," he said. "Truly incredible, especially for a courtesan. Are you all right after all that, my lady? You weren't hurt, were you?"

His sudden interest in her took her off guard. Was that suspicion she heard in his tone? For a moment, she knew she glared at him by accident. "No, I not hurt," she said simply, reassessing him. Perhaps he had caught and misread her signals at the harp earlier. Did he think she had been flirting with *him*? And why was he calling her a lady, when she was clearly only a courtesan?

"Ah. Good," he said with a nod and a smile. "Take care then, my lady." And without another word or glance at her, he turned on his heel and followed his older brother out of the room.

She stared after him with narrowed eyes. Something strange was going on inside his head, she decided. He'd expressed a quick interest in her but didn't follow it up. Perhaps he would make his next move during dinner that night. Lily made a mental note to herself to pay more attention to him next time, at least until she could figure out his motives.

She turned to the king's announcer. "Sir, I have…tired," she said then, pretending to stumble over her words. "Where to sleep?"

"Ah, yes," he answered. "You all must be exhausted after your ride here and all of this excitement. Come, I'll show you to your quarters."

The ladies followed him silently, making their way through winding corridors as they listened to their guide repeat a memorized tour in a bored drone. This is where Prince or Princess So-and-So played a few generations back, here is the balcony where a noblewoman jumped or was pushed to her death, this is where a certain retainer was caught conspiring against the crown, here is the spot where a bloody duel took place, etc. Since they'd established that only Camilla knew any of the language, she translated for her companions. She was glad for the maps she had studied earlier, for the castle was expansive, and without them she knew she would be thoroughly lost by now.

When they finally reached their quarters, in the east wing of the palace overlooking a small enclosed garden with a pond, she found that they had been given a fairly nice suite in the guest area. She was pleasantly surprised that the king had honored them with an apartment with separate bedrooms for each of the women. Their trunks of clothing had already been deposited into their rooms, and there was a portable oaken bathtub hidden behind a screen in the living room, full of warm water for them to bathe in in turn. After showing the trio to this last stop, the announcer bowed politely and made his exit.

Lily headed immediately to her own bedroom, leaving Rosalita and Olivia to argue over who got the bath first. In her quarters she found a large, luxurious four-poster bed, a clean chamber pot tucked underneath, a single window overlooking a tiny courtyard and another wall across the way, and a huge armoire, the doors of which were open, revealing the rump of an elderly maid sticking out of it.

"Hello?" Lily asked politely, startling the maid, who straightened up. She was cute, in an old way, with sagging jowls and plenty of womanly curves. Her eyes, after first taking in Lily's vivid red hair and low-cut décolletage, finally rested on Lily's face, kind but cautious.

"Oh, hello, my dear. I was just finishing putting your things away, though one of your trunks was locked and I couldn't find a key to it." She apologized as she motioned to the final trunk, a large case of black leather that sat on the immaculately made bed.

"Oh no, is good. I put away. You rest." Lily gestured to a small wooden chair that sat beside a vanity, a basin of water sitting on its tabletop and a mirror behind it for her to clean herself in the morning.

The woman seemed surprised by this, and it was obvious to Lily she wasn't used to such kindness, either from those she worked for or from the courtesans. "Oh, are you quite certain?" she asked. "If you just let me borrow the key, I could put everything else away for you." Seeing Lily shake her head and smile, her eyes softened. "Well, all right then. Thank you, ma'am."

Before she could sit down to rest, however, there was a call in Aluvian from Olivia in the living room. The maid looked to the door in confusion. Then, after the call repeated, this time by Rosalita, she glanced at Lily with a nervous look on her face. "Do the other, um, ladies speak our Arestean?"

"Oh, no," Lily answered, "only Aluvian. She asks help. With bath." Lily gestured to her hair, indicating that the courtesan needed help rinsing it out.

"Oh, I see. Well, okay, then. I'll let you know when your bath is ready. I'll even get one of the young lads to fetch fresh warm water just for you." The maid gave her a wink and dipped a quick curtsy as she departed the room, closing the door behind her. Pleased, Lily locked it behind her. She had found that with servants, a little kindness often went a long way.

Lily knew better than to trust in the palace locks; after all, the servants would certainly have keys to allow them access to the bedrooms for cleaning. But it gave her a measure of privacy while she unlocked her trunk, removing undergarments that lay inside and folding them neatly on the bed, then opened the false bottom, revealing her stash of weapons.

It was only a small arsenal: ten daggers of assorted sizes for throwing and stabbing, a blade-edged decorative fan, a couple of vials of poison, a small lock pick set, a wire garrote that retracted inside a bracelet, a length of rope (unfortunately she had to leave the grappling hook at home due to the weight), and a tiny crossbow and quiver of compact, unfletched bolts. Nothing compared to what she had to pick from at home, but more than enough for a subterfuge job like this one, regicide or not. Also in the false bottom was a small bundle of her dyed lilies, protected in a cedar box so they wouldn't be crushed. One for the king, one for the prince, and a couple extras just in case circumstances demanded them. Underneath all of this was an assortment of tightly packed costumes and wigs to fit various positions in society—a serving maid's outfit, a page boy's livery, a ragged, dirty brown peasant dress, and of course her assassin's garb.

This last item she pulled out and examined happily, running her hands over it. Each assassin had one that was custom made. The bodysuit was a strange, foreign material that was as soft as silk and both skintight and flexible. The supple leather armor was just enough to protect the vital organs without hindering movement. It wasn't quite black, but more of dark gray with a tint of midnight blue when the light hit it. She completed the ensemble with a hood and soft, silent leather boots with tiny grips on the bottom that prevented her from sliding around when walking on polished floors or scaling walls.

She quickly replaced her assassin's garb in the trunk before returning the false bottom, relocking it, and sliding it under the bed where no one would see it.

The entrance phase was over, and barring the minor fiasco with Duke Frederick, she'd been inserted perfectly into palace life. Now all that remained was the watching and waiting. She had to be ready to strike at a moment's notice; when the time came, it would come swiftly, and she would be gone before any thought to suspect her, leaving behind only her lilies and an infamous legacy unrivaled by any other assassin in history.

Smiling to herself, Lily unpinned her hair and undid the awful corset. Not long after, the maid knocked on the door. After such a lengthy journey and all of that careful strategy, she decided, a long, hot bath was well deserved.

Four

"Dear Alec, what do you *call* this dish?" the Duchess of Montflos asked of the plate set before her, prodding the food with a hesitant fork.

"*Wurzfleisch*, dear Prudence," the king answered, lifting a forkful and pointing it at the Duchess. "A Beuteland delicacy, so I'm told. First time being served on Arestean soil, actually."

"Ah, yes," the Duke of Montflos drawled as a passing waiter filled his wineglass, "and how *is* Beuteland this time of year?" He scooped a forkful of the dish into his mouth, then closed his eyes and made a show of savoring the taste while Alec's attention was on him.

"You expect me to know this, Henry?" the king asked around a mouthful of *wurzfleisch*. "I do not, for the most part, actually go to the places I conquer, you understand—that's what the army is for. Incredibly useful things, armies. Saves me the long walk. Much easier kinging that way."

"Oh, Alec, you *knave*," laughed the Duchess.

Lily wished she could turn a deaf ear to the conversation, but every scrap of info gained might be important, no matter how inane its presentation. She smiled at the servant as he poured her wine, then took a bite of the slimy brown-and-yellow glop on her plate. Some kind of creamed meat. It was revolting, but she suppressed her disgust and ate casually with an outwardly interested eye to the conversation.

She sat at the head table in the Great Hall, an honor for any noble, and most especially a courtesan. This table was raised above the others at the front of the room, allowing all the courtiers a reminder of who was in favor. Courtiers schemed, fought, bribed, and wheedled to be seated at that table and the king's right hand.

The Duke and Duchess of Montflos were easily written off in her mind — pompous aristocrats in fancy clothes going through the motions of being delighted in the king's hospitality. Montflos was a large but mostly rural and undeveloped region to the west of the royal city, filled with rolling green fields and natural flower beds of every color stretching out to the horizon. Or it had been a few generations ago, until an expanding population drove the need for agricultural production up. Montflos's lush greens were tilled over to make room for crops, but in their rush to capitalize on heightened demand, the growers got too greedy with their land.

Today Montflos was an irony, a large swath of struggling, stunted grass and oversized, failed farms. This made it one of the poorest duchies currently on the books in Arestea, and the duke and duchess relied heavily on the king's favor for societal standing and privileges, including a sizeable tax break that none of the other Arestean nobility were particularly happy about. As such, they spent more time in the royal palace than at home, shadowing and yessiring the king.

"And how *is* the expansion going, Sire?" the Duke of Lakeview asked as he pushed his food in circles on his plate. "Any other neighbors we've subjugated recently? How do we stand with Ovinurland?" The Duke of Lakeview was a young, thin man seldom seen at the palace unless it became necessary for him to be there.

Lakeview, unlike Montflos, had a thriving economy thanks to good fishing and a healthy forest, and the Duke had no problem paying his taxes. Furthermore, judging by information the Guild recorded from past meetings of the royal council, as well as his own disposition now at the table, Lily understood that he took a cynical, almost treasonous view of his country's recent expansion efforts. She made a note to herself to verify his status on the matter to the Guild when next they contacted her; perhaps he could be useful in installing the puppet when he arrived.

"Ovinurland is exceptionally quiet as of late, actually," King Alec informed him. He drained his wine and held the glass aloft to signal a waiter for more. "We've not had a skirmish with them since we began the invasion of Beuteland. Our massing size is making them flinch—they know they can't risk provoking us with seasonal raids anymore, so they're trying to slip off the map of our attention before we turn our sights on them next." He steepled his hands and smirked at the Duke of Lakeview overtop of them. "By enriching our empire, I've also bought us relief from the northern barbarians. A nice turnout, don't you think?"

"*Tremendous,* m'lord," the Duchess of Montflos trilled. Her husband raised his glass to the king. The

Duke of Lakeview merely grunted in assent and turned his attention back to his plate.

"At any rate, I think we'll take a break for the year. Begin again next spring," the king continued. "Our soldiers are just come home from fresh victory, and our empire is seeing an unparalleled period of growth, economically and culturally." He shoveled a forkful of *wurzfleisch* into his mouth for emphasis, swallowed, then continued. "Now's a time for rest and regrouping. Come winter, I'll have come to a decision on Aluvia. Emiliano practically insulted me today in court, you remember, with his blatant attempt at bribery."

All eyes turned to Lily then, none of them discreetly. "Could it not also be said though, Sire," said the Duke of Lakeview, "that King Emiliano, in an offhanded fashion, also saved your life? Had the young lady not been near your side this evening when Frederick attacked you—"

"Honestly, what was *with* dear Freddy?" the Duchess interrupted. "Such a *tantrum*! It is deplorable. There are *proper* channels for these things, you know. Peer of the realm and all, yes, that's very nice, but it is no call for *rudeness.* Honestly."

"Rather impressive show on the young lady's part, I do say," her husband said, smiling at the new courtesan through his bushy mustache. "Does she understand anything we've been saying, d'you think?"

"She understood just fine in court, if you remember," the Duke of Lakeview answered before she could say anything. "Spoke the language as well, if falteringly." He raised his wineglass to his lips and mumbled, "Wonder how she feels about us discussing going to war with her homeland in front of her," before taking a drink.

Lily bowed her head to the group. "Is alright," she said softly. "Aluvia no home now. Arestea new home. Yes, lord?"

The king grinned and raised his glass to her across the table. "Yes, lady. Well said. You see, Raoul?" he said to the Duke of Lakeview. "Nothing to worry about. You worry too much about stepping on toes. But I'm an excellent dancer, Raoul, and by extension, so is Arestea."

"Respectfully, Sire, I don't think that metaphor quite works," Duke Raoul returned.

"You know what I mean," the king argued. "Besides, I doubt it'll come to war with Aluvia. We've great trade with them lately, and Emiliano's not stupid, despite what his gambit may seem to indicate. The fact that he even made it shows desperation, I think. No, with the right approach, I think Aluvia can be integrated diplomatically, bit by bit."

The Duke and Duchess of Montflos clapped lightly at that, and Lily joined in after a belated moment. She smiled at her king, catching his eye for a moment before he turned back to his food. The nobleman's sudden attack had jangled her nerves when it happened, a potentially major snag in the beginning of the fabric she was trying to weave, but she had to admit now that it had done her well in the end. She had planned on passing her first few weeks as a nobody before she got the king comfortable enough to allow her near him when he was with his nobles, yet here she was at a private dinner with three other leading aristocrats.

Their acclimation to her would open even more doors in the palace and more secrets of recent inner-circle politics, and her public show of risking her life to save the king would all but ensure she was overlooked as his murderer when the time came.

As she thought this, she caught her gaze drifting to the chair beside the king, opposite the duchess. Prince Adrian sat at his brother's right hand, eating calmly and contributing so little to the conversation that most of the table, herself included, seemed to have trouble remembering he was there—an ability she found unnerving. He glanced at her more than anyone else, though, including the king himself. Half the time he made clumsy attempts to hide his gazes, but she always knew when his eyes were on her. She had come to dinner with him in mind, with learning his intentions as a secondary motive after gaining the king's growing trust. So far, though, he had given her nothing new to go on. She might have to make the next move herself. What could a foreign courtesan say to a prince that wouldn't look like she was taking untoward interest in him?

"Oh, and did you *hear* about Geoffrey?" the duchess asked then, dropping her voice to a whisper, then raising her whispering volume so everyone could still hear. "They found him bled to death in a *brothel*! With his *nose* cut off!" Her gloved hand flew to her lips as if this were the first time she'd heard the news herself. "Can you *imagine*?"

"Now, dear, is this really appropriate dinner conversation?" her husband chided.

She ignored him. "They say it wasn't just murder, that he was *assassinated*! No one knows why. They thought it was the girl he was with what killed him until they found a black lily in his pocket."

"The Black Lily," the Duke of Lakeview said with a smirk, swirling his wine. "That's quite a high-end name to send after old Geoffrey. The man must have done something gruesomely offensive to somebody to earn that kind of attention."

"And this just after his son's tragic death," the Duchess continued. "You remember the fire? The boy and his wife both, burned alive inside their home! How *horrible*. And his poor Rebeckah…how she'll go on now after losing her brother and father both, I haven't a clue." She jabbed her fork into her plate, launching into her meal with righteous indignation. "Whoever this so-called Black Lily is, I don't know how he can stand to live with himself after something like that, ruining such a sweet girl's life."

"The part I find most amazing is how no one has ever seen him," Duke Raoul said. "He's broken into nigh impenetrable castles before and killed some of the highest-ranking people inside, and yet somehow no one knew until the next morning. Some say he's a ghost…or a wizard."

"A wizard? Nonsense," scoffed the Duchess of Montflos. "Everyone knows magic is dead, over a half a millennium in its grave. Unless you count those fortune tellers in the marketplace, but they are all shams."

"There *are* still a few healers out there who claim to control the old magic," her husband replied. "I don't know who would trust smoke and chanting mumbo jumbo over honest medicine, but there you have it." He raised one bushy eyebrow as he turned to his wife. "And didn't you attend a séance just a few months ago, dear?"

"Yes, well, those are fashionable gatherings now, dear Henry. Something to liven up an otherwise dull salon. But everyone knows that they are fake; it's just fun and games, pretending to talk to the dead. It gives old widows some momentary comfort to think that their husbands still watch over them from the afterlife. Or for some, to have confirmation that that's really where they are." She lifted her wine glass to take a dainty sip before continuing. "Either way, I doubt that this assassin or any other is a wizard. The Black Lily is nothing more than a very clever madman, I imagine."

Lily had to daintily dab at her mouth at this point to hide her grin as she listened to their speculation. She stared down at her plate and willed her humor away. It was a novice move, she knew, letting pride compromise one's cover, but she was particularly happy with her latest work, and the nobility's total ignorance of the manner made her almost giddy with delight.

"Are you well, my lady?" the prince asked, his first words since the *wurzfleisch* was brought out. She glanced up to notice him looking at her with concern, everyone else's eyes naturally following his.

She cleared her throat and put her hand back in her lap, raising her head and smiling at him. "Yes, lord. Only throat tickle."

"Are you sure?" he continued. "You looked upset just now."

"Oh, leave the girl alone, Adrian," the king said, and all eyes turned back to him. "She said she was fine. This talk of grisly murder and wizardry probably set her off her appetite. Don't forget that they still fear black magic in parts of her country and burn supposed witches at the stake. Take this away," he added to a passing servant. "Bring out dessert. And dearest Prudence, please, do try and think of a happier topic of discussion. All of this politics and scandal is making me feel like I'm back in court again."

"Very well, m'lord," said the duchess brightly. "Have you seen the latest performance down at the Sapphire?"

The prince cast one last glance at Lily before turning back to his food. Lily put a faint and faraway smile on her face while she berated herself in the privacy of her head. She had wasted a chance to figure out his game again and had possibly even let him catch her smiling at what should have been a worrisome conversation. And now he was, by all obvious evidence, ignoring her once more. Was he biding his time before making whatever move he planned to make on her? If so, he was taking smaller and farther-between steps than most nobles would with a common servant. Or was he trying to undermine her in the eyes of the king? What little he'd said to her so far were all questions asking after her health, her physical condition, her state of mind.

Perhaps, she thought, he was trying to assert the impression that she was weak and fragile; perhaps her boldness in protecting the king had unnerved him somehow. It *was* unexpected behavior in a courtesan, she knew. Did he suspect her? Had she inadvertently tipped her hand to him where all others had failed to catch on? Her painted smile faltered for a second as the possibility took hold. If so, he was sharper than his peers. She would have to take pains to be extra careful around him from now on, just in case.

The following morning, Lily woke early, before the sun and even most of the palace staff were up. Dressed in a thin silk nightgown, she made her way toward the royal quarters, intent on creating a mental map that she could pen down and send back to the Guild. They were aware that throughout the castle were secret passages—some used by the servants to move about their work unseen, others by the king to spy on his guests, and still others for quick escape in the instance of an attack. However, the exact locations and the usefulness of these passages was more of a mystery; it was up to Lily, during her stay, to discover as many as she could and send the information back whenever a messenger arrived for her.

She spent most of the next hour roaming the halls, passing only the occasional servant cleaning or carrying a load of laundry. She smiled at each as she passed them, then once they were out of sight, peeked in doors and down intersecting halls, memorizing the layout. Besides the throne room and great hall, the main floor of the palace consisted of the chapel and library. Those she did not bother to visit at present, but instead wandered the second floor of the palace, which consisted of the living quarters.

On this floor was the king's private dining room for exclusive guests or special parties, as well as the offices of the king's counselors, his personal butler, the treasurer, certain diplomats, and other heads of the palace in charge of the actual running of the estate. Here also were the living quarters of the king's own personal guards, who were always kept close to the royal family. Down the west wing were two levels of expansive royal quarters, now inhabited by the king and his brother alone; across in the east wing were two stories of apartments for courtiers, their families, and their servants, complete with small private living rooms and bedrooms and shared bathing rooms. Between the two wings was the innermost and grandest courtyard, where multiple gardens flowered and summer parties and games were often held.

Just as the dawn was breaking, a door down the hall from her clicked and gently opened. It should have been an unused room. Due to the dwindling size of the royal family, most of the royal quarters on the second floor of the west wing were empty, save for the prince's suite. The third floor above was occupied solely by the king. Nevertheless, the door creaked open and a servant girl tiptoed out, closing it behind her.

The girl spun, then gave a start when she saw Lily. From the look on her face, she hadn't been expecting anyone on this floor either, especially a woman clad in dark clothing and not carrying a candle, despite the lack of light in this part of the palace at this hour. The girl held her own candle forward, getting a better look at Lily and allowing her a chance to study the servant in turn. She was perhaps eighteen or nineteen, though the lines on her face made her look older than she was. Under the dirt on her skin and her messy hair, she was quite pretty, with delicate features, light auburn hair, and bright green eyes.

"M'lady," she whispered, taking Lily's hand and pulling her down the hallway, "what are you doing up at this hour? You should be in bed, resting."

When she turned her back to Lily, the assassin's eyes caught the sight of blood, and she smelled it on the air. She let the girl take her around the corner, then stopped and tugged her back, staring at her in confusion. "What you do here?" she asked the servant. "These king's rooms, no?"

"Well, they haven't been used in years," the girl answered. "I just sleep here, on occasion. The beds are nicer. Ah, please don't tell."

She tried to move on then, but Lily stopped her once more. She reached a hand up, touching the girl's cheeks, which were wet, then her back. The servant flinched in pain. "You cry. There blood on back. Did someone hurt you? I will call guard!"

"No, no, my lady!" the girl said nervously, stopping Lily. "It's nothing."

The girl's vehement denial piqued Lily's interest. There was something odd happening here, and she wanted to know what it was. "Is not nothing. We go to healer," Lily demanded.

When it became apparent that Lily wouldn't budge without answers, the servant sighed. "Please, it's not what you're thinking. It's just a game we play," the servant continued, dropping the courtesan's hand. "Surely that can't be so strange to a...well a lady of your profession. But I'm married, and I can't have word of this getting to my husband. Please, my lady, return to your bed now and pretend you saw nothing here."

Lily nodded her agreement. "I not tell your secret, promise. But please, what are you called?" she asked.

"Oh," said the maid, then dipped a quick, awkward curtsy. "Irene, miss. Sorry to have troubled you."

"Camilla," Lily said with a smile. "And is no trouble."

Irene smiled meekly back, then left without another word, disappearing down a narrow servant's staircase. Lily went back to the room the girl had left, but found the door locked. Obviously, the servant was careful to keep her secret just that. Crouching down, she pulled a pin out of her hair and stuck it in the lock, getting the door open after a few deft turns. She took a quick peek inside, but it showed her exactly what she'd expected to see. The bed was a mess, and drops of blood stained the sheets. There was a dirty towel in the corner, and the room smelled of sex and sweat. A whip lay on the floor, and leather restraints were strapped to the bed. She closed the door behind her, pinning her hair back up.

She heard footsteps on the stairs and quickly righted herself, turning and walking away from the person at a slow and steady pace, as if she had simply been taking a stroll through the castle. A voice spoke up behind her, and she recognized it instantly as the prince's. "My lady," he said, surprised, and she turned, pasting an equally surprised look on her own face. "I had not expected you to be up so early."

"Oh, I rise early, lord," she said with a smile and a quick curtsy. "Enjoy walk in morning air. Is…how you say…refreshing?" She went to one of the many windows along the hallway, opened it, and gazed out, seemingly lost in thought, while she studied him in her peripheral vision. What was he doing here? Was *he* the one the maid had been meeting with in secret? No, he had a book in his hand, and it looked well-read. A paper stuck out of it to mark the spot.

"Yes, I couldn't agree more." He took a few steps closer to the window, then, as if thinking better of it, stepped back again. He seemed reluctant to be within an arm's length of her, so instead stared over her shoulder at the gardens outside. "I love listening to the hum of the birds and smelling the fresh dew on the grass. It helps, especially when the insomnia is bad."

"The what?" she asked, turning towards him. She leaned back against the stone window sill, stepping on the back of her long gown so that it pulled tight around her body, revealing her curves. She knew that the rising sun was splashing golden across her breasts, as it did across his face. She saw the dark circles under his eyes from lack of sleep and stubble across his chin.

"It just means I have trouble sleeping. I've tried different draughts and remedies, but still, I find it hard to rest. And when I do, I have bad dreams." He continued to stare over her shoulder, not looking at her face or the rest of her body. "So I like to walk in the mornings, or find a quiet place to read."

"What of your lady?" Lily asked with a tilt of her head. "She not lay beside you, keep bed warm and thoughts nice? Should do better job tire you."

He seemed confused by this, and his eyes met hers as he tried to understand what she meant. "Oh no, my lady, you misunderstand," he said once he'd gotten it. His face flushed, and he ran a hand through his disheveled bed hair. "I don't...um...have a mistress, or anything. That is more of my brother's tastes, not mine." Finally, his eyes caught hold of her fiery red hair, fixating on it in the morning light. Lily shook a tendril free, so that it fell out of its pin, tumbling down over her shoulder and resting across her breast. His eyes followed it, staring at the soft skin of her cleavage, her thin nightgown leaving little to the imagination. Suddenly, he yanked his eyes away, his blush growing deeper.

"You shiver. Forgive me, my lady, I did not realize your state of undress. Here, take my robe." He pulled it off without an answer and handed it to her, purposefully keeping his eyes pointed away. It was a lush, blue velvet, simple yet clearly expensive. Beneath it, he wore a baggy white nightshirt and dark green breeches over brown slippers. Even at a glance, she could judge the quality — satin and silk, all of it, despite its plainness. He neither flaunted his wealth and status nor forewent it.

She took the robe from him slowly, allowing her hand to gently glide across his and linger for a few seconds. Once she had it on, he seemed much more comfortable, and allowed his gaze to return to her.

They began strolling down the hall beside each other. "What you read?" Lily asked to fill in the silence.

"Oh, *On the Levels of Regency: A Study and New Treatise*. It's actually quite boring. Politics and whatnot. I'm sure you wouldn't care."

Lily was irritated by this and didn't bother to hide it. "I am courtesan, not dumb, lord. Tell me, please, what is about?"

"Well, I...political classes, mostly." He shrugged. "You would have to understand how our class system works here. It's a bit different from Aluvia."

"Then teach me," she said simply, taking her hair out of its pins and braiding it over her shoulder as they walked.

"Well, in Arestea we have multiple classes. They are normally aligned along an axis, from bottom to top. The commoners, the merchants —"

"Merchants, what is this word?" she interrupted.

"Umm, people who trade things. Then, above them, you have the military. They protect the people from harm. Then the religious order, then the nobility, and at the top, the royal family."

Despite his obvious fatigue, Prince Adrian grew more animated as he spoke. Good, she thought, people let their guard down when they spoke of favorite subjects. Perhaps she'd finally get something from him. She kept smiling as they walked, silently coaxing more from him.

"However," the prince continued, "in his book, Rory de Berecum argues that the classes should not be seen as ladders on a rung, going up and down, but rather as the stones of an arch, with the lowest classes as the springing stones—that is, the support—and the monarch as the keystone. Each class still in its place, yes, but each reliant on the others to hold them in place. He argues that for this reason, a commoner should have the same legal rights as a nobleman."

"He can say this in book?" Lily asked, eyes wide. Never mind that she'd read this same book herself; a sheltered Aluvian girl fresh over the border for the first time would find the idea novel, and if it endeared her to the prince, so much the better.

"He can," Prince Adrian said. "Though it helps he's a landed gentleman himself, if not exactly part of the aristocracy. Still, even then, his ideas are contentious in many circles." He glanced at his companion's blank face a moment before adding, "Some people think he's wrong and don't like him. Though some do quietly support his treatise since it implies even the king can be punished for breaking the law."

"King Alec can break law?" Lily asked. "But he is king. He *is* law, yes?"

The prince sighed and ran a hand through his blond hair, and the assassin took a mental note of it. This wasn't a sign of his fatigue—had she touched a nerve? Broached an uncomfortably familiar subject?

"Yes and no," the prince continued. "He can break the law, and probably nobody would try to bring a charge against him. He can get away with a lot as king, or bend laws at a whim if it suits him. But, at the same time, he is the most scrutinized person in the realm. Scrutinized, it means watched. Everyone is watching him, always." He shrugged. "So, he can ignore the law some, but if he does a lot of bad things, becomes very unpopular, then the people can revolt. And if enough people revolt, or the right people, they can overthrow him. We call that a coup."

"Then who be king?" Lily asked.

"I guess I would," said the prince. He didn't sound happy about it. Another mental note to be filed away. "Unless whichever power leading the rebellion had other ideas. There's a precedent for that, actually. That means it's happened before," he added before his companion could ask. "About 130 years ago, King Duncan grew paranoid in his middling years, imprisoning and executing people for the slightest of offenses, or even for imagined ones, or ones he thought they were about to commit. The vast majority of the nobility finally gathered against him and staged a coup. Duncan was imprisoned in the Ergastulum for the rest of his days, and the nobility installed one of his distant cousins in his place. My great-great-great-grandmother, Queen Cassandra. The first law she passed gave the aristocracy the right to assemble in times of political contention and vote the current monarch off the throne. If the ballot was unanimous, he or she was legally compelled to step down or risk civil war." He paused in his walk and glanced at her again. "Uh, that all means—"

"I know what means, lord," Lily said with a smile, walking on. He quickly caught up to her pace. "But is no worry now, yes? King Alec is good king?" she asked, curious what his answer would be.

He didn't respond immediately, and when he did, it was with a furrowed brow. "He is an effective king," Adrian said at last. "Whether he is good or not depends on whom one talks to. Many people are upset at the direction he's taking Arestea, with his wars and expansion. Others point to the trade he's increased, the road's he's built, the universities he's opened as proof he's bringing about an unparalleled golden age. All of which, of course, cost great sums of money. However you view it, though, he's definitely a king you can't be apathetic about."

"And what you think, lord?" asked Lily. "Your brother is good king?"

"Of course," he said, and this time the response was too quick for her to find it a believable one. "He's got the best interests of Arestea at heart. He's a skilled ruler, and though he can be insensitive at times, I think he's a good man deep down. I'm not about to call a vote for his removal, if that's what you're asking," he added with a short-lived smile.

However much he believed himself, Lily thought, his response sounded too rehearsed for complete sincerity. If the king's own brother had doubts about his rule, that might be useful for her purposes. No use pushing this subject any further now, though. "So, long as I keep King Alec happy, and he not overthrown, then I have job here for long time, yes?" Lily asked.

"I suppose so," he answered, staring forward. They walked on in silence for another few moments, and whenever she glanced his way, she found him pointedly not looking at her, his expression slightly nervous. Perhaps he'd realized that he'd just been discussing matters of historic treason and tyranny with someone who was essentially an exclusive prostitute for the upper class. However guilty or embarrassed he felt about it, though, Lily smiled with a silent pride. This was likely the longest conversation anyone in court had gotten out of the wallflower prince in a long time.

Before long, they came to an intersection in the halls. To the right was the heart of the palace, and beyond that, the east wing where Lily was staying. Ahead was a corridor leading to Adrian's personal suite. "Well, this is where I leave you, my lady," the prince said, regaining some of his slipping formality. "I believe I'll return to my own quarters now and try again to get some rest. I will see you at breakfast, won't I?"

She curtsied low to him, allowing one last flash of cleavage, though she wasn't sure if he looked or not. "If my lord wants invite me, I be there. And I thank my prince for the walk and the teaching."

"Why…well, yes. Of course you're invited," he said with a frown. "Why shouldn't you be? You are a guest here, after all. And you are welcome. Thank you as well."

She didn't bother to point out that there were two other courtesans she'd come with who were also guests and who had yet to receive the same privilege. He returned her curtsy with a slight bow and turned away, heading up the marble staircase. She would have to traverse the remainder of the west wing later, it seemed.

Still, this was good; she had learned something about this prince at last. For one, she doubted he was the liaison the servant girl had been with. Also, the prince was shy, apparently, but not immune to her charms as he had previously seemed. She had even gotten him to open up and talk to her, albeit about possibly one of the most boring topics available to them. Despite Camilla's insistent interest, he hadn't told her anything she hadn't known except his own canned, untrustworthy thoughts on his brother's reign. Still, she had made it seem like she was interested in him, which could go a long way to getting him to like her. And having both the king's *and* the prince's favor would likely open many useful doors.

This was a good sign, and she allowed herself a small smile as she made her way back to her room. She could manipulate people who showed no attraction to her, but it was easier when her natural physical assets also disarmed her opponents, and in a job this complicated, she wanted every advantage. If he really was attracted to her, then his interest in her was predictable and easy to steer. He was a man, after all, and in the end she found that most men had the same carnal desires.

She stopped with her hand on her own doorknob, her smile dying. He'd *had* her alone, she realized, and all he'd done was complain of insomnia, give her his robe—which she still wore even now—and talk to her of politics, which certainly wasn't the most romantic of conversations. He was a prince, she a servant for all intents and purposes, and they'd been alone in the dark in an empty wing of the palace. Yet there was no proposition, no physical contact, nothing.

He hadn't even taken the opportunity to ogle her properly, and she'd been sending clear signals of interest. He seemed to have some sort of devices on her — his brief but pointed attentions so far were proof enough, especially since he was the only one besides King Alec giving her any notice. But if they were merely carnal, as his brother's were, as she had designed her persona to elicit, then why had he not taken initiative?

She entered her own room and closed the door before striding to the window and glaring out in earnest this time, her mind worrying at pinning down what she thought she'd had sewn up. If it was carnality, he'd missed his best shot. Was he stupid, then? Had she misread him? Did he actually prefer men?

He was the prince; he had power but no real responsibilities, so he would be allowed to be dull witted. But that didn't seem right. Their conversation had proven that he was in fact quite intelligent — some might even consider him a scholar. And the moments of flustered attraction he'd shown, inadvertent though they seemed, made her doubt very much that the female form held no allure for him.

He had been quite talkative a few moments ago, but in public he was quiet and elusive. Silence, in her experience, meant either subordination or plotting. He was subordinate to no one but the king, and given what she had witnessed of their familial relationship, probably not even much there. So that left plotting.

He wasn't showing his hand yet, she concluded. That had to be it—whatever he wanted from her, he was waiting for it, testing the water still.

Worries of her near exposure in the court room rose up again, but she fought them down as she always did. Until her cover was legitimately blown, there was no reason to think it was and get sloppy. Plan for it, yes, and she had escape plans, but she wouldn't crack in front of her audience.

He'd invited her to breakfast this morning; that was a sign that whatever his designs on her, he wished them to be made public. She would go, humble and gracious, and study him some more. The king took priority still, but she had to be sure her path to him was clear of unseen obstacles before she walked it. And where the king's disposition and interest was well-known, his brother was too much of an unknown variable still.

She most certainly could not rule out Prince Adrian as a harmless and easy target. The best thing would be to befriend him, to cause him to lower his guard, and discover in the process what designs he had upon her.

Unlike dinner the night before, breakfast was a much less formal affair. The king and prince did not bother to eat in the great hall, but instead in their private dining room. The participants were the same as before—Duke Henry and his wife Prudence in their usual seats, Duke Raoul in his. The only exception was that the king was surprised to see her, judging by his raised brows as she entered. "Good morning, lady…uh…"

"Oh. Camilla, lord," she reminded him, curtsying.

"Camilla," he repeated with a snap of his fingers. "Right. Joining us again, are you? I don't remember extending the invitation."

"I did," Prince Adrian explained from his usual seat beside his brother.

The king turned his surprise on the prince. "Did you?" he asked, a smirk forming. "Well. My kid brother's finally showing an interest in women, then, is he? Good for you. Frankly, it's about damn time; I was starting to wonder about you, Adrian. I thought maybe yours was broken."

The prince blushed and opted to glare at his plate rather than the king in front of the rest of their breakfast guests. "Cut it out, Alec," he muttered. "I was just being polite. She's new here — she ought to be made to feel welcome."

"Ought she?" the king said, smile growing. "She has two other companions that are just as new, you know, and without the benefit of even a rudimentary grasp of the language, yet I notice that you didn't extend the invitation to feel welcome to either of them."

"I haven't seen them," the prince said, though his answer took just a bit too long to convince anyone that he'd remembered the other two courtesans at all.

Lily sat down delicately in the chair, listening to the exchange with rapt attention while she kept her face innocently blank. She poked at the medley of berries in front of her, her eyes occasionally darting over to the other table companions to see their reactions. The Duke and Duchess of Montflos looked embarrassed at the king's language and the prince's anger, and they politely acted as if they did not hear him at all. The Duke of Lakeview, however, seemed to be ignoring them entirely, instead staring down the low-cut bodice of her dress. When he realized he'd been caught looking, he flashed her a handsome grin. She merely bowed her head politely and returned to her breakfast.

Lily smiled at Adrian coyly as she ate. When there was a pause in the conversation, she took the opportunity to say, "Oh, I sorry I not bring your robe to return, Prince Adrian. I wanted to have maid to clean first."

Silence filled the room as everyone stopped eating and glanced at Adrian, who had turned bright red.

Alec lifted an eyebrow at his brother, then began to chuckle. "Well, at least you have cleared my worries brother," he said. "I feared if you kept refusing all of the women in court they would begin to question your preferences."

The silence only grew after that as Adrian stared unseeing at the food before him, nearing the same color as the raspberries on his plate.

The Duchess of Montfloss spoke up after a moment to break the tension. "Tell me, dear, how are your two companions faring?" she asked Lily.

"Oh, Rosalita and Olivia?" Lily replied. "They are…alone? No…lonely. They miss home, and they know nobody here." She glanced at King Alec, brushing her hair over her shoulder, where the sleeve of her dress fell, revealing the creamy, lightly tanned skin there. "They, all of us, do wish king to invite us spend time with him. Show our gratitude for taking us into palace." She gingerly picked up a strawberry from her plate with her fingers and placed it between her lips, sucking on it for just a second before biting into its lush center, glancing at him from under her eyelashes.

Marianne, her senior at the Guild and one of her mentors, would have called the ploy brazen and rebuked her for lacking subtlety, but she knew her opponent and his weak points. That the king's eyes followed her tongue as she licked the juice off her lips only confirmed it.

"Well, in that case, we should invite them all to join us in today's excursions, should we not, Henry?" the Duchess asked her husband. After he nodded his approval, she glanced at the king. "Come, Sire, the more company the merrier, I say, especially when one is playing croquet."

"Yes, why not?" the king said with a sigh, still watching Lily. He'd been forming other ideas, apparently. "If it would please my brother to be in the company of these lovely ladies, then we shall."

Lily glanced overtly at the prince, who had sent his brother a hard, almost jealous look. If the king saw it, he did not comment on it, but simply returned to eating his breakfast.

The croquet game was disappointingly uneventful. She pretended to be as unaware as to the rules of the game as her fellow courtesans and tried, unsuccessfully, to get the king to teach her. Instead it was Duke Raoul who most often came to the aid of all three courtesans, sliding his hips against theirs and wrapping his arms around them under the pretense of showing them how to hit the ball with the mallet.

Now that Olivia and Rosalita finally had the attention of the king, they spent all of their time near him, trying constantly to win his favor with every bit as much subtlety as Lily had shown at breakfast. It left little room for Lily to get his attention herself without looking too desperate, so she stopped trying and instead pretended to be absorbed in the game. She did take care to note that the prince seemed completely uninterested in the game itself, and when she tried to start a conversation, he avoided her, his face changing between embarrassment and irritation — the former directed at her and the latter at his brother. By midday, dark clouds covered the sky and a rain shower started, forcing them to quit their game early and return inside.

Once inside the castle, the prince disappeared almost immediately and without a word to anyone. Before Lily could ask the king for his company, she was pulled aside by the Duchess of Montflos, who insisted that she look at the woman's embroidery. She didn't miss that as the king left the room, he was accompanied by Olivia, and that neither Rosalita nor the Duke of Lakeview were anywhere to be found.

For the rest of the day, and many days after that, she neither saw nor heard from the king or the prince. While the Duchess took a strange liking to her, frequently inviting Lily into her chambers to knit or embroider together while she rambled on and on about her son and her dogs and more courtly gossip than Lily cared to stand (some of which was useful, most of which was simply annoying), it seemed both the king and the prince had forgotten about her completely.

That did, however, give her freedom to roam the halls of the castle as she pleased and indulge in whatever activity she felt like for the day, whether it be reading or taking walks in the garden or plotting how best to murder Alec in any given situation when the time came. So long as she didn't intrude anywhere uninvited, she was left alone.

Not that she stayed out of places she shouldn't go. She took every opportunity to slip alone down unfamiliar passages during the day or to poke about the hidden alleys behind the walls at night while the servants who might use them slept. In a week, she had explored as much of the castle as she could without changing out of her Camilla persona, searching from top to bottom, marking individual passages that were unknown or correcting the locations of certain drawing rooms and bedrooms.

Only once was she discovered somewhere out of place for a courtesan, poking around the narrow passages leading from the scullery on the lower level. One of the cooks had politely but insistently shooed her out while she offered apologies in broken Arestean for getting lost. She had a good enough excuse. The lowest level of the castle was the ground floor, which was below the main floor of the palace and partially underground, the only natural light coming from windows set high in the walls. She had brokenly explained her confusion to the cook, although the woman seemed to care less, and simply escorted her to a staircase to make her way back up where she belonged.

The ground floor she knew was home to the laundering rooms, servant's quarters, and food storage. It boasted a large wine cellar and presumably a few small dungeon rooms. The cells were for prisoners too important or too rich to be shipped off to the Ergastulum, the maximum-security prison complex situated in the rocky seaside cliffs some fifty miles from the capitol (and from which, of course, no one had ever escaped).

These palace cells were presumably for those prisoners whose sentences the royal family took an intimate interest in. That they were there the Guild was certain of — even if reputable hearsay hadn't confirmed them, nearly every seat of power on the continent had them — but they had not been mapped out, as no one who made it out of those cells ever did so in any shape to give a detailed description. She had been attempting to do just that before she was asked to leave.

Unfortunately, she found it likewise difficult to enter the upper level of the royal quarters, as they were more heavily guarded than the second floor. Perhaps with a different disguise she could manage to slip through, as a palace servant or even cross dressed as a new and fresh-faced guard recruit; but she'd designed Camilla to stand out, and the risk that someone would recognize her, even in a different disguise, was too great. It would take too long to make herself truly unrecognizable, and no doubt the courtesan's absence would be missed in the meantime. So for now, she left those avenues alone.

The other area that she still needed to explore was the king's suite. It, however, was almost impossible to breach. Also on the third floor, Alec's personal suite had only a single staircase that she could find leading to it, and it was constantly guarded should he ever be attacked. The only way in there, it appeared, was with King Alec's permission.

At the end of the king's suite was the tower that rounded out the west wing of the castle, and it was this tower that intrigued her most of all. The Guild had no clue what was in there. If any of his guards or servants knew, they were tight-lipped about its interior. Lily wondered at the possibilities that resided in that tower and itched to explore it, to report her findings back to the Guild; but she was never able to find a way in save straight through the king's suite, and so far she hadn't been invited in there. Rosalita and Olivia soon changed places, she noticed, but Lily had yet to be called on.

She'd returned to their suite one evening to hear the two girls giggling and speaking to each other in Aluvian. As she'd entered the room, Olivia asked, "And you enjoyed that?"

"Oh yes. It was sinfully pleasant." Rosalita replied. "You should ask him to do it to you next time. The look in his eyes when—" She stopped talking as soon as she noticed Lily standing in the doorway. Olivia stood behind Rosalita, helping her to tighten her corset. It seemed that Camilla gaining the king's favor as soon as they arrived had alienated her somewhat from her tight-knit companions.

Perhaps they distrusted her for her surprising skill in a fight, but Lily suspected jealousy might be the more likely culprit, despite the fact that both had enjoyed Alec's intimate attention before she had. Regardless of the reason, the two often grew tight-lipped whenever Camilla was around lately. Lily simply pretended not to notice and continued on to her bedroom without a word.

After the croquet game, the only times Lily saw King Alec were when he conducted court, and then she was only meant to decorate the throne room like an exotic tapestry. It was during one of these court sessions that a bronze-skinned older merchant approached the king and requested a license to import honey from the Meli Islands to the south the following summer. Trade with the islands was an incredibly lucrative business, and thus the rights were zealously guarded by those who held them, necessitating a royal audience to open a new line of trade. On his knee before the king, the merchant made a peculiar gesture with his fingers behind his back, three times in a row and aimed at the side of the room where Lily and the other courtesans were standing.

While the clerk drew up the license, Lily followed the merchant to the library. It was as opulent as the rest of the castle, with a wraparound loft that looked down over the main room, accessible by a spiraling wrought iron staircase. The walls boasted floor to ceiling bookshelves that required small ladders on rails to the reach the top of. Scattered throughout the room were desks and comfortable couches for reading. There were no fireplaces—after all, this would be the most dangerous room in the castle for an open flame — but sunlight pouring in through the enormous windows kept the place bright and cheery, despite the light chill.

Lily pulled a book of Aluvian poetry from a shelf near where he was seated waiting. After five minutes of silent page turning, she sighed. "Sometimes I miss the smell of the sea at my window," she said in Aluvian to the bookshelves.

The merchant shifted in his seat on the other side of the aisle. "And a sailor soon misses the solid stone of the mountains," he muttered, also in Aluvian.

Lily smiled and closed the book. "If I bottled the tide and brought it with me, would it ease my nostalgia, do you think?" she asked him directly.

"You cannot bring the sea or a mountain with you," the merchant replied with a shrug, looking up from the letter he'd been writing. "A piece of either will only remind you of what you miss. Best not to think on a dead past."

"To be honest, I expected a fellow countryman." She pulled another book from the shelf at random and gazed at the cover. "But I see that Meli merchants, too, have need to know this land better."

"You will meet many travelers on your road, love," the merchant said, turning back to his letter and dipping his quill in his ink once more. "The only things linking you and them together are the direction you're heading and the destination in mind." His pen hovered poised over the sheet of paper, waiting.

Lily nodded, flipped the book open at random, and began casually summarizing in fluent Aluvian her experiences in the palace to the pages, from the building layout to her impromptu defense of the king her first day in court to the difficulty of getting into his private tower. The merchant nodded to himself at intervals and continued writing his letter, which she could see at a glance across the aisle included crude maps of the palace's halls and hidden tunnels. When Lily had finished telling the bookshelves her story, he continued staring at his pages for several minutes, then rolled them up and tied them with twine before tucking them back into his pocket.

He stood to leave, but paused in the aisle beside her to examine the decorative molding of the bookcase. "Many people come and go in this palace, it seems," he mumbled, and Lily took a sudden interest in a tome just behind him. "When the autumn peaks, someone with an important future will arrive. He will need a good friend if he is to have good luck. But this is all just a sailor's intuition." The merchant glanced over his shoulder at her and smiled amiably, nodding a greeting. "The captain sends regards to a sailor all alone."

Lily returned the smile and dipped a quick curtsy. "And the travelling maiden thinks often of home," she said. The merchant nodded again, then left the room.

She ran her fingers along the spine of the book in her hand, still smiling to herself. She had a month or two yet, then, before mid-autumn, when her master's puppet king arrived at the palace. That would be plenty of time to divulge King Alec's secrets. After all, if he could get bored enough of Olivia to switch to Rosalita after only a few days, she could not be far from his intimate graces — and her chance to see his tower. Both of them, she thought, and chuckled to herself.

She replaced the book and turned around. Prince Adrian was seated across the library in the upper gallery, his nose in a book, at a perfect position to see and be seen by her place in the shelves. He wasn't looking at her now, but she knew better as she made her way up the wrought iron spiral staircase to meet him. He'd been spying on her. That was either cute or dangerous.

He looked up as she approached his seat, and she curtsied low. "Lord Prince," she said softly, holding the pose.

"Oh, Camilla," he said, feigning surprise and failing miserably as he gestured her up. "Good evening. Please, not so much ceremony outside of court, if you don't mind." He cleared his throat and closed his book, then gestured to the seat opposite him. "What brings you here?"

"I look for books from Aluvia," she said, sliding into the proffered chair and adjusting her skirts just enough to flash her legs at him a couple of times. "I find poetry, history. Very comforting."

"I see." He leaned back and looked over toward the window the merchant had been sitting in front of. "Were you talking to that merchant just now? I didn't think you knew anybody else in Arestea."

She followed his glance and nodded. "Very brief. I ask if he sell Aluvian things. Spice, flower, small comfort. He say not now." She leaned her head wistfully on her hand and wondered why he was being so nosy all of a sudden after several days of ignoring everybody.

"Oh. I understand," he said, then smiled sadly at her. "You must be homesick. I can't imagine how difficult your mission must be for you now."

"Yes, lord," she said softly, bowing her head and hiding her eyes. "Very little bit homesick. Sorry."

"No, don't apologize for honest feeling, please. King Emiliano sent you here as a gift of diplomacy. It's natural not to be completely happy with the arrangement, even if it is a mission from your king. If anything, *we* owe *you* an apology." He turned his attention back to the window. "Besides, I think I know the feeling of not quite belonging where you're needed."

She said nothing, only kept her head bowed and her eyes hidden, while inside her mind caught fire and sped up. He was doing it again—trying to lead her on, draw her in to him. He wanted her to think he empathized with her. And his referring to her "mission" most likely only referred to her being gifted here, but the wording made her wary. Professional paranoia, almost certainly, but too much was at stake not to humor the worry. Well, this time, she wouldn't let him make the move and run. She'd figure out his game once and for all before he could disappear into his chamber again.

She decided to call his bluff, if that's what it was. Lily leaned towards him, flashing just the tiniest bit of cleavage, enough to catch him off guard but not enough to distract his attention away from the current conversation. She placed a hand gently on his arm—

physical contact was always the best way to show someone you were truly interested, and the arm was a fairly neutral place, neither too sexual nor too friendly. He seemed surprised but did not flinch from her for once, and she smiled up at him sweetly. "I not understand. How you feel...not belonging? You are prince of Arestea."

"Oh, uh," he stammered, looking away from her, his eyes darting around as he tried to come up with a suitable answer. Avoiding eye contact — the most obvious sign of lying. "No, don't worry, please," he said with a dismissive gesture, "it was just a slip of the tongue."

Lily's lips pursed. He was backpedaling, trying to avoid her question. There was an ulterior motive of some sort in him after all. She'd caught him in his game finally, and now she pushed her advantage. "Please, lord, I wish to know. You trust me. I not tell. Please, give to me your troubles."

He paused, seeming to debate with himself or, she thought more likely, trying to come up with a quick cover to his slip. But then he sighed and suddenly gave in. "It's just that I...I suppose I feel...I mean, of course I'm necessary, I'm next in line for the throne. But my brother could honestly rule without me, and I don't even want to—" He stopped short, his words catching in his throat. He stared at her with large eyes, and she knew that he wanted to escape, but she had him pinned against the high back of his chair, and the only way around her was to grab her and move her out of his way. And she had noticed how much he seemed to loathe touching her. "I...I apologize," he said after a moment, once he'd collected his thoughts. "I've let my mouth take control. Please, forget what I said."

Lily leaned closer, so that she was practically in his lap now, and pressed her chest up against him. "My lord know I here to please. And I think my lord have nice mouth. Is...appealing." Her lips beside his ear, she breathed softly on his neck as she whispered, "You not need feel alone. That is what I come here for."

He jumped up suddenly, practically throwing her to the ground. She managed to gracefully grab the arm of the chair and lift herself up without too much disarray. He backed away, as if afraid she would burn him with her touch. "I apologize, my lady. I did not mean to make you think...I certainly was not trying to...Forgive me." He dashed down the spiral staircase to the level below, and she watched as he escaped out the double doors, leaving her alone in the library.

That was it then? He did not want to be king? It was not difficult to realize; he had practically said it himself. But she couldn't see what the big issue was. Many nobles and future monarchs feared or resented the title they may one day have to uphold. They were the ones who were usually found dead, murdered by their more ambitious next of kin, who saw the weakness in them.

But there was no next of kin after Adrian d'Arestes. Unless his brother married and quickly produced an heir to cut in front of Adrian in the line of succession, he would be the only member of his family left to rule. Not that she would let that happen. As it was, there was no ambitious next of kin that Adrian d'Arestes would have to worry about murdering him for his position.

Which was exactly why she was going to have to kill him herself.

And it was a good thing, too. If he were truly as weak-willed and easily perturbed as he made himself seem, he would never make a good monarch. And if it were all a ploy, a persona like the one she wore, then his true nature was too unpredictable. She was doing her country a favor by removing him and his brother. If he were in charge, the nation would fall into disarray.

Why, then, did the thought of killing him give her a sudden twinge of uneasiness? It was rare that any of her targets elicited such a response. Perhaps it was because he seemed so innocent. He couldn't be any older than she herself, but he seemed like a fumbling teenager at times.

But surely no future monarch was ever innocent of anything. And yet, she had no proof, not even rumor, that he had ever done anything to hurt those beneath him. None of the servants gossiped about him. She'd never heard the same tales of him carousing with and corrupting the young maidens of the land that were so often told about his brother. Either he was very crafty at keeping a lid on his indiscretions and secrets, or — and this was much less likely — he had none to speak of.

But surely he couldn't be completely innocent. One wasn't raised with a silver spoon in their mouth, with everything they ever wanted at the tips of their fingers, without becoming conceited, perverted, or at least entitled. Men like him, raised with money and power, believed they could take whatever they wanted, and they always wanted more and more, until they became addicted to the act of taking, and greed became their dominant characteristic. She should know; those were the kinds of men and women she murdered. A prince surely couldn't be any different than the other corrupt nobility of their kingdom.

And yet, what if she was wrong? She'd never murdered an innocent before. Never. That was her one stipulation, the one promise she'd extracted from Master Gavriel when she committed to the Guild in earnest. She would only kill those who deserved it, and gods knew there were enough of those in Arestea that she'd never even had to worry if her targets were innocents or not. They never were.

But what if he was not as bad as his brother? What if—and the strangeness of this thought bothered her, but she had to admit it was possible—what if this wasn't a subtle game he was playing with her, showing her empathy and then ignoring her until she least expected it? What if he was genuinely concerned with her wellbeing, without the ulterior motive that would keep him hovering about her and trying to wear her down with his presence? What if he really was just a nice person?

And yet, what if he wasn't? What if he was tricking her into believing this? What if he'd been tricking *everyone* into believing it, to accepting the right hand of the king as an easily dismissed nonentity? What if he was leading her on because he suspected something? What if he was really trying to trick her into revealing too much? In all her many dealings with nobility, this seemed the more likely option. Not that it would ever work, of course; she was no fool, and she would never fall for it. But if he had any suspicion, and he went to his brother with that suspicion…

She slumped down in the seat the prince had recently occupied, kicked her feet up on the coffee table, and stared at the dust that danced in the rays of sunlight. For the first time since her apprenticeship had ended, she felt confused about her job. Always it had been simple: enter, kill, leave, get paid. She'd done some spying, of course, that was nothing new, but never had the stakes been this high.

Never before had she been asked to live with her targets for over a month, maybe longer, while she waited for something to happen. And never before had she felt this uncertain about a mark. Alec she was confident she had in her hand, or soon would, but Adrian confused her. And she didn't like being the one who was confused.

One thing was for certain—she needed to make sure he was on her side, or at least not actively against her. She was the predator here, he was the prey. She could never let those roles be reversed.

Five

The entire main floor of the west wing was devoted to the prince as his personal quarters. It spanned several bedrooms, sitting rooms, studies, bathrooms, a small pantry, and several small closets for quick access by the cleaning staff, though no servants entered any of the rooms without his permission or summons. Despite the vast space and total privacy, however, he still found that he preferred the comfort of his childhood bedroom.

It had been his only dedicated personal space before his parents had died and Alec had moved up a floor into their old quarters, and so it felt more familiar, more like his own sanctuary, than the rest of the suite he'd inherited. He took his meals at his desk, did most of his reading sitting on his bed, played chess against himself on the board in the corner, and studied the sky and stars from his balcony. And at times like this, when his position as a prince with no power seemed more of a curse than a luxury, it was to this room that he retreated to reflect and collect his thoughts, away from his brother and the other nobles.

Prince Adrian lay on a bed that he found excessively enormous for one person and thumbed through a book from his personal collection. The palace library was extensive enough, but he kept a shelf of books that held particular value or importance to him in his living room. His library ranged from histories to fairy tales and legends, from dramatic narratives and novels to scholarly texts on philosophies and the latest scientific discoveries. At present he was poring over a book of translated poems by Luka Nikolao, the renowned Meli poet, in order to reroute his thoughts away from their usual melancholy musings about the direction the kingdom was headed and his place in it.

Sadly, it did not seem to be working.

Adrian sighed and flipped the book closed, giving up on distraction, and sat up to look at the sunset outside his window. The sky's colors blended seamlessly from brightest yellow to darkest red, hitting every hue along the way and mixing it into a wash of beauty that shamed any jewel in the palace. Yet, to the prince, the sight just looked like a massive bloodstain, and he tried to imagine how many men and women were out at the borders right now fighting and dying in the name of the crown—his family's crown, which he had only been saved from wearing by Alec's birth seven years prior to his own.

Details of his brother's campaigns pushed their way to the front of his mind. Battles with Ovinurland had sprung up intermittently since before their parents' reign, but under Alec's rule, they had grown steadily more frequent and larger in scale. The southernmost territories of Ovinurland had been taken and occupied, pushing Arestea's northern border up by hundreds of miles. To the east, his brother's armies had invaded and conquered a handful of smaller nations, including, most recently, Beuteland, a country roughly half the size of Arestea's original borders. To the west lay Aluvia, Arestea's only neighbor between itself and the

Western Ocean, and he knew Alec harbored vague plans for King Emiliano's lands as well, despite the recent peace offerings and shows of goodwill.

The only direction they hadn't expanded was southward. All that lay south of them was the Temperate Sea with the Meli archipelago spread out in the middle. The most popular spices and luxury exports for the whole mainland continent, as well as the southern continent on the other side of the sea, came from the Meli, and Alec wouldn't risk the audacity of taking them and sparking contempt from those nations that remained neutral or peaceable to his own. No, he'd said before in private, it wouldn't do to steal the other kids' favorite toy. Not before he'd put them all to bed first, anyway.

Adrian stood and crossed the room to the window, then closed and latched the shutters, hiding the blood red sunset from view. The room went significantly gloomier, the only light now coming from a lit candle near his bed.

Arestea was technically the healthiest it had been since its founding, he told himself as he replaced his book of poems on the shelf. A few pieces of the country had broken off into independent nations in their distant ancestors' time, but all of them and then some had since been reclaimed by Alec. Never had their empire been so vast, and the results were tangible: more money in the treasury from taxes on new citizens, more quantity and variety of foods readily available across the country without tariff, and enough natural resources to spur economic and industrial, as well as territorial, growth. Alec was careful to absorb rather than raze his conquests. Objectively, everything was going great.

But at what cost? Adrian flopped back on his bed again and stared at the patterns on the canopy. He knew the necessity of unpopular policies that came with leadership — sometimes some things had to be done that no one would enjoy for the overall good of a country's future. But Alec had taken that lesson instantly and passionately to heart, and it seemed to Adrian at times that he was pushing the nation's boundaries just to see what he could get away with.

Expansion and annexation, he argued, were natural and necessary for all parties involved. He talked of governments in terms of natural selection, claiming that those who couldn't resist conquest would thrive better under stronger leadership, while those powerful and capable enough not to need conquering would resist it and throw them off. And while he had an intellectual point that Adrian couldn't refute, his practice of it worried the young prince.

Ovinurland had shown time and again that they could resist Arestea's armies, or at least match them in many of the hundreds of battles they'd had over the past five decades; yet Alec kept pushing in that direction in between larger campaigns, taking small chunks of land at a time and defending them vehemently. *How many times do you have to resist conquest before it's enough to prove your worth?* the prince wondered. *How many victories do we need to claim before we can rest easy in our own sense of stability?*

And then there were the citizens. Of course, there were always the citizens. A nation, a kingdom, an empire was no good without citizens. They knew that, their parents had known that, and every ancestor before had learned that lesson or found themselves surprisingly replaceable. But Alec seemed to regard his subjects as an obligation, as much an obstacle to his policies as the recipients of them, or so it seemed to Adrian. Those peoples they conquered held obvious resentment, and every season it seemed more of the native Arestean people were voicing concern for or, at worst, outright opposition to Alec's growth projects.

The constant warring, though mostly victorious on their side, was taking its toll on the border cities that saw the most immediate aftermath of the conflicts, and every year it seemed the dissension spread further into the middle of the country. With Luceran situated in the exact middle of the country's borders — at least until the most recent expansions — and Alec's outlook that what was beneficial or profitable was more important than what was popular, Adrian feared he'd do nothing to assuage the people's growing complaints until it reached the palace doorstep, by which point it would be too late.

A knock on his own door startled him from his thoughts, and he sat up and slid to the edge of the bed in an effort to appear more composed. "Yes, who is it?" he called through the wall.

The door opened without an answer, which was, to Adrian, an answer itself, even before Alec stepped through into view. No one else could afford to be so irreverent to the crown prince. With a passing smile at his younger brother, King Alec strode to the desk and threw open the shutters, letting the sunset back in.

"Awful dark in here," he muttered, pulling out the desk chair and straddling it. "What were you doing? Do I want to know?"

"Reading," Adrian answered with a sigh, sprawling back on his bed again. No need for appearances after all, it seemed. "Thinking. Brooding. You know — my usual repertoire."

"Hm. Ever get tired of being so damnably serious?" The king leaned forward and shook his head. "No, don't answer that, it won't change anything. So what was it this time? Conflicted opinion of current political happenings? Ennui of high stature with limited responsibility? Girl trouble?" He clasped his hands in front of him and bowed his head over them. "Please, Ade, do me a favor and say it's girl trouble, just this once."

Adrian smiled despite himself. "Mostly a mix of the first two again, I'm afraid. Though that Camilla girl does seem to have formed some, uh...some notions in her head about possibilities that might exist between us that I don't exactly share."

Alec's eyebrows shot up at that. "What, she's trying to seduce you? Oh, that minx..." He smirked to himself as he stroked his beard, gaze wandering off into private thought. "And here I'd hoped she'd been falling desperately in lust with me. Well. I'm not sure what to think about that now."

"I don't want her," Adrian said with a frown, turning away from his brother. "She's nice enough, but I don't think we're exactly compatible." A long pause followed. When Adrian looked back to his brother,

Alec was staring at him with a furrowed brow and a concerned look. "What?"

"Adrian...are you a man lover?" Alec asked.

"*What?*"

"Not that there'd be anything wrong with that," the king began, holding up his hands in defense. "Hell, you don't tell me how to wave my scepter, I won't tell you where to wave yours. They say Uncle Julien has those tastes too, y'know. I'm sure his, uh, convenient relocation had nothing to do with where he stuck his—"

"I am not a homosexual!" Adrian argued, a bit louder than he'd intended. "Just because I don't cavort with every skirt that comes my way like you do...There are other stages, you know, between wantonly debauched and, and inverted proclivities!"

"Alright, alright, granted," Alec said, waving his hands in a request for peace. "There's also celibacy. That's right down the middle of the two, and I can't imagine it's healthy for anybody. You're going to turn into a clergyman at this rate, Adrian."

"Did you come here just to berate me for my sex life?" The prince stood and began to pace. Informal proximity to his brother often did this to him, he realized not for the first time. "Are you so concerned with the lineage you must constantly badger me for my discretion with my private life? I've given thought, you know, to the idea that this Camilla's been acting on your behalf when she flirts at me."

Alec shrugged, fingering his chin. "Not a bad idea, actually."

"Well, don't bother. I don't like this whole courtesan–courtier institution, people trying to get into a noble's good graces by whatever means possible. It's all so degrading and so blatantly, sickeningly false." Adrian willed himself to stop pacing and sit back down on his bed, glaring at the flagstones on the floor. "I've no romantic interest in Camilla or any of your other 'pets,' and it's highly unlikely I ever will. So don't worry about competition or anything."

Alec started to laugh a bit harder than Adrian thought was really called for, though he quieted down a bit when the prince turned his sullen glare on him. "Sorry," the king said without apology. "I know that wasn't a joke, but…no, never mind. Just forget it."

"I intend to," Adrian said, looking pointedly at the door. "Now will you kindly leave?"

"No, not yet. I actually did come in here for a reason." Alec forced down his humor and turned to look in earnest at his younger brother. "My forces in Beuteland are taking longer than should be necessary to completely secure the country."

"I thought we'd already won that front," Adrian said hesitantly. "That you were calling some of them who had been there longest back home." The sudden shift unnerved him.

"We have," Alec assured him. "Unequivocally, we have. But there are loose ends to tie up and measures to be installed before the main force of the army can be withdrawn. And orders I've given months ago are just now being exercised, and often incorrectly, if my information is to be believed."

"Tampering with dispatch lines?" Adrian speculated. "Or faulty reconnaissance?"

"I'm not sure. One, the other, maybe both. Could be obstacles I'm not privy to are holding up the message deliveries, or some sort of ineptitude on the soldiers' part. Maybe it's all just unfortunate accident, or maybe there are pockets of resistance that escaped the main brunt of our invasion force scrambling our communications."

"Or passive rebellion in the soldier body itself?" Adrian asked.

Alec frowned. "Or that, possibly. I like that one least of all. Current unrest makes it a candidate, though. Many of our men out there are long since ready to return home to their families." He smiled when he looked up and saw the prince's expression. "Oh yes, I hear the dissent I'm stirring, brother. Whatever you may think of me, I know better than to turn a deaf ear to the voices in Arestea. I've contingencies in place to stem treasonous sentiment before it becomes a national threat. Or I thought I did, at least."

The king's expression sobered again, and he turned to stare out the window at the rapidly darkening sky. "But this fuddling of our main army doesn't bode well. If it's transmission error, then I won't discover its root by sending out more transmissions. And if it's the stirrings of rebellion, then I'll need to find and quash it quickly with a confident, command-bolstering move. Something to stir my popularity and reinforce my image as a king that gets results and doesn't mess about." He turned to Adrian again. "Which is why, a fortnight from now, I'll be heading to Beuteland myself to personally oversee the last steps in the country's annexation."

"What?" Adrian jumped to his feet again before he could think better of it. "Brother, is that wise?"

"Is anything preemptively wise? Or is wisdom just a title we assign in hindsight? No, don't try to answer that," he said, waving his hand. "I read it out of the same book you did, and we both know the following discussion took twenty pages. My decision stands; I can argue the strengths and weaknesses of it with you if you really desire it, but it's already been decided, and no doubt rumor is in the first stages of spreading. I'll not hesitate now after the fact and undermine the very goal I've set for myself."

"And the kingdom?" Adrian continued. "If the worst is true and the need to reassert yourself is so great, won't leaving your throne empty after such a huge and controversial move as this latest conquest only encourage treasonous action?"

"The throne won't be empty," Alec said with a smile. "Because I want you to keep it warm for me while I'm away. See? I just fixed all of those problems you'd been brooding about."

Adrian stared, and it took an inordinate amount of time for his brother's words to register. "Me?" was the first thing he could think of to say. "You want me to be king until you get back? You're serious?"

"You know, Adrian," Alec said slowly, "being king when the previous king can't anymore is kind of tied in with the whole crown prince thing. I seem to remember seeing it somewhere in the definition of the term. It's not just something I make people call you so you'll feel better about yourself."

"No, I'm...But I'm the emergency king," Adrian argued, resuming his pacing. "I don't just take over your duties whenever you leave the room."

"What, afraid you can't do the job, brother?"

"Yes, honestly, that's it exactly." He stopped, turning on his older brother with an anxious gaze. "I don't have the same knack with the nobles as you. I can't deal with the subtle threats and backhanded promises. I don't play well at intrigue."

"Yet you've said nothing about your judgment," Alec said. "You trust that?"

"Well..." There were a number of things Adrian wanted to say just then about their respective judgments, his view on present circumstances versus his brother's, their unmeshed senses of morality. "I am comfortable with my own method of deciding things, yes," was what he eventually settled on. "I can't think like you, though," he added carefully. "I can't come to the same conclusions you would come to in my staid, and I can't pass some of the judgments I've seen you decree. If you leave her with me, Arestea will not be run as you'd direct her during your absence."

Alec studied his younger brother for a long moment, sizing him up, it seemed to the prince. Just when the scrutiny was becoming uncomfortable, the king grinned. "That sounds about right," he said, rising to clap Adrian on the shoulder. "Don't worry, though, brother. I respect your views, if I don't share all of them, and I wouldn't expect you to know how to mimic me precisely. In fact, I'd be disturbed if you could."

The king turned and began pacing himself then, though he looked more comfortable doing it than Adrian had felt. "And you won't be alone in it, either — I've instructed my closest advisors and all heads of staff in the palace to aid you in any way necessary. In fact, most of the responsibilities have already been divided up amongst others: the guard captain will oversee any defense issues that come up, the treasurer has the kingdom's funds well in hand, various ministers are doing ministerial things, so on and so forth. All you really have to do is walk around like you own the place, review their reports, and give the final say on anything contentious. Should be pretty cushy."

Adrian tried to sigh in relief without appearing to be doing such. "Oh. Not much different than usual, then?"

"Not much. Except now your opinions actually matter." Alec chuckled in brotherly good nature and headed for the door. "I'm putting together a small going away party for myself for a week from today, after which I expect I'll be so wrapped up in organizing the place as to leave no time for fun until I'm gone. So you have a full seven days to brace yourself for my usual brand of entertainment." He stepped a foot through the open door and had almost closed it before stopping and turning back. "Oh, and if you see that Aluvian hanger-on of yours," he added with a smirk, "tell her I've a bone to pick with her."

The prince waited until the door was safely latched before he allowed his pent-up groan to escape, flopping back down to his bed and dropping his head to his hands. Two weeks, and then Alec would be gone, and then who knew when he'd be back? Adrian couldn't wait until he could be rid of him for a change.

And then, he knew, he'd be counting the days until the king returned again. Such was his curse.

Lily couldn't quite get enough air. She was certainly no stranger to all manner of uncomfortable clothing, but this particular outfit was done up so tight it made breathing difficult.

She gazed into the floor-length mirror in front of her, tucked away in a relatively slow corner of the ballroom. She had to admit, though, the dress did do wonders for her figure. Her ball gown was a deep forest green, the tight-boned corset hefting all of her cleavage up and together. From the hips, it flared out in layers and layers of shiny satin until it reached the floor, where it dragged a bit behind her — it was a good thing they kept the floors so clean, or else the train would be ruined before the night was over. The gown was sleeveless, so she wore long gloves of black lace that ended above the elbows. Her hair was up in a messy bun, though some of it had intentionally come loose and rested in soft curls on her shoulders. Around her neck hung a chandelier necklace, each swoop of chain adorned with black crystals, the largest of which dipped between her breasts.

Despite the fact that she couldn't breathe and the slightest wrong movement would disrupt her carefully crafted outfit — damn, did she look amazing. Not just amazing, jaw-dropping, and she knew it couldn't be just her own vanity talking. Let's see the king try to ignore her dressed like this. Or even the prince, with his stick up his ass.

"Would you like a drink, miss?" asked a passing servant carrying a tray full of glasses.

Lily turned away from the mirror with a smile. "Yes, please," she said, lifting a glass and watching him spin away into the nearby crowd. Sipping her drink, she gazed around the ballroom, watching the others. All of the various lords and ladies that could arrive within a week of the king's announcement were there, most of them residents of the city. They were all dressed in lovely finery, and under the lights of the chandeliers, the room seemed to glisten off of the ladies' dresses and jewels.

The king and prince had not yet arrived, being the ones for whom the party was thrown. She was a bit disappointed that she couldn't have made a grand entrance for them to see; but then, she was only a courtesan here, and they royalty. The band had already started up, mostly string instruments with a few percussions and woodwinds. Already a few group dances had been performed, the kind where one changed partners regularly and did a lot of spinning and bowing. She'd grown out of breath after just one such dance and found she had to take a break, though the huge skirts of her dress made it difficult to sit with any dignity.

Just then the song ended and the music did not start up again. The crowd turned in unison and stared expectantly at the entry doors, which were opened by two butlers. The king and prince stepped in, and everyone began clapping. Lily had to admit they looked marvelous. The king's ensemble was grand: mostly royal reds, with a long, rich jacket that ended at his knees. His thick copper hair was tied back, drawing attention to the strong line of his jawbone.

Even his brother looked exceptionally handsome tonight. The prince wore a stiff, white jacket trimmed with blue that filled out his chest and shoulders, and black pants that were tight enough to show that he actually had quite a nice backside. Like his brother, he had a decorative jeweled sword hanging from his side, though when he walked, one could tell he wasn't used to the way it bounced against his leg. His clothes were so starched and stiff they actually made him stand up straight, so no matter how uncomfortable he probably was, he appeared regal for a change. As usual, his blonde hair hung softly into his eyes, which were especially blue in the chandelier lighting. With his white jacket, he didn't even look as pale as he normally did.

The king held up the glass in his hand, and the ballroom hushed. He smiled as his gaze swept over the assembled crowd. "Lords and ladies, it pleases me to see you all here tonight," he said, his words carrying with ease across the crowded room. "As you know, I will be leaving you within the week." There were gasps and mumbles, even though all in attendance already knew this. Clearly, some courtiers wanted to ensure that he knew just how much they would miss him. "I may be gone a few months, perhaps more," he continued, "but there is no need to lament. For while I am away at our borders securing the future of Arestea, my brother, Crown Prince Adrian, will be here as your regent, safeguarding the present. And I do believe he will do a fine job." There was subdued clapping. "So, I don't want tonight to be a night of sorrow. My absence will not be so long, and this will be a great time of growth for our prince, for our empire, and for us all. Now, let us dance."

And dance they did. It seemed every lord and lady presented themselves to the king and prince, who were forced by decorum to accept the ladies' invitations to dance. Rosalita and Olivia were of course among them, and Lily tried not to roll her eyes at how desperately they clung to the king. Lily finally found a settee and managed, with some careful planning, to sit and breathe at the same time, though it was incredibly uncomfortable. She was asked to dance by a few gentlemen, and accepted each time, though she could tell that they asked more out of politeness than anything else. After all, they all knew she was not noble like them, and while this might have enticed many men had they been alone, most were here with their wives and were otherwise surrounded by their gossipy peers.

Finally, she saw the crowd around the king thin enough that she could try to get his attention without seeming needy. She made her way slowly towards him, curtsying to nobles and occasionally sparking up short, polite conversations, all to seem nonchalant. When she arrived before the king, she acted neither surprised nor expectant, but merely curtsied, kissing the ring on his proffered hand.

"Camilla," Alec said as she rose again, "you look absolutely ravishing tonight. I was hoping I would get the chance to dance with you. Here I thought you were being coy and avoiding me," he teased.

She blushed gently on command, looking demurely away from his face. "Never, my lord. But you always surrounded by people. I did not want take king away from subjects."

He took her waist in one hand and her hand in the other, leading them through the crowd in long sweeps. "My beautiful girl, I would welcome the distraction from my subjects," he said with his rakish smile. "As kind as they all are, they grow tiresome after a while. And besides, I know that with you, I do not have to worry that everything you say is planned in an attempt to gain status with me."

She wondered what would make him believe so. She *was* a courtesan, after all. While it was true a courtesan could never marry the king, she could always try to win his favor, to become his favorite mistress and thus receive the benefits of such. As friendly as Rosalita and Olivia acted towards one another, she was sure that each would willingly throw the other under a carriage to become the king's favorite mistress. It was not unheard of for kings and queens to give their favorite lovers titles, whether their lovers were noble stock or otherwise, not to mention jewels, houses, even lands.

He must have seen the questioning look on her face, because he smiled down at her. "I know that there is much competition between you and your fellow countrywomen, yes. But I also know that it is not me that you fancy." Now she was even more confused. "My brother has told me of the attention you give him."

The worried look on her face didn't have to be forged. She had flirted with the prince, sure, but she flirted with pretty much everyone. It came so naturally to her, after years of training. And for Camilla, an excess of flirtatiousness only made sense, given her station. Had he taken it the wrong way? Should she have been more forward toward the king? It would seem her ploy to be patient in the hopes of making him come to her had not paid off.

"Don't be upset to be caught, my dear," Alec said as he watched the shallowly buried distress play across her face. "In fact, I am quite pleased with this development. You see, not many ladies have taken a liking to my younger brother. He seems to…put them off, I suppose. He's not good with romance, and he certainly doesn't know how to take initiative. Not to mention, as I'm sure you've noticed, he is very awkward when it comes to forward women."

They wove gracefully through the throng as he spoke, his dancing skill surprising her in the part of her mind she could spare for such things. "I have tried, believe me I've tried, to leave you alone so that he will develop feelings for you in kind. But so far, it doesn't seem to be working, and I can wait no longer. I almost feel guilty about the things I will do to you tonight." He pulled her tightly against him, his breath at her ear. "Almost."

"My lord," she began uncertainly. How to put this correctly, so as not to offend the king? She had no problems bedding the prince if that's what he wanted.

She supposed he might not be that bad, even if he was as inexperienced as he seemed. But she didn't want to lose her opportunity to get into the king's tower. "I do find prince handsome, is true." She blushed and looked away again, trying to act the embarrassed, naïve girl with a crush. "But you are reason I sent here."

"Yes, I know. And I've denied myself for too long. Seeing you tonight, I'm not quite sure how I've managed. Hopefully poor Adrian won't mind too much." He smiled then, and it sent chills down her spine. On the outside, to anyone else looking, it would appear a kind, gentle smile. But she saw a flash in his eyes. A possessiveness. An eagerness. His hand tightened around her waist, his fingers digging into the folds of her dress. He pulled her noticeably closer, until her breasts were pressed tight against him. When he spoke, there was a seductive edge to his voice. "Come to my rooms tonight. My guards will let you in." It was a demand, not a question.

The dance ended and they stepped away from each other. He bowed and she curtsied, feeling his eyes stray over her body, especially lingering on her breasts. When she rose again, he did not bother to hide the fact that he had been staring.

"There is one more thing," he said.

She curtsied once more. "Anything, my king."

"Dance with my brother." He nodded across the ballroom, though Lily couldn't see over the nearby heads herself. "I know he's been having a dreadful time tonight. He hates parties such as these, all the formality and whatnot. And, despite his embarrassment, when we spoke of you, I got the feeling that he does feel something for you, even if he does not want to admit it. Tenderness, lust, curiosity, I'm not sure which."

They'd spoken of her to one another? That was potentially heartening; it suggested that her insinuating attentions were more effective with one or both brothers than they had been letting on. Provided they'd spoken positively of her, anyway.

She wanted to play the flattered gossip, ask the king what was said and by which of them, but she didn't get the chance. "Besides, I do love to make him uncomfortable," Alec continued. He winked at her then and took her arm, leading her through the throng to the prince.

Adrian was standing against the wall speaking with a few nearby courtiers and looking as if he'd rather be anywhere else. He looked surprised to see them approach, then blanched a moment later as if his brother's coming could only herald grief.

"Adrian, brother, I am ashamed of you," Alec scolded, not bothering with discretion and ignoring the curtsies of the ladies nearby. The prince seemed to grow even more nervous. He looked around, then at himself, as if trying to discover what embarrassing or shameful thing he had done. "You've given your attention to all of these lovely beauties," the king answered for him, "and yet you have not asked the most gorgeous woman here tonight to dance with you."

Lily didn't miss the indulgent smiles and subtle glares of the women around them at that comment.

"Oh, yes, of course," Adrian stammered with a furrowed brow. "My apologies brother...er, Camilla."

He bowed to her then, haltingly, and tugged at the collar on his jacket. "Would you dance with me, please?"

"I be happy to," she answered sweetly. He took her arm, leading her onto the dance floor, and she glanced over at the musicians to see the king speaking with them. They struck up a tune, one with a very fast, complicated tempo. She recognized it as a song from her supposed homeland. It was a sensual Aluvian dance, meant to impress and seduce. King Alec asked Rosalita to sing, and she did so gladly, pleased to be in the spotlight. The words were sultry and wove a love story, though Lily wondered how many of the present here understood Aluvian well enough to know what she sang.

The prince's spine went straight and his arms suddenly stiffened, or at least more so than before. She could tell that he was not a very good dancer. She had been observing him enough to notice that the few times when he did dance with some of the other women, it was mostly waltzing or part of a formation dance. In those, he moved competently enough, but stiffly and dispassionately, the rote repetition of whatever social lessons were part of a royal upbringing. In a more fluid and hot-blooded song like this, he was hopelessly out of his depth.

At least he knew where to place his hands, though he kept trying to not quite touch her waist, letting his hand sort of float above the fabric of her dress. She grabbed it and quickly pressed it down, grinning wickedly when his face turned a bright red. Then, *she* led *him*.

It was a perfect song because there was no one unique dance for it. Instead, a few well-known steps were mixed and intertwined together according to the dancers' instincts. She turned them around the room gracefully and easily, her body flowing to the rhythm, and other couples moved out of the way. Soon she realized that most everyone else had stopped dancing and were now watching them. The tempo of the song picked up more. Their bodies had to press tight, their legs often intertwining, and occasionally he almost tripped on her dress; but she lifted it up out of the way, scandalously high in fact, and held him tight at the shoulder, keeping him standing upright. He tried to stare down at his feet, to see what he was doing, but her dress poofed so much it occasionally covered even his legs, and then he would catch sight of her breasts, find himself staring, and quickly look away.

She observed him as next he turned his nervous gaze to her shoulder, but seeing all of those people staring at him made him even more uncomfortable, she could tell, and in the end he was forced to look into her eyes. Forced to share his panic with her. She could tell he was none too pleased with this idea, and while the wicked side of her was quite enjoying it, she decided she might try to make him a little bit more comfortable. So she gave him a small, encouraging smile, and whispered, "No worry. You dance good."

The movements and beat were irregular, but even if he didn't know how to move to it, she did. Each time the drums crashed, she turned her hips against his, her upper body swaying to the other side. Occasionally she pushed him backwards as she stepped forward aggressively, and then, realizing he had to do the same, he followed suit, though never as hard as she did. The tempo was very quick now, and all eyes were on them.

She knew that they were about to reach the climax of the song. She pulled him tight against her, glad that he wasn't as tall as his brother, so that she could easily whisper in his ear, "When I say, dip me back low as you can. No worry for hurting me—just don't drop."

He gulped, staring straight at her, giving the tiniest of nods. The percussion rolled, the strings hummed, and the woodwind sang, all leading up to a final crescendo.

"Now," she said, and as he lowered her she held loosely to his shoulder with one hand while she quickly grabbed the sticks holding her coif in place with the other, yanking them loose so that her hair tumbled down, touching the floor beneath her.

The room roared with applause. Adrian blinked suddenly, as if waking from a dream, and stared around in shock.

Lily delicately cleared her throat. "Prince, please to lift me up?"

"Oh, of course." He gently raised her back to her feet, and they stood panting together, his hand still on her hip, though he seemed to forget that it was there as she saw the realization of what they'd just done finally dawn on him.

"Camilla," Alec's voice purred behind them, startling the prince. "You were most excellent. Had I known you were such an exquisite dancer, I would have kept you to myself for that song." He grinned at them and patted his brother on the shoulder.

Lily curtsied once more, though it was no easy matter, as hard as she was breathing. She felt dizzy now and wanted nothing more than to sit down and have a cool drink of water. Oh, and to rip her damn corset off as quickly as possible. "I not have done without prince guiding me." None of them bothered to point out that she had clearly been in the lead for that dance. It was only polite to pretend Adrian had actually had any clue what he was doing.

"My lady?" Lily heard behind her. She turned to find a group of men standing there, each looking expectant. "If you wouldn't mind, I would ask that you reserve your next dance for me," one asked, bowing low.

Oh, so now they wanted to dance, whether their jealous wives saw or not. She didn't miss the scorned women glaring daggers at her from across the room. Or the fact that Rosalita looked irritated that Lily had stolen the attention for herself. Between her performance just now and the king's earlier comment, she was on track to gaining the ire of nearly every other woman in attendance tonight. Lucky for her that her mission didn't hinge on the goodwill of any of them.

"Um, I sorry, but…I really very tired," she said to her newest suitor. "I think I just go rest." She glanced at Alec as she said this, and saw from the glint in his eye that he caught her meaning. She could feel his eyes boring into her as she left the ballroom, making her way back to her own quarters. He should still be occupied with his party for another hour or more, and that would be ample time to explore his suite in private.

Six

After returning to her own rooms to change into something more comfortable, Lily made her way to the king's chamber. There was only one entrance, as far as she could tell, and it was under constant guard. The sentries must have been made aware that the king would have a lover visit him tonight, however, for they let her in as soon as she told them who she was. A guard led her down a hall to a beautifully carved mahogany door, opening it for her politely. Going through, she found herself in a large, comfortable living room. Without a word, the guard bowed and departed, clearly used to escorting women to the king's chamber.

A fire was burning in the hearth, warming away the natural chill that would otherwise seep through the stonework. Fluffy rugs were draped over the stone floors; the one in front of the fireplace appeared to be from some large animal, possibly a bear. A wide, luxurious couch sat before the fire, and adjacent to it, a matching loveseat, both done in rich red velvet. A small bar occupied the corner, and hanging on the wall behind it were racks full of expensive looking wines. There were no windows in the living room, but there were doors leading to other rooms on every wall. On the wall to her right with the fireplace was an open door leading to a bedroom.

A quick peak in the bedroom showed Lily that she was alone for the moment. She stepped into the room and took a quick glance around. Most of the space was taken up with a huge four-poster bed draped with red silks and piled high with more pillows than were necessary for one person. A wardrobe against the wall held an array of expensive clothing. She opened a window and peeked her head out. She could faintly hear the sound of music from the ball, and as it would be impolite for the king to leave before his own party was over, she surmised that she still had time to explore.

Returning to the living room, she went to the wall on the left of the entryway, which had two doors. One led to a bathroom with a large marble clawfoot tub and a window overlooking the side gardens. The other led to an office, which she entered. She quickly looked through all of the drawers on the desk, searching for anything of use, but found nothing. As they weren't even locked, she doubted that any imperial secrets were being kept here.

She left the office and stared at the last remaining door across from the entryway. It was larger than the others, made of a heavier, sturdier wood, with a complicated lock on it. And unlike the others, it actually was locked.

Lily knelt down in front of the door and pulled the stick out of her hair. While it appeared to be nothing more than a simple accessory, it was hollow on the inside, with a long, thin metal rod hidden in the interior. She pulled the rod out, which was sharpened to a point and bent at the end. Sticking the tiny metal rod into the lock on the door, she felt for the tumblers, and when she had activated them all, she used the hair stick to twist the lock. There was a click, and the door opened with a slight creak.

The room before her was dark. Scant, red-tinted moonlight filtered through the large stained-glass window on the opposite wall, casting the room in an eerie, blood red glow that was still too dim to illuminate its contents. It was enough light to show that the room had curved walls, though, which indicated that this was indeed the western tower she had been looking for.

Her heartrate quickened in excitement. The Guild hadn't been able to procure floor plans for this tower; the eastern one, they knew, was largely used for storage of miscellaneous furniture and supplies, but not a single person throughout the Guild's extensive network of informants knew anything more than rumor regarding the interior of the western one, and each rumor differed. Finally, she'd be able to fill in one of the largest and only remaining gaps in the palace layout. It wasn't necessary for her main mission, but it was an enticing feather to add to her cap nevertheless.

Lily grabbed a candle from the living room and held it before her, chasing away the deep shadows and revealing her surroundings. She lifted an eyebrow, whistling in surprise. Where she had been expecting to find his real office, full of government secrets and important letters she could copy down and send to the Guild, she instead found a torture chamber.

Or so it seemed at first glance, as she took in the shackles on the wall and ceiling, the wooden horse tucked in a corner, whips of various sizes and lengths.

It certainly looked ominous in the flickering orange candlelight mixed with the red tint from the window.

She had seen torture devices before. The Guild had taught her about all of the different methods that would be used on her if she were ever caught. She had watched the torture of others, often traitors and ex-allies who knew too much. She had even been tortured herself as part of her training — nothing permanently damaging, but just enough so that she'd know what to expect and how to endure should she slip up and find herself captured by an enemy.

But these were not quite the tools of torture she had been warned of. No, a closer glance as she traversed the room revealed among them a good many instruments of pleasure. In the very center of the room, two long chains with shackles at the end hung down from the rafters, just high enough for someone of average height to stand on their tip toes if their arms were stretched up above them. The plethora of floggers mounted on the walls, from whips to crops to paddles, came in as wide a range as she had ever seen, each one displayed like a trophy. One multi-thonged whip had sharpened metal tips; another looked like it was made of several long ribbons braided together with regular knotted protrusions; and still another featured regular leather thongs, but attached to an ivory handle that ended in an undeniably phallic knob.

Propped nearby on the wall was a long metal pole with two more shackles at the end; Lily imagined it must be used to keep one's legs spread. A shelf on one side of the room held blindfolds, small knives, cuffs, collars, and various phalluses made of marble, jade, even one that was gilded. There was even a pillory, which had been outlawed over forty years ago; she wondered if it had been especially built for this room, or had been brought here from the center of town when the others were being torn down.

Lily felt a tickling at the back of her mind, a memory trying to surface. Then she remembered. The servant girl, who was meeting in secret with someone in the castle, someone who apparently liked to play rough. So the servant girl's secret liaison was the king himself.

Lily couldn't say she was surprised. Someone with as much power as the king would certainly get bored with the women throwing themselves at his feet. And when one had power, they often craved more, in every aspect of life. If he wanted to tie up the other courtesans and beat them until they begged for mercy, that was none of her business.

But he wasn't going to beat her. Lily was no prude; she'd had her fair share of lovers, some of them even at the same time. She was no stranger to lust and base desires. But not even in her wildest sexual fantasies would she find it arousing to be helpless. It was not in her nature to submit to the mercy of another, king or not. Her training, her instincts, old memories that still wouldn't fade — they all made it impossible for her. Her body shuddered at the memory of those past tortures inflicted by Master Gavriel, a warning of what would come should she disobey. Even if the king's tortures brought pleasure to others, she knew they couldn't for her.

Just knowing that these were his proclivities soured Lily's attraction to the man somewhat. But she was in the king's private chambers now, and she had already agreed to sleep with him this night. If he kept this room so close at hand, no doubt he would want to put it to use. If and when it came up, she would have to convince him that she had no interest in such things. How best to do that without seeming to reject him?

She had little time to ponder, for she heard footsteps down the hall—the king returning to his rooms. He was whistling a jaunty tune that had played earlier in the evening. Lily cursed inwardly and rushed to the door, closing it behind her as quietly as she could. She grabbed the padlock, sliding it into place just as the handle on the door to the living room turned.

She quickly stood up, shoving the hair stick back into her hair. But she hadn't quite gotten the lock pick back in it all the way and somehow she ended up scratching her face in the process. She wiped at the blood hastily as she began walking to the door, the candle in hand, a bright smile on her face.

King Alec stepped through, his eyes glinting darkly in the light of the fire, and grinned at her. She curtsied deeply. "M'lord," she simpered, "I am happy you finally come. Would you like glass of wine?"

He nodded, throwing his brocade coat over the couch and kneeling to take off his boots. Lily glided over to the bar, opening a bottle and pouring two glasses for them. She was stoppering the bottle when she felt him step up behind her, his stockings muffling his steps, and she jumped in mock surprise when he wrapped his arms around her, burying his face in her hair.

"You changed your clothes," he murmured. "I thought I might feel disappointed, but...this is much nicer."

Indeed, the dress she wore was silky and light, practically transparent in some areas, with a slit running up the side. A garter belt held up her thigh high lace stockings. Over her dress, she wore a matching floor-length robe, all done in a light purple with black lace, which he now began to slip off of her shoulders.

He paused. "What happened here?" he asked, tracing the cut on her cheek. His thumb was rough against it, and she hissed in a breath.

"Oh, I scratch self. Getting out of corset," she replied.

Alec grinned, putting his thumb to his lips and sucking her blood off of it. Then he dipped his fingers in the wine and trailed them down her throat before licking it off. A power play she would have tolerated normally, but now the thought sent chills down her spine. The dark red wine looked too much like blood, which she was sure was why he did it. He was probably just now envisioning running one of those metal-tipped whips down her back and licking up the trail of blood.

Disconcerted by the thought, she slid away from him and walked over to the fireplace, carrying her glass of wine with her. "I have chill," she told him as an excuse. "It is drafty here, yes?"

"I thought it was getting too hot, actually." He was undoing his shirt now and dropped it to the ground. The muscles of his chest rippled as he stalked towards her.

115

Lily began to worry now. He was much more muscular than she had thought he would be. She knew he'd ridden into plenty of the battles he'd ordered waged, but still, she had expected a king, with servants waiting on him hand and foot, wouldn't have the need to be so toned. Evidently he did more than sit his horse and passively watch others do his fighting. Now he seemed much stronger. Not too strong, certainly, if it came to that; but enough that it would be a fight for her. And with nothing but his slacks on, she could clearly see the bulge in his pants.

The king licked his lips, lust in his eyes. Lust and power, or the hunger for it at least. As if he needed any more than he already held daily just from his birth. The more she thought about it, the more Lily decided that her prejudice against royalty was too strong not to taint the idea of dallying with one of them. As he moved in closer, she brought a hand up to his chest. She tried to appear loving, but in reality she just wanted to keep him at arm's length.

He moved quicker than she would have expected, though, and grabbed her wrist tightly in his hand, pulling her against his hard chest, his lips crashing down on hers. He didn't bother to move gently. His tongue was inside her mouth, and then he was shoving her down on the floor, onto that distasteful bear rug, his body crushing hers, his hands pinning her wrists down. His mouth moved away from hers and down her neck. She wriggled under him as he began to suck on her flesh, then bit it hard. Lily gasped in pain and surprise, and the king smiled at her with a chuckle. "Like that, do you?" he whispered. "Yeah, I get that a lot." He trailed one hand down her thigh, ripping away her undergarments, and before she could stop him, his fingers were inside her, uninvited.

Lily was quickly losing control of this situation. If she didn't pleasure him tonight, he could throw her out of the castle, and her mission would be a failure. But any desire she might have had for him was gone now, knowing what he wanted to do to her in return; and at the rate he was going, he was going to discover her lack of desire very soon if she didn't act fast. She had to find a way to leave him satisfied while still keeping control of the situation.

A thought sprang to mind, and she grinned. Years of practice allowed her to hook her legs around him and flip their positions in one quick movement. In another she grabbed his hands and pinned them down on either side of his head.

He looked shocked. Whether it was at the idea that she would push him away or the fact that she could, she wasn't sure. "What is this, then?" Alec asked curiously.

"The other girls tell me what you like, my king," she whispered with a smile, glancing at the padlocked door. His eyes followed hers, a wicked grin spreading across his lips.

"You courtesans do love to gossip. I was hoping that would be a little surprise for you tonight. How much did they tell you?" he asked.

"That you like to control. To cause…pain," she answered, trying not to sound accusatory.

"Not just pain, my dear," he purred beneath her. "Pleasure, as well. Some girls shy away from it at first, but they always come around in the end." She didn't bother to mention that that might be because he was the king, and they were too afraid to tell him no. "You can't honestly tell me this is the first time you've serviced a lover with rougher desires."

"Of course not, my king," she answered smoothly. "But that what you always have to do, yes? To be in control. Of country. Of family. Of women." She lowered her head until their lips were almost brushing. "But have you ever try the, how do you say, reverse?"

He lifted an eyebrow questioningly. "What did you have in mind?"

Lily sat up, removing the sash from her discarded robe, and tied it around his head, obscuring his vision. "Now, you must let me be king tonight, yes?"

Alec's lips pursed as he seemed to mull the idea over. After a moment, he shrugged. "I suppose I can give it a try," he said. "Are you sure you can handle having that much...power?" He lifted his head and glanced blindly down in the general direction of his erection.

Lily rolled her eyes. Why was it that men always thought that their particular member was the gods' gift to women? "I suppose we will have to see," she teased.

"Very well," he said with a smirk. "Then I shall give you a chance to prove yourself. But if I should find your skills at leadership lacking, Lady King, then I shall have to wrest control from you again. Understood?"

"Understood, my king." She didn't miss the seductive threat. Nonetheless, he relented, placing his hands behind his head and waiting expectantly.

Lily didn't leave him disappointed. She started at his throat, sucking and biting at his neck, then began working her way down. She left him a love bite on his nipple, which seemed to surprise him, though he didn't complain—especially as her mouth moved lower, following a trail of hair to the edge of his trousers. In one swift movement she pulled them down, his cock springing free, and left them around his ankles as a sort of restraint.

She slipped her lips over him and took him into her mouth, teasing him slowly at first until he was groaning for more. He soon forgot to be subservient and wound his hands through her hair, urgent for her motions to be faster. She fondled his sack, then wondered just how far she could push him. It was arrogant of her, but having the king of Arestea so literally in her hands—and mouth—it was impossible not to. As he lifted his hips to thrust further into her mouth, she squeezed.

He hissed in shock, but before he could say anything, she brought him over the edge. Lily pulled her hands and mouth away just in the nick of time, watching his manhood spasm as his seed splattered onto his toned stomach. By now his makeshift blindfold had fallen from one eye, and he seemed to be studying her.

"Well, that was certainly…different. I'm not sure I appreciated that bit at the end there," he said.

Lily smiled. "You must try new things, yes? And being king can be very…" she pretended to struggle with the right word.

"Intoxicating?" he growled. Lily nodded. "I agree. Which is why I'm afraid I'm going to have to wrest back my title now, my lady." His grin was wicked. "And after that little performance, I believe I shall have to work extra hard to make sure you know who is really in control."

Her heart leapt in fear. Was that not enough to satisfy him? Did he still intend to torture her? She feigned a yawn and rose up from him, stepping gracefully towards the door as she grabbed her robe from the floor. "Oh, someday, yes, but not tonight, my king. One thing I learn as courtesan, always leave man begging for more, yes? That way he keep you, and he come back to you." She smiled as he watched her from the floor, apparently still too spent at the moment to chase after her. "And you go far away to battle. I need make sure you have reason come back safe to me."

Alec yawned as he rose to a sitting position on the rug. "Camilla, that is probably the stupidest thing I've ever heard," he muttered, closing his eyes. "But I am too tired to argue with you right now. Fine, you win for tonight." He waved a hand vaguely toward her and the door. "You may go."

"Thank you, Highness," Lily said with a curtsy. And with that, she left him alone and began her way back to her own rooms.

Prince Adrian ascended the eastern stairs towards his chambers, trying not to drag his feet. Even after his brother had left and the party officially ended, women continued to bother him for dances, despite the fact that none were so heated or skilled as that with the courtesan Camilla. If they were disappointed, it didn't show; and finally, nearly an hour after his brother's disappearance, the party began to properly disperse. Some nobles returned to their own quarters, others to another's. He cared not, as long as he could return to his room and get out of this damned uncomfortable outfit and these pinching shoes.

As he reached the top step, he saw Camilla striding toward him, a small smile on her face. She had changed out of her billowing ball gown into a night dress that he could practically see through. She looked up when she heard him coming, paused in her step for the briefest moment, then dipped into a quick, deep curtsy, hiding her face from his view.

He saw it, though, there on her cheek. And the only thing on that side of the corridor she could have been interested in was his brother's room.

"What did he do?" Adrian demanded, an angry edge to his voice that he hadn't intended. She went into a deeper bow, not looking up. "What happened?" the prince tried again, softer this time. "Are you hurt?"

"N-no, my lord," she answered quietly, barely audible, and finally glanced up at him through her eyelashes, her cheeks burning pink. "You mean this?" She touched her fingers lightly to the cut. "Just small scratch," she said. "I have accident with corset."

"Yes, many of our maids and serving girls have accidents in this corridor," he said, ire rising again. "Camilla, you don't have to be afraid of him. If you can tell anyone, you can tell me, I promise. I know what he's like."

"No, no, is not what you think," she insisted, rising finally but keeping her eyes averted.

"Funny, that's what all the others say as well." His hands were clenched at his sides, he realized. He also realized that it wasn't just his brother he was getting angry at. "And here I thought...I don't know." He sighed and turned away, back toward the stairs.

"My lord?" There was honest concern in her voice, though whether for him or her own safety he couldn't tell. "You are all right? Is something not good?"

"Yes. And yes." Adrian turned back to her, and more than the others he'd met along this hallway, for some reason, the sight of her both angered and saddened him. Whatever charms she may have held over him before, he couldn't see them now. "I'd just sort of...I'd hoped you were better than that, Camilla," he said quietly, then turned and made his way back down the stairs, ignoring her stammering as he left her staring after him.

Seven

The days before King Alec's departure ground by too slowly in their passing for his taste, and every one of them awash in more clamoring aristocrats seeking to get in one last audience, more Officers of This and Ministers of That requesting clarification of duties or alternate arrangements, and more shouting from the king at anyone who tried to see him that he hadn't specifically sent for himself.

The bustle inside the palace increased threefold as servants worked constantly to accommodate the influx of visitors they were expecting, preparing larger and more frequent meals, tidying every room multiple times in the same day (before and after use), and readying supplies and equipment for his majesty's travels. In the stables outside the palace proper, every mount and packhorse was inspected, groomed, exercised, put on a strict feeding regiment, then inspected and groomed again.

In the guardhouse and all along the gate, soldiers trained doubly hard in order to ready themselves against any threat that may try and strike during the king's absence. Everything in the armory, from the weapons to the armor to the standards hanging on the wall, was taken out and cleaned, polished, repaired, tested, honed, recleaned, re-polished, and replaced in exact order, down to every link of mail.

Finally, the time had come for him to depart. Alec was loathe to the leave the capital city, wondering how Luceran would fare in his absence, but he believed his brother was adequately prepared to rule in his stead. And where Alec was needed most was not in the capital but on the front lines, leading his men in the final stages of conquering their neighbors.

Unlike too many of his predecessors, Alec believed the king should actually rule the land actively. Too often, previous kings and queens had seemed to be of the belief that their simple existence was enough to keep a country running, without any actual work on their parts. They were oblivious to all of the planning, management, peacekeeping, budgeting, and lawmaking that was needed, and left most of that to their advisors and counsel. Instead of actually leading, they would travel around the country visiting the nobility and attending lavish parties in their honor, acting as little more than expensive figureheads.

While Alec loved such lavish parties himself, he also loved exercising his authority and putting it to good use. It helped that he had a knack for it; it certainly wasn't something that came naturally to everybody. Alec and Adrian had both been subject to the same rigorous studies of history, politics, law, society, and the arts, had been trained in reading, writing, arithmetic, language, martial strategy, and most importantly, diplomacy. However, where Alec had taken to it with ease and even enjoyed it, Adrian seemed to loathe even the idea of ruling a country. Perhaps it was because he believed the crown would never pass down to him — that Alec, being young and healthy, would rule until he had an heir, who would follow in his footsteps.

If only that were so. But circumstances thus far seemed to be proving otherwise. Alec was no stranger to dalliances with women from all walks of life within his country — he was a king, why should he not indulge himself? At first he had been careful, always making sure that he would not have to worry about an illegitimate child. But as time went on, he had stopped bothering. He reached the point where he just assumed the first noblewoman who became pregnant with his child was the one he would end up making his queen. But no woman ever did, and he was beginning to wonder if there was something wrong with him in that regard. Not that he was incapable — the number of women he had bedded over the years and who kept coming back for more were proof beyond his own boasting of the prowess he held in the bedroom. It just seemed he was not physically capable of fathering children.

This was actually fine with Alec. While he kept it a secret from all to avoid rumor or even fear among the people that their royal bloodline was dying out, he was setting up his brother to be his heir. Alec only wished he knew if Adrian also had the same problem with creating children as he did. So far, it seemed to run in the family. Alec knew that his mother and father had had great difficulty in producing the two of them. That was why they were born so far apart and there were no other children, when most royalty had as many as they could, in case some were stillborn, died at a young age, or were targeted for assassination. Alec had heard the rumors that his mother and father had even turned to secret magic, which had long been presumed dead, in order to conceive of their two sons.

Years after Adrian's birth, when Alec was a teen, there had been a third and final pregnancy, but this had resulted in their mothers' death. The child had been stillborn, and it was uncertain for many years whether or not the problem had lain with the king's virility or the queen's womb. Now, it would seem, the former had been the case, and that it was hereditary. Alec just hoped Adrian would be able to conceive of a child when he did eventually marry, so that their family line did not end with him.

But at least this left Alec free to enjoy the company of women. Many, many women. It was more than just pleasure. It was his civic duty to bed as many women as possible in the hopes that one might end up with his child. He smiled as he thought back to a few nights ago with Camilla. She had surprised him, taking control like that, leaving him the vulnerable one. It was the first time a woman had had the gall to do such, and it left him intrigued. Sadly he'd been too busy to have her, or any of the courtesans, return to his chambers since that night.

A rapping on his door pulled Alec away from his pleasant memories of that night. He called for his visitor to come in, already knowing from the light, hesitant knocking that it was his brother.

Adrian entered and then slumped in the chair across from Alec's desk in apparent exhaustion. Alec knew his brother had been running around the castle for the past few days trying to absorb and memorize everything he could before his departure. He could see from the look on Adrian's face that he still didn't feel prepared to step into a king's duties come tomorrow morning.

Adrian's gaze wandered the room, taking in the neatly organized books and immaculate rugs spread across the polished marble floor. "I don't believe I've ever seen this room so clean," he said. "Was this rug always here?"

"Adrian, you didn't come here to admire the carpets. And yes, it's always been there, just usually covered in paperwork. You'll be *fine*, brother," Alec reassured him with a grin.

"You keep saying that," the prince replied. "And it's not that I doubt my own competence. I know enough of politics and of running a palace to know I won't drown under the weight of them. But the pressure..." He sighed and ran a hand through hair long since disheveled by the same gesture. "Not from the work, but the *people*. Everyone's so reluctant to see you gone for even the shortest bit that it seems they expect the whole country to fall apart as soon as the door closes behind you."

"So prove them wrong," Alec said, steepling his fingers and peering at his brother over them. "You just said you know you can handle things; people thinking you can't do something doesn't make it any harder, just more satisfying when you achieve it."

"Alec, I'm not as cavalier as you, and I'm not as experienced," the prince complained. "I can't just ignore the citizens' voices and do my own thing the way you do, especially when my ruling is subpar to

127

yours in the eyes of every noble you still let into the palace. In a time of peace, they might accept a less-aggrandized ruler, but with all the wars we've been fighting…and then the man whose idea it was in the first place just steps out and puts someone less popular on the throne…"

"'Still let into the palace?'" The king quirked an eyebrow and held the prince's gaze, unblinking.

Adrian looked away almost immediately. "You know what I mean. The ones who openly agree with your policies. The ones who still make appearances at court."

"And you think there are others who don't?" Alec continued. "You think I surround myself with sycophants only, and any who speak against me are kept from doing so within my walls?"

"Um…" Adrian slumped back to his chair and took a sudden interest in the new office arrangement. There were several seconds of awkward silence before he finally glanced back at his brother and saw that he'd been smiling.

Alec slapped the desk with enough force to make the prince flinch. "That's exactly what's been going on," he said, pointing at his brother. "Good eye, Adrian. Though if you're going to accuse someone of something, you can't be so quick to back down when they call you out on it. Especially when you know you're right." He frowned, then waved a hand. "No, scratch that. Especially when you think you might be wrong. If you're right, it'll fall out eventually anyway, but if you're not and you insist you are hard enough, you might still make your enemy doubt his case enough to win."

Adrian sighed and dropped his face to his palms in lieu of reply.

"Adrian." Alec paused until Adrian looked up to see the concern on his face. "Are you well? You're stressed, I know, but you often are with the things I do, and you don't usually look this bad."

"I've not been sleeping," the prince answered. "I've been trying to learn all of the new developments and the ways you're arranging things for when I'm in charge, and it's keeping me up at night."

"You know you don't have to commit every detail to memory, right?" the king asked gently. "Hell, even I don't know all the details of everything I've been commanding. That's what parchment and secretaries are for. It's called delegation."

"Yes, well…" Adrian exhaled a deep breath and added nothing more.

"Yes, well," Alec repeated, then smiled again, "in that case, you're either going to love me or despise me for this next one. Or at least, love or despise me more than you do already, I'm never sure with you."

"Huh?" Adrian's head snapped up, instantly alert.

The king's grin widened. "I've arranged for that Camilla girl to move into your rooms while I'm gone. To help you sleep at night." He'd wondered if Camilla was the right choice for Adrian or not. After all, she was incredibly forward, ready to take what she wanted. Alec was afraid that Adrian might shy from such a woman, but throwing demure girls at his feet in the hopes he would fall for one of them had thus far failed.

Adrian himself was too reserved to court a woman, and Alec was afraid that if his brother didn't lose his virginity — and his timidity — soon, Adrian would remain a bachelor forever, ending the D'Arestes line. Perhaps a strong-willed woman like Camilla could finally break through his shell.

"You…" Adrian shot to his feet again. Alec wasn't sure if he was furious or merely livid. "Why? Why would you think I would want you to do that?"

"Oh, I knew you wouldn't," Alec said as if it were obvious. "But since when have I cared?" He grinned and leaned back, linking his hands behind his head, pleased with himself. "You either secretly like her more than you're letting on, or you really are sick of being near her; in either case, it should be like living with me. But with tits." He spread his hands and beamed. "You see? It's like I'm not even really leaving. You've been worried all this time for nothing."

"Yes, it's exactly like that," Adrian grumbled. "Even when you're miles away, you still find ways to vex me."

"Thank you." The king bowed his head. "I try."

"Good. Then try and leave," Adrian said. "And I hope you realize that I'm just going to send her right back to her own room as soon as you're gone."

"And I hope you realize that you can't," Alec said cheerfully. "Or that you won't. See, I've let it be known that her continued usefulness in the palace will be directly tied to how pleased you are with her company while I'm away. So if you kick her out of your rooms, she gets kicked out of the palace altogether, and her contract as an accessory to my arm is terminated. And from what she's told me, she seems very concerned with the possibility of being let go. Almost frightened of the thought, I'd wager."

"You..." Adrian, at a loss for words, simply stared at him with his mouth opening and closing, like a fish taken out of water. "You're a total bastard," he finally finished.

"And that," said Alec, rising to pat his sibling on the shoulder over his desk, "is why I'm the king. Better study up, brother."

The king's departure was a parade. Lily wasn't sure if he had intended it to be one, but that's what it became.

She lined up like everyone else in the palace to bid him farewell, noticing his younger brother's grim face as they hugged in parting. Then Alec mounted his steed and rode out of the palace gates flanked by his guards. Peering beyond the gates, she could see nobility, peers of the realm, tradesmen, workers, and even the poor lining the streets together all the way down the royal hill, cheering and throwing flowers at the king. Whether those present truly loved him, were only glad to see him leaving, or simply wanted an excuse for a celebration, she could not tell. He *did* look magnificent, she had to admit, in his newly smithed and gleaming armor that had yet to see actual battle. A decorative sword hung at his side, and his entourage carried bright banners with the royal crest. It was all very flashy and showy, but she knew once he was outside of the city walls that he would climb into a gilt-trimmed carriage and ride the rest of the way in that, surrounded on all sides by guards for his safety.

After he had disappeared from sight, the castle inhabitants stood around awkwardly for a few minutes, unsure of themselves and what to do now. After some time the crowd dispersed, people milling off to go about their day. The servants went back to their chores, the visiting nobles to their idle pastimes, and the guards to their rounds.

It was pleasant outside: the sun was high and a cool autumn breeze blew through the trees. Lily knew soon enough it would grow chilly and she wouldn't be able to enjoy the pleasant warmth that still remained. So once the excitement died down, she took a stroll through the gardens, watched fish jump in the ponds, sat under a cherry blossom tree that was just beginning to turn, and watched some dukes play croquet. Eventually she decided to return to her rooms.

She found them gone. Well, not the rooms themselves, of course, but everything of hers. It had all been packed up and moved out while she had been strolling outside. Had she been kicked out? Was she now deemed useless without the king there to please? She glanced into the rooms of the other two courtesans, and found they had not been disturbed in the least. Had the king discarded of her for not pleasing him adequately?

"Oh, m'lady. There you are. We've been looking for you." A maid entered her room, making a quick curtsy.

"As you can see, we've gathered your things. Are you ready to leave?"

"Leave?" Lily asked dumbly.

"Well, yes." Seeing the confused look on her face, the woman asked, "Didn't the king inform you? Or Prince Adrian? How odd. The thing is, you've been moved in with the prince. You have a beautiful room, twice as large as this one, right next to his. And your own bath, of course, with a boudoir. I am certain you will love it."

"And others? Rosalita and Olivia?" she asked.

"Well, no," replied the maid, "they're staying here, of course. It's just you moving in with the prince. And if I may say, personally, I'm certainly glad of it. That young man needs a strong, beautiful woman like you to break through his shell."

At least Lily didn't have to try hard to seem surprised. "I...I see. I find his rooms on my own, please. First I wish say goodbye to others."

Seeing she had been dismissed, the maidservant curtsied again and left. Lily closed and locked the door behind her, then immediately went over to the bed, pulling out her chest.

At least they hadn't thought to check if she'd stored anything under her bed. And it hadn't been tampered with. Good. Well, this was certainly unexpected, but nothing to get flustered over. If anything, she would now be in the royal quarters, and thus have more excuse to go wandering around them, searching in crannies for any information of value. But the thought of moving in with the prince, or next to him anyway, after what he had said to her, how he had looked at her...For the first time since she came here over a month ago, she suddenly felt true trepidation.

When she left her room, she saw Rosalita and Olivia were out. That was fine by her. She didn't really want to talk to anyone at the moment anyway. Lily made her way to the prince's chambers, carrying her chest in her arms. It was bulky and certainly heavy, but she hadn't gotten too out of shape at the castle, so it wasn't much of a struggle carrying it up and down the staircases. She was going up a narrow stairwell meant for servants when she heard footsteps coming down the hall towards her. Looking up, she saw the prince standing at the top, staring down at her. He seemed surprised, though she wasn't sure why. After all, according to the servant girl whose name she'd never learned, he had known of this arrangement before she had.

He quickly regained his manners and descended the stairs towards her. "Camilla, let me help you with that."

"No, no, is fine. I can handle," she told him, trying to give him her sweetest smile.

"Please," he said, "it looks quite heavy. I insist." He took one of the handles in his hand. In her sudden panic, she held on tighter to the other as he pulled. A short and awkward tugging match ensued as they both tried to get the other to let go of the chest. There was no way she was letting him have it, though he apparently didn't seem to understand that.

She wasn't sure how it happened. They'd both pulled on the heavy chest at the same moment, and then it was flying through the air, tumbling down the stairs, crashing and banging into the stone walls as it went. It landed at the bottom, broken, strewing its contents across the floor. They both stared in shock, unsure of what to do. Then he started moving, babbling apologies, and the stairs were too narrow for her to pass him up without pushing him out of the way, and that would only look more suspicious. He reached the bottom first, then froze, staring.

And Lily's anxiety reached a crescendo.

Eight

He saw flashes of metal first. Adrian didn't quite realize what they were. He almost mistook them for jewelry, tangled among the dark fabric of some dress. But it seemed wrong, and when he looked twice, he realized it wasn't jewelry, and the fabric wasn't a dress. It was a pair of pants and a shirt, with dark leather attached to some of it, like some sort of crude, thin armor. And the metal was from knives, bolts, a small crossbow, and some other weapons he couldn't even identify.

Then he took it all in. The papers fluttering down to the floor around him. He picked one up. It was a sketch of the castle. An extremely detailed one, showing a number of private rooms, every hallway, every servant's staircase and hidden passage, with notes scribbled throughout—names of residents, locations of hidden doors, details of secret nooks and crannies. There were letters, cursory glances of which revealed detailed discussions of matters of national security, in blunt language much like his brother's. In fact, one he recognized, having read it earlier in the week. But they weren't written in his brother's hand; no, the scrawling letters were much more feminine, as if someone had copied down his brother's writing word for word. And they were written in Arestean. Adrian knew that Camilla couldn't speak the language well, and so he had doubted she could read it, either. Scattered amongst it all were various lacy undergarments. But what caught his eye, above everything else, were the flowers.

They had the shape of lilies, but the petals were black. He bent over, picking one up gently in his hand. It smelled nice. He was surprised something so haunting could smell nice.

He saw movement in the corner of his eye. He turned, staring at her. She had a dagger in her hand. Where had it come from? They watched each other, he holding the flower as if he were going to hand it to her, she holding the knife. He knew he didn't want her to give that to him.

Time seemed frozen. He was sure he could hear the shadows creep across the walls. How long did they stand there?

It must have been only a moment, though an incredibly tense one, because he soon heard voices in the hall, and footsteps. She heard it too. He saw her eyes widen.

"M'lord, are you alright?" came a masculine voice from the stairs above them.

"Hide it," she hissed suddenly, then burst into a flurry of movement. He realized, somewhere in the back of his mind, that her accent was gone. He had enough sense to hide his hand behind his back as she passed him, running towards the mess. He didn't get the chance to see what she was doing. The guard appeared at the top of the stairs.

"I heard a commotion. Is everything okay?" the guard asked.

Nobody said anything, and then Adrian realized the man was talking to him. He swallowed, cleared his throat, but before he could answer Camilla spoke up from behind him, her accent suddenly returning. "Yes, yes, everything fine. We drop my chest. Down stairs. Is all." She wrapped an arm around the prince, and he suppressed a shudder. He felt something cold and hard press against his flesh under his shirt. A warning. He nodded his assent to the guard.

"Oh, well, would you like some help?" the guard asked, beginning to descend the stairs. "I can get that for you."

"Oh, no. I get all myself. Prince Adrian so kind to help," Camilla simpered at him.

"My lady, I insist. I'm sure I can carry that little chest for you easily." The guard was smiling at her. Falling for her every word. But he wasn't leaving.

"I, I too embarrassed. It is...lady things," she said quietly, giggling and blushing. "Undergarments. I no want anyone see. You understand?"

Adrian saw the guard color slightly as well. "Oh, I see. I won't bother anything then. But if you need any help..."

"No, thank you." She smiled and glanced shyly away, like a young girl. The guard began to leave. Adrian wanted to yell, but he couldn't seem to find the voice to. Why wasn't he stopping the man? Why was he letting the only person who could protect him go away? But then, seeing her there, blushing, hanging off of his arm, her face bashful, he couldn't see how dangerous she could be. She was smaller than him, about a head shorter, and so slender and delicate. She didn't seem at all like she could kill somebody.

And then the guard was gone, and she turned on him, her face changing before his eyes, becoming stony and unreadable. She held the knife between them, her body crouched and tensed, and he wasn't sure if she was preparing to flee or to kill him.

Instead she simply watched him, her eyes narrowed. He grew uncomfortable and looked behind him, though he didn't turn his back on her. She had grabbed a tapestry off of the wall and thrown it over the spilled contents of the broken chest. He hadn't even noticed the tapestry there before.

Finally, he looked back at her. He realized she wasn't going to say anything. She just kept staring intensely at him, unmoving, not showing any emotion. So he was going to have to talk. "Who *are* you?" he finally asked.

Lily's eyes darted between the prince, the chest, and the stairs descending behind them, quickly assessing the situation while she tried to come up with a plan for damage control. "I think, perhaps," she replied, "we should go somewhere more private to speak of these matters."

She wondered if he had blinked once in all the time they'd been standing there. She didn't think so. She wasn't sure if he was in shock or just daft. But slowly he nodded, his lips forming a grim line, and glanced down at the mess beside them. "What should we…?"

She hated the thought of him touching her most prized possessions, but she certainly wasn't' going to turn her back on him and risk him escaping or, worse, attacking her. "Clean it up," she demanded curtly, waving at the mess with her dagger. He seemed shocked at first that she was issuing him a command, but when she stepped menacingly closer, he bent down and began to do as he was told.

When he'd finished messily repacking her chest, she made him pick it up and carry it up the stairs before her. She followed silently, keeping the dagger at his back at all times. They entered his suite, and he set the chest down on the floor of the sitting room. Lily took a quick glance in the adjoining bedrooms to ensure that they were empty. It appeared the servants were gone by now, having finished packing away her clothing and what few personal items she had bothered bringing.

She made her way to the armchair. She could tell by how worn it was, and by his apparent discomfort at her sitting there, that it seemed to be his favorite chair. She lounged back in it like a throne, her feet up on the tea table, playing at having power she did not possess. She would not let him see how nervous she was.

He sat down on the settee across from her, his back ramrod straight, his hands folded in his lap. "So, would you kindly tell me what the hell is going on now?" he asked.

She quirked an eyebrow at him. "Why do you even bother asking? Isn't it pretty obvious?"

She watched him as his face went from that blank confusion to anger. She remembered his disappointment the night she'd left the king's rooms, but she had never seen him truly angry before. It was...interesting. Not at all frightening, like on his brother, but it almost made her feel a sense of achievement. She had made the pacifist Prince Adrian angry. "I saved you back there," he said heatedly. "I could have called the guard on you, but I didn't. I think you at least owe me some answers."

She laughed then. Threw her head back and laughed. The prince was thrown off guard. His anger deflated as his expression once more became confused. "You're not very bright, are you, princeling?" she asked, and she saw his eyebrows furrowed as he tried to figure out what she meant. "I could cross this room and kill you before you could even blink. You were a fool not to yell for help when you had the chance. Though I suppose this did help to sway you." She slowly lifted her long skirt, extracting a dagger from her left leg sheathe and toying with it. His eyes followed her every move.

For a while he didn't say anything, and she sat there smirking at him, making him uncomfortable. Finally, though, he seemed to come to a conclusion. "Okay," he said. "Perhaps you're right. If not, you bluff well enough. But you haven't killed me yet, and I haven't turned you in yet...so why don't we just talk?"

It was a simple enough request. And besides, what could he ask of her that he couldn't surmise himself from what he had seen? She shrugged. "Fine. Ask your questions."

"Who are you?" he asked once more.

"That again?" She sighed. "You really are daft. If you must have it spelled out, I'm an assassin."

He looked irritated again. "I gathered that much. You're the Black Lily, aren't you?"

"I am," she replied nonchalantly. "See? Your questions are useless; you already know everything."

He shook his head. "No, that's not what I was asking. I mean, what's your name? Your *real* name."

It was he who threw her off guard this time. Her name? Why did it matter what her name was? "Isn't it obvious?" she said. "It's Lily."

"Really?" he asked. "That's your real name? I thought it was just an alias."

"It's what I've been called since childhood," she said with a shrug. It wasn't a lie, though not the whole truth. "It's short for something else, if you really must know."

"What?"

Lily smiled. "Now that, I'm not telling. It's not a name I'm particularly fond of."

He let that drop and moved on to a different question. "Why are you here?"

"I am an *assassin*," she repeated, slowly and carefully, as if speaking to a particularly dim student. "Why do you think I'm here?" She sighed again in exasperation as he only glared at her. "My assignment is to assassinate the king and replace him with a better one."

His fingers drummed the arm of his chair, his look thoughtful. "And why would you want to do that?"

"It's not a matter of what I want, young prince, it's a matter of what is good for the country."

His anger returned once more and he stood up, his voice on the verge of a yell. "Good for the—!" he stammered. "How is regicide good for the country? I'd think a living king would be better, don't you?"

"Even if that king is your brother?" she rejoined.

"Yes!" he said, yelling in earnest now. "Yes, my brother is good for the country! He's a great king!"

She merely looked at him. Realizing he'd lost his temper, he sat back down. "Do you really believe that?" Lily asked.

"...Yes," he answered after a pause. He didn't sound very convinced. "He may not be the nicest man, and maybe he's done some things to make him unpopular, but he is a good king. A skilled one. He understands what he's doing."

Again, Lily shrugged. "Either way, he's grown unpopular enough, as you've said, and there are certain people in high places that want him removed. My Guild has assigned me to take him out."

"Who wants him removed?" he asked.

She shook her head. "You know I can't answer that. Even if I did know, I have a duty to protect the confidentiality of my patrons."

"An assassin with honor?" he asked sarcastically, but didn't pursue the matter. "And what about me?"

"You are also a mark, this is true. Ah!" she added, raising a finger before he could begin to protest. Lily knew she would have to talk fast to get him on her side, to give him something to consider besides turning her in. "But you don't necessarily have to be. My

143

assignment has a bit of wiggle room. A small bit, admittedly. For your silence, you and I could come to an…arrangement."

His gaze turned even warier, if such a thing were possible. "Such as?"

She shrugged. "We could stage your death instead. A gruesome one from which your body was never retrieved. You could go on living your life with the promise to me that you would not later try to regain the throne, and I could fulfill my contract."

"You want me to fake my death and then run away while you kill my brother and put some assassin-condoned stranger in charge of our empire?" From his tone, Lily knew he didn't consider it an option.

She tried anyway. "I think it's a fair arrangement. You get your life, I finish my job, we go about our merry ways."

He shook his head, looking disgusted. "I would never abandon my brother."

Lily took a deep breath and looked past him at the wall. "Well then, we only have one other option left, don't we? You can try to turn me in, in which case I will kill you prematurely to save my own life."

"But that would ruin your assignment, wouldn't it?" He steepled his fingers and looked over them at her with that thoughtful look that set her on edge. "You said 'prematurely.' I'm not supposed to die until after you've killed my brother, am I? And I won't let you kill him."

Well then. He wasn't as slow as she had believed him to be after all. In fact, he was actually quite observant. She smiled at this. "You are correct. Killing you could mean I don't fulfill my assignment as planned, but I can always find another way to do so. But you can rest assured, I do value my own life over yours. And my mission is more of a failure if I die than it would be if I only finished half of it."

Another tense moment of silence followed as they stared each other down. "The thing is," he said at last, slowly, "there is another option that you haven't considered."

It was her turn to look confused. She had already gone over all possible outcomes in her head as soon as she was revealed. There was nothing else.

He didn't keep her waiting, though, like she would have done to him to make him nervous. "I could just throw you out of my rooms, tell everyone I don't want you. Then you, being unwanted by both my brother and I, would be of no use, and would thus be removed from the castle. That's the arrangement you've been set up under."

So, there had been more to her being moved over here than she thought. This really was some form of punishment from the king. He must have known that Prince Adrian wouldn't want her around, and had expected the prince would just get rid of her, thus publicly humiliating her and leaving her homeless in a foreign country, or so Alec believed. What a bastard. "And when I come back to finish my assignment?" she asked. "When I force my way in here and kill your brother and everyone in my path? I will reveal to all that you knew who I was all along and let me go free."

"What? Why would you come back?" He leaned in as if to give his argument more weight. "Don't you see?

I'm giving you a chance to leave here. To get out of this predicament with nobody dying. It would be better for both of us—"

"No, princeling, I don't think *you* see." The sharpness of her voice cut him off. "I can't leave here without finishing my task. I can't just stop being an assassin. It's not a hobby. It's my life, it's what I am. And even if I wanted to, which I don't, it wouldn't matter. If I left here a failure, if I abandoned my mission, the Guild would hunt me down and kill me. And trust me, what they would do to me would be much, much worse than anything you could possibly imagine. A public execution would be a mercy compared to the punishment they would give me. Which is why I would have no fear storming back in here on a killing rampage if it meant I would have even the slightest chance of getting at you and the king."

She could see the shock in his eyes. And the horror. So innocent, to think he could just let her walk out of the castle without looking back. But he had never been expendable like her. Never in his life.

No matter that she was partly bluffing. Sure, Master Gavriel maintained that she and her peers were all tools that could be discarded if the overall good of the Guild required it. That had been true for her once, and likely still was so for the less experienced assassins he commanded. But she was the Black Lily, the most infamous killer in modern history, and likely the second best in the world at what she did, after her mentor. Even if she *did* completely botch this mission, she was still too valuable a tool to be so easily tossed aside, even for damage control. But he didn't need to know that.

She leaned back in her chair in satisfaction. Time to keep the bluff going. "Besides, it wouldn't matter. Turning me in, I mean."

"How so?" he asked.

"Another would just replace me," she replied. "You see, my prince, we are everywhere. We have eyes and ears and hands in everything. And you would never know us. We could be your cook. Your washerwoman. Your chambermaid. Your guardsman. Even I don't know every single one of those in the Guild, there are so many, and we are built on secrecy. But anyone in the castle or outside it could be one of us. If I die, there is another to replace me. And another. And another. Not all are assassins, of course. Some are simply spies. Or thieves. But we are all in the same shadow network, and we watch each other's backs."

Every word of it was a lie. While there was a network of sorts, it was a small one. Lily only had a few contacts herself, and she'd only ever met the few other assassins that she lived with, all of whom kept to themselves and rarely even saw one another. But lying came naturally, and she could see from the look on his face that he believed it.

"So unless you want to start killing every suspicious person you meet and become labeled a mad regent, you should tread carefully there," she continued. "That is also why I cannot simply leave. They would know immediately, and they *would* find me." That last part was not a lie, though she might be able to outrun them for a short time with a head start.

If she ever did betray them, the only way she would escape would be to flee to another country, and even that was not a guarantee of safety.

When he finally spoke again, his voice was quiet and sad. "So what do we do now?"

They'd run out of options, and neither of them were willing to budge. She didn't like it, but there was only one course of action that still presented itself. "I guess for now, my prince, we just learn to live with each other."

Nine

Adrian marched quickly down the corridor to his brother's study, ignoring the few servants along the way that stopped to bow their heads or curtsy at him. He normally made a habit of acknowledging the staff and their polite gestures, as he knew very few others passing through the palace ever did so. Tonight, he doubted he would notice even his own parents had they risen from their mausoleum to bid him good evening.

He'd spent the last few hours drilling the assassin for more information about herself and her plans, and very occasionally getting an answer. He'd learned that Olivia and Rosalita, the other two courtesans who'd arrived along with "Camilla," were actually who they said they were and not also part of the plot to murder his brother. And while he didn't trust her word alone on the matter, he also couldn't think of a way to ascertain as much himself without revealing that such a plot existed—something he ached to do, but not to innocent bystanders, and not without at least a dozen soldiers at his back.

So he'd left Lily in her new chambers with an express command to the two guards outside that she was not allowed to leave them and wander the halls until he gave his permission, a stern order that had visibly surprised the two when it came from their normally soft-spoken prince. Then he'd made his way to the now-tidy royal office where the king's official seal was kept, sat himself in Alec's leather-backed chair, and began to write a letter:

> Alec—
>
> I pray this letter reaches you quickly, for we've no time to spare. There is an assassin in the palace—Camilla is really the Black Lily, and she means to see us both dead. Do not take this for jest; I am deadly serious, brother, though I wish my fears were groundless. Tell no one whom you do not explicitly trust, for I know not where else their agents may be planted. Instead, I urge you, return with haste and the swift command to have her discreetly dealt with; for I cannot move against her without her knowledge, and my attempting such would accomplish only my own death and her immediate disappearance beyond our reach.
>
> —Adrian

He was just reaching to unlock the drawer in which the royal seal was kept when a velvety voice behind him said, "You don't realize how correct you are, do you, my Prince?"

Adrian spun in his seat so fast he nearly slipped from it. The assassin was leaning against the wall behind him, within arm's reach, a short, thin blade hanging limply and casually from one of her hands. It bobbed idly in her grip, but if the stories he'd heard about the Black Lily were true, it could be buried in his throat before he registered its movement.

He opened his mouth to say something, but it took a few seconds for the words to come out. "H-how did you get in here?"

Lily smiled. "You saw my maps, didn't you? Few walls in this palace are solid all the way through, it would seem. Discreet pathways for your ancestors' servants to move about the palace without being seen by the more important folk. I doubt most of your current staff even knows they exist. I wonder how many of them you know of?"

He stared at her as she smiled at him, his hand slowly creeping over his letter.

"I've just finished reading it, you know," she said casually. "No sense trying to hide it from me now. No sense, for that matter, trying to send it, either."

"I..." He looked from her to the letter and back, then to the dagger in her hand. "You can't kill me in here. It's too obvious."

"No, I mean it would never get to the king," she said, pushing herself off the wall and standing straight. "My Guild learned he'd be traveling shortly after he knew it himself. We've arranged for any news we don't agree with to not reach him."

"You...?" He scooted back away from her in his chair. "How?"

"Trade secret," she said with a wink. It made him flinch slightly, which made her grin. "Besides, you'd need the royal seal to get it to him directly."

He looked instinctively at the drawer it was kept in before realizing his mistake and jerking his head back around to face her. "I have it," he said, his first sure words since the conversation started.

She raised her eyebrows in surprise. "Do you?" she asked, then unfolded her arms. The hand he hadn't been watching rose up between them, holding a fist-sized ivory knob. "What's this, then?"

He could hear her chuckling to herself as he stared in shock at the object in her hand, then whipped around to the locked desk drawer. A quick tug on the handle revealed that it was not, as he had assumed, locked, and that it was, as he hadn't assumed, empty. He spun back around and lashed a hand out, grabbing for the stolen seal.

It disappeared behind her back and into an unseen pocket before he even got close. "You can't beat me, princeling," she purred. "It's cute to watch you try, but you're out of your league. You said so yourself, you cannot move against me without my knowledge."

He slowly stood and backed against the desk, gaze steady on hers and face reddening in anger. "I could have you killed while you slept," he said.

She shrugged. "As I could kill you myself with much less hassle."

"I don't sleep much these days. Besides, that would raise too much suspicion," he argued. "You'd never get a chance near Alec then."

"And the prince ordering the death of an innocent and helpless courtesan wouldn't also raise alarm?"

He glanced away then, glaring instead at the wall behind her. "Not if it were made known that she was neither a courtesan nor an innocent."

"And you would do this?" she pouted. "Have me slain in cold blood, without a trial or a chance to defend myself?"

He swallowed visibly, still not looking at her. "If necessary," he said, choking on the words. "Because I know now that you would have no scruples doing the same to those less deserving."

She laughed low in her throat and stepped toward him, her dagger tapping against her hip as she did. "Disregarding the debate over what constitutes 'deserving,' I concede the point. Hmm." She raised the blade and tapped it against her chin, grinning again when he flinched back from the movement, before finally sheathing it in her sash. "You have caught me, then, my lord. Like you, I shall simply have to cease sleeping from tonight onward."

His brow furrowed as he looked back at her finally, and he blinked at her a few times before responding. "You can't do that. Not for very long, anyway."

"But you can? Oh, my lord, your lack of faith hurts me," she said, stepping closer. He tried to back away more, but the desk kept him trapped between it and her, and he had to settle for bending backwards as she leaned into him with a sultry smile. "I have been thoroughly trained by the best in the world to do the things I do, you must know. My...endurance would surprise you." She laid a hand gently on the inside of his leg as she pressed herself to him.

His head jerked away from hers, his face burning. "I am not my brother, Camilla—"

"Please," she breathed, "call me Lily."

" — and I will not stoop to your bait. Get off of me," he commanded.

She giggled. "Is that an order, my lord?" she asked, placing another hand on his arm as the one on his leg slid slowly upward.

She seemed genuinely shocked when he suddenly grabbed her by both her shoulders and shoved her bodily back, pinning her against the wall with more strength than even he thought he contained. His fingers dug into her skin, and her eyes, only inches from his own, went wide at his sudden anger. Truth be told, he was a bit surprised himself at his reaction. And while there was a hint of longing he wasn't surprised to find in himself as his eyes bore into hers, he was surprised by the amount of hate that drowned it out. From the corner of his eye, he saw her fingers reaching for the hilt of her blade, but he didn't care.

"Do not talk to me like that," he growled, his voice low and wavering, unused to the tone he was using. "Do *not*. I am not Alec."

There was a moment when the two simply stared at each other, he in fury, she in wide-eyed wariness, before a polite knock on the door interrupted the tense silence. "M'lord?" came an elderly male voice through the wood. "Are you well, m'lord? I, uh, I heard thumping."

Adrian backed away from her then, but kept his hands firmly wrapped around her arms and his eyes firmly on her face. "Come in," he called brusquely.

The door slowly opened to admit a gray-haired steward wearing palace livery; Alec's manservant Bodan, whose services had been lent to him during his regency. Adrian didn't need to turn and look to recognize the man. His voice, and the dry politeness it held, were enough. He wondered briefly what the old man thought he was walking in on.

The prince turned slowly and cautiously to the steward, eyes still on the assassin and one hand still dug into the arm that held her knife, currently hidden from the steward by the placement of the desk. "I was just tidying up," he said flatly. "Camilla here got lost." He yanked her by the arm toward Bodan, and he watched as she used the distraction of her stumbling to tuck her dagger lengthwise into her sash and out of view entirely. "See that she makes it back to her room, please."

The old steward looked uncomfortably between the two, both slightly flushed and somewhat disheveled, before clearing his throat and nodding to his prince. "As you say, m'lord," he said, backing out of the doorway. It was only Adrian's familiarity with the man that made his uncertainty noticeable. "If you please, m'lady…"

Lily turned one last, lingering, unreadable look on the prince before smiling politely at the white-haired servant and allowing herself to be led away. Adrian waited until the sound of their footsteps had died out in the hall outside before slowly closing the door and returning to the desk, dropping himself into the chair. He glanced at his letter, only to find it gone, along with the royal seal. At some point she'd managed to snag them both. He slumped to the desk, his head landing in his arms with a deep sigh. The anger he'd felt had passed, but it left a bitter aftertaste in his mind, and his brother's words rose, unbidden, to his memory: *"If you're going to accuse someone of something, you can't be so quick to back down when they call you out on it. If you're right, it'll fall out eventually anyway, but if you're not and you insist you are hard enough, you might still make your enemy doubt his case enough to win."*

Adrian took a deep breath before sitting up and staring at the blank parchment, considering whether he should rewrite the letter. She might have been bluffing, he knew, but he also knew that it wasn't likely. And if he did send his letter, and her Guild intercepted it, they might send in reinforcements, and that would only make things worse. He had to assume that she had not had a chance to alert them to the fact that he knew her secret. Perhaps she had too much pride to admit she had made a mistake?

She hadn't looked really threatened until he'd finally pushed back. Still, he knew he couldn't win a physical fight with her—he had almost no combat experience, and if even half of the stories about the Black Lily were accurate, she could kill him in a dozen ways before he'd get the chance to touch her.

So he couldn't out-fight her, and he couldn't out-subterfuge her. But he could still surprise her on occasion. And she still hadn't gutted him.

His brother was right, loathe as he was to admit it. If he wanted to be strong enough to help his kingdom, he had to learn to think less pacifistically. He had to be a better bastard.

"Alec," he said quietly to the empty room, "I never thought I'd say this. But for your sake, help me think like you."

For a fortnight they did nothing but watch each other. Everywhere she went — which, when he was looking, wasn't much of anywhere outside of his suite — he followed her. And anytime he left her alone, she had a tendency to show up suddenly and seemingly out of the air, and he realized she had found most of the castle's hidden passages. He rarely spent any time in his rooms anymore, not just because he was busy trying to rule in his brother's place, but also because, if he was honest with himself, he was trying to get away from her.

Just her presence seemed to fill up a room, and he felt more of a stranger in his own chambers with her there than he did in the throne room surrounded by nobles. He wasn't sure what it was about her. She rarely spoke to him without him initiating the conversation, and when she did talk to him, it was always with that seemingly innocent slyness that he knew was completely fake. Often he felt as if she were watching him whenever they were together in his sitting room, and anytime he tried to take a sidelong glance at her to confirm this, she would be openly staring and often smirking. He had no way of knowing what she was thinking or why she kept showing up in the castle wherever he happened to be. He felt like a spider in her web. And he had no idea how to change their roles.

But he had grudgingly realized, after much deliberation, that she was right; he could not expose her just yet. First of all, she had mentioned that her friends, other assassins and spies, had their hands in everything. There could be a number of them in the castle already. If he did get rid of her, another would come, and then he wouldn't know who it was. Right now he had her pinned, unable to make a move until his brother returned since, for whatever reason, she needed to take Alec out first. Better the enemy he was aware of than one hiding in the shadows.

Also, she had mentioned that someone, or perhaps many someones, had requested his brother's death. He doubted that any of the disgruntled commoners of the realm would be able to afford the Guild's services, or that the league of assassins was taking on this contract out of any sense of charity or civic duty. That meant the Black Lily's client was a member of the nobility.

Adrian had always known that Alec was not the most popular king, but sometimes being an effective one meant being unpopular as well. His brother had told him time and again that he would give the people what they needed, which was not necessarily the same thing as what they wanted. Most of his enemies — or the ones who were open with their disdain, anyway — at least had to grudgingly admit to this much. Who had he pissed off enough that they would send the most infamous assassin in living memory after him? Adrian had to know, had to find out who was the traitor in their midst attempting to supplant the throne. Much as he disliked the idea, keeping Lily alive and near him was the best chance he had at finding this information.

And finally, he realized, he needed proof. Otherwise he would just seem mad, especially if he started finding traitors at every turn. Already he was becoming jittery and suspicious of everyone in the castle. Just the other day he had yelled at a maid for spilling tea on him, scalding his hand and triggering his barely contained sense of panic. The girl had run from the room in tears, afraid he was going to have her kicked out. He could tell his retainers were shocked, having never heard him raise his voice before.

But he couldn't help it. He jumped at every sound. Every time he ate, he wondered if his food was poisoned. He locked his bedroom door and moved his armoire in front of it before lying down, but still he couldn't sleep, knowing that she could still get in if she wanted to. When he did drift off, he dreamt of all of the different ways she might end his life. Soon, he had graduated from difficulty sleeping to choosing not to sleep at all, and he found himself drifting through the halls during the day confused and irritable. While she, on the other hand, seemed unaffected.

If he made a move against her now, it would be as an edgy and jumpy regent ordering the death of an innocent woman who didn't understand what was going on. Removing her as the stopgap in the Guild's plans would also justify his anxiety even further if her hidden allies had an excuse to move against him in earnest. The whole palace would fall apart around him, and the nation would soon follow.

No, if he was going to accuse her of being the Black Lily, he would have to have some sort of proof. If he could just show the guards one of her weapons or even her flowers, they would set on her like hounds, and she wouldn't be able to escape. But getting the proof was the difficult part. If she saw the guards coming, she would find some way to hide it. And it seemed she was always close by, watching him. If she caught him snooping, she just might stab him and be done with it.

But then, finally, he got his chance. The Duchess of Montfloss called on the courtesan Camilla to entertain her and the other courtiers with some music, and Adrian slipped away from the court and into the royal suite. He grabbed two soldiers as he went, asking the men to follow him with a sharp and unelaborated order.

The guards did so without question, though Adrian could tell they were flustered and confused when he brought them to his private rooms. It only grew worse when Adrian led them to Lily's chamber. "Here," he said, pointing to the wooden chest sitting at the foot of her bed. The broken hinges had been replaced, and the chest was padlocked shut.

"The Aluvian girl's chest?" the first guard asked.

"Open it," the prince commanded.

"It appears to be locked, sir," the second guard pointed out.

"Yes, I know that," Adrian said between gritted teeth.

"Um...may I have the key sir?" asked the first guard.

"Obviously, I don't have it, or I wouldn't be asking," said the prince. "Now break it open, and quickly."

"Not trying to argue, Sire," the second guard piped up, "but wouldn't this job be better suited for a blacksmith? So we don't damage the lock or the chest?"

The prince spun on them. "What are your names?" he asked.

"Hobbs, Sire," said the first guard. "And this is Jameson."

"Well, Hobbs and Jameson, trying or not, you *are* arguing—and with your crown prince and current regent, I should add. I gave you an order and I want it carried out. If it were my brother giving the order, you would not ask twice. Now break the damn chest open already."

Hobbs swallowed and quickly pulled his sword from its scabbard. "As you command, Sire," he said, then lifted his blade and stabbed it down at the lock. The metal latch broke open with a piercing crack. Hobbs sheathed his sword and opened the chest while Adrian and Jameson watched on.

"Remove the contents," the prince commanded. "I want them taken in as evidence."

"Sire?" Hobbs asked. "Evidence?" He looked into the chest, then back up at his prince, brow furrowed. "It's all lingerie, Sire," he said, standing up and delicately lifting a slinky white lace and satin dress in his hand.

Jameson whistled in appreciation, then straightened up and became serious when Adrian glared at him. "There's a false bottom," the prince snapped.

"Of course," said Jameson with a smirk. "Allow me, Sire." He knelt down beside the box and took his time rifling through the underwear to find the bottom of the chest, then pried it open and peered inside. What he saw made him whistle again in appreciation. "I see what you mean, Sire. A few of these are definitely illegal." With a grin, he pulled out a book and held it up for examination. The cover displayed a detailed painting of a nude woman in what was, to put it lightly, a very provocative pose. "I mean, I think this one was banned under your grandfather's reign, but don't we all have a copy, Sire?"

Adrian stared at the book in shock, felt his cheeks warming, then growled in irritation. "Move out of the way." He shoved between the two and knelt down by the chest, rummaging through it and pulling items out. Lacy underwear and sheer shifts, more lewd books, some in Arestean, some in other languages. All of their meanings were clear from the pictures. "Where is it?" he grumbled.

"Where is what, Sire?" Hobbs asked.

All of it! He wanted to yell. But it was gone. The weapons, the maps, the copied letters, the costumes, the damned lilies. It was all gone. He stared into the chest, not quite seeing, wondering where it could have all gone. "Her room," he said, rising. "Have her room ransacked. I want every piece of furniture searched."

"Sire, if I may, what exactly are we looking for?" Jameson asked.

"This, lord?" a female voice asked in that sickeningly sweet, fake Aluvian accent he'd come to recognize so well.

Adrian turned and stared at Lily standing in the open doorway, his mouth gaping open at the diamond and ruby necklace that hung from her hand and the innocent look plastered on her face.

"What—" he started, but before he could even get a word out she started babbling, switching into her supposedly native tongue with ease, as one would do when excited or scared.

"Miss, please, calm down. What are you saying?" Hobbs asked. "Speak more slowly, please."

"I did not know," she whined in Arestean. "King Alec say is fine. He give to me. As gift. He tell me is his mother's. I did not know my prince be so...so angry. Please, not punish me. I not know." She began crying as she spoke, her chest heaving, distracting the guards.

"Uh, Prince Adrian? Is this what you were seeking?" Jameson asked, holding out his hand for the necklace and passing it to the prince. Adrian accepted it numbly and could only give a mute nod. "Do you still wish us to take this in as evidence?" Jameson continued.

"No...of course not," Adrian answered in a daze. "It...is fine now. You can both go." He couldn't say anything else. She was there in the room. She could have all of their throats slit in a matter of seconds. But that wasn't what bothered him. If her gear wasn't in the chest, then she had moved it all somewhere else. Who knew where all of the evidence against her was now? Perhaps not even in this room, or even the palace. She could have hidden it all somewhere he would never find it. They would think he was crazy if he had them ransack her room and turned up nothing. What's worse, they would now think it was just some sort of harsh act of revenge for allegedly taking his mother's necklace. They would believe him a mad king if he would go so far as to accuse an innocent woman of

163

treason out of what they would assume was a petty squabble brought on by a misunderstanding about a gift.

The guards left, closing the door behind them with a small click, but not before he saw the confused look that passed between them. The assassin waited until their footsteps were echoing down the hall before smiling at him cruelly and dropping her accent once more. "Well, now, I see you've been busy."

"This isn't my mother's necklace," was all he could manage to say, his mind whirling with anger and disbelief at being duped so handily.

"No, it isn't. And I'll be having it back now, thank you." She lifted the necklace from his hands before tossing it on her nightstand. "It's a pretty nice imitation, though, isn't it? You couldn't tell by looking at it that the gems are fake. Well, maybe *you* couldn't. I, however, can always spot a fake."

"Why?" he asked.

"Why did I save your skin just now, you mean?" She began tossing the books and lingerie back into the chest. "Well, for starters, I don't really want my room destroyed searching for something that isn't here, and we also can't have the rest of the country thinking the crown prince is an insane pervert, can we? Not while you're the one in charge and I'm not allowed to do anything about you, anyway. Though with the way you've been acting lately, some may already be drawing that conclusion."

"What does it matter, if you're just going to kill me?" he asked bitterly.

"I already told you, I don't have to kill you. I'm still offering you a chance to escape with your life, if not your pride." She smiled as she closed the chest and turned to him. "Now, is there anything else I can help you with, princeling?"

"Where is it?"

"What?" she asked innocently, batting her eyelashes.

"Your tools!" he shouted. "Your weapons! Your damn flowers! Everything!"

"Oh that?" She put a finger to her lips and glanced at the ceiling as if in contemplation, then smiled and shook her head. "Don't worry your little head about it. It's all safe…somewhere else."

"You're evil," was all he could think to say.

"I've been called worse, my lord," she said sweetly. "Now, tell me, don't you have something sufficiently kingly to be doing? Running a country and whatnot while your brother is away?"

He realized with a start that she was dismissing him. *She* was dismissing *him*. He sputtered in shock, unable to say anything, his mind whirling with so much hatred and rage that he couldn't even think. He found all he could do was slam the door as he left.

He was sure she enjoyed that immensely.

Adrian groaned in exhaustion and rubbed his eyes, leaning against the nearest pew in the palace chapel. Finally, court was over for the day. It had been less than twenty-four hours since his last encounter with Lily, but he was still too distracted to come up with another plan. He had more pressing matters on his hands at the moment.

A riot had broken out in the city last night. Adrian's advisors had given him the news just that morning. It happened in the Low Quarter, where most of Luceran's peasants lived. Nobody was sure what had started it; his most likely reports said that a bar room fight had spilled into the streets, creating chaos, and in that chaos some thieves broke into a tavern and stole a bunch of liquor. This seemed to escalate into vandalism, and eventually a stable was set on fire. There was a great deal of property damage and a few deaths, the news of which Adrian's advisors had delivered with the same bored monotone they would have used to report that, say, the palace kitchens were low on salt. And after they'd told him all that had happened, they asked Adrian what to do with the people that the guards had imprisoned for allegedly starting the whole mess.

The prince was at a loss. He knew what his brother would do: have them all executed or thrown in the Ergastulum as a lesson to the peasants about rebellion, or, if he were feeling generous, have them put to work doing hard labor, toiling away for their remaining years building roads or walls for the cities. Forcibly instilling a sense of civic duty, as Alec called it. Adrian wasn't his brother, though, and he didn't believe something as simple as a tavern brawl, if that was really all it was, should be so severely punished. But his advisors seemed to think differently. They believed this was a sign of civil unrest, a result of Alec's harsh rule and his absence from the city, and that the peasantry was testing Adrian's limits. They told him that if he didn't want pandemonium, then he should be just as harsh, if not more so, than his brother.

Unable to handle the stress at that moment, Adrian had fled to the chapel, where he now paced alone beneath the multicolored gazes of stained-glass gods. The chapel had vaulted ceilings like the throne room, with dark wood support beams against a vibrant blue paint meant to remind one of the skies, and at one end was a giant stained-glass window depicting the major gods and goddesses. Along the walls were alcoves with altars for one to pray and make offerings to the individual gods. He wasn't particularly devout, but the chapel was often empty, which made it a peaceful place where he could think without interruption. Perhaps the gods would notice him here and help him decide what to do.

He was staring out one of the lower, clear glass windows, gazing over the palace garden outside and the deepening sunset over the outer walls, when a movement caught his eye. He wouldn't have thought much of it had he not noticed the shocking red hair that the retreating figure had up in a bun, just before it pulled up its hood. It was the assassin—she was the only person in the palace that had hair that vivid, more of a ruby hue than the natural copper of most redheads he saw.

Where was she going? And why?

Without even thinking, he was racing down the stairs and out of the chapel, leaving through a side door and following her path. By the time he reached the garden where he'd seen her, she was gone. Where else would she need to go on palace grounds? Or was she heading into the city?

When the palace was still young, its gates had held a single entrance with a portcullis brought down at night for protection. Over the last few hundred years, though, the city had grown so expansive around it that new openings had been created in the stone ramparts to allow for easier flow of traffic for those coming and going about palace business, suppliers bringing in their goods or soldiers leaving for patrol. These openings did have gates, of course, but they were rarely lowered, as nobody had attacked the royal city in over three hundred years, and Alec believed lowering them would only waste time and interrupt trade.

But there were still supposed to be guards posted there. *Did none of them think to stop her?* Adrian wondered as he hurried to the nearest side gate. Surely a richly dressed courtesan leaving in the middle of the night unescorted seemed suspicious.

He asked as much of the guard on duty when he reached the gate. "No Sire, no one dressed like that," was the guard's response along with a concerned frown. "Red hair, you say? There *was* a serving woman left just a few minutes ago with red hair. Said she had to go take care of her sick grandmother and would be back later tonight, to let her in. She didn't look like any courtesan, though, not in those rags. Certainly you didn't mean her, Sire?"

Had she changed her wardrobe? When he'd seen her from the window, she'd had on one of her many lavish gowns.

"No, of course not," the prince answered. He was getting good at false reassurances lately, it seemed. Not a talent he was proud to be developing. "Sorry, I must have just been mistaken…"

He turned from the guard's scrutiny and stood staring across the darkening grounds, thinking. Adrian wanted to follow her, but he knew no one would let him leave without an escort, especially with the recent violence in the city. He could hear the guard behind him shifting awkwardly from foot to foot. Of course, if he simply ordered the man to let him pass, he wouldn't be stopped. But he also wouldn't get far before a belated entourage chased him down to offer their concern and protection. By now, everyone in the palace had heard of his eccentric behavior since his brother's departure. Guardsmen and servants alike walked as if on glass around him. Whatever he did here would likely only fan the flames of those concerns.

But he couldn't in good conscience let a ruthless killer like the Black Lily come and go as she pleased, not without his closest attempt at scrutiny, at the very least. Hang his public image; there were more important matters at stake.

This must be how Alec always thinks, he thought to himself as he turned back to the gate, reaching as he did into the small purse in his doublet pocket. A small fee paid by a merchant in court today against back taxes he owed the crown on his lease. It was meant for the coffers. Adrian would need to remember to replace it from his own funds. "Here's a silver," he said, passing the coin to the guard, who took it only hesitantly. "I admire your perceptiveness and your honesty. Why don't you take the rest of your shift off, get yourself a drink or something? Prince regent's treat. I'm just going to go for a stroll around the gardens and see if my missing friend turns up."

"If...you say so, m'lord," said the guard, his confused look giving way to a gracious smile. "Thank you kindly."

Adrian smiled back and walked off, though he didn't go too far. Once he saw the man leave, the prince made his escape, heading down the hill through the city. If she had dressed herself like a servant, she was likely heading to the Low Quarter — at the outer rim of Luceran on the northeast side of the river, where the city's poor lived.

He hadn't traveled far from the palace when he thought he noticed her, just a short glimpse of ruby red beneath the hood of an otherwise nondescript female figure turning a corner ahead. It helped that they were still in the High Quarter, and thus he had only to look for the servants among the nobles milling about on the streets to find her. Had she still been in her finery, she would have blended better, though she likely would never have gotten out of the castle gates.

He trailed her through the High Quarter where the aristocracy's manor homes clustered around the palace in well-kept splendor, then into the thickening, bustling crowds of the nicer part of the Merchant's District. The further they went from the richer neighborhoods, the more his own fine clothes stuck out and the more momentary notice he attracted from passersby. It couldn't be helped, though, he told himself; even if he'd had any rougher outfits, it's not like he could have gone back to his room to change, not if he wanted to have any hope of following her trail. Hopefully nobody would notice who he was without the crown and the throne nearby to give him away. Nobody had shown signs of recognizing him yet, at least. He supposed that was one of the benefits of being fairly reclusive and unimportant until recently.

Every now and again, just when he thought he might have lost sight of his quarry, he spotted her: that same hooded figure, the same slight peek of what might be vivid red hair as she turned a corner. She was leading him toward the river. His hunch was right, then. She was heading for the Low Quarter.

Full night descended as they walked. While the Merchant's Quarter had been fairly lively with people eating and drinking at taverns and bars, the closer they got to the Low Quarter and the poorer the houses became, the thinner the crowds grew.

As they crossed the bridge onto a cracked, cobbled street lit only intermittently by failing lamps, his certainty was cinched. The foot traffic had since died out completely, leaving only him and his distant target on the streets. And there were no women who would walk this part of town alone at night, he thought, not even in such an obscuring, drab brown cloak, and especially not with *that* amount of confidence. Even at a distance, he could tell by the figure's posture and stride that she wasn't the slightest bit afraid of her surroundings. It had to be Lily.

Adrian was just about to call out to her, or maybe go up and grab her just to see the shock on her face, when he himself was taken by surprise by something heavy and meaty landing on his shoulder from behind, stopping him in his tracks.

He quickly turned and looked up to realize it was a hand, and that it belonged to a burly, hairy man, grinning down at him with the smell of booze on his breath. He was easily two heads taller than the prince, and nearly twice as wide. "You lost, young man?" he asked in a voice like loose gravel.

"Oh no, of course not. I live around here," Adrian said quickly, glancing back down the road where Lily had been earlier. She was gone.

"Really?" the man asked. "Where do you work, then, kid?"

"At the blacksmith's," he blurted out, choosing the first laboring profession he could think of.

"The blacksmith's, huh?" The man's hand still rested on the prince's shoulder. "Which one?"

There was more than one around here? "Uhh..."

Before Adrian could think of an answer, the man reached out with his other hand and grabbed his collar. The prince flinched slightly, but the stranger only rubbed the material between his thumb and forefinger. "These are some mighty posh threads for a blacksmith's apprentice," he said. "Don't you boys think?"

Boys? Adrian looked around. There were two other men coming out of the alleys around him, one slimmer and shorter than the man who had yet to release his shoulder, the other of average build, but with piercings in his ears and a scar on his hand in the shape of a 'T'. Thieves, then.

"I stole them," he said, hoping it would at least gain their respect, if not some credibility. "From some rich fool in the High Quarter. His wife gave them to me...after she tore mine off."

They grinned at that. Whether or not they believed him, he was still surprised by how easy the lie came to him.

"Still," said the thinnest one, crossing his arms so that Adrian could see the black tattoo of a snake circling around his bicep, "his hands look awfully clean and pretty for a blacksmith's. Not even so much as a chipped nail."

"I'm, uh, just really careful," said the prince, taking the wrist of the man holding his doublet and trying politely to remove his hand. It didn't budge.

"We bet," said the man holding him, and his grip tightened on his shoulder and collar, locking into place. "That don't explain how skinny you are, though. You'd have more muscle on ya if you were swingin' a hammer all day. And ya don't stink like a blacksmith, either. No sweat or soot. No calluses, either."

"Well, I only just started, see," Adrian said, and grinned broadly in what he hoped was an amicable fashion. "And obviously, I've cleaned up since my last, uh, shift. I was with that nobleman's wife, right? I freshened up afterward. Before I stole his clothes."

The man holding him sighed, still grinning. "Y'know, you had me going for a second there, kid," he said, "and it ain't the worst story I ever heard, but I don't think I believe you. My guess is, *you're* the poncy one in this story. You got led down here, probably by some pretty lass like you say, slummin' after the less fortunate. Lookin' for a brothel to have a nice night with a cheap peasant tart. And I'm thinkin' you went and got yourself a bit lost. Well, ain't no carriages run down here this time of night," he continued, sidling up beside the prince and resting a massive arm over both of his shoulders, "so you must need an escort, am I right?" He looked to the other two, who grinned and nodded encouragement. "There's an awful lot of crime around here, what you'd call a bad element. You wouldn't want to run into some unsavory fellas, would ya? Tell ya what, how about if me and my boys escort you back home?"

"Well, alright, you've got me," Adrian said with a laugh, hoping it didn't sound as nervous as he felt. "I admit, did get a bit lost. But I don't really need an escort. Thanks for the offer just the same. If you could just tell me which way—"

"Are you refusin' our hospitality?" the scarred one asked, stepping closer. Whatever veneer of friendliness he'd been able to muster melted. "That's not very nice of you, kid, and after our generous offer. Y'know what I say?" he added as he turned to the other two. "I say we just take his money. With those kinds of clothes, he's got to be loaded. And then we leave him here to think about just how rude he was to refuse our help."

"You wanna rob and rough some noble's welp in the middle of the street?" the thin man asked. "Let's at least take him somewhere a bit more discreet first, yeah?"

"We coulda mugged him thrice over by now if we'd all just shut it and get to work," the scarred man snarled back.

While they bickered, Adrian tried to duck beneath the big one's arm and slip away. But the man's grip was iron, his arm like a wooden beam, and he had the prince like a mule in a yoke.

With no options left, Adrian drew his arm back and punched his captor as hard as he could right in the gut.

The bickering stopped then, as did the smiles. None of them liked that, least of all the giant of a man whose stomach Adrian had just bruised his knuckles on, who hadn't budged an inch, and who was now frowning down at the young prince.

It didn't help, Adrian had to admit to himself, that he had never actually hit someone before tonight. He had no clue how to do it beyond the obvious motions. As a teenager he'd had fencing lessons, sure, but that was more for show than anything, and he didn't have a sword on him now at any rate.

So without any knowledge of how to defend himself, the prince had no idea how to block or dodge the giant fist that smashed into his face seconds later.

He went down like a sack of expensive laundry, his head bouncing off the cobbles, and the world spun painfully around him. A short cacophony of grunting and yelling broke out somewhere nearby, and as he assumed the noise was aimed at him, he curled around his head on the ground and braced himself for the inevitable pummeling.

A few long moments of fearful anticipation later, he realized that it had never come. And when he finally uncurled himself, opened his eyes, and looked up, she was standing over him with her hood thrown back and her ruby hair ruffling in the night's gentle breeze.

Ten

Lily knew she was being followed before she even got to the poor district. Whoever it was kept to her exact path and didn't have enough sense to make their footsteps fall in time with her own. She stopped at one point to look in a shop window, pretending to browse the merchandise, and instead watched the person in the reflection waiting down the street. He'd pressed up against the wall beside him, but didn't even try to stay out of the light of the streetlamps overhead, and instantly she recognized him. The prince. Idiot. Not only was he likely going to get himself killed, but he was going to ruin her errand.

She tried to lose him...and nearly did. Unfortunately, they were only in the Low Quarter for a few minutes before he was making new friends. She quickly turned another corner and leaned against a tavern wall, trying to figure out what to do.

Lily knew immediately that the man talking to Adrian was up to no good, likely a thief, and with her trained eyes she had seen his two friends hiding in the shadows of the alleys. Adrian would be easy pickings for them. Hopefully they would just rob him and send him on his way. In all likelihood, though, they would also rough him up some, maybe even kill him if he put up a fight or they realized who he actually was. If she let him die now, it would theoretically make her job a lot easier, removing her biggest obstacle. But it would also implicate her both for being in the same area and for Camilla's having momentarily disappeared on the night the prince was murdered outside the palace walls. If nothing else, with the resulting pandemonium and increased security after his death, she would never get a good shot at the king when he returned.

Plus, as much as she hated to admit it, she felt just a little bit guilty at the thought of allowing him to get killed by his own naiveté, especially since it was she who had inadvertently led him out here. Mark or not, he seemed like a nice enough guy — for a prince, anyway.

So when she heard the sound of impact followed by the thud of a body hitting the ground, she sprang from behind the wall and took out the man closest to her, a skinny little guy who didn't even see her coming, by snapping his neck. The second thug rushed her then, but it took less than a second to bury a dagger in his throat, his yell turning into a gurgle as he fell scrabbling at the hilt running slick with his own blood. She knew he would be dead before she finished with the last one.

He was a big guy, twice her size and weight, and all muscle. He'd done a number to poor Adrian's face already, but his attention had been diverted by the death of his two comrades. He looked shocked when he saw how small and apparently delicate she was; they always did. But unlike most, his shock was quickly replaced by wariness. He pulled a blade from his belt, the notched steel easily as long as her forearm, and they began to dance, circling around each other, each watching the other's moves.

He lost his patience too soon, though, and charged at her with a loud bellow. She sidestepped his wide swing and jumped on his back, locking her arms around his neck and putting him in a chokehold. He managed to swipe at her a few times with his blade before eventually running out of air and passing out, but he didn't do much damage besides a few light cuts to her arms. Before he could wake up again, she grabbed a nearby loose cobblestone and bashed his head in with one quick, precise swing.

Looking around, she was pleased with her work. Likely it wouldn't look like anything more than a fight between a few lowlife thieves—an event that would have been written off as unsurprising even before the riot.

On the ground, Adrian groaned in pain and tried to sit up. Lily wiped the blood off her hands and extracted her dagger from the dead man before making her way over to the prince. When he opened his eyes, his surprise and relief was evident.

Until he saw the dead bodies and blacked out once more.

Adrian awoke once more, this time to the sound of raucous laughter and an out-of-tune lute. He slowly opened his eyes to find he was lying on a stained, wooden bench, his head in a woman's warm lap. He sat up with a groan, gazing around in confusion at the people, mostly unwashed, milling about in a large, dimly lit room. Firelight flickered from one far wall, while a long wooden counter stretched across the adjoining wall out of view into the dim haze. Every available surface that he could make out held at least half a dozen mugs or tankards, as did most of the people he could see. A tavern, then. He'd never actually been in one before now.

"Idiot," a familiar voice scoffed from behind him, and a full mug was slammed unceremoniously on the table beside him.

He gasped in surprise, then immediately began choking on the smoke that pervaded the whole of the hot, crowded barroom. He turned on the bench to find that the lap his head had previously been resting on belonged to none other than the assassin. She set down her half-finished drink and smacked him hard across the back until his coughing subsided. His eyes burned and itched from the smoke, and every breath tasted stale and rancid. "Where are we?" he finally choked out.

"The River's End," Lily answered. "Most popular tavern in the Low Quarter. Also the most crowded and the easiest to get lost in. We shouldn't be recognized unless—" She caught herself and smirked. "Well, I won't be recognized at all, regardless. You should be fine, too, so long as you don't draw a lot of attention to yourself. Think you can handle that this time, blacksmith?"

The familiarity in her tone probably wouldn't have bothered him coming from anyone else, but he wasn't about to start demanding titles in this element. "Why are we here?" he asked, waving the worst of the smoke from his face. "And why am I an idiot?" he added as an afterthought.

"I can't explain that second question exactly," she said, "though I have a few theories. And we're here because I couldn't be seen dragging you up to the palace. That's not exactly an inconspicuous image. I needed a safe place nearby where I could keep an eye on you until you came to."

"So you brought me here?" He gestured around the room and its many patrons. There were more people concentrated just in sight than there normally were in the palace hall when court was being held, and very few of them looked like his idea of safe. In fact, many of them were just as intimidating as the gang of thugs that had tried to mug him. That realization brought back the memory of sitting up in the street to see his assailants' corpses lying in pools of their own blood, and the image made his head swim and his stomach roil all over again.

Lily snorted. "You've obviously never been here before. A man passed out in a corner isn't going to set off any alarms with this crowd. Hell, neither will dragging that man in or out of here. I probably could have done a little puppet show with your limp body and gotten nothing worse than some drunken laughs." She hefted her mug and took a long chug, her hair spilling out of her hood as she tilted back her head.

"You murdered them," Adrian muttered, staring down at his hands on the table.

The assassin wiped the foam from her lips before giving him a deadpan look. "You're welcome."

"How could you do that?" he demanded. "I mean, I know they tried to rob me, but surely they didn't deserve to die for it? How could you just kill three strangers so easily?"

Her eyes narrowed, and she frowned. "You do know what I do for a living, right? Please tell me I haven't been playing it cautious around you this whole time for nothing."

"Of course I know what—!" he froze, realizing that he had raised his voice. "I just...I just don't understand..."

"You don't need to understand," she said, pushing his mug closer to him. "What you need to do is collect yourself so we can get you back home. I can't work with you trailing at my heels like an overly groomed puppy and drawing every criminal in the city behind you."

He eyed the mug, then her, suspiciously. "That's no incentive for me, you know. I consider it a success if I make it so you 'can't work,' as you call it."

She quirked an eyebrow at him. "Are you saying you'd willingly follow me into a band of cutthroats on the off chance that doing so would irritate me?"

He glared at her for a moment before answering. "Maybe. If my misfortune is so irritating to you that you need to stop what you're doing to prevent it. I like you better as a bodyguard than a murderer."

"Weren't you just saying how reprehensible you found my style of bodyguarding?"

"I said I liked you *better*," he clarified, "not that it made you likeable. It's a small improvement, not a complete fix. Like a drop of perfume in a cesspool."

The assassin smirked. "You should have been a poet, Adrian, instead of a...blacksmith. Then I wouldn't have to kill you later on."

"And I suppose I should be flattered by that sentiment," he said dryly.

"Now you sound like your brother," she teased.

"You hang around someone long enough and eventually they start to rub off on you," he said. "Or at least, that's how it usually works. *You* hang around someone long enough and eventually stab them in the throat, I suppose."

"Shut up and drink," she said, and pushed his mug at him again.

He peered into it at the dark yellow liquid sloshing around just below the rim, white foam clinging to the edges. It smelled like what he would imagine a chamber pot would smell like if it had been left out in the sun for a few days, and its appearance did nothing to belay the comparison. But everyone around him was drinking it just fine and seemed to be enjoying it, Lily included. So he lifted the cup to his lips and took a modest swallow.

The assassin was pounding his back again as he coughed and sputtered onto the already sticky table, his throat burning to match the sting in his eyes and nose. "Oh, for the love of..." Lily muttered next to him. "Are you seriously this dainty, or do you just enjoy making me take care of you?"

"You poisoned it," he wheezed, kicking himself for his recklessness.

She snorted again. "Yes, I saved your delicate ass from being beaten to death by thugs in an empty side street so I could poison you myself in front of fifty witnesses. Bravo, you've caught me. Honestly." She raised her hand to the room and whistled loudly over the constant din, waving to a nearby serving girl while Adrian cleared his throat over and over, his face turning red from embarrassment and lack of air.

The waitress approached and bent over the table across from them, her already ample cleavage falling forward and almost out of the deeply plunging neckline of her dress. "Freshen your drinks?" she asked them, hoisting the metal pitcher in her hand.

"No thanks," said Lily, "but a glass of your finest wine for my friend here."

"This handsome gentleman?" she asked, smiling at Adrian and squishing her breasts closer together with her arms. Adrian blushed redder and turned his gaze quickly to the floor, staring at a knothole in the boards as she giggled. "You must have excellent taste, sir. I'll get that for you right away." He heard the rustle of her dress as she stood up and walked away, and he waited until he was sure she was out of sight before looking up again.

Lily was grinning at him. "What?" he demanded.

"What is it with you and sex?" she asked. "I thought maybe Camilla was just too intimidating for you, but a tavern floozy? Are you just terrified that somebody might get naked in front of you someday?"

His gaze went right back to the knothole on the floor. "Now *you* sound like my brother," he said curtly. "I'm just surprised at her forwardness."

"She's a poor Low Quarter girl working for tips in a bar, and you look like a nobleman's pretty boy brat who likes slumming. Can you blame her?"

The prince drummed his fingers on the table in lieu of looking up. "Is her station really so bad that she would sell herself like that?" he asked after a moment.

Lily took a pause herself before replying. "Does it have to be?" she asked, and her tone sounded genuinely curious. "It doesn't matter how good or how bad your life is, it could always be better. A little more money, a few less enemies, more prospects, less competition. Would you begrudge someone for an act that was less than polite if it benefitted them in the long run?"

Adrian sighed, feeling a pang of sadness he couldn't quite explain. "Then where do you draw the line? How much honor or self-respect do you have to sell before it becomes too much?" There was a long silence at their table for a minute, enough that the prince finally had to look up at her. He saw her staring at him with that same unreadable look she'd given him in the king's study the other day. "What is it?" he finally asked. He liked her scrutiny even less than her sarcasm.

"This is about your brother, isn't it?" she asked uncertainly, and he blinked in surprise. It was the first time he could remember her asking him a serious question. "You're trying to compensate for the way he treats people, aren't you? That's what this whole persona is." She leaned toward him, her voice sounding more certain as she spoke. "He uses people as a means to an end, and you come along afterward and apologize. He doesn't seem to care for their feelings at all, and you care for nothing else."

It was his turn to be confused. "You say that like it's an act we have going."

Her eyes narrowed suspiciously. "Isn't it?"

"It's who I am," he said. "What do you want me to do?"

She didn't say anything. When his wine arrived, he drank it in silence, mindful not to catch the eye of the serving girl as she hovered around their table afterward. He finished half the glass before pushing it away when they rose to leave, all the while enduring Lily's constant watchfulness. She left the rest of her own drink untouched.

The walk back was awkwardly silent. Lily wasn't sure what was going through the prince's head, or if he was just trying to avoid conversation with her, but she herself had a lot to think about. Had he truly been sincere all this time, not just playing games with her and the rest of society? Was his noble, kindhearted act not an act at all?

And if so, how? Was it possible that two men of the same family, both potential heirs to the throne and raised with the same silver spoons in their mouths, could be so completely different? If it was, that meant that Lily had completely misjudged him all along. She had thought they were playing a game, when in reality he didn't even know he was in one. It meant she would have to completely change her tactics.

Though what tactics could she use around him anymore, anyway? He knew who she was. He had her completely in his control, only he appeared not to realize it. He seemed too weak or perhaps just too naive to exploit her. And that still left them at a stalemate, one which she would soon have to break. Her puppet would be arriving within the month, and she couldn't be spending all of her energy worrying about what the prince might do to intercept her, as he'd tried to tonight.

His voice cut into her train of thought, interrupting the silence of the night. "What were you doing sneaking out, anyway?"

"Going to play the interrogator now, are we, blacksmith boy?" she said with a smirk.

"Why do you insist on calling me that?" he asked.

"I just think it's hilarious that that was the best cover you could come up with." She grinned wickedly. "With your pretty face and nice clothes, you would have done better to play at being a high priced whore."

She couldn't see his face in the dark, but she was certain he had turned red with embarrassment again. His voice was certainly exasperated when he sighed and said, "Never mind."

"I suppose there's no harm in telling you," she said after a minute. "I'm sure you've heard of the recent riot in the city? I went to the Low Quarter to get a feel for the unrest. After all, stirring up trouble is often my business."

"And? What did you find out?" He seemed truly interested, not just trying to make small talk. She wasn't surprised. It had happened a few days ago already, and he had yet to make a decision about what to do with the prisoners who'd been taken.

"Well, thanks to my having to drop everything and save your regal ass, not a whole lot," she said, ignoring the sideways glare he threw her. "But thankfully, there wasn't much to be found. I asked around a bit at the tavern before you woke up, and turns out it's nothing pointing to any deeper movement this time. Just a small street riot, nothing of the Guild's doing, nothing with any rebellious traction. I'm sure they never meant for it to escalate to the point that it did. Unfortunately."

She thought he might say more, but by then they'd reached the wall surrounding the castle, the gate within sight. "Best not to go in together," she told him. "You don't want to be seen sneaking around at night with the likes of me, especially when I'm dressed as a peasant."

"I don't think we have to worry about it," he said. "I gave the guards the night off."

"And they listened? I'm surprised."

"I am the prince, and lately, I'm also the regent," he reminded her. "But I was surprised myself."

By now they had walked through the gate unhindered, and she made her way to the overgrown bush where she'd hidden her courtesan clothing, in an out of the way nook close to the wall where no one would see her switching guises in a hurry. She began undressing, but to her surprise Adrian didn't leave. Instead he stood next to the bush, his back turned to her, and she wondered if he was intent on escorting her

187

all the way back to their suite. Probably, she realized, though it was likely more from fear of what trouble she might get up to rather than any real chivalry. And he'd clearly seen tonight that she could take care of herself.

"It makes me wonder," she said to him over the hedge. "You did pretty good tonight, managing to sneak out of your own castle—and just days after a minor insurrection, no less. And you didn't do half bad trying to make up a story on the spot to get rid of those muggers. Besides the whole blacksmith's apprentice thing. I mean, you *are* terrible at following someone, I knew you were there the whole way."

"Is there a point to this, or are you just trying to insult me?" he interrupted.

"What I was getting at is that, all in all, you weren't terrible for your first time." She sucked in a breath to tighten her corset as best she could, then exhaled slowly and continued. "Maybe you have a natural knack for this subterfuge thing. With a bit of training, you might even make a decent spy. Ooh, think of that. The crown prince himself, a secret agent."

"I wouldn't spy on my own kingdom," he said over his shoulder.

"No, no, of course not," she said as she pulled her dress on and began to lace it up as well. "But you could spy on *other* kingdoms. For the sake of your own. Think on it—they would let you in because you're the prince, but then when they're not looking, you make a quick switch, blend into the crowd, and find out all of their nasty secrets to come home and tell your brother about."

She finished dressing and stepped out from behind the bush, her other clothes hidden in the basket she carried. He turned to glare at her, his eyes flashing in the torchlight. "I am not, nor will I ever be, a spy."

"Fine, fine, no need to get testy," she said. "It was just a joke anyway. You're far too sweet to be a ruthless killer like me." She patted him on the cheek and began making her way back to the castle. He followed, and once more they fell into silence.

By the time they'd reached their suite, he still hadn't said anything. She stopped before going to her bedroom and turned to him. "In all seriousness, though, Adrian, I think you should let those people go," she said. "Their lives are hard, they have jobs to do, families to feed. And from what I've gathered, they're really quite harmless."

He stared at her in surprise, as if he hadn't expected she could actually be serious or show compassion. Finally, he nodded. "Thanks," he murmured before closing the door on her.

Adrian's arrival to the throne room the following morning was met with gasps of surprise and pity from the assemblage already present and waiting for him. At the front of the crowd, the Duchess of Montflos approached the foot of the dais with a polite grimace. "Why, Prince Adrian, whatever happened?" she asked for all of them. "Are you quite alright, Sire?"

"Ahh, yes," he replied with a self-deprecating smile, gingerly touching his bruised face where the fist he'd taken the night before had left its mark. He knew it was a nasty sight, black and blue and swollen, and it made his head ache like nothing before. "Apologies if I startled everyone. I was...trying to saddle my horse earlier this morning. For a short ride."

"Why not give the task to a stablehand, Sire?" the Duke of Montflos inquired, stepping up beside his wife.

"It was still quite early, before the sun and the stablehands were up," Adrian replied. "I couldn't sleep. I thought a ride might clear my head, and I confess, I didn't think it would be so difficult." Seeing that his audience still wasn't satisfied, he forced a grin. "It seems, having never done it before and it still being dark, I couldn't tell which end was the front. I think I gave the poor mare quite a fright."

The small crowd laughed, not believably, but seemed to accept the excuse nonetheless. Adrian seated himself on the throne, feeling much the imposter, and beckoned for the announcer to begin calling forth subjects to present their suits. He spent the next few hours answering requests for tax breaks, approving amendments to a law regarding inheritance, hearing reports of Arestea's border disputes with its neighbors, and greeting those subjects who had arrived that day to visit the palace, some for only a few days, others for weeks. Finally, the morning had turned to midday, when Alec would normally end his court session for lunch followed by an afternoon of entertaining the nobility. However, before Adrian could escape, one final decision had to be made.

The captain of the city guard and the warden of the Luceran jail both stood before the throne, helmets under their arms, asking him what was to be done with those who had been arrested in the recent riot. There were a dozen people the guard had been able to apprehend and pin charges on: nine men and three women, a few of them local business owners, none of them anyone of note otherwise. The warden informed him that they stood ready to transport the rioters to the Ergastulum if the prince wished. The guard captain also dutifully informed him that his men could have them all executed, publicly or privately, should the prince give the word.

Though he didn't look up at any of them, Adrian could feel the whole court watching him expectantly, wondering how he would handle this largest and most recent threat to his authority. He stared at his linked hands for a few moments in contemplation. If he let the rioters go, he would seem weak, and more riots may break out as the people tested his limits. But then, there were those who wanted his brother removed from power because he was often viewed as too harsh and uncaring toward the lower class. And if what Lily claimed was true, that her "friends" had had nothing to do with the rebellion, then these were innocent lives on the line.

But what if she were lying simply to protect her own? Why, then, would she have gone into the city last night looking for answers? Unless she somehow knew that he would follow her...so she could do what?

Protect him from being robbed? It wasn't that he doubted that she or her Guild had the resources to have staged the whole attempted mugging. He just couldn't imagine she would go to that trouble for his benefit, as some complex attempt to try and win his trust — if for no other reason than that it didn't work and they both knew it.

"Prince Adrian?" the guard captain asked, bringing him back to the issue at hand. He looked up at the roomful of expectant faces.

"Fine them for the trouble they caused, high enough to cover all the damages of their tantrum, and then release them," he finally answered. "With the warning that a much longer prison stay is in their future if they're caught partaking in such activities a second time," he added.

As the captain and the warden both bowed and turned away, Adrian felt his eyes drawn to the corner of the room. There, amongst visiting nobles and other retainers, Lily stood watching him. She gave a small nod, smiled, and walked away.

Adrian called an end to the day's court session and escaped to his private library for some peace and quiet. How Alec could not only handle the burden of being king all day long but actually revel in it was beyond him. He fully intended to tell his brother once he returned that he should either quickly find a wife or find a way to become immortal, because Adrian never, ever wanted to do this job again.

He had just sat down and begun to relax and lose himself in a book of poetry when he felt her warm breath on his ear as her velvety voice whispered,

"'Verily, m'lord, doth I praise thy strength, / For 'tis certain without thee, mine virtue yet would be ta'en.'"

He started at her first words, the book tumbling from his hands. She caught it before it hit the floor, opening it up as she finished her verse and walking around his seat to the front. "Ahh, Valen de Brightfalls," said Lily with a sigh. "A classic choice. I like his work well enough, but I always found his tales of chivalry and romance to be a bit…outdated." She draped herself over his chaise lounge at the far end, her long legs spilling out of her dress. Despite it only being early evening, she was wearing her nightgown, one of many that he'd seen her in lately; it seemed as if she wore a different one every night. This one was a pale ivory color and draped loosely, like something a goddess of olden times would have worn, with a slit running up the side that went all the way to her thighs. Not that he was looking.

His library was a few hallways removed from his bedroom suite. He might have once asked her how she had gotten out of her room, down the hall, and into this one, but he had long since stopped expecting her to stay put somewhere prying eyes might be watching her. For a while he'd tried posting a guard outside her door and one in front of the nearest secret passage he knew of; but when she evaded even them, he realized he shouldn't bother. At least when she did sneak out, it was usually to come find him and torment him. He was fine with that, because if nothing else, he knew then where she was and what she was up to.

He finally realized she was watching him, expecting him to say something. He quickly averted his eyes, realizing he'd been staring at her for far too long, though she hadn't made any complaint. "What do you mean?" he asked. It took him a moment to remember what she'd been talking about.

"Brightfalls' stories are all about knights rescuing damsels from dragons," she said. "Women jumping to their deaths after discovering their husbands have died in battle. Evil pirates turning good for the love of the women they've captured. That sort of thing."

"And what's wrong with all of that?" he asked.

"Oh nothing," she said with a shrug, "it's just not...*passionate* when he gets hold of a story. His writing is so dry. He tells the tale of the evil pirate Captain Maelcon, who falls in love with the princess he kidnaps and ends up returning her to her country only to be captured by her people and hanged for treason. She dies of sadness after watching his execution." She rolled on the chaise lounge to lie on her stomach, propping herself up on her elbows and giving him an unobstructed view of her cleavage. "But what he doesn't write about is the part where the captain ravages his not-so-unwilling captive in the hull of his ship all night long, the rolling of the waves in sync with the rocking of their bodies, his men not sure if the crashing is coming from the sea or from the captain's quarters, and the sound of her ecstasy as she calls out his name, sensual as a siren's song." She grinned. "That's the sort of poetry I could get into."

The more she talked, the more uncomfortable he became. He was sure his face was turning red; he certainly felt hot. It didn't help that as she spoke, she moved closer, slinking towards him on the lounge like a snake slithering over the grass, until she was practically in his lap, purring in his ear. He swallowed hard, not sure if he wanted to stand up and unceremoniously dump her on the floor or grab her around the waist and pull her the rest of the way onto him. Instead he just sat there staring ahead, trying to ignore how soft her skin was and the way the silk of her dress sounded when it slid across his own clothing.

She leaned back against him, her red hair spilling over her shoulders, her heaving cleavage in plain view. He averted his eyes. "The Aluvians, now, they have the best poetry," she said. "Sensual and erotic. It helps that the language slides off the tongue so beautifully."

"You're not even really Aluvian," was all he could think to say at the moment.

"So?" she asked, tilting her face back and up toward his. "I've been there often enough. Did you think I was speaking gibberish when I sang for you and the king? I speak fluent Aluvian, as well as Beutelandic and Melisian, though I am still learning Ovinuric. You would find, my lord, that I have a very skilled tongue."

"I'm sure," Adrian mumbled, turning his gaze away further and pretending to scan the distant shelves. "By the way, I've decided to assign one of the royal wing servant girls to be your personal lady's maid," he announced suddenly, as much to change the subject and distract them both as to warn her. "No arguing. The young woman in question has already been informed. She was quite pleased with the promotion, actually."

"Lady's maid? But Camilla is not a lady and everyone knows it." Lily smirked. "What you mean to say is that you've hired me a personal and, I assume, unknowing handler."

He nodded. "There is an empty room across the hall from my suite," he said. "She will be moved into there this evening, so that she can be at your beck and call at all hours of the day. And of course, anytime you leave my suite, she is required to go with you should you need anything. I can't have you running off in the night again, so she will supervise you when I am not around."

"And how effective do you think she will be at corralling me?" she asked, rising up slightly and turning partially toward him. "I've already proven that I can elude any guard you post on me whenever I wish. What makes you think a maidservant will fare any better?"

"Because none of the guards I've assigned to watch you were told to follow you wherever you went," he said, shifting under her weight and hoping she didn't notice. "That would have raised suspicion against you, which we both know would be potentially dangerous for both of us. Even if you didn't feel the need to cut your losses and start slitting throats, it would raise too many questions about my apparent paranoid obsession with you; especially after that scene in your room with your clothing trunk and my asking the guards about you when you snuck out the other night. Nobody talks openly of either incident, of course, but I know they likely exist in gossip. Plus, I think you get a thrill from stymying armed authority figures."

Lily chuckled. "I can't exactly correct you there," she said.

"A servant made to shadow you under the guise of tending to your needs is different," he continued. "For one thing, she can keep closer to you than a guard could and it won't seem out of place. For another..." He looked at her again, risking her open attempts at seduction to gauge her reaction. "You seem to hold some strange, atrophied semblance of a conscience in there after all, if your reaction to the riot proceedings was anything to go by. So I'm banking on your having more compassion for a young serving girl trying to follow orders than you would for armed guards. I don't think you'll harm her outright, and I doubt you would allow harm to come to her through any clandestine actions on your part. And if you *do* manage to lose and evade her with any sort of regularity, I will obviously hear of it, and I will have no choice but to think she is incompetent in the duties that were assigned to her. She may need to be turned out of the palace, if such a thing were to happen. That would be very unfortunate, I think."

She didn't give him as much response as he might have hoped. Her expression didn't change at all for several moments. When it did, she merely narrowed her eyes slightly. "To clarify, then," she said slowly after another moment. "Is our kind, polite, fair-minded prince regent threatening harm against the reputation and livelihood of one of his own staff if she should prove she can't always keep up with the spirited charge that he himself assigned to her? That sounds a bit cruel and capricious, doesn't it?"

He was afraid she would call him on that, but he didn't let himself waver. "The crown has been known to exhibit a certain amount of capricious cruelness of late, it seems," he said. "Perhaps it would shock some coming from me. Perhaps I would not even enjoy giving the order. But nobody will question me too hard on the matter. And I will be able to tell myself it is for the good of protecting my country and my family. I believe I will be able to live with that, all things considered."

Her narrowed eyes widened. "So, you would really involve an innocent handmaiden in our little power play?" she asked, smiling. "Quite daring of you, princeling. Are you sure we're ready to take this step together? It can be daunting and confusing at first, you know, bringing a third party into our relationship."

Adrian snorted and looked away again. "Hide behind entendre all you like," he said. "The worst you can do with it is fluster me. I hope the fleeting victory amuses you. Whatever you say, though, however you think to distract me, I know what you are and are not prepared to do right now. And I think we both know our maid will be safe enough in your employ, and perhaps your more unsavory qualities will be tempered somewhat."

Lily smiled, tilting her head to the side as she leaned in. "So, you've got me all figured out, do you? Read me like one of your books?"

Her lips were at his ear, her breath tickling him. Her hands always had a way of finding their way to his chest or his thighs, her fingers so feather light he wouldn't have noticed it if it hadn't been for the way his skin burned wherever she touched.

He told himself he was burning with anger at her shameless manipulation, but he couldn't make himself believe it. However he may hate her, and despite his condemnation of the tactic mere moments ago, a man would have to be dead to be touched by her and not have his body respond.

And then his thoughts turned to his brother. Certainly she had used this same behavior on him, though with a more eager reaction. He wasn't sure why, but the thought of her and Alec both purring and pawing at one another suddenly made him hot with anger. Was he really jealous that his brother would sleep with her, knowing how obviously promiscuous they both behaved? Or was he angry that she should be able to manipulate the king so easily with such base seduction and that she thought the same tactic would work with him?

It didn't matter. Adrian grabbed her hands, pulling them off of his body. She seemed surprised, like always, but not so much now as she had been the first time he had physically refused her in the royal study. "I think you should go now," he told her.

She sighed. "Alright, what's the matter, Adrian?" she asked, that rare tone of seriousness in her voice again. "I know it's not that you have different…proclivities. After all, I can see the way your body responds to me." Her eyes lowered to his groin, then raised back to his. Even with his irritation with her still fresh, he averted his gaze—mostly habit by this point. "If you're just embarrassed because you're a virgin, don't be," she said. "I promise to be gentle."

"Enough!" He stood up, unceremoniously dumping her off of his lap onto the floor, his temper now undeniably hotter than his libido. "My sexual orientation is neither relevant nor any of your business, and even if…if I *was* a virgin, sorry to say, the thought of my first time being with my brother's whore, and one who plans to murder us both no less, doesn't really interest me." He realized he'd raised his voice and that his fists were clenched. He took a few deep breaths to calm himself and finally met her gaze.

It was icy enough to freeze his blood. She stood, smoothing down her dress, and glared at him. "Is that what you think, princeling?" she asked, an eyebrow lifting. The flirty warmth in her tone had also frozen. "Not that it's any of *your* business, but let me make something perfectly clear: I am *not* a whore." She emphasized her point with a shove that sent him back down onto the settee. "I may be an assassin, a spy, and, yes, even a hot-blooded woman who, *shockingly*, has sex from time to time and enjoys it. But do *not* call me a whore to my face, especially if you mean it to be some sort of petulant, chauvinist insult. Even if I had slept with your brother, it would not have made me into used goods, too soiled for your pure touch. And if you think such a thing, that women are nothing more than handkerchiefs to be used once and discarded, then you are worse than your domineering brother."

Adrian stuttered for a reply, but found himself floored by her logic. Finally, he asked in confusion, "Wait, *had* slept with him? But that night…and you were bleeding…"

She shrugged nonchalantly. "I cut myself on a lock pick. Waste of time too. All I discovered was his pleasure chamber." His confusion must have shown on his face. "I know this can't be news to you; you yourself told me how often women 'trip' on the stairs to his chambers."

"No," he said, "I mean, I knew that women came from...from being with him...hurt." She crossed her arms over her chest, her face skeptical as he spoke. "I just never realized it was a sexual thing, or that he had...tools for it."

"So you're telling me then that you just thought that he beat women?" She scoffed. "And you never did anything to stop it?"

"It's not like that. I only noticed it a few times...and I wasn't sure it was him," Adrian stuttered. "And how would I have stopped it, anyway? He's the king."

"And you're the prince! And currently the regent." She shook her head. "For all of your preaching, you turned a blind eye to what you believed to be assault, simply because it was your brother?"

He didn't have the chance to argue further with her. She had already turned on her heel and strode away, the sound of the door slamming behind her reverberating through his skull.

For a few minutes afterward, he sat staring at his hands. He knew what he had to do. He wouldn't be able to sleep that night unless he saw for himself. Not that he would sleep anyway. He was starting to lose track of how long it had been since he'd slept, *really* slept, at least for more than a few fitful hours of tossing and turning.

Lily returned to her quarters to find her new lady's maid waiting inside. The woman jumped to attention when Lily entered, her face bright and her demeanor willing to please.

Lily paused. She recognized the girl as the one she'd met only her second day here, the one she had caught coming out of an unused bedroom with post-coital wounds on her back and visible bruising on her neck and arms. Irene, she'd said was her name. Knowing what she did now, Lily knew that the lover this girl had been meeting in secret could have been none other than the king himself.

"Greetings, m'lady," Irene said with a curtsy. "I trust his highness has told you already, but I'll be your new personal stewardess. Pleased to meet you. Again."

Lily smiled at her. "Yes, thank you," she said. "I looking forward to company."

"Thank you, m'lady," Irene said, beaming as she rose. "I confess, I never dreamed I would be a lady's maid. It is ever so exciting. I will be the best you've ever had, I promise. Just tell me what you need." The young woman fidgeted nervously as she spoke. "And I will be just across the hall, so if ever you call, I will hear it. You won't be disappointed. Is there anything you need now, m'lady?"

"A bath, please?" Lily asked. The maid nodded, rushing from the room to find servants, now lower than her, who would bring up hot water for Lily's bath.

Lily had observed how the chambermaids managed to get those big pots of hot water up multiple flights of stairs and down long corridors to their rooms; near every major intersection of corridors on every level of the palace were subtly hidden doors that opened on hollow chutes traveling straight up and down between the floors above and below. At the top of these chutes were pulleys that lifted trays up and lowered them back down.

In this way, a maidservant below could load the hot water onto the tray, the maidservant above could lift it up and carry it to the proper room, and by the time she returned with the empty bucket, another full one would be waiting. This saved them perhaps ten trips up and down from the laundry to fetch hot water. Lily had visited the laundry herself once, before she'd been found and politely shooed away out of the crowd of hectic servants. There was a giant pot of water with a constant fire under it, ready at any time of day in case a lord or lady wanted a bath or needed clean clothes.

If one were careful, these little service chutes also made great elevators for getting quickly and discreetly between floors, especially after dark when few people wandered the halls.

Lily had wondered how long it would take the prince to figure out this particular method of her sneaking around. Now she was beginning to doubt he ever would.

A few minutes later Irene was back, instructing the other servants where the tub was and how hot to make it, testing the water with her own hand before accepting that it was the right temperature and sending them away. Lily was impressed by how quickly she fit into the role of an upper servant, now allowed to boss the others around.

"Shall I wash your hair, m'lady?" the girl asked.

Normally Lily refused, not wanting any maids to see the scars and battle wounds that she owned and get suspicious. She could explain them away in the heat of passion to a lover who was too preoccupied to care much, but not so with a curious bath attendant. But knowing this particular maid's proclivities for violent copulation, she suspected the girl would not ask too many questions. "Yes, that sound good. Your name Irene, yes?"

The maid started, meeting Lily's gaze before dropping it to the floor again. "Um, yes. I'm surprised you remembered, miss."

"I have good memory, Irene," Lily told her as she undressed and sank into the warm bathwater, sighing in pleasure as the maid began to massage oils into her hair.

The girl blushed. "Then I suppose you remember how we met? I apologize for being so elusive that morning, m'lady. I knew you would find out soon enough the king's preferences, but I did not wish you to think that I would be any sort of competition for his affections. And I certainly didn't wish anyone to know of our…secret meetings. That is why we met in an unused room, instead of me going to his chambers. I didn't want any guards or other servants talking and word getting back to my husband."

"It is no trouble, not to worry," Lily said. "I tell no one." She shut her eyes and lounged back against the tub, luxuriating in the warmth and Irene's pampering.

"Thank you, m'lady," the maid replied. Lily only hummed in acknowledgment. It seemed the girl didn't care much for quiet, though, for after a few minutes she spoke up again. "When we first met, it seemed you could hardly understand a word I said. Your Arestean is much improved now, m'lady."

"Yes, thank you," said Lily. "Prince Adrian has been teaching me."

"How incredible that you should win favor with both of them," Irene mused. "Is he nice, then, the prince?"

Lily wondered if she was just making small talk, or if she was wondering if he treated women the same as his brother. Lily reached back and took the girl's hand, smiling up at her. "Yes, he is very kind and gentle."

"Ahh, well that is good," Irene said, and gently squeezed her hand. "Is it too bold to ask then, miss, who do you prefer?" Seeing the mischievous glitter in the young woman's eyes, she began to think that perhaps having a personal servant girl wouldn't be so bad after all.

Lily shrugged. "I am not sure yet. The prince is very…hesitant." She grinned wickedly. "Still a virgin."

Irene's eyes widened in surprise. "No! However so? He's so handsome! And surely some girls like sweet boys like him."

"Some girls. But not so much you?" Lily tilted her head to the side questioningly. "Do you enjoy what the king does to you, Irene?"

205

The girl blushed again, but the naughty twinkle in her eyes had not gone. "I...yes. Oh yes. It is terribly wicked of me, I know. Sometimes I wonder if there is something wrong with me, that while he's lashing me, I'm begging for more. But my husband, well...he's such an old, boring man. I married him out of necessity. I was poor and afraid of being alone, you see, and he helped me get a position in the castle. He's been a stablehand for years." The girl sighed discontentedly. "But after I married him, I realized my mistake. Being with him, taking him to bed, it is so...gross! He is old and flabby and doesn't bathe often, and he...he has a mean streak. Every once in a while I oblige him, but he doesn't often seem to know or care what I want, and I became so frustrated. And then one day I caught the king's eye and he invited me to his rooms, and we began our affair, and soon he showed me his tower. I wasn't sure I would like it at first, but he does find a way to make it ever so strangely pleasurable. Do you enjoy it, m'lady?"

Lily shrugged. "I do not like to be...how do you say, vulnerable?" She shook her head. "When I was with king, I made sure I was in charge, not him."

Irene's jaw dropped, and then she began to laugh. "Oh, I bet that one sent his head reeling! I wonder if a gal's ever done that to him?"

"I do not imagine so, judging by his surprise." Lily smirked and stood from the bath, Irene handing her a towel.

"And yet, you and the prince haven't rolled in the hay yet? Oh, that's a saying here, it means—"

"I know what it means," Lily interrupted.

"Right. So you haven't?" Irene asked.

Lily shrugged. "So far, he is avoiding me. I believe I make him uncomfortable."

The girl shook her head. "I don't know how he possibly could. I mean, look at you." Irene waved at Lily's naked body as she toweled off. "You're gorgeous! With a body like that, how could anyone resist?"

Lily lifted an eyebrow and stepped closer to the young woman, until her bare breasts brushed the girl's uniform. "Tell me, Irene, have you ever been with a woman?"

The servant's eyes widened in surprise. "Oh, no, I haven't. Have—have you?"

"But of course. I am a courtesan. I serve the nobility, men and women alike." Lily smiled, twirling her finger in the girl's hair.

She had known before she even talked to him that Adrian would refuse her advances today, as he had every other time before; her attempts at them were mostly to keep him nervous around her. But that didn't mean she hadn't been suitably in the mood, nor that the uncomfortable way they'd left one another had cooled her down at all, carnally speaking.

And now Irene was here, polite and pretty and hoping to please.

"But how...how does that even work?" the maid asked, flushing, but the sparkle in her eyes indicated that she was not completely averse to the idea.

"Would you like me to show you?" Lily asked. And she leaned down and kissed her.

As it transpired, Irene was not averse, only nervous. By the time they fell back into the tub together, that nervousness had been suitably banished, leaving behind an exploratory amateur eager to learn more. And Lily, as the more experienced party, was happy to teach until the water went cold and they moved, dripping and giggling, into the bedroom to continue the lesson through the night.

Lily was in the chapel the next morning, staring out the window at the bleak day outside. The clouds hung low and dark, rumbling ominously and occasionally flashing, threatening to unleash a storm at any moment. Gazing at the barely leashed anger of mother nature through the towering windows of the chapel, she felt they suited her mood perfectly. She knew she should have gotten over it, especially with Irene's help, but she was still smarting from Adrian's comment the afternoon before. She hadn't even bothered to continue spying on and disrupting him after their argument, and neither did he seek her out to do the same. Instead, she'd risen quietly from bed—leaving her new maidservant dozing naked and covered in faint love bites beneath the covers—and immediately recalled her conversation with Adrian from the night before, which soured her afterglow and sent her into restless wandering until she'd ended up here.

It was the longest she and the prince had gone without keeping an eye on one another since he'd discovered her secret, and if she were honest with herself, by this point, she found his absence and lack of concern over her activities strangely off-putting. If he had too much time to himself to actually stop and think about it, she worried he'd realize how easily he could have her thwarted without the bloodshed he feared if he just spoke a few discreet words to the right people. The recent civil unrest, and his continuing problems with insomnia, were seriously working in her favor to keep the prince from thinking too clearly about their stalemate.

Lily heard the doors to the chapel open and close, but didn't bother turning to see who it was. The sound of footsteps making their way towards her echoed through the huge room, bouncing off of the tall, two-story-high arched ceilings and the statues of the gods that adorned the chapel. "You know," said the visitor, "as much attention as Camilla draws around the palace, you're surprisingly hard to find when you're being elusive. I've been looking all over for you. This is honestly the last place I thought to find you."

"Never pegged me for the religious type, princeling?" she asked, not bothering to turn and address him to his face.

"Honestly?" Adrian asked. "No."

She snorted. "You're right, I'm not the type to rely on the gods to solve my problems for me if I just ask nice enough. Are you?"

"I do seek the gods for guidance from time to time, hoping to find a nudge from divine inspiration. Especially on difficult matters." He was standing beside her now, staring out the window himself, allowing her to watch him from the corner of her eye, though she still refused to acknowledge him.

"Matters such as what to do with me?" she asked

He nodded. "Such as."

"Hm." She glanced at the nearest god statue she could see, but all she could make out was a formless marble robe over sandaled feet. Could be any of them. "So, which god of choice do you turn to now?"

"Right now? Artos," he said. "My usual god of choice, actually. I'm hoping that meditating on the avatar of wisdom will mean some epiphany will rub off on me." They both turned to look at the nearby icon. As the leader of the pantheon, the image of Artos was twice as tall as the others, his stony beard reaching to the floor, his eyes perpetually blindfolded; true wisdom, the priests taught, came equally from looking within as from looking without. "And you?" he asked, turning back to the window. "Who is your god or goddess of choice? Oh no, wait, let me guess: Morana."

"The goddess of death." She smiled faintly. "Cute. It fits me, true. You could say I am responsible for deciding who dies and who does not. But you're wrong. I don't worship Morana. Too obvious."

"Oh?" He looked at her finally, leaning against the windowsill and crossing his arms over his chest. He seemed genuinely interested in their theological debate. "Then who?"

She rose and, for the first time since he'd entered the room, met his eyes. "I don't worship the gods. Any of them. They abandoned me—this world, long ago. Why should I waste my time praising them? They have done nothing to deserve it."

"That seems like a sad existence." He frowned and for a moment said nothing before continuing. "But I did not come here to talk about, or to, the gods. I came here to talk to you."

Lily turned back to the window. "Then make it quick, princeling."

He lifted an eyebrow, as if he were going to ask, "What, you have something better to do?" But instead he said, "I wanted to apologize. For what I said last night. It was…uncouth." He sighed, turning his gaze to the floor. "And you were right. I went there last night and saw for myself."

She scrunched up her eyebrows in confusion. "There? Oh, you mean the king's tower? How did you get in? He keeps it locked up."

"I have a skeleton key," Adrian replied. "It unlocks every door in the castle." She could tell from the smug look on his face that he was pleased at her surprise. "And no, I won't tell you where it is. You seem to be doing alright on your own. The point is, I came here to apologize."

"And you did. Now you can scurry along and go back to living in your ignorant, perfect little world." She turned to leave.

"Wait," he said, grabbing her arm. That surprised her. Very rarely did he ever touch her, instead of the other way around, and when he did it was usually in a sudden fit of anger. This time, though, he seemed more pained than angry. "Look, I…I always knew my brother wasn't perfect. I mean, I've heard the rumors, that he was sometimes…violent with the servants. Everyone had. I've seen maids and the occasional

211

noblewoman leaving his wing with visible bruises or a limp. And you're right, I turned a blind eye, because he's the king, and my brother, and I did not think he would act purely out of sadism in anything. But I was not expecting…that. I honestly don't even know what half the things in that room were, or where he got them."

It was her turn to raise an eyebrow. "Truly?" she asked. "You're a prince, and you don't know about torture devices?"

The prince turned to the window, bracing his hands on either side of it. "Yes, well, my parents were very progressive monarchs," he said. "They believed torture was wrong. And certainly not something for royalty to partake in. They had any such devices removed from the castle. The dungeon is now used mainly for storage, with only a few holding cells left. Those other things are the sole purview of the Ergastulum now."

She rolled her eyes. "Even now, your prudishness is showing. Those devices were not for torture; trust me, I've experience with *those*. Alec's collection is just for deviant sexual pleasure. And honestly, I don't even mind that part so much. I'm not one to tell others what to do behind closed doors, if it's what they want. They just can't do it to me." When the prince tilted his head questioningly, she continued. "No one, no matter who they are, will ever have control over me. Not by torture, not by payment. I am the one in control of my body, always. I make sure of it."

Adrian's lips pursed, his expression hurt. "I truly am sorry," he mumbled. "For what I said to you. For what I called you." He paused. "Wait, what do you mean, you have experience with those devices? Please don't tell me you've tortured people?"

She shook her head. "No, torturing marks for information has never been my particular area of expertise," she said. "That is not to say that some particularly bad ones, the rapists and murderers and whatnot, haven't died painfully at my hands. But no, I meant that I've personal experience on the receiving end of many torture devices."

His eyes went wide at that. "Truly?" he breathed, paling slightly. "By whom?"

"My Guild, of course," she said with a smirk and a hand on her hip. "You think training to become an assassin is easy and painless? They had to let us know what would happen if we were ever caught. They gave us a little prelude to each of the main methods of torture, just so we could feel them for ourselves. Nothing enough to damage us so much that we would no longer be useful, of course, but enough to provide a thorough education."

He shook his head. "What kind of purpose could that possibly serve?"

"To motivate us to never, ever get caught, for one," said Lily. "And to make sure that if we are, we aren't taken alive." He still seemed shocked, to say the least, not to mention horrified. "It's like this," she explained. "If I'm caught, and my captors actually figure out who I am, I will be tortured for days, perhaps even weeks on end, in every manner that you can imagine— physically, emotionally, and because I'm a woman, most likely sexually as well. If I manage to die during the process, I'm lucky. If not, it's because I gave into the torture and actually told my captors information about my Guild. And if I ever manage to escape or I'm set free? It wouldn't be likely, as I'd probably be publicly executed, but on the off chance, what the Guild would have in store for me would be a hundred times worse. Because then not only am I a poor assassin, I'm also a traitor and a dangerous liability."

It took several long moments of him staring dumbfounded at her before he spoke again, and when he did, it was barely above a whisper. "How can you live like that?"

Lily shrugged. "See this?" She tugged on the chain of her necklace, pulling it out from under the neckline of her dress where it usually sat between her breasts. On the end of the chain was a tiny vial full of a shimmering purple liquid, teardrop shaped and without any air bubbles — a design that made it seem a solid amethyst crystal rather than what it really was. "This isn't for decoration," she said, "it's poison. Don't worry, prince, it's not for you. It's for me. If I ever get caught, I drink this, and I'm dead within a few seconds. It saves me a lot of pain and suffering. I never go anywhere without it."

"That's horrible," he whispered, staring at the glass vial as she twirled it in the air, the dark purple liquid inside catching in the light.

She tucked it back into her dress out of sight. "That's life," she said. "My life, anyway. Be glad your own is so comfy, princeling."

Eleven

The next evening, Adrian held the first formal court dinner since the king had left for the newly expanded border. In the full month since temporarily accepting the throne, the crown prince had been taking his meals privately while he mulled over the day's decisions and those the next day would bring, leaving the various visiting aristocrats to make their own meal arrangements with the palace staff and with one another. Tonight, however, was the last night that Duke Raoul of Lakeview would be at court, and polite custom called for at least one more intimate gathering before he departed for his own lands the next morning.

Though he couldn't honestly say that he enjoyed rubbing elbows with the other peers of the realm, Adrian had to admit that Duke Raoul was at least less pretentious than most. He, like the prince, made his appearances at court more for duty's sake than for any real pleasure in sampling the upper crust, never stayed longer than propriety deemed necessary, and hardly ever tried to invoke his status to gain extra pampering or a more expedient meeting of his demands. In fact, the only time Adrian could ever remember the man actively drawing attention to himself was when he had an opinion that he felt wasn't being shared by enough of his colleagues. Fortunately, with his disposition, he seldom surrounded himself with his colleagues by choice, and so was written down in Adrian's book as a likeable enough man as far as the aristocracy went.

The dinner was a small and somewhat awkward affair attended by only four of them: Prince Adrian in his brother's high-backed seat at the head of the table; Duke Raoul, already dressed in his finest riding attire, as if he couldn't see the city gates fast enough; Duke Henry of Montflos, alone tonight since his wife had been nursing a slight fever since the evening before; and the Duchess Sidonie of Berecum, the largest coastal city on the southern border, still recently arrived in the palace for her socially mandatory round of court appearance.

They sat, amicable but mostly silent, around the large oak dining table while servants bustled about setting out the first course. Greetings and pleasantries had already been exchanged, leaving room for the night's discussion, which Alec usually kicked off while Adrian sat passively listening and eating. Now that the onus of conversation was on him, the prince sat placidly stirring his soup and willing some relevant topic to occur to him. "So…" he hazarded at last once the food was properly laid out. "Duke Raoul. I trust your visit was to your liking?"

The duke sipped his wine and grunted noncommittally. "I have no egregious complaints, m'lord," he said, turning his languid gaze on the Duchess of Berecum.

Adrian followed it. "Duchess Sidonie," he tried again. "Good to see you again, as always."

"My thanks for the sentiment, m'lord," she said coolly, returning the duke's casual gaze as she sipped her soup.

Adrian took a mouthful of his own soup and made it a point to swallow slowly, then sat in uncomfortable silence a moment longer. "Duke Henry?" he said uncertainly, his last point of attack.

The older noble smiled through his heavy mustache and waved his spoon at the younger duke across the table from him. "If I may apologize on behalf of my younger peers," he drawled, "we are all grateful for the honor you show us tonight, my liege. I'm rather afraid these two pups here only have eyes for one another lately."

"Oh?" said the prince. He wasn't overly endeared to the haughty old man or his gossipy wife, but he had to admit that the pair did have a talent for commanding and steering any conversation they were involved in. "I'm sure I've not heard of this. Is there to be an alliance between Lakeview and Berecum, then?" he asked, turning to the two in question.

"I've not yet heard myself either, Your Majesty," Duke Raoul answered, eyes still casually resting on the young duchess. "My frank but courteous inquisitions on that front have thus far been met with resounding ambiguity."

"It is being considered, m'lord," Duchess Sidonie said, dabbing daintily at her lips after every small mouthful. "We have received the offer, yes, but the interests of Berecum must take precedence over any personal satisfaction in such a link. And we have been offered more than a single option in the matter."

"It's Liam, isn't it?" Raoul asked, cutting off Adrian's readied platitude. "You are no doubt aware of the man's advancement in years, dearest Sidonie, as you can be in no unequal doubt of your own want thereof."

"Duke-Milite Liam does possess an admirable maturity of disposition, yes," the duchess answered. "Indeed, we have often heard it accounted amongst his finer qualities, of which there are apparently several."

"He's forty-three, is the subtle gist of my former point," Raoul said, swirling his wine and ignoring his food. "Whereas you yourself are barely twenty, is the general lean of my latter."

"Duke-milite, is he?" the Duke of Montflos broke in. "Sounds rather fancy. Pray remind me, what's the 'milite' for?"

"Alec's title," the Duke of Lakeview answered, sounding less than enthused. "Sorry, our most honored king, may he live a thousand years," he added to Adrian. "His title. A present for showing support for his majesty's little invading hobby."

"It was our understanding," Sidonie said, cutting off the prince once more before he could speak, "that the Duke-Milite of Treventre was instrumental in the quick and relatively clean capture of Beuteland's capital, which awarded a swift victory to Arestea, where many feared a long and drawn-out conflict."

"Interesting," scoffed Duke Raoul. "It was our understanding that the man has yet to even get his sword dirty, much less meet a horde of them himself."

"Not true, not true at all," Duke Henry argued, quickly setting aside his soup and wiping the broth from his whiskers to better throw himself into his explanation. "You'll remember that business — when was it? — three or four years ago, I believe, during the spring. With the assassin." He paused to take a generous drink from his wine while Adrian's ears perked up, suddenly invested in the conversation. He didn't have to ask the old aristocrat to go on. "A young man, in the prime of his youth and reportedly strong as an ox, slipped into poor Liam's own family manor early one morning and slit the throat of every guard along the way. Hired by the former Duke of Cragstaff, they said, angry over a land dispute that was awarded in Treventre's favor."

Confident that he was now in command of the others' attention, the duke helped himself to another few noisy spoonfuls before continuing.

"Anyway, the young buck's in thick leather all over with a bloody dagger in one hand and a short sword in the other, slinking into Sir Liam's room just as calm as you please, ready to do one last wicked deed and go collect his pay. But Liam hears him come in and flashes out of his chair like a divine fury, yanking his sword down from over the fireplace and turning to face his murderer, and the two have it out right there in the office while the duke's breakfast is cooling on his desk."

By now even the terminally unimpressed Raoul was watching the older man weave his story. The Duke of Montflos took the opportunity to finish his soup before continuing.

"By the time the remaining guards patrolling outside on the manor grounds hear the commotion and rush in past the trail of dead bodies, the duke has the assassin pinned to the flagstones with his own dagger through his shoulder and the duke's sword at his throat. He holds him like that until the guards arrive, and they haul the evildoer down to the Treventre dungeons, where Liam himself makes the killer confess his crimes and the whole story behind them. Had him publicly executed the next day. Hanged in the town square for all to see, then put his head on a pike at the gates of his manor to keep it from happening again."

Duke Henry smiled to himself as he finished off his wine, as if imagining in his head the round of applause that his young audience surely would have given if propriety had allowed.

"Anyway, that's how I heard the story," the old man continued after a moment. "That's why old William stepped down from Cragstaff and handed control to Liam's nephew Gareth. They couldn't prove he'd had a hand in it, but Liam had it from the assassin's own mouth that it was Duke William that hired him, and that he had more targets in mind after he'd finished with Liam. Stopped a conspiracy, they said. His majesty gave him honorary command of the newest squad of royal infantry right after that, and that's how he went to Beuteland. Must've been how he earned this 'duke-milite' title of his as well." He nodded, satisfied with his story, and held his wine glass out for a nearby servant to refill. "Remarkable lad, that. Mark my words, that man's going places. Got real drive and skill, like our King Alec himself. Like you saw in the nobility fifty years ago. You don't see so much of that in this new lot, all raised on plenty and privilege their whole lives, with no reason to earn it. Present company excluded, of course."

"Of course," Duke Raoul repeated, draining his own wine, any show of interest gone again. "M'lord, with your permission, may we serve the next course?" he asked the prince. "All this talk of war heroes has impressed me something terrible, it seems, and I find myself tiring under the excitement."

"Oh. Of course," said the prince, turning to the waiter standing patiently behind his chair. "The next course, please. Thank you."

"He's on his way, you know," Sidonie informed them casually as the soup bowls were collected. "Duke-Milite Liam de Treventre," she clarified as she caught Raoul's eye. "He mentions in his correspondence with us his intentions to visit the royal city and await the king's return. It is our understanding that he should arrive in little over one week's time." She brought up a gloved hand and casually examined the lace trim. "'Tis a pity you leave us so soon, Lord Raoul, before you get the chance to meet this man of whom you have evidently heard much about and already have formed such interesting opinions. We have heard rumors of there being a small parade to welcome him through the gates."

"Yes, more's the pity," the Duke of Lakeview said with a sigh as his wine glass was refilled. "Such a shame to be called home on such brief notice. I had considered extending the visit to better reacquaint myself with the lady of my favorite coastal neighbor, but I'm afraid I've only just remembered several exceedingly pressing issues that require my most immediate attention back home. You will of course forgive me for my prudence, m'lady."

"Of course," the lady answered without a flicker of expression. "Which reminds us, how fares the ailing Duchess Prudence, m'lord?" she added to the older duke as the servants laid out the main course.

"Oh, much better today, thank you for asking," he answered, carving into his meat as soon as it was set in front of him. "Fever's just about to break, I believe. I warned her against taking such long walks at night with this damp air we've been having, but you know how Prudence is."

Adrian went back to slowly picking his way through his food while the conversation ran on without him, glad to have a few moments alone again at last with his own thoughts. Several new ones were now vying for his attention. He'd be sure to bring them up the next time she intruded on him.

"What?" Lily finally asked, setting down the book she had been reading. "You're itching to say something, so say it already."

Adrian started in surprise. They were alone in his sitting room again, both of them pointedly reading to themselves while they kept an eye on one another. It had become such a regular occurrence, this open pantomime, that he could almost pretend it wasn't a matter of life and death, that they merely enjoyed one another's company. Lately, he even got some actual reading done; his thoughts on what to do with her always ran the same futile circles of late, and he reasoned if she wanted to make a move against him while they were alone together, she would have done so long ago.

He hadn't realized how obviously he'd been staring at her today, though. He hadn't meant to, but with as much as she'd been sharing lately about her life as an assassin, he'd started to wonder how it must feel to be a killer. Did she have friends? Family? Had she known the assassin who had been caught and killed? Were the two close? Or were all assassins just cold-blooded murderers like he'd always believed? Was there any honor among thieves, or in this case, among killers?

He wondered how to broach the subject. "I'd heard today at dinner…" he began, uncertain. "That is, I knew about this already, of course, but hadn't paid it much mind, but now that it was brought up, I was wondering…"

"Get on with it, princeling," she said, raising her book again.

Adrian cleared his throat. "Well, a few years back, there was another assassin who was caught and executed. In Treventre. By Duke-Milite Liam. I was wondering if you knew him."

Lily snapped her book shut and stood suddenly, turning her back to Adrian. "Why do you ask?" she demanded, crossing to the window and staring out at the rain. It had been pouring for the past three days, stopping only occasionally for the clouds to refresh their stores. Even during these breaks, the sky rumbled and flashed, and then later in the day the rain would start up again. It seemed as if the gods were trying to wash a stubborn stain from the city.

"Oh. I was just curious," Adrian answered. "I thought maybe you two were comrades or something. I guess I don't really understand how your...uh...career choice works. Are all assassins part of your Guild or just some? Do you all know each other?"

Lily sighed, running her fingers through the leaves of a window plant. "Interrogating the enemy again, princeling? Looking for a new angle to be rid of me?"

"Would this information help me at all if I were?" he asked.

"Not really, no," she said with a smile. It was very slight, and very brief, and then her strange melancholy returned. "No, not all assassins know each other or are part of my Guild. Many are personal assassins for your dukes and duchesses. I'm quite sure Alec even has one himself. It's just that my Guild has a...majority share on the art of killing. And anyone with any exceptional skill works for us."

Adrian listened to her in surprise. He hadn't really expected an answer. He figured any more information about Lily or any other assassins that she hadn't already willingly shared would be too sensitive for him to know, despite her dismissiveness. Perhaps she was only telling him as much as she was because she was planning on killing him before he could use the information. The thought wasn't a comforting one, but since he had her talking, he didn't see any harm in continuing his questions. "So, the one that was caught," he pressed. "Did you know him?"

"Is that really important?" she snapped. Adrian started in surprise. He hadn't known her to lose her temper, besides a few days ago when he had called her a whore; then, though, she had had a look of cold malice on her face, not this sort of...nervous tension. He hadn't realized at first, but her hands were clenched, her foot tapping, her eyes astutely avoiding his. Had he hit on something vital?

"No," he said, "I suppose not, but I would like to know, regardless. I'm sorry if I'm making you uncomfortable. Were you two...friends?"

"Adrian," she said. She rarely used his name, he noticed, except on those rare instances she turned serious. "Just drop it, please. I...look, I'll answer any other single question that you have if you just forget this one, okay?"

"Truly?" She must be more agitated than he'd thought to make such an offer. "Any?"

"Any." She gave him a wicked grin. "Just don't ask something that will make me have to kill you after I tell you. I won't be held responsible for your own bad judgment."

Adrian gulped, waiting until she turned away again before resuming his observations of her. Enemy or no, Lily was perhaps one of the most intriguing persons he had ever met, and he had a million questions to ask, many of which might risk his life. But most of all, he realized, he still wondered what her life must be like as a professional murderer. He wondered if she had friends, true friends, or family, or if she was completely alone beyond professional relationships.

He wondered if she had any real empathy, or if she was truly cold-hearted beneath her deceptive persona.

But most of all, he wondered what had happened to her to harden her so much that she didn't flinch at the thought of killing another human being. How does one so completely inure oneself to murder?

All of those questions were too loaded to ask her now, though, when she looked uncharacteristically nervous. He was afraid to spark something in her that might cause her to lose her temper and attack him. But he certainly wasn't going to waste such a perfect opportunity, either. Finally, he realized what he wanted to know. "How many?" he asked.

"Twenty-nine," she answered without pause.

"Gods, woman, you've slept with twenty-nine men?!" He couldn't keep the horror out of his voice at the thought. She didn't even look twenty-nine years old yet. That meant more than two men a year since her majority, probably more. How did she find the time or the energy?

"What?" She spun on her heel, a bewildered look on her face. "No, of course not. I've *killed* twenty-nine men. Well, nineteen men and ten women." She quirked an eyebrow. "Wait. What were you asking, Prince?"

He tried to wrap his head around that fact. She had murdered twenty-nine people. As far as he could remember following the popular exploits of the Black Lily over the years (which, admittedly, he followed very little), he could only count eleven victims that had made the gossip rounds—still more than enough to mark her for infamy. He would have to ask his guard captain or a record keeper later. If she was still being honest, and the public knew her true body count…

Adrian realized she was still waiting for an answer. "Uh, no, I was wondering…" he began. Now that he had to elucidate, though, he wished he'd picked a different question. "Well, you seem so…well-rounded…in the areas of…" She lifted an eyebrow and smirked. She knew what he was trying to ask, he realized, but she wasn't going to help him any with finding the proper words. Typical. "That is, I was wondering how many lovers you've had."

"Oh, that," Lily said, and rolled her eyes. "Now, mind you, you said lovers, not dalliances. Of those I've had many. But actual lovers…" she drummed her fingers on her chin, and he wondered if she really had to think about it or if she were playing him again. "Five," she said after a moment.

"Five?" he repeated.

Slinking back over to the couch, she lounged across from him. "I know, for a whore, it's not very many, is it?"

He flushed again at her reminder of their argument but otherwise refused to take the bait. He'd apologized once already; he wasn't going to do so again. "So, five men?" Adrian asked.

"I didn't say that," Lily replied. "I said I've had five *lovers*. Not all of them were men."

Adrian thought about this, probably harder than he needed to. He'd heard of such things, of course—Uncle Julien was supposedly experienced in similar pursuits, one of the many unspoken reasons that he had been politely but assertively asked to live away from the palace, without the same obligations of the nobility to put in the occasional appearance. But Adrian wondered…how did women even do that? They didn't have the anatomy to connect properly. How did it work?

"And how many, umm, dalliances have you had?" he asked.

"Enough. A girl doesn't give away all of her secrets." She smirked. "But I can happily add another to that list now."

"My brother, you mean?" he asked, and couldn't entirely keep the disgust from his face.

"Oh, yes, that too," she said. "I suppose if we must count it. It was only really half a dalliance, though. I honestly only pleasured him just enough so that I wouldn't have to actually sleep with him. I got no personal pleasure out of it, you can rest assured. Just a quick bit of mouth—"

"Yes, thank you, I don't really need the details," Adrian interrupted, and loudly, to make sure he couldn't hear if she kept trying to inform him.

Lily smirked again. "Fair enough," she said. "No, I was referring to that naughty little lady's maid you assigned to me."

"That…What?" he asked dumbly.

"Oh yes. I didn't even have to work to seduce that one," she said. "Happened almost by accident. For her first time with a woman, though, she was very curious and…enthusiastic."

Adrian swallowed. "She was supposed to keep an eye on you," he said, "not bed you."

Lily shrugged. "She's proven she can do both. Don't worry, she keeps her eyes on me when we fool around. Until I make them roll back in her head, anyway."

An image of Lily lying naked with the servant girl came unbidden to the prince's mind, and he felt himself growing uncomfortably warm at the thought. That her smirk grew ever so slightly said she noticed and knew where his mind was going. Maybe he shouldn't wonder about such things.

Realizing again that she was waiting for him to say something, he asked, "So...did you ever dally with your, uh...targets?"

"I keep offering to 'dally' with you, princeling," she purred, "but you keep turning down the bait."

He rolled his eyes. "And I will continue to do so. But thank you for reminding me you still plan to kill me at some point."

"Sorry," she said. Again, she ran her fingers thoughtfully along her chin. "Let me think...One. A hired swordfighter that was getting a bit too successful fighting duels for the nobles. He was just too delicious to pass up, so I played the admiring fan and spent a night with him before attending his fight the next morning. He knew, of course, that there were assassins out to get him; he just didn't suspect me." She grinned for a moment at the memory and stared up at the ceiling before continuing. "Anyway, I rigged the fight to make sure he would lose. But he only counts as a dalliance, not a lover."

"And the others, then?" he asked, realizing he was becoming interested despite the protestations of his conscience. "Your official lovers?"

"Let's see. There's the sailor, Jerica," she continued, counting off on her fingers. "She's a feisty one. She was my first and taught me everything about the art of pleasing both men and women. Every time I hear she's in a nearby port, I drop by for a visit if I can. Then, after she got me comfortable with the idea, we had a little *ménage a trois* with another pretty companion of hers by the name of Emanuel. He had the most beautiful long, silky blonde hair and thick, pretty eyelashes, prettier than most women I've seen. I like to stop by and visit him as well when I'm in the area." She paused for a moment, and he could've sworn he saw her shiver just a little before she continued. "Another lover was one of my contacts for a while, but last I heard she'd been promoted to working in the city guard in…let's just say a city in the northwest. I can't really give you any more details on her, you understand. We still have the occasional minor business dealing. And then there's that naughty scoundrel and thief, Jinx. You might have heard of him, he's a pretty big crime lord. Needless to say, he's stolen many, many nights of sleep from me."

"That's only four," he said, once again trying to force unbidden images out of his mind, as well as a rising jealousy. Wait, why the hell was he jealous? That she'd had so many former lovers? That *they'd* had *her*? Or that he hadn't had any?

Her impish grin suddenly fell, as if a dark storm cloud had blown in over her thoughts. "Ahh, yes," she said, turning away again. "Robert."

"Robert," he echoed. "What about him?"

"Let's not talk about him, shall we? It's an...old wound."

Adrian pondered over this for a moment. Perhaps a lover who had cheated? Though Lily didn't seem the type that would care about infidelity, especially after this new information. Unless she had been very close to this man Robert. Or maybe he had simply treated her poorly. Perhaps he was part of the reason she had turned to a life of murder? If so, whatever happened between them, it must have been horrendous indeed.

"Now you have to answer the question, princeling," Lily said with a smile, all traces of her earlier pain gone and buried.

"The question?" Adrian chuckled nervously. "What question?"

"How many, and what were their names?" she asked. He blushed, running his hand through his hair and staring at the ground to avoid her gaze. She huffed indignantly. "It's only fair, princeling. *Quid pro quo*. I answer a question, you have to answer a question. And technically, I answered two questions for you when I gave you my kill count."

"Fine, fine," he grumbled, then sighed. Of course she'd find out eventually with the inescapable interest she'd shown in his life these past few months. Might as well get it over with. "There's not much to say. None."

"None? Really? Not one at all?" she asked. "Sure, no lovers, all of court knows that. But not even a night with a whore or a serving girl?"

Adrian glared at her. "You don't have to sound so shocked. I would think it's pretty obvious."

231

Lily shrugged. "Besides how weird you act around a woman flirting with you, it actually is a bit hard to believe," she said. "You're quite good looking, Adrian, and you're a sweet guy. If you just learned how to talk to girls, I'm sure you'd have ladies hanging all over you."

He blinked at her in shock a moment, then frowned. "I think we've long since moved beyond the point where I'm susceptible to your casual flattery, Lily."

"No we haven't," she said bluntly. "And I'm being serious. You don't think I flirt with you just because I like to make you squirm, do you?"

He gave her a look that made it pretty obvious that was what he thought.

"Okay," she conceded, "true, I do like making you squirm. But if you were up for it, I also wouldn't mind going for a romp in the hay with you." She stood up, running her hands down the curves of her body to emphasize her point, and began walking closer to where he sat. "Would I even be your first kiss?" she asked in a whisper—then leaned down over him, her lips only a few inches from his.

Before he could answer her question, those lips were pressed against his, her velvety smooth mouth exploring his own. He felt his jaw drop in surprise and she took it as an invitation, plunging her tongue between his lips, running it over his. Adrian's body flooded with heat as his mind tried to think what to do, what to say, but his body didn't seem to be having any trouble responding. He found his tongue intertwining with hers while his hands seemed to have magically worked their way up to her hips. Oh gods, those hips.

Suddenly, he found he couldn't breathe. She was sitting on his lap, her legs on either side of his, those thighs — gods, they were firm — pressed up against his aching manhood, only the clothing between them keeping him from possibly losing his virginity. Shocked back into awareness, Adrian pulled away from her, gasping for breath, trying to find something to say.

Finally, he managed to remember his words. "Lily, stop."

He was surprised at his voice. He had expected it to be squeaky and high pitched with nerves, but he heard instead a voice deep and heavy with desire. He hadn't realized that he himself could sound so...sensual.

He was also surprised when his command worked and she pulled away, panting for breath. "My...apologies, princeling," she said carefully, and he was shocked anew to find her actually blushing somewhat. "I got a bit...carried away. You'd warned me you wouldn't reciprocate. No touching, right? Keep my hands to myself?" She stood up, backing away from him, and he found he could breathe normally again without her so close.

Adrian nodded, afraid to speak again and hear that foreign voice coming from him.

"Right," she said. And then she unlaced her dress, letting the skirts fall away to leave her in her corset and a short, sheer underskirt. Beneath that, she had black stockings running up to her thighs, held up with a garter belt wrapped around her hips. Slowly, she pulled off one stocking, then the other, letting him glimpse her creamy tanned skin.

"What are you doing?" Adrian asked, entranced, sitting up a little straighter as he stared at her bare thighs.

"Why, exactly what you wish," she purred, blushing no longer. "I'm keeping my hands..." He stared at these same hands as they glided up along the curve of her corset, untying the bow at the top, "...to myself."

With each string that came loose, the curve of her bosom became more and more exposed. Before the corset was completely gone, she reached a hand into it, grasping one of those full, round breasts and cradling it gently, watching him all the while.

"I...I have to go." Adrian stood up, grabbing a blanket off of the couch and holding it in front of him as he backed away, not quite able to look away from those tantalizing breasts, part of him wanting to catch just a glimpse of her pink nipples, but knowing that if he did, he might lose what little self-control he still had. She grinned at him wickedly as he turned tail and ran to his room, locking himself in, his back against the door, as if afraid she would knock it down with her sheer, unleashed sexuality.

"Princeling," she called through the closed portal, "you may be a virgin, but I can guarantee I know what you're doing in there."

Her mocking laughter followed him, unanswered, as he did exactly what she was suggesting.

Twelve

Lily smiled at the closed door, smug in the satisfaction that she had driven poor Adrian to taking matters into his own hands. She had hoped, though not really expected, to go further with him before he escaped, but this was a fun consolation prize. Honestly, she was a bit surprised he'd let her get as far as she did.

She wondered if he even knew what he was doing in there, or if she should give him pointers. But then again, if he had remained a virgin all twenty-six years of his life, he likely knew how to please himself just fine. Even monks weren't *that* celibate.

Lily stuck her head out the door and called Irene from across the hall. At least if she couldn't have the prince, she could alleviate her own desires with her maidservant. Irene was proving to be willing and eager at nearly any hour, and easy access to such a receptive partner had been keeping Lily's own libido high lately, she'd noticed. Maybe she would moan extra loud so that Adrian could hear them behind his closed door.

Irene ducked out her door and across the hall, entering the prince's suite quietly. Lily noticed immediately that something was wrong with the young woman. Usually she was bubbly and full of mischief, but today she would not even lift her eyes to look at Lily. She also moved awkwardly, as if she were in pain.

"Irene, what is wrong?" Lily asked bluntly.

235

"Wrong, miss? Nothing, of course," the maidservant mumbled.

Lily narrowed her eyes and grabbed the girl's chin, pulling her face upward. The eyes that met hers were puffy and black, and the girl's lip was split. These were not the wounds of sexual play; the king was still away, and these wounds were not even in Irene's darkest tastes. Even if they were, the girl would not be embarrassed to show them to Lily.

"Who did this to you?" Lily asked, grabbing her hand and pulling the maidservant into her bedroom for more privacy. "Where else are you hurt?"

"Please, my lady, I don't wish to say. It would make no difference anyway," Irene replied.

Lily ignored her. "Undress." When she made no move to listen, she added, "That was an order."

Irene did so reluctantly, stripping down to her undergarments. Her body was covered in bruises and cuts. Not the kind made with whips or paddles or other toys, but with fists, probably with at least one ring on them. "Have you been to a physician yet?" Lily asked.

"If I go to one, they'll ask questions. And…and I…" the woman suddenly began to cry.

Lily led her to the bed, pulling the maidservant into a hug. "Tell me," she said quietly. "You know there is nothing shameful with me." She stroked the girl's hair. "Clearly this was not by choice."

"It was my husband, miss," Irene answered. "Trevor. He's a stablehand. I married him because my family is poor and I needed someone to take care of me financially, and he got me a job here in the castle. But I've never cared for him, or his crudeness, always drinking and eating like pigs do. And he smells worse than one." She took a shaky breath. "I went to him yesterday, miss. To tell him I was leaving him, that I was a lady's maid now and didn't have need of his money anymore. It hurt his pride. And...and he had found out about me and the king, someone had told him. Found out about some of the rougher stuff we do..." She trailed off.

"What happened?" Lily asked.

"He...he attacked me," the woman answered. "He'd been drinking, he was raving mad, and he started beating me, right there in the stables. I screamed at him, yelled for help, but no one came if they heard. He said if I liked pain, I should enjoy what he was doing to me. For such an old man, I never realized how strong he was...and then...then he, he forced himself on me."

Lily paused. "He raped you?" she asked. The girl nodded, and Lily found herself struggling not to clench her fists in rage.

"It was awful, miss. Whenever I've obliged him before, I didn't enjoy it, but this...He hurt me. Wanted to make me bleed. And when he was done he just left me there on the stable floor and spit on me like I was scum." She began to weep again.

"Then we should report it. I will find a guard immediately," Lily said.

The girl shook her head. "Oh no, my lady. Please. It wouldn't matter. He's my husband, after all. There isn't even a law that says a man can't force himself on his own wife. And it's...it's too shameful. I don't know how word spread about me and King Alec, but I don't want the other servants gossiping about me. At least I can take comfort knowing that I never have to see him again, and that there shouldn't be a child from it, judging by the other times."

"Have you bathed yet?" Lily asked. Irene nodded. Lily took another quick glance at the girl's wounds. None of them looked to be fatal, at least. There were no signs of broken bones or internal bleeding. Her ribcage looked the most worrisome, especially since she seemed uncomfortable breathing; but if any ribs were broken, the only thing to do would be to let her rest until they healed. "Fine, I will not make you see a healer if you do not wish," Lily said. "But you will rest until you are better. I want you to stay here, in my bed. And drink this." Lily plucked a vial from her dressing table, an alchemical concoction she drank to dull the pain of cramps during her monthly. Irene drank it without any more protest, lying back in the bed delicately. "Tomorrow, we will see about covering up some of those bruises with my makeup, so you do not have to hide from the rest of the palace."

"Thank you, my lady. You are too kind. Is it too greedy then of me to ask, will you...will you lie with me?" the maid asked softly. "At least until I fall asleep. I would find it comforting."

"Of course," Lily answered, and joined her in the bed. The woman curled up against her, and Lily stroked her back gently until she fell asleep.

She stared at the ceiling, listening for the sounds of Adrian moving about his suite. Thankfully, she didn't have to wait long to hear him leave. Likely he couldn't sleep after their encounter earlier and was headed to the main library, where he would read well into the night in the hopes of getting her out of his head. Lily waited until she was certain he wouldn't return, then went to his room, kneeling down on the floor beside his bed. She rapped her knuckles against the wall, waiting until she heard the hollow echo of her knocks.

The palace was old. It had been built almost four centuries ago when Luceran became the capital city of an early Arestea. While much of the inside and some of the newer additions were made with aesthetics first in mind, the original castle had been built all in stone to fortify and protect it from siege. If the early city was ever laid upon by its enemies, all of the townspeople would pour into the castle's outer walls for protection, and the royal family would hide inside the castle proper and issue commands from there.

However, war had changed. It was now done loudly and with pomp out on the open battlefield or quietly behind closed doors with words and secrets; and for the houses of Arestean royalty and the highest of noble families, comfort took precedence above protection. Thus the Royal Castle became the Royal Palace, updated and redecorated for its new needs. One such reconstruction, done at least two centuries ago by her reckoning of history, was to line many of the inner stone walls with sturdy wood paneling that was then decorated over with paint, stucco, and friezes of carved mahogany. The paneling beneath did not always fit snugly against the original stone wall, however; sometimes, if one knew what to look for, one could find small gaps between the inner wall and the outer stone.

In one such gap in the prince's room, Lily had cut out a pane, stored her assassin's gear inside, and replaced the pane so perfectly that the seam was invisible to all but the most observant eye. It hadn't been an easy project, especially given that Adrian rarely slept these nights, but the effort was worth it. She had no doubt that the last place he'd go looking for her gear was inside the wall right beside his own bed. If he ever *did* find out, of course, he'd be completely speechless. Imagining his reaction was just one more positive to the arrangement, as far as she was concerned.

Lily had to forgo her favored assassin garb this time. While it made it easier to move and protected her better from harm, she couldn't be caught wearing it inside the palace. It was only to be donned in the event that things went south and she had to flee or fight her way out. Instead, she put on her peasant girl's clothing, a loose fitting brown smock with a tight corset of simple, tanned leather overtop that showed off ample amounts of cleavage, as per her norm. It offered little in the way of protection and the skirts hampered movement somewhat, but the object was to distract the opponent into a false sense of security before striking. At least the boots were comfortable and allowed her to run, which was more than could be said for the ridiculously high-heeled slippers she wore daily with her extravagant courtesan gowns.

Lily also left behind her namesake, as this particular outing was not going to be a public statement. For one, she hadn't been assigned or sanctioned by the Guild, and secondly, unless she made what she did next look like an accident, she'd be jeopardizing her mission with unwanted attention. Telling everyone that the Black Lily had made it onto the palace grounds was the absolute last thing she wanted to do. She also felt she was finally getting somewhere with the prince and didn't want to risk losing what tenuous relationship they had developed. No, this one was not for business, merely pleasure.

It didn't take long to traverse the servants' quarters to the castle grounds this late at night. There were so many servants and visitors in the palace that nobody gave her a second look, especially because she had hidden her vibrant red hair under a brown wig done in a long, simple braid. At one point she was pulled aside by a laundress she'd never seen before, who asked Lily to give a certain guard whom she was sweet on a love note from her. Lily delivered it silently on her way out of the grounds, smiling at the guard's blush as he read it over.

As a light, misty drizzle began to fall, Lily made her way to the palace's stables. A quick glance revealed them to be empty except for their equine tenants, but laughter coming from a nearby bunkhouse caught her attention. It was one of the many bunkhouses on the palace's sprawling grounds where the guards lived while off duty. Servants and such had their own quarters inside the palace proper, so that they could always be on call if need be, but guards who patrolled the grounds or the walls were given small, separate bunk rooms with two to four men per room in which to live, as well as a communal bathhouse, kitchen, and living area. Currently the living room was occupied by a few guards reading, sitting by the fire chatting, and playing cards.

It was these gamblers that caught her attention. While none of them were in their armor or uniforms, one in particular stuck out for his worn, homespun garb, which looked more suited to tending the fields than defending the palace. He'd clearly had more than a few drinks and, as a result, was the only one at the card game without even a small pile of money at his side.

"It just seems the Lady of Fortune does not smile on you tonight, friend," one of the guards said with a smile, patting the roughly dressed gambler on the back. "Perhaps next time."

"So, Trevor, how's it going training that new stallion for us?" another asked. "I heard it's quite a wild one. Already thrown off two men and broken another's leg."

"Yeah, yeah," the man grumbled, shrugging off the hand on his shoulder. "I'll whip its hide raw until it learns to behave. You'll see."

Lily smiled, recognizing the name. She leaned against the wall just outside the window, shifting to a comfortable pose under the meager awning as rain began to fall in earnest, waiting for her chance.

It didn't take long for an opportunity to appear. Fed up with losing, Trevor folded his hand and tossed the last few copper coins to his name across the table. The guardswoman across from him laughed as she scooped them into her pile. "Much obliged, Trevor boyo," she said with a grin. "I'll be thinking of you while I drink away your coin."

"Ehh, fuck you, ya sod," Trevor spit, rising from his seat.

"Now, is that any way—"

"Ahh, shaddup. You know where you can stick that coin. I'm goin' home." He stalked off, grumbling, and slammed the door as he left. As he stumbled his way towards the stables through the now pouring rain, Lily snuck around the back, sidling into the barn through a window before he could get there.

Trevor saw movement out of the corner of his eye and looked up from his grumbling, surprised to find a woman lounging in the hay in his barn. She smiled up at him as she played with the braid of her brown hair. She'd kicked off her boots, and it was all he could do not to stare at her bare feet peeking out from under the skirts of her dress. "Who the hell...?" he began to ask, but she cut him off, standing up and walking toward him.

"Trevor, ain't it?" she asked, putting a finger to his lips. He nodded dumbly, wondering what this beauty wanted with him. "I've been watchin' you for a long time. You're such a handsome lad. But whenever I saw ya, you were always with that wife of 'yours. Never could get close enough to tell ya how much I fancy you." She ran her hands through his hair and down his chin.

"Funny," he said, swallowing hard, "I don't remember—"

"Shh." She silenced him by pressing those luscious lips against his own, and he forgot what he was about to say. Who gave a shit who this woman was? He needed this—deserved it. Ever since that frigid bitch of a wife of his had stopped putting out for him, just because he enjoyed his drink and put her in her place a few times, he'd been pent up with sexual frustration. He was sick of pleasuring himself in the hay while the horses watched. And if Irene was getting some from someone else, as he'd recently learned, then why shouldn't he?

He lost control, grabbing the girl against him before pushing her down in the hay, straddling her. His hands were all over her, pulling her clothes off, digging into her hair. He pulled hard, wanting to make her cry out in pain, the way Irene had last night, but he found himself staring at a fistful of brown hair that wasn't attached to a head. "What the bloody hell?" he grumbled.

He wasn't sure what happened next, just that somehow he was on the ground and she was on top of him, her knees pinning his arms down to his sides. Suddenly there was a dagger at his throat, drawing a trickle of blood with only the slightest pressure. His head spun from drink and confusion. His servant girl was gone, replaced by a demon with blood red hair and a wicked blade, her grin glinting in a flash of lightning through the window.

"What are you?" he tried to shout, but the blade pressing into his throat constrained it to a hoarse rasp. "Whaddaya want from me?"

"I'm a spirit of vengeance, Trevor," she whispered in his ear. "I know what you did to your wife. Do you think it's okay because you're wed? Did it make you feel like a man, Trevor, to see her bruised and battered, knowing that you did it?"

"My wife? She sent you?" Despite the blade and the redheaded demon, the whiskey heat began to leak through his fear and stir his anger. "That…that cunt has been sleepin' with other men! I know it! She deserved it! I'll kill her for this!"

"I don't think you have to worry about that, Trevor," whispered the demon. "Now, how shall we do it? Shall I make it look like you hanged yourself? Or should it be a little more…dramatic?"

As she contemplated his doom aloud, he managed to free his hand. He reached for the nearest thing he could find, an empty bourbon bottle, and brought it up to smash over her head.

Her hand reached up and caught his arm before he could bring it down, and an impish grin broke across her face. "Amateurish," she said. "Did you really think it would be that easy?" In a swift motion, she snapped his arm, breaking the bone at the elbow. His vision went black from the pain before he could even scream.

When he came to, he was bound and gagged on the stable ground, his face pressed against the dirty straw, the rank smell of sweat and horse heavy in his nostrils.

"For the noise, you understand?" the demon woman informed him. She was pacing the rows of horses, still smiling. "Let's see…a runaway horse, I think. Yes, this one. It *is* a mighty frisky one." The stallion she laid her hand on, a young but muscular

245

Ovinur thoroughbred, stamped and reared its head as if in answer. "I do believe this must be the one you've been breaking in, yes? I wouldn't doubt it would love to get a bit of revenge for feeling the whip on its hide."

Trevor tried to speak, to scream, but no sound came out through the rag stuffing his mouth. The woman, the devil, still smiled sweetly at him as she grabbed a horseshoe from the wall. It turned into an evil grin as she brought it down across his face, and the resulting wet crunch was the last sound he heard.

Thirteen

"I'm afraid Ovinurland is massing a force on our northern border, m'lord," Bodan reported. "Our scouts from Graywatch have just informed us last night."

Adrian didn't look up from the stack of letters in front of him on his desk. "I wouldn't worry too much about it," he said. "Ovinurland is always massing a force on our northern border. They seem to really like it there."

His steward bowed his head again. "As you say, m'lord. But with most of the army still held up in Beuteland and not yet reorganized, there is some concern that this may be a larger threat at present than in previous instances. Especially with the king still out of the country."

"I still wouldn't worry about it too much. Alec never takes from the northern garrisons without putting at least as much back, and I haven't touched those numbers at all in his absence. That line has been as firm throughout this whole Beuteland mess as it ever was before."

"Very good, Sire," the steward acquiesced. "Then what message shall we send to the inquisitive northern holdings? Lord Graywatch in particular has already sent word of his urgent concern."

Adrian was looking at that particular letter himself just now, scanning the fluff of obligatory political good manners to pick out the subtly outraged demands beneath of a loyal vassal to his uncaring sovereign. "Tell them — Graywatch in particular — that our border is under no new threat," he ordered. "They just mass forces over there for lack of anything better to do, I think. All that cold and frost and wind, they can't plant anything or go anywhere. Massing forces is probably just how they keep warm."

"As you wish, Sire," Bodan answered.

"But word it a bit more delicately than that, please," Adrian added. "Something sufficiently puffed up with all the vague toppings. Like an official kingly decree."

"As you say, Sire. Er…if I may, m'lord…" The man trailed off.

The nervous tone made the crown prince look up at his steward. "Yes, Bodan?"

"Are you well this morning, Sire?" The older man was frowning, but it looked to Adrian more like confusion than concern.

"I feel fine, thank you," he answered. "Why?"

"Not to offend, Sire, but you seem more…distracted than usual. Does something trouble you?"

What doesn't trouble me these days? Adrian thought. To Bodan he sighed and said, "I'm just feeling in a rut, is all. Stuck in a holding pattern with no clear direction to move in and no way to get there anyway." He lifted the stack of official letters and ruffled them tiredly for emphasis. "I mean, look at this. Everyone wants something, everyone else doesn't want them to have it, and nothing I do or say will fix any of it. I feel bound in every direction, and I can't take a step in any of them without strangling myself, and there's no one else around who can help me untie myself except for a few who would politely but happily refuse if asked." Which was true, he thought, if not the entire truth. There were concerns he wasn't about to voice aloud to anyone who didn't already know, not even his family's most loyal steward.

"Ah, yes," said Bodan with a sage nod, "I believe I understand, m'lord. We are all feeling the absence of King Alec. Not to belittle your management, of course, Prince Adrian," he added hurriedly. "You have a fine, unpretentious grasp on the throne, and many of the nobility have confided in me how at ease they feel within it. Just that the king is always so sure of his judgment, and that surety of purpose infects the entire palace. Makes people feel secure."

Adrian sighed. "That's a good way of putting it. Honestly, I never thought I'd miss the bastard this much. However he ran the place, whether I agreed or not, I have to admit that at least it did *run* with him at the helm. And he made it look so easy."

"Exactly so, Sire," said the steward. "If I may presume, though, Your Highness…you do seem to have a bit of your brother's air about you lately as well. It does quite become you."

"Do I, Bodan?" Adrian asked. He wasn't sure whether he should take the thought as comforting or worrisome. Any time before he would have dismissed the notion as impossible, but the more time wore on and the more complicated his situation became, the more he began to sympathize with his reigning sibling. Entitled landowners on one side, needy populace on the other, surrounded on all fronts by nations who smile pleasantly while their soldiers march around peering over the fence. And the only people he could trust were the ones who openly hated him, because at least those people were being honest.

He thought of Lily again, with her easy conversation and warm manner and the half a dozen implements of murder she probably kept casually hidden around a body she kept inviting him to explore. As if the job needed any more complications. Hell, for all he knew, this wasn't even the first time a situation like this had happened in their kingdom. Maybe chatting up regicidal courtesans was just another unspoken responsibility of kings. He couldn't remember either of his parents ever having this many problems at once, but then again, who else besides himself really knew how much weight was on his mind right now?

"You do indeed, Sire," Bodan answered with a wry smile. "This past week especially, you have made the rulership seem a tedious bore for its familiarity rather than the daunting challenge it first appeared to you. King Alec would no doubt laugh to hear it."

Adrian almost laughed himself. "Thank you, Bodan. Let me know if I start picking up his arrogance, though. I've always half-feared it might be contagious."

The steward bowed his head. "As you say, Sire."

"You don't have to pretend he's not, you know," the prince added. "Everyone who's met the man knows he can be a selfish prick. I'm not even entirely sure anymore if that's a failing or a necessary side effect of wearing this mindset all day long."

"As you say, Sire."

"Thank you, Bodan." He dismissed his steward then, watching as Bodan took his leave of the king's private study and gently shut the door behind him. The man was old enough to have served Adrian's parents during their long and peaceful rule, then stayed on when Alec succeeded the throne and began forming his expansion campaign. Unsympathetic as his brother could be at times, presumably there was still enough sympathy in him to inspire loyalty from the very servants and commoners he seemed to deride. The longer his absence stretched on, the fonder Adrian found himself becoming of Alec, even of things that had before only rankled.

There were still facets of him that Adrian couldn't justify, though. His absolute dismissal of what his subjects thought of him, for instance; Adrian felt that a king should still at least address his people's complaints, even if he didn't let them define his rule. Alec's policy of open and consistent disregard worked when his single-minded faith in himself paid off for the country at large, but with all the controversy of late, there was no way that everybody could win from Alec's continuing gambles. And that blasé attitude had already been the torch used to incite the flames of riot in more places than just Luceran's Low Quarter.

The biggest damnation for the prince, though, was Alec's personal habits. Adrian had to take a deep, steadying breath whenever he thought of what he'd found in Alec's private tower. Everyone had their own tastes, he knew, and he'd often been the only person in the room who would argue that an individual's private proclivities were not the business of every interested gossip who asked after them—but he knew there was a line in that argument as well, and his conscience told him that his brother had made a sport of crossing it. He hadn't known before how to justify his brother's effective leadership with the tyranny it involved; now he didn't know how to mesh his growing respect for the king as he learned what was really required of him with his sudden disgust as he learned what rewards that same king took for himself as payment.

He occasionally wondered, usually at night and alone in his private bedchamber, whether it might not be justified after all to let Lily assassinate him when he got back. However much she enjoyed her work, she didn't do it for free—presumably somebody very important somewhere thought this course of action was worthwhile enough that they had paid somebody else a great deal of money to send the realm's most infamous assassin after him. Plenty of people had come forward with vehement, if brief, complaints against the king lately, of course—you couldn't spit in this kingdom without getting some outraged noble or other wet—but in Adrian's experience, the one thing the aristocracy loved more than its opinions was its wealth. The price tag on sending the highest-tier killer available after the highest-tier target possible must have been outrageous. If multiple nobles were pooling their money to cover the cost, that was even more damning. Lily's presence here alone was a stronger argument against his brother than any of the angry rants Adrian had heard wind of.

It was not, strictly speaking, lawful. Actually, it was not lawful by any stretch of the term. But it did ring of a perverse civil justice. And it would solve a lot of problems for a lot of people—problems Adrian had thought he'd shared in until now.

He wondered. And then, when he caught himself wondering, he very quickly turned his thoughts in a new direction lest he risk finding an opinion of his own. With the nation's mounting tension, opinions were becoming dangerous things to carry. Adrian was risking enough as it was already as regent. Besides, even if he justified the idea to himself somehow, how could he sit back and let his own brother be murdered?

His thoughts were interrupted momentarily by a polite knock on the door. The prince mumbled his assent half automatically, then bit back another sigh when the Minister of Internal Affairs entered his office with a bow. Here, at least, were issues he was used to hearing and felt qualified to lord over, though they tended to consist mostly of gossip and boring clerical details.

He put on an expression of stoic attentiveness as the minister delivered his report of goings-on in the palace grounds, nodding where appropriate as the man rattled off inventories for each branch of palace staff, instances where the shoring up of supplies was needed and the recommendations of staff chiefs as to how best to cover them, general reviews of servants and guards by visiting dignitaries, general reviews of visiting dignitaries by servants and guards (a system implemented by Adrian's own suggestion in the beginning of his regency), the status of the palace proper and its outbuildings, training schedules for the guards, seasonal plans from the head gardener, a casualty report from the stablemaster —

"Wait, what?" Adrian interrupted, blinking as his attention was kindled back to life. "Casualties?"

"Just the one, Sire," the Minister of Internal Affairs assured him. "Nothing more than a passing annoyance, really. I'd hoped not to trouble you with the tedious details, m'lord."

"Passing annoyance?" the prince asked, frowning. "You're telling me somebody in the palace died! I should hope that a dead body would merit a stronger reaction from my staff than passingly annoyed!"

The minister shrunk back a step and raised his hands before him in what was probably supposed to be a calming gesture but looked more to Adrian like shielding a surprise attack. "Indeed, Sire, as you say, there was a bit of distress raised when the man was found. It was apparently quite gruesome. But the incident has all the evidence of a sad accident, so we have ruled out foul play." He turned his hands upward in a small but elegant shrug. "Unfortunate, yes, but these things are known to happen time to time."

"Nonetheless, I wish to hear the tedious details, as you call them," Adrian said, then listened intently to the story of a drunken stablehand stumbling out of the guards' barracks in the rain last night only to be found in the morning lying dead in a pool of dried blood next to an open stall, his forehead caved in and the resident stallion trotting nervously and freely around the room, trampling the body and leaving bloodstained hoof prints across the floor as the other hands tried to coax him back into his pen. The stallion was a new addition and yet unbroken, the stablehands told the guards, and the dead man was known to be violent with it in its training. One of the guards said they had overheard him mentioning his intentions to take out his anger from losing a card game on the horse just before leaving for the night, and that was the last anyone had heard of him. His wife had been given his estimated pay for the next three months in advance as compensation for his death, then allowed to leave for a week to mourn, inform his relatives, and get his affairs in order.

None of it, everyone agreed, was suspicious or surprising or, really, all that unfortunate. Trevor had not been anyone's friend; his wife Irene would be the only person crying over him, if even she felt the need.

"Irene?" Adrian asked. "Why does that name ring of familiarity?"

"I do believe she is the same maidservant you recently promoted to position of lady's maid for your courtesan, Sire," the Minister responded. He did a quick check of his ledgers. "Yes, the very same."

Adrian bit back a curse. He couldn't very well refuse the girl a proper mourning period just because he needed someone to serve as Lily's unwitting handler. "Give her her own wages in advance as well," the prince ordered quietly after the minister finished speaking. "And the rest of the month off. We've plenty of staff left and fewer visitors than normal for the season; we won't be hurting for want of one grieving widow."

"As you will, m'lord," the Minister of Internal Affairs replied with a small bow, then finished his

255

report. Adrian thanked him and dismissed him, alone again in the royal office.

He had feared a death ever since discovering Lily, that, her cover blown, she would start murdering her way one by one through the guards and nobles, leaving no evidence but inciting panic, until…well, granted, he wasn't really sure what that would accomplish on her part, but it was a chilling thought nonetheless. The growing familiarity between them had only turned his fears more wary.

It seemed too coincidental that the man killed should be the husband of her lady's maid. Would Lily have killed him just to get rid of her maidservant's watchful eyes? Surely that would go against her edict of never killing innocents.

She did seem to be behaving herself rather admirably but for her stubborn refusal to abandon her plot and submit to official justice. In the time since she'd been discovered, this was the first violent incident to occur on his watch. And the guards who had investigated the incident had themselves ruled out foul play. There had been no mention of a flower of any sort being found with the dead man. If Adrian asked her, would she admit to it? And if she did, would it even be the truth, or would she just take credit in an attempt to bluff him into panicking more?

He had to trust the guards and believe that this was just an unfortunate and timely accident. Not even the dreaded Black Lily could command wild animals to do her dirty work. Could she? No. No, surely not.

Having decided that this accident was just that, Adrian's thoughts turned back to his brother's potential murderer. However quarrelsome and unpopular this stablehand had been, his death left a short chaos of reports and contingency plans and, most importantly to Adrian, a distraught wife whose world had suddenly been shattered. And however quarrelsome and unpopular King Alec may be, his murder would trigger a much larger, much more complicated chaos that would claim much more than the happiness of a single maidservant. Trevor had duties and responsibilities, both to his employers and to his family; so did Alec. His death wouldn't make them go away or fix his mistakes, just as Trevor's death couldn't tame a wild horse or make the man retroactively likeable.

The kernel of doubt that had been slowly growing in Adrian since the war had started vanished then. His brother was far from perfect, but he deserved a chance to fix his messes himself and do what he thought best for his country. However much sense Lily might have been making, however rationally she worded it, and however nobly she behaved herself within her stated duties, Adrian couldn't let her succeed in her plans any more than she had already. He couldn't let her kill Alec, no matter what name of justice she invoked.

If it came down to it, if they didn't reach a peaceful compromise in time, he would have to have her executed. It wouldn't be easy, he knew; he would be sending some of the men in her arresting party to their deaths, most likely. But if things continued as they were now, perhaps she would grow comfortable enough around him not to see it coming. Perhaps, if she kept thinking him a harmless obstacle, she'd make the mistake of thinking he carried no threat. He wouldn't enjoy giving the order, and he wouldn't enjoy trying to deceive her trust until then, but he would do what was necessary to see his job through. He thought she would appreciate that sentiment, at least, since she preached it so often herself.

Help me be a better bastard, Adrian thought again, remembering his silent plea when he'd first discovered what he'd be up against. *By all the gods, brother, I didn't think they would actually listen.*

Adrian returned to his quarters, feeling tired even though it was not yet midday. Then again, perpetual tiredness was becoming familiar. Perhaps he could take a nap? But no, as soon as he laid his head down, some crisis would come up that needed his attention or some visiting nobleman would call on him for tea. As he stepped into his living area, he heard voices coming from Lily's room. Curious, he leaned against the wall, listening.

"I...I just don't know what to do," came a female voice he didn't recognize, though the woman sounded as if she were near tears, or had recently stopped crying. "I know that I should be sad for him, but I never loved the man, and after...after what he did to me..."

"Shhh," he heard Lily reply. "He is gone now, yes?" Adrian noticed that Lily had returned to a less exaggerated version of her false accent that she used around everyone but him. After hearing her speaking perfect Arestean for so long, it sounded odd.

"I feel wrong, like I should be upset, hearing how horribly he died. But, all I can feel is...relieved. Is that wrong of me, my lady?" The other woman drew in a shaky breath. Then this must be Irene, Lily's recently widowed lady's maid.

"Listen, Irene," said the assassin. "You have every right to be happy. After how he treated you, you deserve it. You are free now. He can no longer hurt you."

Adrian found himself confused as he tried to follow the conversation. What did they mean, what he had done to her? "I know, my lady. And now they tell me that I should leave, for an entire month, to mourn him. But I don't wish to leave your side, miss. This is the best job I have ever had, and I would fear someone replacing me should I leave for so long. I never thought that I would be a lady's maid, much less that I would be friends with my lady. Is that alright, if I call you friend?"

There was a pause on Lily's behalf. Adrian, too curious not to see what was happening, peeked his head around the corner. Lily sat on her bed with the maidservant, Irene, hugging her. Lily's face betrayed surprise, as if the concept of friendship was strange to her, but within a second she had adjusted, putting on what Adrian assumed was a fake smile. "Of course, Irene. You are a dear friend to me."

Lily glanced up then, catching Adrian's eye. She politely disentangled herself from Irene and stood, nodding to him with her fake smile. "My Prince, you have returned."

Irene shot up, her eyes wide. She fiddled with a handkerchief nervously as she curtsied to him. She quickly ducked her head. "My…m'lord," she said, staring at the ground, "if there is anything you need…"

"No, I'm fine. And I am deeply sorry to hear about your recent loss…Irene, was it?" Adrian asked.

"Y-yes, m'lord," the maid stammered, blushing deeper. "Thank you for your kindness."

"If you don't mind, I would like a few moments alone with…Camilla," he said, remembering at the last moment to use her alias.

"The rain has finally stopped," Lily said, reaching out to take his arm. "Perhaps we should take a walk, my prince." She stumbled briefly, wavering on her feet.

"Oh, my lady, are you alright?" Irene asked, reaching out a hand to steady her.

Lily held a hand to her head, eyes closed. Adrian tried not to roll his eyes at her antics. What she wouldn't do for attention. And with a grieving widow in the room, no less. Gentlemanly, he took her by the arm. "Yes," Lily replied, though her voice briefly lost its fake accent. After a moment, it returned. "Just a bit…lightheaded, is all."

"You should be careful, miss. A lot of that going around, lately," Irene warned her. "Why, Lady Montfloss has been ill with the fever all last week."

"Of course. Thank you, Irene. I will call on you tonight to draw me a bath, yes?" Lily asked.

"Of course, miss." Irene curtsied, then guided them to the door. It seemed Adrian would be stuck with Lily for longer than he had planned. Ah well, he needed the fresh air anyway. And perhaps he could start acting a bit nicer, try to get her to trust him more.

Lily and Adrian strolled through the gardens at a slow pace, breathing in the scent of flowers and wet grass, the pervading rainstorms of the past several days having finally dissipated. There was a chill in the air from the last heavy downpour the previous night, and the trees were beginning to turn colors as autumn descended. More than once Lily found her head spinning and had to clutch Adrian's arm tighter to keep from losing her balance. She didn't mind, really. He had a nice body under those fancy clothes of his, despite having been born and raised a spoiled prince.

She was worried, though, she had to admit. She almost never got sick, but perhaps all that dratted standing around in the cold rain waiting for Trevor to stumble drunkenly away from the guardhouse had gotten to her.

"That was very nice...what you did for that maidservant," Adrian mused aloud. "I almost have to wonder what's in it for you, helping her out. Unless it's all for show. If I hadn't assigned her to you myself, I would be afraid that she was an assassin too."

Lily snorted, dropping her pretenses and fake accent, knowing they were alone. "Her? An assassin? She is too sweet and gentle for it. I consider her a friend."

"You don't have friends." Adrian pointed out. "You have targets and people that you use. So why are you actually being so nice to her, then? Easier dalliance opportunities?"

Lily sighed. "Is it really that unbelievable that I would care for another person regardless of what I might gain from the arrangement?" She saw the skeptical look on his face. She considered telling him the truth, or at least part of it, that Irene's husband abused her. But then he would ask questions, and he was too clever not to figure out that the man's death wasn't as accidental as it seemed. Besides, it was not her secret to tell. "Just because I'm a cold-blooded killer doesn't mean I can't be nice every once in a while," she replied, a hint of humor in her voice.

"Perhaps," said the prince, not sounding totally convinced. "You know, I have to wonder. What could make a girl want to become an assassin? To murder innocent people—"

"Stop there, princeling," she interrupted. "The people I kill are far from innocent. I've told you this. They deserve it, every one of them."

"Even your swordsman?" Adrian asked. "The one you deigned worthy enough to sleep with before murdering?"

"He was a hired sword, princeling," she argued. "He fought and often killed people for money. He was basically a sanctioned version of me." She had to admit, though, if she had ever felt sorry for one of her marks before, it was him. Adrian didn't need to know that, though. "I was attracted to his body and talents, not his ethics. He had none. He may not have been outright evil, but he was far from good nonetheless, and he knew the risks of his lifestyle when he chose to live it. All I do is bring people the justice they have coming to them."

"So, that's why you do it?" the prince asked. "Some weird sense of justice? And you've never considered that there is a way to do this lawfully?"

"No," she answered immediately, her tone hard and brooking no argument. "The law is a fine theory, but easily dirtied when filtered through those who should enforce it. You know as well as any that the highest powers can commit the worst of sins and the law will not intervene. If you have enough money, you can pay anyone to look the other way."

"I don't believe that," he replied.

"Then you are a fool," she snapped.

"But even so. Even if everyone you have ever assassinated so far really was guilty and had it coming to them...what if you were ordered to kill an innocent? Or a child?" he asked.

"No one is innocent. Not even children. I should know." She tucked a strand of hair behind her ear, suddenly feeling very tired.

"You can't believe that. Not if you also believe that what you do somehow protects the innocent. So what if you were?" he pressed.

Lily sighed. "I don't know, Adrian. I don't know what I would do. I don't have the energy for philosophical discourse right now." They both paused to watch as a parade of carriages pulled up to the front of the palace, and Lily's mind suddenly focused. Finally. Her contact had arrived; she had been preparing to meet them when Irene had come to her with news of her husband's death, then Adrian after that. She knew only that they were a noble due for a court appearance, or else posing as such in order to make the transition to puppet king easier after she eradicated Adrian and Alec. She squared her shoulders and mentally shook herself as she turned her attention back to the prince. "We have guests, it seems. Come, let's greet them. I can search my soul in private later."

Adrian followed her as she made her way out of the garden and to the front entrance of the palace. Servants, both the king's and her contact's personal ones, were unloading baggage and containers from the carriages. It seemed whoever her contact was, they were not shy about making themselves comfortable. She stepped around a pile of hatboxes, trying to guess who it might be. She had only recently been informed of the date of their arrival; her covert go-betweens had never mentioned who exactly to expect.

Then the carriage door opened, and *he* stepped out.

Lily froze, staring as he descended, his gaze sweeping past the bustling servants to the palace grounds. This was not her contact — in fact, this might be the only man in the kingdom that she could say with a certainty her Guild would never work with. She knew his face immediately, as it was one of only two faces that ever haunted her nightmares. The angular, almost concave features. The long, light brown hair streaked with gray, falling in waves down past his shoulders, revealing a sharp widow's peak in the front. The lightly tanned face that sported no facial hair save for his thin, angular eyebrows that gave him the appearance of a hawk searching for prey. He was a tall, lean man, but that didn't make him any less daunting. He carried himself with the air of any aristocrat, but mixed in was a sense of danger, of tension, as if he were prepared at any moment to lash out at some hidden threat. And when his gray eyes fell on her, she felt a chill run through her entire body.

Evidently her contact was not the only new arrival today. But if *he* was also here, her mission took on a whole new level of depth. Maneuvering around Adrian was already difficult enough, and she had yet to figure out the best means of dealing with him when the time came. She had even less of an idea how she was going to kill this man when the prince was already trying to watch her every movement. But she knew she was going to, somehow. It was not part of the mission, but she would never get such a chance again. The Guild would understand. She would bring them a report of how painfully she had managed to draw it out for the sake of poetic justice, and they would all sleep better at night for it.

The newly arrived nobleman stepped forward, bowing before the prince with a small smile. "My lord, you honor me with your presence and hospitality," he said, his voice light and cool. Then he turned to Lily, and his smile widened as he took her hand and kissed her fingers, her trying desperately not to clench them into fists at his touch. "And you must be as new as I to the palace, for I am sure I would remember such a vision of loveliness. My liege, it seems, grows only the most beautiful of flowers for his garden."

As his gaze slid off of her back to Adrian, Lily's already troubled breath caught in her throat, her vision swimming. It was impossible. He knew the secret phrase, the one that only her contact should know. The one that assured her he had the Guildmaster's sanction, and that everything was going according to plan.

Duke-Milite Liam de Treventre *was* her contact. He was the man she would help place on the throne. The same man who had tortured and hanged her lover, Robert.

Lily collapsed as her world went black.

Fourteen

Despite his better judgment and every voice of reason in his mind urging otherwise, Adrian fretted, waiting outside the door to Lily's chamber as the royal physician evaluated her. She had simply collapsed in the garden and hadn't woken up since, and he had to have her carried back to her bed. If he ever came to his senses, he knew he would realize what a stroke of luck this was for him that she was finally incapacitated, even if only for a short while. At present, however, surprise and worry got the better of him.

"Your concern for the lady is commendable, Your Highness," Duke-Milite Liam assured him, "but if I may, I'm afraid you might be worrying overmuch. The poor girl was flushed and swaying on her feet when I first laid eyes on her. No doubt she'd merely been fighting a fever when it got the better of her." The duke-milite had followed him to Lily's room when they rushed her here, even offered to help the guards carry her, and now stood in the sitting room across from the frowning prince, leaning against the wall with an air of calm to counterbalance Adrian's panic.

"I'm sure you're right," Adrian answered, glancing involuntarily through the door at the physician's back. "It just happened so suddenly, right in the middle of introductions. She'd said she felt tired, but she hadn't given any hints that it was anything more than simple fatigue."

"Well, perhaps she was mastering her illness before my arrival," the duke said with a grin. "Perhaps I came on with a bit too much charm. I have known some women to react in such a way around me if I am not overly careful."

The Black Lily, swoon over a nobleman almost twice her age? Adrian chuckled, partly at the duke's joke and partly at the absurdity of the idea. He couldn't picture Lily swooning in earnest over anyone or anything, and would have chalked the whole performance up to her occasional tendency for insinuating theatrics had he not felt her burning head for himself. No, she was legitimately out, though why and for how long he wasn't sure yet.

But he would find out as soon as possible. And then he would make his plans. If luck held, he would have this whole assassination conspiracy well in hand and wrapped up before her fever broke, and she would wake to find herself already under arrest and being hauled off to the Ergastulum for questioning, without any more chances to try and confuse his loyalties or morals.

The creeping disappointment he felt at this prospect did not entirely surprise him, not anymore. She'd had an interesting effect on him, he had to give her that, and he wasn't sure what, out of all of their conversations, had been genuine and what she had simply fed him to weaken his resolve. Maybe, once her plan was in ruins and she had nothing more to lose from open honesty, he would ask her about it. She might even tell him — though, of course, she might just feed him more lies.

He would be sure to push for as much mercy as was appropriate when it came time for her trial. Execution was the first and obvious choice, but perhaps with some convincing and a show of remorse on her part they could commute it to life imprisonment instead, a rare and therefore valuable example of the king's mercy. Maybe she would eventually see the error of her ways and start to truly repent. Perhaps she could even be convinced to name her conspirators in return for her life, making the kingdom a safer place for its citizens.

And then maybe she'd sprout wings and fly away to join a monastery, he thought. It was just as likely an outcome, he knew, but still, he could hope for the best.

He would have to remember to remove her poison vial before her arrest. It wouldn't do if she killed herself while he was trying to save her life.

Adrian sighed. He hoped she would forgive him. And then he chastised himself for having such an incredibly stupid concern.

The physician returned with a serious expression, her mouth set in a pensive line. For a moment the prince feared that there would be no need for his plans after all, but before he could speak, the physician shook her head. "Merely a fever," she said quietly, "but a heavy one. I've seen a lot of it lately with the weather being what it has. She has simply exposed herself to too much cold and moisture. Let her rest and it will pass."

Adrian sighed in relief, then immediately second-guessed that relief. He wasn't sure if the amount of sympathy he felt for her was appropriate to the situation. After a moment of thoughtful silence, though, he realized that both the physician and the duke were still looking to him for response. Of course, they couldn't know that she was anything more than an unfortunate courtesan; if he continued to debate the appropriateness of his sympathy for her, they would only see it as aloof inconsideration. Somewhat abashed, he cleared his throat. "That is good to hear. Do you know about how long her convalescence will last?"

The physician shook her head again. "Duchess Prudence was my most recent case before this, and she has been bedridden these past couple of weeks. This lady is younger and healthier, but her fever is deeper. It's as if she simply stood out in the pouring rain all night." She shook her head a third time, puzzled. "I estimate the worst of it between two to five days, and if her fever has not broken by then, there may be something worse at hand. Provided that the weather is all that is wrong, however, she should recover quickly once the fever has gone. Perhaps a week all total, thereabout, given her youth and vitality."

Adrian nodded, thinking this over and committing the doctor's details to memory. "Is she lucid yet?" he asked after a pause.

"At the moment?" the physician asked. "No. She moans softly in her sleep and lolls her head now and then, so I suspect fever dreams. This will be the worst of it up front." She turned back to the doorway then, peering through. The prince followed her gaze. "I've left a tonic on her bedside table for when she wakes," the physician continued. "Have whoever watches her try and get her to take some when she comes to, even if it's just for a moment. A spoonful four times a day, ideally, but for now do what you can. If she can get some of it in her, it should shorten her recovery. And I would recommend keeping away from her yourself, Your Highness. We certainly can't risk our regent falling ill." She nodded then and turned back to Adrian. "Anything else I can help with, Sire? You've dark circles under your eyes. A sleeping draught perhaps?"

Adrian still stared at Lily's unconscious body through the doorway, bundled as it was beneath a heavy pile of blankets so that only her head was visible, her red hair currently damp and plastered in strands across her face with sweat. For the first time since he'd met her, she looked completely vulnerable, and that unnerved him even more than her subtle threats had lately. "No, thank you," he said to the doctor without looking at her. "I find they muddle my head too much during the day. I'll send for you if any more concerns arise."

"As you wish. Do try and get more sleep, Your Highness. We can't have you passing out as well. Then if you'll excuse me, gentlemen," the physician said with a bow to the prince and a smaller one to the duke-milite. "I must attend to the duchess. Her husband has insisted on checkups twice daily." She smiled briefly at the both of them, then turned and walked leisurely down the hall, in no obvious hurry to get to her next assignment.

Adrian leaned his head back against the couch, eyes shut, and took a deep breath. She would need someone to look over her until the worst of the illness passed — social politesse and simple human decency demanded she receive that much no matter what else he decided to do with her. Irene was the obvious choice, but she was due a leave of absence starting today; and while it was entirely possible that she would stay on anyway if asked, as much as she seemed to admire "Camilla," Adrian felt it would be best not to bring it up. Let her grieve properly and get a small break, at least, for her troubles.

He could easily arrange for any other servant to stand vigil, even have a rotation of servants set up rather than assign her one specifically. But he also felt that he himself should sit with her as well, at least on occasion. Obviously he couldn't spare the time to keep a constant watch over her until she recovered, but if she had moments of confused wakefulness or started to talk in her sleep, she might inadvertently confess to something that could give away her cover. However he chose to deal with this, he didn't need the hassle of another innocent drawn into the plot, nor the panic that might lead to. The fewer potential targets he gave her, the better.

He had much to consider, and he needed to come to a decision fast to take full advantage of the opportunity. For now, at least, he would get the first maidservant who wasn't too busy to keep an eye on her. Any of his own responsibilities could be delegated or simply wait until he'd formed a plan of action.

"My lord?" Duke-Milite Liam interrupted his thoughts. "Is something the matter?"

"Huh?" Adrian opened his eyes, and it took a moment to get his mind back to the same place as the rest of him. "Oh, no, not particularly," he answered with a dismissive wave of the hand. "Just considering how best to see to the lady's recovery, is all."

The duke-milite had a concerned frown on his face. "Your Highness truly has a generous spirit. But if I may be so bold, you heard the physician; 'tis only a moderate flu. Simply assign her a personal attendant and wait to hear that she's gotten over it."

Adrian half smiled to himself. He'd never personally met the duke-milite before except in passing during court functions, where they had exchanged only brief and empty acknowledgments with one another. He was pleased, however, to find an aristocrat unafraid to simply tell someone above his own station what they thought the best course of action was, unimpeded by simpering platitudes and unburied by political vagueness. He could use more such straight talk and blunt advice, he thought, especially in the next few days as he dealt with this Lily problem. Perhaps a confidante in the matter would be useful.

"Yes, thank you," he said to the duke, "my thoughts exactly. I must talk to my steward and see what help we have to spare for this." He glanced back in at her prone form, brow scrunching in worry once more. "Do you think she'll be alright on her own for a short while until we can get the details worked out?"

"Most likely, Sire, yes," answered the duke. "However, if it would ease your concerns, I have no qualms supervising the lady until proper help arrives. My luggage and lodgings are already being attended to, so I have the time to spare."

"That is most generous of you," Adrian answered, attention pulled back to the duke. Liam smiled charmingly, and the prince couldn't stop the sudden concern that came to him, surprising though he found it. "That is, uh…if you think it would be entirely appropriate," he added awkwardly, glancing back into Lily's room, "leaving an unconscious lady alone in the company of a man she doesn't know." Voicing his concern aloud, he immediately realized it sounded ridiculous.

Duke-Milite Liam chuckled lightly, evidently thinking the same thing. "Your chivalry does you credit, my prince, but I can assure you that you've nothing to fear from me. Even if I hadn't arrived with my own designs on courting Duchess Sidonie while she is in attendance, I can assure you I would not be so brash as to attempt anything on an unconscious woman. Especially when the crown prince himself obviously favors her so highly."

Adrian fought back a rising blush, an endeavor in which his frequent time alone with Lily had actually made him rather skilled. "It's not quite like that," he assured the duke, then shook his head. "Are you not worried about catching ill yourself?"

The duke-milite's smile was sardonic. "I have been in many battles and seen men slain by mortal wounds and sickness in equal measure. I have had comrades fall upon me bleeding, their wounds filled with rot. If that didn't kill me, I doubt a small fever will."

"Yes, I suppose I am being a bit unreasonably worried, aren't I?" Adrian asked. "My apologies. If you would be so kind as to watch over her for a short time until something can be arranged, I would appreciate it."

"No problem at all, Sire," the duke answered with a bow of his head.

Adrian thanked him again, then stood and left the suite, making his way to his private study, mind already racing once more. No matter how comfortable they may have grown around one another, he knew that he and Lily were still locked in the same game of strategy they had always been in. Now that she had lost a few turns, he finally had a chance to outmaneuver her. And if part of him felt some sadness that their game would soon be over, a much greater part felt only relief that he finally had such a clear and easy shot at winning it.

Duke-Milite Liam de Treventre waited until Prince Adrian left his suite before stepping into the courtesan's room and quietly closing the door. He liked the prince, he really did. One did not often see such quiet modesty in royalty, and he found it refreshing, especially considering the brother that he usually had to deal with.

He would feel genuinely sorry, he decided, when the time came to have Adrian killed. But he was by now used to overseeing the deaths of people he did not particularly hate. There was simply nothing for it sometimes. And while that modesty was refreshing, it would make Adrian a poor ruler. He gave in much too easily to the wills of those around him, allowing Liam to chastise him like a little boy.

The duke approached the unconscious woman slowly, as if he could wake her by stepping too loudly.

Mandy & G.D. Burkhead

She breathed deeply under her puffed up mound of blankets, head slowly tilting from one side of her pillow to the other, brow furrowing intermittently in her dreams. Now and then her lips fluttered soundlessly, but she seemed nowhere near waking anytime soon. He couldn't tell if the sweat coating her brow and occasionally dripping down it was primarily from her fever or the heat of her covers, but even in illness, he had to admit she was beautiful.

Was she the one, then? The infamous Black Lily, here to commit the crime of the century and the crowning jewel in her already impressive career? She certainly wasn't what he would have expected at first, but Guildmaster Gavriel himself had assured him that her skills were perfect for their needs, despite what she may look like. He supposed it made sense when one thought about it; more kings were killed by betrayal than by war or siege. Poison or a well-timed dagger were infinitely more efficient than force of arms. And what better way to slip past a king's trust than with a beautiful smile and a demur demeanor? All the more distraction from the blade behind your back.

Still…she hadn't given the appropriate response to his passphrase, the one meant to secure her identity to him. She hadn't responded at all before passing out. Bad timing, perhaps? Or were there complications in the plan he hadn't been informed of, something preventing her from using the predetermined channels to relay her messages? She certainly matched the description her Guild had given him: long red hair, a short but shapely form, a face other women would kill for. There weren't many that could match that description so closely. Her status as a recently arrived courtesan also fit the profile. He was almost certain she was the one. But "almost certain" was not a strong enough foundation on which to build the coup of an empire.

Liam checked the hall outside the prince's suite, finding it as empty as he'd left it, then quietly shut the door, locking it this time. Better safe than sorry. He returned to the courtesan's bedside and, slowly, gently, peeled back the layers of blankets covering her chest. She shivered briefly in her sleep, but gave no indication of waking up.

With the bottommost cover pulled back, her chest and shoulders were exposed. The physician had removed her day gown and corset, leaving her in just her shift. All of her exposed skin was currently covered in a light sheen of sweat, and her bosom heaved with her deep, labored breathing. He took a moment to appreciate the sight before his eyes found what they were looking for.

A thin chain of simple silver hung around her neck, the pendant disappearing into her exposed cleavage. Carefully, and with one eye on her sleeping face the whole time, he reached his fingers into her bosom, grasping the small teardrop pendant nestled between her breasts and drawing it out. It was a glass vial, transparent, the edges cut to resemble a false gemstone, and full of a shimmering liquid of deep purple. There were no air pockets inside the container — if one didn't know what one was looking at, it might pass as a solid purple decoration, amethyst or died glass made to resemble such.

Duke-Milite Liam knew what he was looking at, however. Only sanctioned Guild assassins received this particular liquid toxin and these false accessories in which to hide it. One of the admirably few useful nuggets of information that young Robert had let slip before he died, and which Guildmaster Gavriel had confirmed later. So she was indeed who he thought she was.

He gently replaced the vial in its plain-view hiding place, then pulled the layers of blankets back up to her chin. She moaned quietly as he did and rolled halfway over, but the action no longer gave him pause for caution. Instead, he pulled up a chair next to her bed and sat, waiting for the greatest assassin in the country to wake up, or for their shared target to return and relieve him of his vigil.

Lily stood in a crowded courtyard, a silent, still statue surrounded by the press of stinking, hot, excited bodies. The light drizzle of rain fell like mist on the scene before her as she peered up from under the hood of her midnight black cloak. The rest of the mob around her was celebrating, pushing and jostling to move closer, but she was dressed in mourning, knowing what this day would bring. The rabble cheered as a hooded figure dragged a man up the stairs onto the platform. He looked dead already, swaying on his feet in exhaustion. Her quick eyes drank him in, scrutinizing every last detail, committing them to memory. She saw the techniques they had used on him, having learned of every known form of torture in existence. They ranged from the mundane — a crisscrossing of scars across his back made by the whip — to the extreme — the nails had been plucked from his fingers, the skin of one arm sliced clean off, the burn of hot coals evident on his body. And those were only the wounds she could see. Reports would later reveal his tongue had been cut from his mouth and he had been sodomized with a hot poker.

And yet he was still alive. If he still felt the pain even now, she didn't know. She only offered a rare prayer that Morana, the Goddess of Death, had numbed him to his agony, ready to take him into her cold embrace. As the man's name and crimes were read out before the cheering crowd, the executioner lowered the noose around his neck. Lily felt it as if it were a weight around her own neck, but she did not flinch. She did not show any emotion at all. As his eyes inexplicably sought her out in the crowd, recognition, thankfulness, and another emotion — regret, perhaps? — flickered through them. She held his gaze, not able to pull her eyes away, as much as she longed to. She would be strong for him, for them both. She whispered her prayer to Morana, her lips barely moving, and he smiled wryly as the board was yanked out from under his feet and the rope drew taught, snapping his neck and ending it once and for all.

A cheer went up through the crowd and Lily closed her eyes against the sight of her lover hanging from the gallows. Silently, she thanked the Goddess of Death for making it quick. She knew all too well that others might writhe and choke for minutes before expiring.

The tears slipped silently down her cheeks as she turned and made her way through the crowd. Though she rarely felt compelled to speak to the gods, she believed in them nonetheless, absent though they often were. If the priests were right, Robert's soul had been taken to Morana's bosom and would rest peacefully now.

And someday, she would find the man who did this to him, and she would send him to Morana as well.

Late that night, Adrian sat at Lily's bedside, staring at her and trying to decide what should be done with her. She murmured in her sleep and he leaned closer, wondering if he could glean some hidden secret from her while she fevered. But all she did was softly call out a name — Robert — before falling back into a fitful sleep, hot tears rolling silently down her red cheeks to mingle with her sweat.

The prince entered his chambers the next day to find a harried looking handmaiden sitting on a chair outside of Lily's room. "How is she?" he asked, not having time to look in on her himself between meetings. Always meeting and plotting and listening to grievances. He wished he had a just a moment to himself.

She stood when he entered the room, curtsying. "She rests now, m'lord, but all morning she was tossing and turning in her sleep and crying out," the maid reported. "At one point she even began thrashing and tried to hit me! I know that she knows not what she does, but still, it frightens me. I did manage to change her nightgown and bed sheets, though, between the spells."

"Thank you," he said. "You may rest if you like and send in another to watch over her." She curtsied once more and left the room, and Adrian poked his head in to check on Lily. She'd thrown off her covers at some point and her hair and clothes were in disarray. He could not tell if she was grinning or grimacing. He closed the door behind him quietly, hoping her fever would break soon.

A little girl sat in the back of the prison wagon, staring through the small barred window up at the gallows. There was a sizeable crowd, though they didn't seem all that excited. Curious, yes, to see the girl who'd murdered a full-grown man three times her size, but trepidatious to see one so young be hanged.

The crowd watched as they dragged her — the little girl, herself but not herself — up to the rope and wrapped it around her neck. But something was not right. She was crying, blubbering. She knew she would not cry when she went to her death. She would meet it with the emptiness that she felt now.

They removed the floorboard. The little girl dropped, her neck snapped, her small body hung there lifelessly. The crowd didn't cheer, only watched silently in the evening gloom. And then the wagon she sat in rolled away.

Time passed. She was in a black room. The figures with her were masked. They told her that she was dead to the world, that she belonged to Morana now. They could make her one of them. A handmaiden of death. She accepted. Not with pleasure, not yet. It would be a while before she felt glad, felt anything.

Time passed. She stood in the room with her first target. He liked to hurt little children. He used his power to get orphan children, beggars from the streets, brought to him from the nearby towns. He hurt them, kept them chained as unruly dogs in his cellar. Those that tried to run away or didn't learn not to fight back, he killed. She knew their dead bodies were buried in shallow graves on his property, hidden under pretty flower gardens that received infinitely better care than his captives. Nobody cared. Nobody would question if an unwanted child went missing.

She made sure his death was slow and painful. She removed his tongue for the lies he told to get those children brought to him. Cut out his eyes for gazing on them lustfully. Next went his hands, for the pain he inflicted with them. And finally his manhood. The constabulary found the pieces of him scattered amongst his prized lilies. It seemed fitting, somehow. Poetic.

Time passed. After a while, she thought to leave a calling card. Robert had given her a bouquet of lilies for her birthday. It was not the day she was physically born into the world, but the day she was reborn as a harbinger of death. As she sat at her desk writing a letter, she forgot they were there and knocked the vase over, taking her inkpot with it, and the lilies fell into the black puddle. She watched in fascination as they soaked up the ink, the black tint clashing with the innocent, white petals. She left one on the dead body of her next target—a nobleman who had embezzled too much money and made too many enemies. From then on, when people talked about her work, they spoke of the Black Lily.

Time passed. She was making love to Robert in her bedroom at the Guild. He held her in his arms, caressing her body with his hands, his mouth. He murmured in her ear that he loved her, that he wanted to marry her and take her away from everything. Go somewhere with no more orders, no more aliases, no more others. Just the two of them, alone, together. And she told him that she would go with him. She would give up everything, even her growing reputation, everything she'd trained for her whole life, to be with him and him alone.

Time passed. She felt the whip cut into her back. The knife slice the skin from her arm. The wrench as he pulled her nails from her fingers. How could he find this sexually stimulating? She glared at King Alec as he pulled another toy off his wall. He walked around behind her, caressing her with his fingers like Robert used to. Poor Robert.

"Now, Robert," said the king, but not in the king's voice, "you'll tell us everything you know about the Guild." As he circled back around, his face changed. It no longer sported Alec's strong jaw, goatee, brown eyes, and copper hair. It morphed, becoming angular, almost concave, with gray eyes that honed in on her like a hawk. Duke-Milite Liam grinned and brought the knife to her cheek, cutting into the skin.

The scream woke Adrian from his light doze. He must have fallen asleep in the chair beside Lily's bed. He'd long since dismissed the maids to get some rest, assuring them he could watch over her for a few hours. But more than a few hours had passed, and the fire had burned down to hot ashes. Adrian stood up and moved to Lily's bedside where she screamed again, thrashing about. He grabbed her arms, afraid she would try to hurt herself or him. He realized her eyes were open, but they were glazed with the fever, and he wasn't sure if she could actually see him.

Time passed. Adrian. Adrian was there. There was something she needed to remember. Something important. She had to tell him something, but she couldn't remember what it was. Her eyes scanned the room. They were alone. Good. But why was that good?

Because he's here, Robert reminded her. He stood at her bedside. The scars of torture were gone, his face restored to the beautiful one she had fallen in love with. *He's here and he knows who you are. You are in danger.* Duke-Milite Liam was here! She had to warn Adrian, before the duke got to him, did to him what he'd done to Robert. "Adrian!" she yelled.

He heard her whisper his name hoarsely, her throat raw from screaming. Lily clutched at his shirt, her eyes wild with fear. "Adrian," she whispered again. Even though she looked straight at him, she seemed not to see him.

"Yes, I'm right here, Lily," he said in what he hoped was a soothing voice. "What is wrong? How are you feeling?" He put a hand to her forehead. Her fever felt lighter than it had, but not by much.

"Don't," she rasped, struggling to swallow. "Trust. Him."

Before he could ask what that meant, her eyes had already closed and she was fast asleep again, chest heaving with rapid, fitful breaths. "Don't trust who?" he asked the empty room, but received no answer.

Fifteen

Now that matters had come to a crux, Adrian was paralyzed by indecision.

The smart move, he knew, would be to go straight to the captain of the guards and confess everything, lay the whole plot bare, present the concrete evidence, and have her hauled away. With her current incapacitation, it would be quick, easy, and painless for all involved. He'd never have to see her again, even during her trial—

Wait, no. Of course he would need to see her at her trial. As acting monarch dealing with the highest of treason, he would need to preside over it. Unless he could postpone it until Alec's return, and—

No. Too much time would pass. She would recover, formulate some new plan, and escape somehow, or else she would wait until the trial and find a way to murder Alec right then and there. No, it had to be Adrian. He would be the one to hold her fate directly in his hands for all the kingdom to see, the one to look her in the eyes and condemn her to a brutal death—

Unless, of course, he could mitigate her sentence. Which he could only do if she showed real remorse and a sincere desire for penitence. Which she would not. She could act, certainly, she could make it convincing if she wanted, but he knew she wouldn't, not if it came to a direct confrontation like that. And anything less than execution for anything less than a one hundred and eighty degree personality shift would incite the populace, and the kingdom was already enough of a powder keg as it was—

Adrian buried his fists in his hair in frustration. The choice should have been easy, as he really only had two options: either act and bring one of the worst criminals in living memory to justice, or do nothing and allow her most heinous crime yet to come to fruition unopposed and unravel the very country from the inside out.

His thoughts released him somewhat when he stepped out into the gardens and realized only then that he'd been wandering the palace. The murky gray clouds overhead threatened rain later, but for the moment, the air was cool and the breeze pleasant. Here and there rays of light shone through the cloud cover to illuminate a bed of flowers or patch of grass.

In the distance, standing in one such column of light, was Duke-Milite Liam with the Duchess Sidonie wrapped gracefully around his arm. They stood with their backs partially to the prince, observing the rows of alternating fruit trees that lined one of the main paths through the courtyard.

Normally, Adrian tended to avoid aristocrats whenever he encountered them in his own walks. He had almost turned around and headed down a different path out of habit before something stayed him. After a moment of hesitation, he continued on his way toward the noble couple.

Duke-Milite Liam noticed him first, a polite smile on his face as he turned to greet their approaching regent. The duchess curtsied properly, and once he had drawn within comfortable speaking distance, Liam inclined his own head. "Good morning, Sire. How does the day treat you?"

"Good morning Duke, Duchess," Adrian returned, nodding briefly to the both of them. "I confess I have felt better, but nothing to bother the two of you with."

"The latest in shameless gossip has it that you stayed up most of the night watching over the ailing Camilla," the duke continued, smile never faltering. "Does it not, m'lady?"

"I am sure I have heard no such thing," Duchess Sidonie replied airily, glancing about the garden as if bored with the topic. "I have little time for idle rumor."

"Of course, m'lady," Liam replied, lifting her hand to his lips. She allowed it. "And how is our young lady friend doing of late, Sire?" he asked Adrian.

"Better, I suppose," the prince answered. "She is stable at least, so we don't think she's getting any worse. But she dreams violently and mutters in her sleep."

"I see," said Liam, smile faltering at last. "A strong fever indeed, or else something more significant is at play."

"Yes, that is what worries me," said Adrian. It wasn't entirely a lie—Lily's condition *did* worry him, even if it wasn't anywhere near the biggest concern on his mind at the moment.

The duke-milite watched his face a moment, then turned to the duchess, his smile returning. "Sidonie, my dear, would you mind terribly giving the prince and me a bit of time alone, with my apologies?"

"Terribly?" the duchess repeated, already turning away from the two men. "No, not terribly. There is a letter from Raoul that I must see to anyway. M'lords." She ducked a quick, shallow curtsy to each man in turn before strolling away down the garden path on her own.

Liam watched her go with a wry smile. "She means to bait me, I think," he said to the prince once the duchess was out of earshot. "She has one eye on me and one on the Duke of Lakeview, and I think she's waiting for one of us to openly admit to jealousy of the other. Some women and the games they play."

"Believe me, I know exactly what you mean," Adrian muttered, perhaps with a little more feeling than he intended to voice.

The duke-milite caught it and raised an eyebrow at his prince. "Sire, would you mind if I spoke candidly for a moment?" he asked.

"Please do," Adrian answered with a dismissive wave.

Liam turned to face the prince directly, his expression serious. "This woman, Camilla…She obviously means more to you than you like to admit. You worry for her health, but I do not think that is all of your worry. I think, my Prince, that there is some deeper turmoil she rises in you that you do not want to acknowledge or else don't know how to deal with. Am I wrong?"

Was it so obvious? Adrian chided himself for even wondering. Of course it was. He'd never been good at schooling his expressions or hiding his concerns even before they had become this complicated, and lately he hadn't been bothered to make even a token effort at doing so. "No," he answered the duke with a sigh. "No, you are right, I suspect. On the surface, Camilla is a charming woman, and I enjoy her company. But underneath that, well...it gets more complicated."

The duke-milite smiled, pleased with himself, and nodded. "I think I understand, Sire."

"Do you?" Adrian said with a wry smile of his own. "Forgive me, but I do not think that you do. I'm fairly certain that I don't even understand myself."

This time it was the duke-milite who sighed. "You forget that I'm much older than you, m'lord. Why so many young people think that they're the first ones to experience troubles with love, I'll never understand."

"I didn't forget, I just — what did you say?" Adrian asked with a start as the duke's words kicked in.

"Oh come now, Prince Adrian," Liam chuckled. "You think me blind? I'm courting right now as well, and it's not the first time I've done so. I know the signs, and just in the brief time since I've gotten here, I've seen many of them in you already. There is no shame in being besotted with a woman, especially one as beautiful as your courtesan."

"What? No, I..." He paused. How to explain this without revealing too much? "We're just...close friends, is all. Well, but not really even friends, honestly. More like...close companions, I guess?" Mentally, he winced. If there was a convincing way to put it, that wasn't it.

The duke-milite's answering smirk said as much. "If you insist, m'lord. But does the young lady think of you the same way?"

"Um..." For a moment, Adrian found himself wondering what Lily *did* think of him. He no longer thought she saw him as simply another target to dispatch, though he didn't allow himself to doubt that he was definitely still this to her as well. She certainly fawned over him in company more than she probably had to for her job, and he had to admit, she still seemed keenly interested in him even when they were alone, for whatever reason. If it was all simply an act, then she had to be the best actress in the entire kingdom in addition to the best assassin. Still… "I'm not sure what the young lady thinks of me," he admitted at last. "I can't be sure how much of her attention is feigned or for what reasons she might be feigning it, precisely."

"Then do you want my suggestion, Prince?" Liam asked, then gave it anyway before Adrian could answer. "Once her fever breaks and she wakes up, ask her. Tell her that she means more to you than simply another accessory of the court to pass a few moments with, and ask her how she feels for you." The duke-milite smiled. "I've found in my own experience that straightforward honesty is almost always the best approach to a situation when available, and at least then, you'll have your answer. And if she's lying when she answers, I daresay you'll be able to tell."

Well, the prince thought, if he did declare a great hidden love to Lily as soon as she was lucid again, that very well might discomfit her enough to make any immediate lies easier to spot. But then, he was sure that he wouldn't be the first man to suddenly pour his heart at her feet. And he was also sure that he wouldn't be the first man to get her knife in his back with a smile shortly thereafter. "She's…a very good liar, I think," he settled with for a reply.

The duke shrugged. "She's a woman," he said. "Most of them are. Many of them have to be. But I think that, in matters like this at least, a lie is easier to pick apart from sincerity. Even if it doesn't work out as you had hoped, it couldn't hurt any more than it does now, could it?"

Adrian thought very hard about his situation now and how much it hurt, never mind the confusing reasons for *why* it might hurt so much. He wanted, suddenly, desperately, to reveal to the duke-milite just what his relationship with "Camilla" really was and what was really bothering him. Liam seemed like an easy enough man to talk to, wise and experienced without being condescending about it. On top of that, the man was famous for having handled an assassination plot himself, catching his would-be killer in the act and bringing him to justice after gaining the information that he needed from the man. If there were a useful ally to have in all the palace when it came to saving oneself from a known assassination plot, Duke-Milite Liam was it.

The prince had already turned his head to the duke and opened his mouth to tentatively broach the subject when something stopped him. An intuition, a niggling voice in the back of his head. "Don't trust him," Lily had whispered, though whether it was a message meant for Adrian or for a figment of her fever dreams, he couldn't be sure. And even if she had been warning him about Liam specifically, why should he care? If anything, shouldn't he take the fact that she thought him dangerous as a positive sign? If Lily didn't trust him, then that meant that Adrian could. Didn't it?

"Yes, Sire?" the duke-milite said, cutting into his thoughts. "Were you going to say something?"

Adrian blinked and shut his parted mouth, his gaze turning back to the present. "Ah...no, sorry," he muttered. "Just thinking about what you said, is all."

"You're sure, Sire?" Liam pressed, looking a tad concerned.

"I'm sure," Adrian answered, gradually feeling the surety that he claimed. If nothing else, he told himself, Liam wouldn't understand Adrian's need to save Lily's life if at all possible. Adrian didn't quite understand it himself—he knew he had what others called a "bleeding heart," but it wasn't just blind sympathy for human life that drove him, at least not entirely.

He felt, truly felt, that underneath the persona she presented of a cold, efficient killer, there was a decent person in there. Whether or not reaching out to that person was worth preserving the killer was an issue he was still grappling with. But whatever the reason for his compulsion, it was still there, and if he couldn't quash it, then he would have to act on it.

With a smile, he took the duke's hand and clasped it appreciatively. "Thank you for the talk, Lord Liam," he said as the duke looked at him with amusement. "I think you are right. I think that a little more honesty and a more straightforward approach are called for."

Lily opened her eyes, waiting for them to adjust to the room around her. She considered sitting up but, when her head began to throb, thought better of it and instead took in her surroundings. How had she gotten back to her room? Why was she lying in bed in the middle of the day? The curtains were shut tight, but she could see the sunlight peeking in around them.

The memories came back slowly. She had felt sick all morning, probably from being out in the rain the night she killed Irene's husband. Then she had heard that her contact was arriving, and she had gone to meet him, and it had been Duke-Milite Liam. And then what? She vaguely remembered falling, then having terrible nightmares, and perhaps waking briefly to speak with Adrian, though that too may have been a dream.

Had watching his carriage arrive at the edge of the garden also been just one more bad dream, then? She wanted to believe it, wanted desperately to find any incongruity in the memory that made it unreal—but she knew it wasn't. The truth of it stabbed at her, but it was the truth.

The duke-milite was her contact. Liam de Treventre was going to be king. And she was supposed to put him on the throne.

Her head began to swim again, and she had to make a conscious effort to control her breathing. This was wrong. The Guild would never agree to such a thing. He was known throughout Arestea for catching and executing a Guild assassin. Why would Master Gavriel agree to work with him after that? Was it a mistake? Blackmail? Had they not met with him in person, not verified his identity? No, that was too sloppy for the Guild. They would never hand someone the entire empire unless they knew that person was going to be a good, agreeable puppet and followed whatever demand the Guild made.

So the Guild had done this purposefully. But why? Liam was wrong, all wrong for the part, vicious and grasping and sinister as any serpent. He was worse, much worse, than Alec had ever been. He would bring the country to ruins.

No...not him, she thought. However terrible a king he might make, Liam was still a puppet first and foremost. The Guild, of course, would be the real power behind the throne.

She knew this, had known this from the start, but now she wondered: What would happen to this country with the Guild in charge? Assassins were meant to be tools, influencing things from the shadows, from behind closed doors. Master Gavriel ruled a house of a few dozen focused murderers well enough; but no matter his talents, was he truly fit to rule a country? Why had she never considered this? Why had she never thought about it before?

The answer came to her nearly as soon as she'd finished asking herself the question. She had been blinded by the imminent spectacle of a royal assassination, caught up in the conviction that Alec needed to be removed and the ambition of being the one who removed him. What came next was intended to be left in her master's hands, and she had been happy enough to leave it there without pressing further. But as much as she trusted Gavriel, she realized she distrusted Liam at least as much, if not more. That they were throwing their lots in together didn't elevate the duke-milite at all in her eyes, only brought her master down.

She remembered. Before she'd left for this assignment, Master Gavriel had assured her that she would be helping to strike at the heart of all that was wrong with the empire. She had believed at first, but now, there was too much doubt. Sure, Alec was an asshole, but he was an effective leader. He was expanding their borders and increasing their trade, either through peace treaties or, when they were refused, through war. But he never started a war he could not win, and he never took those wars to the point of genocide, like so many other kings before him had. He had effectively kept the peace within his country and reduced crime, even if his means of doing it — squashing any rebellions before they started — were not exactly ethical.

He was showing his country and the rest of the world that Arestea was not to be trifled with. His high taxes were not well-loved and often led to the poor being exploited at the hands of the rich, but that was nothing new. The powerful would always take advantage of the weak, like it or not. She, her Guild, could no more change that sweeping truth than they could alter any other laws of the universe, only excise its most egregious examples. No, King Alec was not what was wrong with this country.

Duke-Milite Liam was a shining example of what was, however. He was bloodthirsty, power hungry, and underhanded. Normally she might respect someone like that, but knowing that he was working with the Guild, even after killing Robert, was too much for her to handle. The Guild was the closest thing she had to family. If nothing else, what happened to loyalty to their own?

A little part of her, that cold, calculating part that had long ago lost its humanity, realized how naïve she was being. Loyalty meant empathy; of course they wouldn't have any. Gavriel himself had taught her how to close off that part of her conscience that made her feel guilty whenever she took someone's life. At first, he had given her reasons for the contract—he would tell her the atrocious crimes the person had committed—but the longer she stayed with the Guild, the less he did, and the less she needed them. She always just assumed that the people she killed deserved to die. But now that she was finally being brutally honest with herself, who was to say they did? Some were monsters, of course, but all of them? Maybe none of them had been innocents, strictly speaking, but who was? The only real excuse a true professional needed was that the money was good enough for the job.

Lily didn't know what was truth anymore, or who she should trust. Maybe this was still her fever messing with her mind; maybe the ground hadn't really fallen out from under everything she thought she knew. At this moment, though, all she knew was that she could not let Liam take the throne, could not let the Guild take control of the country, could not let them kill Alec or Adrian.

Adrian...

He was so naïve, so stupidly innocent. He was the one shining light in this dark, twisted country of intrigue and backstabbing. The one person who still had honor. She realized with a sudden start that she cared about him. She couldn't stand the thought of killing him, but even more, she couldn't stand it if he were to change, to become disillusioned and empty and lose everything good about him that made him who he was. If he were to turn into his brother, or worse, into her.

There was a brief knock at her door that finally pulled her attention from the mire of her own thoughts. Lily looked up as it opened and the most recent object of her concern walked in. His shoulders were hunched as if in defeat, and his eyes were dark with anger, hurt, and disgust. She could not tell if those emotions were directed at her, someone else, or himself. He closed the door behind him and sat down on the chair next to her bed. "I'm glad you're awake," said the prince, sounding hollow. "I figured you'd appreciate my sense of timing, if not my actions themselves."

Her brow furrowed as she sat up in bed. The covers pooled around her waist, and she realized she wore nothing but a shift.

She expected his usual reaction: blush, look away, pretend not to notice. Instead, he met her gaze and held it steadily. That alone tipped her off that something was not right. "This…game," he said slowly. "Whatever it is we've been doing. It's over, Lily. I'm turning you in."

"Wh…what?" she asked, too shocked to saying anything else.

"I don't want to," he said with a sigh. "For the longest time, I've been afraid that making this move would only trigger a killing spree on your part. I thought that if I just stalled long enough, I could dissuade you from your course of action, send you away. But you've made it clear you won't leave without finishing your contract…and I won't let you." He forced out those last few words as if they took great courage and strength of will to say.

She smiled bitterly, running a shaking hand through her hair. She wasn't sure if she was afraid or if she just hadn't eaten in so long that she hadn't the strength to move. "As you can see, I'm in no condition to stop you," she said, and despite all the sleeping she'd been doing these past few days, even to herself, she sounded tired. As her hand dropped back down, she let it subtly brush her neck. The chain of her necklace was still there. Good. At least she had a way out, if nothing else. "But why now?" she asked. "Besides the fact that I'm incapacitated."

"I wanted to tell you before the guards came in to arrest you," he said. "I thought it only seemed honorable that you should have a moment to collect yourself, get dressed, that sort of thing. The Duke-Milite Liam is at the castle now. He has dealt with assassins before. He can help me deal with you, if need be."

She nodded. "Do you know how he dealt with the last one he caught? Do you know anything about what happened besides what you have heard from gossip?"

"I—" Adrian paused, as if trying to remember. "He captured an assassin and interrogated him before having him publicly executed."

"'Interrogated.' Such a deceptive word. So clean…" She hugged her knees to her chest through the blankets and tried, and failed, to keep the bitterness from her voice as she continued. "He tortured the man. Broke his bones, pulled out his nails, cut out his tongue, and…well, I won't even tell you what he did with the poker. When Liam was done, he wasn't even recognizable." She stared off into space, remembering Robert's broken face, his one good eye searching her out in the crowd, focusing on her as the floor dropped and the rope pulled taught.

"You…you mean you saw his corpse?" Adrian asked.

"No. Well, yes," she amended, "the reports we gathered afterward revealed the torture he had undergone before death, but I…I watched him die. I stood in the crowd."

Adrian took a deep breath and pinched the bridge of his nose, his eyes closed. "I assume there's a reason for this story besides trying to disturb me," he said. "So were you there for any particular reason besides professional courtesy or just morbid curiosity?"

"Are you thinking I went looking for tips on how to be more evil?" she asked. She wasn't sure if she meant to sound joking or offended, but it only came out quiet and empty. "He was…" This next part was harder. She found the words catching in her throat, had to swallow them down and take a deep breath before they finally came out no louder than a whisper. "He…Robert…was my lover. The one that I wouldn't talk about when you asked. He was…more to me than the others. He had asked me to marry him. I had told him yes, the day before he was captured."

She could see the thoughts flit through the prince's mind as he opened his eyes and stared at her, could read them in his face. First shock, then disbelief as he considered if she was lying, and finally acceptance. He was so transparent, she wondered how he had survived for so long in this world. "I...I'm sorry," he said quietly at last. "I didn't know —"

"No, you didn't," she interrupted, finally feeling a measure of her old strength returning. "There are a lot of things you don't know, Adrian. You don't know me, and you don't know Duke-Milite Liam." She watched as he sank slowly further into his chair, all of his attention focused on her. Good. Maybe he would listen. Maybe, just maybe, she could change his mind. "He is my contact, Adrian. The duke-milite. He's the one sponsoring my mission."

"What?" Adrian asked, then shook his head. "I...don't understand."

"Yes, you do. You just don't want to believe it. Honestly, neither do I, but it's the truth. Liam came here to become the puppet authority after you and Alec were...removed." She lay back on the pillows again, feeling too tired to keep sitting up. "Adrian, I don't know what game he's playing. The fact that my Guild would work with him...all I know is that this is wrong. He is the wrong person for this country. The Guild..." Her next words were hard to admit aloud after all of her years of training and loyalty, but she forced them past her lips regardless. "The Guild is wrong. They — we — should not rule this kingdom. They're too powerful already; if they gain any more influence, things will only get worse. It will just be more bloodshed, more backstabbing, a never-ending cycle feeding back through the Guild until everyone else is dead and the only people left are so corrupt their hearts have blackened and withered to nothing. They will cast the whole empire into ruin. But you won't be here to see it anyway."

"What do you mean?" His voice was a whisper.

"Liam will kill you," she told him bluntly. "You and your brother, and anyone else who stands in his way. Have me locked up if you want, have me tortured and executed, but it will make no difference. Put me away now, Adrian, and you tip your hand to him. He'll get away, go back to scheming. You'll have no evidence on him. He'll try again, more carefully and more prepared next time, with agents more loyal to him alone. You won't get another chance like this to expose him." She sought and found his eyes then, held his gaze as she continued. "You want to stop the regicide plot? I'm just the hired help. You need to take out the plotter. Otherwise he'll come back for you and your brother when I'm not here to warn you."

She could see his skepticism. Could see him trying to decide if he should believe her or not, or if this was just another ploy or a desperate attempt to save herself. "Does this mean that you're suddenly not planning to murder Alec and me?" he asked, brow furrowing.

Lily sighed. She had been honest with him this far; she might as well keep at it. "Truthfully? I don't know," she said. "I've never quit a job before, but I'm no longer entirely comfortable with this one."

"You don't know," Adrian repeated, his voice a perfect deadpan. "You *might* murder the reigning king and plunge the whole empire into the bloody chaos you just described, but you're not sure. You're still mulling it over."

"Your snark is duly noted, Adrian," she said with a sigh. "And not without merit. But I assure you, this is a much bigger concern right now, especially on my end. I've already compromised this much of myself for you, something I've never done before for anyone. I…" She wavered, losing confidence. "I know how ludicrous this prospect must sound to you, but I am asking you to trust me on this. You have every right not to, but I ask that you please try. However much we've been at odds, I can say with a certainty that I have been nothing but honest with you with the information that I've volunteered since you discovered me. I'm still doing so now."

She shoved the blankets off of herself and clambered awkwardly out of the bed. Adrian reached forward as if to help her, but seemed to think better of it and stepped away. Did he really think she was going to hurt him? That she could? She could hardly even stand. Luckily, that made this next part easier.

Lily dropped to one knee with a thud and bowed her head low to the ground, the ruby curtain of her sweat-slicked hair hiding his reaction from her view. "Please, Adrian," she begged into the floor with as much real sincerity as she could muster. "Whatever Alec deserves, you at least are a good and admirable man and worth saving if at all possible. I would not see you fall to the likes of a vulture like Liam. So I implore you, both as a subject to her rightful liege and as a woman to the closest thing to a friend that she can claim in her life right now—do not face him without my help."

A long moment passed during which Adrian was silent. She chanced a glance up and saw that he was too stunned to speak. She could tell he was also still suspicious of her, though considering her offer. He seemed to be debating with himself, but after a few moments he straightened his shoulders, took a deep breath, released it slowly, and nodded. "Very well," he said, solemn as a church bell. "I'll give you one chance, Lily. Prove to me that Liam is a traitor, that you are changing sides and mean harm no longer, and I will keep your secret safe. But," he added, a stronger steel in his voice than she had ever heard from him before, "take one step out of line, make one move that has me wondering where your loyalties lie, and I'll see you thrown in the Ergastulum for the rest of your life, however short that may be."

Despite the weight of the moment, she couldn't help smiling a little. "That's entirely fair," she said, lifting her head to him and taking a deep, steadying breath. "I accept these terms. Thank you, my Prince. Now help me up." She lifted a hand toward where he sat. "Please," she added.

With another deep sigh and a shake of his head, he rose and took her hand in his, then pulled her back to her feet once more.

The next morning, Adrian sat silently on a stool behind a false wall in one of the castle guest rooms, a small study and library that had been given to the Duke of Lakeview for use but which now sat mostly empty after his departure. The space behind the wall was the size of a small broom closet, with a low sliding panel in the interior wall hinting at a tunnel that connected to some other hidden space further on in the palace. Though the fake wall was hidden behind a couple of hanging tapestries, a gap between the decorations and a strategically placed knothole in the wood gave him a small peephole through which he could see almost the entirety of the room.

He had not noticed the small hole in the wall when Lily led him here earlier. He hadn't known that this space existed at all, or how long it had been here, or to what other room it connected. Yet Lily had known of this and myriad other hidden crannies even before she first stepped foot into the palace. The realization of how thoroughly her Guild had scouted out his home and planned for his family's death unnerved him, and the knowledge that their best agent purported to be on his side now was only a slight comfort.

Adrian sat and waited for little less than half an hour before the door to the room opened and Lily entered, Liam behind her with his hand on her lower back. The prince watched as the duke spun her around, taking her chin in his hand with a smirk and lowering his head as if to kiss her. Lily turned her head and stepped out of his grasp, leaving his lips touching nothing but air.

"Don't bother, your lordship. I've seen to it that we're alone here," she told him, her false accent gone.

Liam looked around the room skeptically, his mouth a firm line. After a moment of silence he asked, "You are sure? A palace like this has eyes and ears everywhere."

Lily quirked an eyebrow at him, her hand on her hip in exasperation. "You would ask the Black Lily if she knows how to do her job correctly?"

The duke-milite crossed his arms over his chest, examining her. "Well, you are either certain we are alone, or you are not as skillful as I thought, to identify yourself where others might hear." He smirked and took a seat, pouring them both a glass of wine from the decanter on a nearby table. "We didn't get any time for professional introductions before your little spell last week," the duke continued. "I assume that this clandestine meeting is to make up for that?"

"Of a sort." She narrowed her eyes at him. "You know who I am, and I know who you are...and what you've done."

"Oh, that sounded defiant," Liam said with a chuckle. "Are you telling me, my dear, that you are questioning your Guild? Such a declaration is almost...treasonous." He offered her a wineglass, but she ignored it, pacing the small room before him. He shrugged and took a sip from it himself. Either the thought of her poisoning him hadn't entered his mind, or else he had reason to confidently dismiss the notion.

"I have questions, duke-milite," she said as she moved. "If our work together is to proceed efficiently, I will need you to answer them for me."

"Oh? By all means," the man replied with a bow from his seat, "ask away, my dear."

She spun on him, her eyes icy cold. Adrian would have flinched under that stare, boring into the man's soul as if she could peel away the layers of his skin and see what lay beneath. But the duke didn't seem the least bit disturbed. "Why would the Guild work to such benefit for a man who so shamed them as you?" she demanded.

Liam shrugged. "Money," he said. "Power. Take your pick, my dear. I have the former in ample supply and, after our little scheme is seen to its fruition, I'll have more than enough of the latter. Imagine. You could be a duchess. Would you like that?"

She didn't answer, but resumed pacing. "That's not good enough. You killed one of us. You embarrassed us before the entire country, hurt our reputation. You think that I would honestly believe the Guild would just overlook that this easily?" She stopped and shook her head at him. "There are plenty of other paths to money and power, those that don't require your assistance. And I'm sure there are plenty of other ambitious nobles out there who would make just as good of pawns as you in this scheme. What are you hiding, Liam?"

He smirked lazily, swirling his wine in its glass. "No, you wouldn't like to be a duchess, would you?" he answered himself, ignoring her question. "It would be much too quiet a life for you. You enjoy being an assassin too much to give it up. You enjoy the challenge. The killing."

"Don't presume you know me," she snapped. "Answer the question."

"So demanding! Tsk tsk. I would expect a spy to be better at diplomacy." He steepled his fingers and regarded her overtop of them. "But then, you can't control yourself, can you? You see, that is your problem, my dear. You take things much too personally. You let your emotions rule you, when you should be cold and calculating."

"You still aren't answering my question," she told him, impatience clear in her voice.

"But I am, don't you see?" he replied with a grin. "The Guild taught you to be cold, merciless, emotionless, because *it* is. The Guild does not hold grudges. It doesn't make attachments. Not even to its own. The past is in the past. Why miss out on a perfectly good opportunity over some petty slight? So when I approached your colleagues and suggested that we work together, it didn't take long to persuade your Master Gavriel to see reason. This is the best arrangement for all. You kill the king and the crown prince, I become the new ruler, and the Guild has complete control of the kingdom from the shadows through me. Certainly you can understand that?"

She spun then, launching herself at him, her knife at his throat. Behind the false wall, Adrian tensed, wondering what he should do. Should he run out there and stop her? Watch her kill the man? It would fix their problems, but then, it would be hard to explain away the dead body. "You killed him," she hissed. "You tortured and maimed him, and then you had him executed. And you expect me to trust you? To work with you?"

He still grinned, not at all fazed by the dagger at his throat, though Adrian didn't miss the steely glint in his eye. "You have no choice. If you fail in your mission, I have a feeling the Guild will be none too pleased. I'm sure they have ways of dealing with traitors, do they not? And besides," he said, leaning closer, even though the dagger must be pressing into his skin by now, "you will because you must. Because you are a killer. It is what you are. It is *all* you are. You can't deny it any more than you can stop it. I got the full report on you when I signed on with this job, Black Lily, and believe it or not, not all of it was glowing. You're good at being what you are, but in the end, all you know how to be is an assassin. And the thought of being cast out by them, letting down your precious Master Gavriel, is more frightening to you than any threats of what they might do to punish you. Because *that* would be the worst punishment of all."

Adrian watched the shock cross her face, then the angry, bitter tears slipping down her cheeks as she glared at him. His hands clenched, and he found himself wanting to fling the false panel aside, to confront the duke-milite and...

...And what? Accuse him of treason? Or deny what he said about Lily and argue for the hidden goodness he saw that she pretended didn't exist? He couldn't tell which misguided desire was stronger in him at the moment, royal duty or chivalrous defense. That confusion, as well as common sense, stayed him as he leaned harder against his hidden peephole.

When Liam spoke again, his voice was icy cold with the knowledge that he had won this battle. "Now I suggest you remove your blade from my neck," he said slowly and calmly. "I will not tolerate such traitorous behavior. And if I have to report to Master Gavriel that his star pupil was threatening their biggest patron yet and putting such a major plan in jeopardy, I'm sure he'd be most upset with you."

Lily hesitated a moment, but then did as she was told, stepping back from him, the dagger disappearing into her sleeve. Her face was a mask of hatred and fear.

The duke-milite stood and sneered down at her. "You're pathetic. Tell me, do I need to get a replacement for you, or can I expect you to fulfill your obligations as you were ordered?"

She stood there trembling, staring at the ground. Finally, she wiped her eyes, raising them to meet his. "I will do as I was commanded," she said, voice empty and defeated. "It seems…I have no choice."

"Good," he said, nodding like a placated tutor faced with disciplining an unruly child. "I don't want to see another ridiculous outburst like this again. I will contact you when it is time to make a move. So if we are done here, *m'lady*." He bowed in mock solemnity, then turned and strode from the room, the door slamming shut behind him.

After Adrian was sure he had gone, he tripped the latch that opened the false wall and stepped out, placing a hand gently on Lily's shoulder. He didn't miss her flinch at the motion. "Are you okay?" he asked.

"Of course," she said, straightening her shoulders, her voice once again normal. When she turned to him, her mask had fallen back into place, her usual smirk on her lips. "Simply a bit of acting, to make him feel more confident. If he believes me to be too weak to move against him, he won't suspect me when the time comes."

He saw too much of a mask in the expression — her emotional performance a moment ago had not been entirely feigned, no matter what she said. "Of course," the prince agreed regardless. "What do we do now?" he asked.

"Now, we must set a trap," she said, setting her shoulders and nodding decisively. "One that is so cleverly placed, he does not see it until he is already ensnared."

"And how do we do that?" Adrian asked.

For a brief second, so quick he wouldn't have noticed it if he hadn't been watching for it, he saw doubt cross her face. "I don't know yet," she admitted. "But I'll figure something out."

Sixteen

She was getting suspicious, questioning her orders and the will of her Guild. It was not surprising, considering the link they shared, and he'd known to expect it after his arrival. Still, it did give events a greater sense of urgency. The plan, the *full* plan, had to be completed before her resolve began to crumble in earnest.

Liam's face was a mask of thoughtful contemplation as he made his slow way back to the quarters he'd been granted within the palace, passing servants and other visiting nobles along the way with only the most basic acknowledgements of their polite greetings. He had much to think about, and he needed a private place away from prying eyes in which to do it.

The rooms that had been assigned to the duke-milite were on the second floor of the palace's east wing overlooking the central courtyard, just down the hall and up the stairs from the empty study in which he'd had his meeting with the Black Lily. He made his way there now, pushing open the door to the private study attached to his bedroom and stepping inside. The room beyond was much like the one that he'd just left—cozy without being too cramped, with basic but lush furnishings and decorations. The wall across from the door was taken up mostly by large picture windows that looked down onto the sunny courtyard garden below, currently devoid of anybody save the groundskeepers. A velvet sofa and twin end tables sat in the center of the room looking out at the view, with a large desk set against one of the side walls. Against the other was a table and bookshelf. Most of the surfaces were already covered in the books, papers, and other assorted possessions that he had brought with him to the palace.

A young maidservant kneeling before the bookshelf looked up as he entered, momentarily startled. She was a mousy and plain-looking girl with straight, short cropped brown hair, and she clutched several of his books in her arms. He recognized her as one of his personal servants that he had brought with him from his estate in Treventre. "Oh, your lordship," she said, quickly rising up only to dip back down again in an awkward curtsy, still clutching his books. "I'm sorry, I didn't expect you back so soon. I was just tidying up a bit."

Liam smiled at the girl and waved his hand dismissively. "Don't worry about it, Melindra," he said, and noted the slight way that her brows and lips momentarily twitched upward as he said it. He had learned early in life the value of knowing and remembering the names of servants, his own or others' around him, to make them feel at ease. If the help thought you were their friend, they were less likely to gossip unduly about you behind your back, quicker to accept and obey your orders, and had a habit of spreading the good word about your character and leadership capabilities. Sadly, he thought, the idea that one's servants were still people first was a basic lesson that many of his colleagues in the nobility had yet to learn. "Actually," he continued to his maid, "if you don't mind, I'd like a bit of private time. Leave the mess; I'll see to it myself."

"Yes, sir," Melindra answered, dumping the books on the nearby table where he had left them strewn the night before. "If you're sure, sir. I can come back and finish cleaning when you're ready, sir, if you want."

Liam shook his head and crossed the room to rest his hand on the girl's shoulder, feeling her tense for an instant at his informal touch before relaxing. "Thank you, my dear. Your dedication is commendable, but that won't be necessary. I am a grown man, after all. I should be able to put my own things away just this once, I think." He laughed quietly, and his maid shared it as he escorted her toward the door. "But please, if you would, see that I am not disturbed for the next few hours unless His Majesty asks for me or it is an emergency."

"Yes, m'lord," Melindra said, turning to him in the doorway and curtsying properly this time. "Thank you, sir."

He smiled and nodded, then closed the door behind her and turned back toward his scattered books and papers, wondering idly what she thought she was thanking him for. For a brief moment, he considered what Melindra might be like in any other role besides a servant. For the most part, he had noticed, the people of this kingdom fit their given roles so well that it was like they forgot how to be anything outside of them. Servant, butler, duke or duchess. King. Prince.

Assassin.

Liam's polite smile faded into a scowl. He had already proven to the realm and himself that he was not like them, not confined to one role, one lot in life. He had not always been a duke; he had not always been nobility even. And if all went according to plan, he would not be merely just another noble for very much longer.

If, he thought. Suddenly, there were a lot of ifs to consider.

He strode back across the room to the table and its scattered papers. Among them were a dozen letters from a dozen different fellow peers of the realm, people who were all convinced that they were important, offering him their congratulations for a number of various reasons. Old letters that he had kept or that had been belatedly received remarking on his ascension to the status of duke-milite, a title coined by King Alec himself specifically as a reward for Liam's exemplary performance both on the king's battlefield and with matters of conflict within his own holding. Even older letters growing brittle and yellow with age, formally welcoming him to the ranks of nobility as the new Duke of Treventre and expressing sympathy at the sudden death of his estranged father and half-brother, who had been the wardens of the land beforehand. Letters of condolences and admiration at his being targeted by an assassination plot only to foil it himself and see the murderer brought to justice. Optimistic congratulations on his now publicly apparent intentions to court Duchess Sidonie of Berecum and unite their lands in mutual prosperity. A few letters received before he left for the palace from lords and ladies already within it, welcoming his imminent arrival and expressing a desire to mingle once he'd gotten there. Newer letters, some of them still unopened, from those lords and ladies who couldn't make the appearance themselves at the moment, beseeching him to pass along his regards and best wishes to the king, and now the prince, on their behalf.

In all of them, admiration and approval practically dripped. In just a few short years, he had risen from relative obscurity as just one more peer of the realm to fashion himself as something of a hero amongst the nobility, a model leader of land, trade, battle, justice, and social grace. A leader of people. A figure behind which aristocrat and commoner alike would gladly rally.

There was no doubt by now that he was far more popular throughout the whole of Arestea than its own king was. If something were to happen to the royal family, if a political emergency were to occur and a new regent were suddenly needed to bring the empire back into order, to lead it forward out of the chaos, Duke-Milite Liam would be the first and most obvious choice with near unified support.

If…

If the Black Lily could still be trusted to perform her duties as her Guild had assigned. If the Guild itself could be trusted to uphold its end of the bargain, to remember that the chaos and fear of a leaderless nation would still not be as profitable for them as a stable ruler who was friendly to their business model. If Prince Adrian's charming naiveté could hold up and keep him blind until his brother returned and they could both be taken out at once.

Liam's scowl deepened. Far, far too many ifs for his liking.

Nobody, not even the incredibly informed Guild and its Master Gavriel, could have predicted the king's sudden impulse to abdicate his throne for months on end and vanish to the front lines himself. And nobody would have predicted that the milquetoast little brother left holding the reins of the kingdom would actually begin to develop a measure of statecraft and a head for sensible leadership in Alec's absence. Even if he did not realize it yet himself, Prince Adrian was no longer an awkward model for pity and dismissal in the eyes of many members of the nobility. If he hadn't done anything particularly exceptional or noteworthy during his time in charge, still, he had kept Arestea running smoothly without any big upsets or issues. It was a welcome change in the eyes of many from Alec's near constant scandals and inevitable new declarations of conquest against neighboring countries. People were slowly taking notice. Little by little, Prince Adrian sitting the throne was becoming less and less of a private joke.

And to top it off, no sooner had Liam set eyes on the infamous Black Lily than she had fallen to some rudimentary illness that kept her incapacitated for most of a week. Now, barely over her sickness, she was chomping at the bit in regards to her Guild's orders. Every time he saw her, he watched her dependability slip just a little more. And in a clandestine coup d'état necessitating a double regicide, dependability was the last thing that any of the players involved could afford to lose.

Liam had known, had been informed by Gavriel himself, that the Black Lily would resent working with him as soon as she knew his part in her mission. He knew that her attachment to Robert, the assassin that Liam had caught and executed, would make him an enemy for life in her eyes in any other circumstance. Her Guild knew it too; it was one of the main reasons that she had been chosen for this assignment, and for the unexpected role that she would need to play once it was completed.

As soon as King Alec returned, the whole sordid business could be wrapped up at last and he could be relieved of his apprehension, turn his attention to more important matters. But as no one knew when that return would come, and none of them could do anything to hasten it along, the duke-milite was forced to sit idle and wait, keeping one eye on the assassin and one on the prince. Beneath the monotony, it was a tense situation, and every day of waiting that passed saw the optimal conditions for the plan erode even further. Liam had never harbored much in the way of paranoia before, but he was beginning to feel the first stirrings of it now. And the worst part was that it was completely justified.

He didn't know how long he stood in thought there in his guest study, pacing the floor or staring at the letters on his desk and table, willing a useful plan of action to come to him. He was gazing out the window at the courtyard below when the storm of his thoughts was finally interrupted. A couple had emerged into the garden, a woman with long red hair in an elegantly simple evening gown walking arm in arm with a blonde man in a white shirt and silver coat. The sun was sinking into early afternoon, casting a slight shadow from the palace's west wing that extended down the garden path toward a small wooded area near the rear of the courtyard. It was toward this copse that the couple strolled.

The duke-milite stepped up closer to the window and peered down at them. The man turned his head just enough toward the woman that Liam could make out his profile from a distance. There was no doubt; it was Prince Adrian, and the ruby hair of the woman on his arm could only belong to the Black Lily. Quickly, the duke crossed to his desk and opened one of the drawers, reaching in for his spyglass. If all he could do for the moment was watch and wait, then at least he could do so thoroughly.

Another note set aside by itself on his desk, this one unopened, caught his attention. It bore the royal seal. Melindra must have brought it in when she came to tidy up, he realized. He cracked the seal and skimmed the contents as he walked back to the window, then froze and read it again, this time more carefully. Only once he had finished a second time did he carefully set it aside on a nearby end table and turn his attention back to the scene outside.

"Walk with me, my Prince," Lily said, linking her arm through Adrian's and pulling him away from the path. They were in the gardens by the west wing, and she guided him towards a copse of trees that was currently empty. Not many people were outside today — although the sky was deceptively clear and sunny, the air was frigid as mid-autumn crept ever closer. Lily had bundled up in an expensive fur wrap over her velvet dress to keep out the chill. Now that she was finally over her sickness, she certainly didn't want to catch it again.

"Did you just happen to be out here, or are you following me?" Adrian asked.

"Which do you think?" she replied. "I did not wish to speak in the castle. The walls have ears."

The prince cocked an eyebrow at her. "We've spoken candidly in the castle before and it was safe," he pointed out. "And the ears in the walls were usually yours, were they not?"

"The walls have different ears now," she said impatiently. "New ears that aren't on our side. Humor me."

Lily said no more until they were within the trees and seated on a bench. She discretely looked all around them, but they were alone. The nearest group out for a stroll was much too far away to hear, and anyone who might spy them from the castle would see nothing more than a couple having a quiet moment. "I know that it must be hard for you trust me, what with my profession and all. I certainly don't blame you. I wanted to tell you something that…might make it easier for you to put your faith in me." She didn't look at him while she spoke, but instead gazed out at the garden, which was growing bare with the coming winter.

"And that would be?" Adrian asked after a pause.

"You asked me before what could have happened to turn me into what I am, and I scoffed at the question," she said. "Maybe it was just rhetorical on your part. But I'm ready to answer it now." Lily took a deep breath, closing her eyes. "I wanted to tell you how I became a killer."

She was born to a family of millers. They worked for Lord Dirk, a gluttonous, greedy man who owned twenty acres of land—not a bad amount for the minor nobility, but far from enough to qualify him for the duke status he desired. The tenant farmers, who were little more than serfs, worked from sunup to sundown in his fields, bringing in the crops. They took it to her mother and father, who ground the grain into assorted flour and meal. The farmers gave most of it to Dirk to cover the rent on the land they worked but didn't actually own; Dirk in turn sold it to neighboring lords and ladies who could afford to pay more for it if it meant they didn't have to produce their own. So focused was Lord Dirk on increasing his profits in order to eventually buy his way to a duchy that very little of the finished crops were left for the farmers, millers, and other workers to feed their families. And unlike some millers, her parents never cheated the farmers out of their grain. To do that would hurt not Dirk but the poor families who had to meet their quota.

When Lily was five, Queen Justinia, Alec and Adrian's mother, raised the people's taxes. The wealthy lords and ladies, dukes and duchesses did not want to have to sell a few silver candlesticks to pay said taxes, so they took it out of their servants' and farmers' pockets, her parents included. They managed to keep up with the taxes at first, but then one day the mill broke. Her parents had no money to fix it. The farmers went to another miller so they could meet their quota. Her parents begged Dirk for a loan to pay for the repairs, but he refused.

Her father left town to find work in the city. For a few months he sent them money, but then the money stopped coming. It wasn't until mid-winter that they learned he'd been set upon by muggers and killed.

Her mother became a seamstress. For the next three years, she and Lily's elder sister, Rose, worked tirelessly so that they could keep their home and their broken mill. Perhaps she believed that they would someday have enough money to fix it, and that their fortunes would turn. Perhaps she even believed that her husband would return, that the news of his death was mistaken. They'd never gotten to see his body, after all—he was assumed a vagrant when he was found dead in an alley, and his remains had been buried in an unmarked grave in a pauper's graveyard.

But they never had enough money. As the years passed and they borrowed more and more from neighbors to pay the kingdom's taxes, Lily watched as the mill slowly started to rot and decay. Their mother became ill with a wracking cough. For months it continued, draining her health and her strength. The apothecary gave her a medicine that was really a poison if taken in large doses. She was only to drink a teaspoonful a day to numb some of the pain.

One morning, she and her sister found their mother dead, the poison medicine clutched in her cold fingers. To this day Lily wasn't sure if the sickness overpowered her, she took too much medicine by accident, or she did it on purpose to make an end of it. They didn't even have enough money for a proper burial in the local cemetery. All they could afford was a shallow grave behind the mill that some neighbors dug themselves.

Rose was only fourteen. Lily, only eight.

Without their mother or their father, all the sisters had to rely on was Rose's mediocre stitching. Lily was still too small and uncoordinated for any real work, though the farmers would sometimes pay her a loaf of bread or a couple of apples to weed their fields all day. When Dirk came around for the season's taxes, they had nothing left to pay him with. They begged him for leniency, but he'd had enough of their late payments and borrowed money. He took Rose, demanding that she become his indentured servant, and in return they could keep their house.

Rose fought him and screamed for help, but none came. Nobody wanted to risk losing their jobs or lives defending a poor peasant girl.

Lily went to the local constabulary and demanded their assistance. They didn't care. Their wages were paid by Dirk and his neighbors like him, whose lands they protected from thieves and miscreants.

She became desperate. That man had her sister, would do unspeakable things to her, she was sure. Lily was young, but she was not foolish enough to believe that Rose would receive any care or dignity at Dirk's manor, nor that he would return her sister unharmed.

She took what was left of the poison medicine and poured it into a bottle of wine that she stole off the cart of a passing merchant. Then she waited until late at night to take it to Dirk's guards, who didn't know or care who she was. They drank the wine without thought, passing the bottle around; and once all of them fell into an unnatural unconsciousness, she crept up the stairs to the lord's room. The rest of the manor was fast asleep, but even so, she dared not use a candlestick for fear of waking someone. She had no plan besides to rescue her sister, and no weapon but an old butcher knife from her family kitchen, the blade nicked and dull with years of use.

When she finally found his room, Lord Dirk was face down and sound asleep in his bed, naked but for the blanket thrown over his fat, gluttonous body. Rose sat on the floor near the door, and Lily knew without asking what had passed between them in this room. There was a broken, faraway look in her sister's eyes.

Lily had meant only to take Rose and leave. She'd brought the knife only to defend herself with. But when she saw her sister, lying on the floor like a dog while their lord slept peacefully in his feather bed, she found herself overcome with rage. It was like someone else possessed her body. Before she knew it she was leaning over his form, the dagger held aloft. He lay on his stomach and she could not roll him without waking him, so she aimed for his heart as best she could from his backside.

She missed his heart. It was harder than she'd realized to stab a knife that deep into a man and hit something vital. It got only halfway and must have hit a bone, for it would go no further. Lord Dirk awoke with a roar, throwing her off of him, then reached out and grabbed his assailant. He pinned her to the bed with his heavy body, cursing, as his blood ran down his back. "You!" he shouted, recognition joining the pain and anger in his eyes. "You little bitch! You think you can kill me? I'll see you hang for this!"

His hands were on her neck. She tried to shove him off, but he wouldn't budge. Black spots were forming at her eyes. Her sister was gone, the door swinging on its hinge—she would get no help there. Desperate, Lily reached up and jammed her fingers into his eyes, making him roar again in rage and agony; but still he would not loosen his hold, and she couldn't go much longer without taking a breath. Her hands left his face and groped around the bed and nearby nightstand, trying to find anything she could use as a weapon. Her fingers found an unlit candlestick, cold and heavy, and clutched it instinctively. With all of her small, waning strength, she hefted and slammed it into the side of Dirk's head.

He fell over and off of her finally, and she sucked in deep, frantic breaths as she stumbled to her feet on the mattress, bringing the candlestick up in front of her like a club. Curled below her on the bed, the man was bleeding profusely from the temple, mixing with the blood still leaking from his back where she'd left her knife embedded in his flesh. He was moaning and clutching his head but didn't move.

She should have run then, but all she could think of was how much he had ruined her life. What he had done to her sister, what he had driven her parents to before that. Her family had been running and cowering from him and his kind her whole life, helpless beneath his power and whims.

No more. In this moment, at least, she was the one with power. Let *him* fear *her* for a change, because she would never cower again.

She raised the candlestick and brought it crashing down again onto his skull. There was a wet crunch, and blood splattered out to stain the sheets. His moaning stopped, his whole body going limp. She hit him again, and his head caved in on one side. Again, and he twitched, then went still once more. And still she hit him, swinging the heavy silver candlestick over and over, past the point where her arms burned with fatigue, even past the point where his head was no longer recognizable.

It wasn't until the guards, those that she hadn't poisoned, found her and pulled her off of him that she realized she had been screaming.

Adrian stared at Lily, waiting for her to continue, to say something else, but she had gone silent. Tears rolled down her cheeks, but she didn't seem to notice. She was far away from him now, still there in that room, killing the man who had slowly killed her family. He realized that her hand was clutching his tightly, and he tried to be as still as possible, afraid that if he moved she would run away, like a wild animal. But when she still did not speak, he whispered, "And then what happened?"

Lily startled from her memory, her eyes flicking to his and away again. "I was sentenced to execution," she said

"But you were just a child," he replied.

"They didn't care," she said. "I had killed a man. An important, wealthy man. Not to mention his guards that I'd poisoned, though that had been an accident. I'd only meant to knock them out, but three of them never woke up." She shrugged. "They didn't give me a trial. They just locked me in a jail cell until it was execution day. They stuffed me into a locked wagon that pulled me to the gallows. I watched as a man was hanged for treason. Then they opened the doors, pulled a bag over my head, and yanked me out. But when the bag next came off, I was in a small, dark room. I must have been knocked unconscious at some point; even now, I still can't quite be sure what I actually remember of that evening and what's just dreams and my mind trying to make sense of it. Sometimes I remember another girl being hanged in my place as I watch. Sometimes I can almost swear that I remember the feel of the rope on my neck and the sudden drop as the floor opens beneath me."

She took a deep breath and closed her eyes, falling back into memory. "But I do know this. When the bag finally came off, there were three people sitting in front of me, each of them wearing a mask. Like the ones worn to masquerade balls, though these were devilish, with horns and evil grins. One spoke, a man with a deep voice. He asked me why I'd killed Dirk. I told him the truth. What did I have to lose? He asked me how it had felt, and again I didn't lie." A small shudder ran through her, and Adrian felt it through her hand in his. "It was oddly wonderful," she continued. "Freeing. I had never felt so…alive. Powerful. Invincible. Dirk had been the source of all of my family's grief over the years, the biggest villain in my life up until then, and I, a little girl with a candlestick, I'd destroyed him. I felt like I'd conquered all that was bad in the world that night." She took a deep breath, her eyes closed as she relived the feeling, then opened them and continued. "The man told me I had two choices. I could either join them and help them kill more people like Dirk, stop their evil at the source…or I could go back to the gallows the next day and hang like I was supposed to. Obviously, you can guess which option I chose."

"And…just like that?" Adrian asked. "You became an assassin at eight years old?"

"Not all at once," she answered with a shake of her head. "I was trained for eight years. I didn't have my first official contract until I was sixteen years old. By then they had taught me everything. How to read and write. How to speak Aluvian with and without an Arestean accent, and how to speak Arestean with convincing Aluvian and Ovinurland accents. How to read the other languages of all our continental neighbors, and the rudimentary basics of native Melian. How to decipher coded messages in a variety of cyphers. How to walk without making a sound, dance like a high-class lady, and talk my way out of most situations by dissembling and playing the scared, ignorant little girl. When I was older, how to use my budding womanly charms for persuasion and distraction. And of course, nearly every way to kill a man."

Adrian sat in silence a moment, absorbing her words. "And you never looked back?" he asked at last.

Again, she shrugged. "What was there to look back to? I had lost everything. My home, my family, my life. I was dead to the world. And I was anonymous. Nobody suspects a teenage girl to be a trained spy and killer."

"What about your sister?" Adrian asked. "You never talked to her again?"

Lily shook her head. "When I became an assassin, they told me I had to break ties with everything and everyone I loved. That was easy, seeing as I had nobody left but her." She took another deep breath, then loosed it in a sigh. "Still, I missed her, and after a year as a protégé I found out what happened to her. She'd run away that night after she was raped. She was later found and informed of my untimely death." Lily smiled sadly. "After the Guild rescued me from the prison cart, and I accepted their terms, they had to make sure that it appeared I had died. The story that was passed around is that somehow I escaped the cart before I could be hanged, but later was caught holed up in a barn. The citizens who found me tried to flush me out by lighting the barn on fire, but it spread out of control, and I burned within. In reality, they burned the body of a recently deceased girl near my size, enough that the features were unrecognizable, and passed it off as me to the constabulary, who informed my sister. After Rose learned of my supposed death, she went to the city, took the only job available to a woman with no prospects, no dowry, no skills, and who had already lost her biggest innate value. She became a prostitute. I'm told they treated her well enough in the brothel, but she got pregnant pretty early on and died in childbirth."

Adrian looked down at their clasped hands, unsure what to say. "My mother's tax raise," he said after a moment, wincing even as he said it. It sounded like such a callous subject after all of her story. "It was…the money went toward funding universities being set up on the edges of the country, away from the major cities. She meant to help people who couldn't afford to travel inland for an education. It was never supposed to…"

"I know," she said. She sounded tired as she said it. "I know now not everyone with power is a monster. But you can't help everyone. And there's always someone like Dirk getting in the way, fouling up good intentions."

"I'm so sorry, Lily," he whispered, knowing it was a paltry sentiment even as he uttered it.

She shrugged as if she did not care, but Adrian could see the tears still wet on her cheeks. "I'm not telling you this to win your pity. I'm not even trying to convince you that what I did was justified. I'm telling you this because I want you to trust me. Everything I have done as an assassin up until this point was to try to make the world a better place. I was trying to change things, and the only way I saw to do that was to remove the people who were wrecking everything in the first place."

"But...surely you don't still believe that just killing people is going to solve anything?" Adrian asked. "Not everyone you killed had to be guilty of a horrible crime like Lord Dirk. You didn't answer me last time I asked, but what if your masters had ordered you to kill an innocent? A child?"

A small wrinkle formed between her eyebrows. "I...I don't know what I would have done," she said. "Likely they would have just given that job to another of us with fewer scruples than me and I'd never hear about it. That might even have happened before, come to think of it. I believed, up until recently, that everything that the Guild and I did was justified. That I was killing people who deserved to be killed. And I still believe that, for the most part, I admit. I've solved a lot of problems for a lot of people, whether you agree with the methods or not. But now...now I'm starting to question."

This time it was the prince that shook his head. "Why?" he asked. "What made you decide to suddenly question your life now?"

"You did." She smiled up at him sadly. Her face looked confused and...vulnerable. It was weird to see her like this, he thought, and know it wasn't a mask. "Honestly? You are nothing like I expected you to be. You are a good person, Adrian. And you want to make the world better. The Guild clearly made a mistake by putting a mark on you. That, or its aims are not as noble as I had once believed. Maybe Master Gavriel and the others don't really care about improving the world by reaching beyond the law and that was just the lie I've been swallowing to justify our work. Maybe they really are as evil as the general populace believes. In which case, I have to stop Liam from taking the throne, and then I have to talk to Master Gavriel. I have to convince him that this is a better solution."

"And my brother? He was not the one that ruined your life. He doesn't deserve to die, either," Adrian argued. "After Alec took the throne, he saw how our parents' elevated taxes were upsetting the kingdom. He realized that the landowners were forcing their farmers and servants to pay most of the burden, and he made that punishable by law. If anyone was caught exploiting their workers to such an extent as Lord Dirk today, they would be tried and fined."

"And how often has that actually happened?" Lily retorted, her usual fire returning. "How often are nobles of any rank arrested for corruption? How much has the aristocracy paid back to those beneath them? Very seldom and very little." She stood up, pulling her hand away from his, and crossed her arms over her chest. "Maybe Alec isn't the monster I used to think he was—or not the same kind of monster, anyway—but he's still part of the bigger problem. The rich take advantage of the poor whenever they can while pretending that they have everyone's best interests at heart. Alec thinks he can charm the peasants with his pretty smile and they will forget how hard their lives are, how those born into luxury treat the less fortunate like second class citizens."

"My brother's a contentious figure, I'll readily admit, but he's still done a lot to make this country better," Adrian argued back, standing as well. "I'd think you of all people would understand the argument of dubious means possibly being justified if people overall benefit. He's increased trade, expanded our borders, built roads and even schools —"

"On whose backs?" Lily hissed. "Ours! The peasants! And all the good he's done has been to benefit you and the nobility. It doesn't matter where the borders of the country are when your whole life is a single village or a few dirty streets, and it doesn't much matter who's sitting in a throne when it's hundreds of miles away and you'll never see it. Do you really think all of his wars and expansions are waged for the sake of the common man?"

The prince opened his mouth to affirm his belief before he realized that he was defending his brother against the very same argument that he had leveled at him so often before. The realization stopped him short, and he had to look away from her while he considered. "I...I don't know," he admitted at last. "Sometimes I do. Many times I don't. I honestly don't think the issue is so cut and dry as I once thought it. But Alec believes it. He's an ass, and I'll be the first to admit it, but he really does believe that he is helping his country. All of it."

Lily turned her eyes to the ground, but they didn't lose their hard glare. "Your brother can believe what he wants," she said quietly. "But believing a thing doesn't make it so, as we've both been discovering of late. And Alec doesn't strike me as the kind of man who will reverse all of his decisions just because someone has proven him wrong. Otherwise, he would have done so by now, and we wouldn't be here having this conversation."

Adrian frowned but couldn't gainsay her. "Even so," he said, "does that give you any right to take his life? To take anyone's? There are better ways to change the world. When I become king…" He stopped and took a deep breath. Just saying it aloud was frightening, but he couldn't turn back now. "When I am king, I can fix it. You could help me, if you would promise to stop killing."

Lily sighed, rubbing her forehead as if she had a headache. "Why is this all so confusing now?" She stared at him, taking three slow, deliberate steps until there was no space between them. She lifted her hand, tracing it down his cheek. "Not too long ago, I knew exactly what I wanted in life. I knew who I was and who my enemy was."

"And now?" Adrian asked, finding the words came difficult, that his breathing had suddenly quickened.

She didn't answer, just reached up and pressed her lips against his. It wasn't like any of the other times she had tried to kiss him. Then, she had been seductive and powerful. Frightening, even. But now, she seemed vulnerable, uncertain. He didn't kiss her back, but he didn't pull away either. And then she was gone, and his lips felt suddenly cold without hers. He watched as she turned and walked wordlessly away toward the castle. He wanted to follow her, but he didn't know what else to say. It seemed that was the only answer he would get out of her.

Liam lowered the spyglass, a frown wrinkling his forehead. He suddenly wished he had learned to read lips. But while he had been many things so far in his life—an orphan, a soldier, a client of assassins, a duke, a national hero, and now a conspirator to regicide—one thing that he wasn't was a spy. The skill had never been necessary before.

As he tucked the spyglass into his desk, he contemplated what he'd seen. The Black Lily had spent a long time talking to the crown prince. He'd seen the tears streaming down her face, the look of pity and sadness on the prince's. She was either a very, very good actress, or...

The duke-milite's frown deepened. What if she was not acting? When she had kissed Prince Adrian, there had been no seduction, no passion. And then, even after she'd walked away from him, she was still crying. There had been no look of triumph or pleasure on her face. Once she'd turned away, she should have had no reason to keep up the facade. But she kept shedding tears, too many to be forced or fake.

There was only one likely explanation: She felt something for the prince, perhaps even loved him. A woman as cold, cruel, and calculating as she was purported to be would never be pathetic enough to cry over someone to whom she had no emotional attachment. He had seen her out in the crowd the day that he had hanged her assassin boyfriend. She had thought she went unseen, but Liam had been told what to look for. Even then, she had shed only a few tears before turning away and disappearing into the crowd.

He drummed his fingers on the desk, the quick staccato rhythm mirroring the controlled frenzy of his thoughts. This was not good. If the Black Lily had actually fallen for the prince, then there was no telling whose side she was on now. After all, she'd already proved with Robert that her allegiance could waver when her heart got in the way. What if she no longer planned to go through with the assassination at all? What if she had already switched sides, had already told Prince Adrian and King Alec everything? But no, she couldn't have or Liam would already be in shackles. So Liam had to assume that nobody knew his plans, or that if they did, they were too afraid to stop him.

Where did that leave the prince in all of this? He was an unfortunate obstacle who would need to die either way, but if he was now an active threat, then it needed to be sooner rather than later. But Liam couldn't tip his hand either, and he certainly couldn't be the one to deliver the killing blow.

But…if he could set them both up, make it look as if they were working together to overthrow Alec, then his problems would be solved. They would hang, and Liam would once more look the hero for catching them in the act. The king would have to trust him — and him alone, since he'd be proving that even Alec's trust in his own kid brother was misguided. Liam would be the right hand of the nation in earnest, and it wouldn't be too much longer before he was stabbing Alec in the back himself and taking the long overdue crown at the urging of a grateful populace.

But first, he had to find a way to bring Adrian and Lily down together. And he was running out of time.

Slowly, Liam turned back to the message he had set aside and picked it up once more. It was an official notice from the king's messenger to all of the nobles assembled in the palace. Alec was returning at last, and would be back in the city in less than a week.

Seventeen

Three days later, the palace was in an uproar. The king was returning, and everyone was preparing for the day of celebration that would occur. The nobility was so excited, in fact, that they had decided to begin the festivities prematurely. Nobles needed little prodding to partake in dancing, drinking, and cavorting behind closed doors.

Lily stood before the tall mirror in her room, examining her dress. It was a deep ruby red, made of shiny silk, with a corset that lifted her bust nicely as per her usual tastes. The bustles upon bustles of skirt were a bit annoying, though, even if they did allow her to hide the daggers and garrote wire strapped to her legs—with Liam in the palace now, there was no way she would risk being caught off guard and unarmed if the need to take him out in private arose. The gown was a new and risqué fashion. The decorative corset was not covered by another layer on top, but rather left exposed, and her shoulders and cleavage were thus bared. She'd been sure to attach her normal teardrop vial of amethyst poison to the jewelry, of course, in case of emergency. A lady always needed to be prepared, after all.

She smiled at herself as she finished applying her lipstick. Normally she would not dress quite so extravagantly for a party in which the king was not even present, but she found that she inexplicably wanted to draw Adrian's eye. Of course, she had tried many times to draw it before, but that had been merely for seduction's sake. She found she now truly wanted Adrian to notice her, to find her attractive, to know that he was not completely immune to her beauty no matter how he tried to deny it.

Lily opened her bedroom door, stepping into the sitting room, where Adrian was already waiting for her. He turned, and she watched as his breath caught, his gaze wavering across her body before quickly snapping back up to meet her eyes. She didn't miss the blush that formed on his cheeks, and the proof that he could indeed still be captivated by her even in the midst of their present predicament was oddly reassuring. After she had opened her heart to him and told him of her past, she had found she felt uncomfortably vulnerable around him, and it was a relief to once more be in control of the situation, at least in this small way.

"Are you ready?" he asked, standing and clasping his hands behind his back.

"Almost," she said. "Help me tie my mask on, please."

"Ah, yes," he said with a sigh as she slipped the mask over her face and he began tying the lace strings behind her head. "I will never understand why nobles love their masquerade balls so much. Everyone knows who everyone else is under the masks, especially considering most of them only cover the eyes."

"It's the thrill of it, Adrian," she explained with a smile. "The excitement of pretending that one is hidden and thus can get away with all the more naughty deeds in public. They all know that everyone else will gossip the next day about who did what, but for the night, at least, they can let their inhibitions go." The string tied, she turned, gazing up at him. Hers was a half mask of black filigree cut to resemble lace which covered her eyes and forehead, but left her nose and mouth exposed to view. Adrian's, on the other hand, was a much more extravagant golden thing that covered his face from his nose to the top of his head and was topped with its own crown. The inlaid golden filigrees looked heavy, and she smiled at him pityingly.

"It looks awful, doesn't it?" he said with a wry smile. "I never thought metal could be so itchy." He fiddled with it until she grabbed his hand, pulling it away.

"It's fine," she said. "Just be happy you don't have one of those ridiculous beak noses or piles of feathers to tickle your face. Come, they'll be waiting for you."

She turned to head towards the door, but Adrian stopped her with a hand on her arm. "Wait. You still haven't told me what you're planning to do about Liam. Shouldn't we act before my brother returns?" he asked.

She shook her head. "That would be unwise. He wouldn't expect me to attack you until after Alec came back because he knows that once the word spreads of your assassination, the king's guards would advise Alec not to return for his own safety. For that very same reason, we can't move against him yet. We must wait until Alec is back in the palace before we make our move, exposing Liam to the king and the rest of the country at once. But once Alec *is* back, we must act swiftly and reveal Liam's plans without compromising either of our safeties."

"Certainly you could just let me talk to my brother." the prince said, though his tone sounded less sure than his words. "I know he would listen —"

"No, he wouldn't," she interrupted. "He may forgive you, eventually, but he would never trust you or your judgment again after knowing you befriended me and did not turn me over to the law. And as for me…he would hang me right beside Liam. He would not care that I had helped to bring Liam to justice. No, whatever we do, we must do it without Alec ever knowing our involvement or we'll both be ruining ourselves in the bargain."

"And what will we do? You still haven't told me anything," Adrian said.

Lily sighed, turning away and heading towards the door. She hadn't told him anything yet because, honestly, she hadn't figured out what to do. For the past three days she had been pacing her room and thinking, trying to come up with some brilliant plan, something foolproof that would allow them to set up Liam without compromising herself or Adrian. But so far she had come up with nothing.

She couldn't bring evidence of Liam's working with the Guild before the court, as she had none, and he would not be stupid enough to bring any with him to the palace. There was no time or opportunity to leave the palace and root for the evidence back at the Guild or at Liam's own residence in Treventre — her absence would be too long not to be noticed, and she had no believable explanation for her guildmates as to why she would have returned before the mission was complete. She couldn't convincingly forge the evidence; however many skills she had, that wasn't one of them. And there was no way to let slip his treachery in conversation without revealing herself as well. However noble her change of heart may have been, she wasn't about to throw herself on any swords just to bring down one man, no matter what kind of threat he posed or how badly she wanted revenge.

She didn't want to admit it, but she was cornered, and she was running out of time.

The only thing she could think to do, and she dreaded the thought and what the consequences might mean, was to assassinate Liam after Alec's return, then escape the castle. Everyone would soon figure out that Camilla was really the Black Lily, which would be a serious blow to the mystery of the persona she had cultivated over the years. But Adrian would still seem innocent and oblivious of the whole ordeal, which was well worth the compromising her reputation. If she waited until the king had resumed the throne, then the prince wouldn't even face the stigma of failing to react effectively; she'd have come in under Alec's watch, killed and left again under Alec's watch, and only Alec would shoulder whatever responsibility there was for having housed her and allowed her the opportunity. She knew Adrian would likely feel betrayed that she would simply abandon him like that after the bond they had formed — and that she had resorted to solving another problem with murder — but she could think of nothing else.

As for what it would mean for her when the Guild found out...

Lily put the thought out of her mind. If or when it came to that, she would decide then how to deal with the Guild and Master Gavriel's anger.

"I'll tell you when I have a better plan," she said. "For tonight, don't worry about it. Put it out of your mind and enjoy the party, Adrian." She linked her arm through his and pulled him away from his chambers and towards the grand ballroom.

The party was in full swing when they arrived. Lily slipped away from the prince at the last moment and instead entered through a side door, leaving Adrian to make a grand entrance alone through the main doors, as was expected of the prince. She could feel him glaring at her through the room for leaving him stranded amidst a sea of clinging aristocrats, but she ignored him as she walked over to a table, taking a glass of champagne for herself and picking through the hors d'oeuvres. She flirted with a few noblemen as she ate and occasionally chatted with a duchess or two, but most of the assembled peers of the realm ignored her, likely figuring she could gain them little to no favor. Besides, she still feigned to speak Arestean poorly, though not as poorly as when she had first arrived. That left little opportunity for conversation on her part.

All the while, Lily discreetly watched the prince, his smile tight as he went about politely greeting everyone in the room and trying to avoid dancing with most of them. Some were apparently still convinced that he was secretly a good dancer after his one graceful turn around the room with her so many months ago. He was also forced to join in numerous toasts to his brother's return, until he had gone through three glasses of champagne and his cheeks grew rosy with it beneath the mask he kept fidgeting with. He'd have to learn to stop that before the next masquerade, she thought.

Lily soon lost track of time in the inconsequential excitement of the evening. She was surprised when, hours into the affair, she felt an arm circle her hips and a hand lightly grab her waist. She turned to smile gracefully up at the owner, then froze when she saw to whom the hand belonged.

Liam too was looking at the prince. "Stalking our prey, are we, dear?" he asked quietly. Despite the noise in the room that guaranteed they would not be overheard, she noticed he still made sure his words were laced with a double meaning. Anyone who overheard would think he merely referred to bedding Adrian and nothing more.

"Always, duke-milite" she answered, glancing away from him. "To what pleasure do I owe?"

"Is it not enough for a man to ask after the time of a beautiful woman?" the duke-milite answered with a smile. "I confess, I feel a certain responsibility toward your wellbeing ever since our unfortunate first meeting. I trust you are over what ails you, my dear? No more lingering fatigue or clouded mind?"

Lily gave him a polite smile that didn't reach her eyes. "No more, m'lord," she said. "I am fit and healthy, thank you. No more...how do you say?... unfortunateness between us."

"I am glad," Liam answered, pulling her by her waist closer to his side. "Would the lady consent to a moment of more...private conversation, perchance? A minute or two away from the crowds?"

Again she smiled. "M'lord is courting beautiful lady already, yes?" she asked, placing a hand on his, neither holding it to nor removing it from her waist. "A duchess? Should he also be having private moments with lowly courtesans?"

"Oh, you've nothing to fear from me, my lady," he answered with a grin as he turned her away from the dance floor. "I shall be a perfect gentleman, I assure you."

Lily allowed the lie to pass without remark as she walked away at his side.

He led her back toward the door through which she had entered, turning just beyond it into a small sitting room off the main corridor. There were no guards or servants immediately nearby, their attention being focused on the party. When the duke-milite shut the door behind them, they were left in complete privacy.

"Something on your mind, Treventre?" Lily asked quietly after a brief scan of the room. There were no furnishings or decorations sufficient to hide behind, and she knew from studying the castle layout that the only other door led to a small water closet. They were alone, for the moment.

"A good many things on my mind, actually, Black Lily," Liam answered, turning to her and leaning back against the closed door. "For now, I'll settle for a question. I'd like an honest answer, please."

Lily mimicked his pose, leaning back against the windowpane of the wall opposite him and crossing her arms. "Ask away."

"Do you love the prince?" he asked.

For the briefest of moments, Lily's mind blanked; but her training kept her reaction infinitesimal, and she settled on arching an eyebrow at the duke. "What kind of ridiculous question is that?" she asked.

"A blunt one," Liam replied, "and one that you'll not dodge. Your answer, please."

Anger swelled unbidden in her, rising up through her chest until she had to fight the urge to swallow it back down. "You presume much, duke-milite," she said coolly, her voice pitched to a low threat. "My private thoughts, whatever they may be, are not included in this unique relationship that you and I have. But if you will insist on your answer, fine." She half turned her head to gaze out the window behind her at the darkening sky, watching his reflection in the glass. "I think that our little princeling is a better man than we all reckoned," she said. "I think he is less incompetent than his peers have believed, with sincere and noble ideals, however naïve and misguided. It will discomfit me to see his blossoming career cut short, but it will not be the first time I have felt a measure of pity for someone under my focused attention. But am I in love with him?" She turned back to Liam then with her best smirk. "Please. I'm no blushing maiden, duke. Even if I were to entertain the idea of falling in love, I'd need a real man, not a righteous boy still trying to figure out his own private parts." She shrugged. "Or a real woman," she added. "I've played on both sides, and I see no reason to choose a favorite."

"A real man," Duke-Milite Liam echoed, tilting his head slightly. "Like your friend Robert?"

She was standing upright and halfway across the room before she knew what she was doing, and it took all of her self-control to stop herself. When she did, she stood tense as a drawn bowstring as she glared across the remaining space at her unwanted client. "Yes," she said through gritted teeth. "Like Robert, you smug prick."

The duke's lips spread to a thin, slight smile that made her fists clench at her sides. "Are you going to ask me how I knew?" he said, voice barely above a whisper.

Lily took a deep breath and forced herself to relax, waiting for the worst of the tension in her body to pass before she answered. "No," she said. "I expect my master told you when you contacted him, or else you got Robert to let it slip while you were slowly cutting pieces off of him. And once again, I fail to see how this private affair of mine has anything to do with our agreement."

"Oh, it has everything to do with our agreement, I'm afraid," Liam answered, then sighed and stepped away from the door. "I admit, if half the stories they tell about you are true, then you may very well be the best talent that your associates have to offer. But nobody is perfect, my dear, not even the best. Everyone has at least one fatal flaw. And yours, it seems, is your unfortunate willingness to love when you shouldn't." He walked slowly past her as he spoke, mercifully giving her a wide berth lest she succumb to her growing anger, and stopped in front of the shut water closet door. "I don't believe you, you know, when you say you feel nothing for the prince. I've seen you two together, walking the halls or the palace gardens. You have either tripped over your duties into love again, or you are the finest actress outside of the Sapphire Theater."

"And you don't think someone in my line of work knows how to act?" she asked, keeping her eyes trained on him at all times.

"I know you can," he said. "But I think that you took too long defending yourself against my allegation. You acted too well, my dear. I know a performance when I see one, even a sterling performance. An honest answer would have just been a simple no and perhaps some confusion, not the angry rebuttal you gave. Perhaps your short temper is another flaw of yours."

The next time that she had the opportunity, she thought, she would properly berate herself for letting her personal hatred of the man show through so much, obvious though it may have been. For the moment, she simply snorted and crossed her arms again. "You're a shit employer, you know that?" she asked. "Thought I'd heard all the servants saying how nice you were to the help. Nitpicking the flaws of someone whose services you so dearly need isn't good form, Treventre." She narrowed her eyes at him. "And what would a petty, grasping man like yourself know about love, anyway?"

She had the momentary satisfaction of seeing him scowl in real anger at that, his answering glare the first

348

crack in his smug expression since they'd entered the room together. "More than you think, *my lady*," he growled, then raised a knuckle and rapped on the door behind him. "My pet, would you join us please?" he said louder.

Lily's heart stopped for a moment as the water closet door swung slowly open behind him and the Duchess Sidonie stepped out. She wore a half-mask of gold to match her hair and gown, but Lily knew immediately who she was. What she had been doing here, though, and why Liam would be stupid enough to involve her in this affair even in the slightest, were beyond her understanding.

The duchess frowned as she took Liam's arm around the elbow, glancing back and forth between the duke-milite and Lily. "Liam?" she asked quietly. "What is going on here? What were you two talking about, and why was I made to listen?"

Perhaps she hadn't heard the conversation well, then, thought Lily. She could still salvage this situation if she thought quickly. Placing a hand over her bodice, she forced an embarrassed flush to her cheeks and blinked vacantly at the duchess. "M'lord?" she asked, parroting Sidonie's confusion. "I thought you say you want private moment between we two, yes?"

"Yes, I did, didn't I?" Duke-Milite Liam answered, reaching his free hand into a pocket of his evening jacket. "So sorry, my ladies. Sidonie, dear, if you would please excuse us."

The duchess turned her uncertain frown back to the duke, looking up at his face. As such, her neck was perfectly situated and bared so that, when he pulled his hand from his pocket and stabbed, the thin blade pierced her straight through the hollow of her throat.

Both Lily and the duchess froze, neither knowing how to react as the duke-milite leaned his face down to the duchess's. "I am so terribly, terribly sorry, Sidonie dear," he said with genuine regret in his voice. "But it is for the good of the realm." Then he laid his lips gently against her forehead in a final kiss before pulling back and yanking the dagger out through the side of her neck.

Before the duchess crumpled, Liam shoved her hard from behind toward Lily, who caught her out of instinct. She felt the hot splash of the duchess's blood on her chest, running down her décolletage and over her dress. Already, Duchess Sidonie's eyes were glazed as the light left them and she slumped quietly against Lily's shoulder.

Then the stunned moment passed, and the assassin let the noblewoman's body drop to the floor as she turned her attention back to Liam, who was already moving quickly for the door. He turned with one hand on the knob and flung his other hand out. It was only after she had snatched his clumsily thrown dagger from the air that she realized he had not meant to try and pierce her with it, but by the time she realized her mistake, it was too late.

"Your services will no longer be required," the duke-milite said sadly, then wrenched the door open and bolted out of the room shouting, "Help! Guards! *Assassin!*"

Lily's mind was a blank, but thankfully she had been trained for such sudden life-or-death situations, and her body reacted without her mind needing to tell it to. She raced into the corridor after Liam, tackling him to the floor and bringing the dagger to his own throat. He was faster than she had reckoned, however, and brought an arm up just in time, so that it cut into the flesh of his forearm instead of his neck. It did not matter, for the guards were already in the hallway, their eyes quickly assessing the situation before they grabbed Lily and hauled her off of him, disarming her.

"That woman..." the duke-milite gasped. "She is an assassin! She killed Sidonie! Oh gods, my dear Sidonie!"

Talk about bad acting. Not that it mattered. She was covered in blood and had been attacking him. Besides that, she'd been holding the dagger still warm with Sidonie's blood. Lily had only a few seconds to decide what to do. There were three guards in the hall and more in the ballroom. A crowd had already gathered, staring into the hallway, the word "assassin" passing amongst them in shock and confusion. Lily had her weapons under her skirts, but there was no way she could get to them and take down those guards before the others were on her. If she tried to fight her way out of here, many innocents would die. Adrian might even be put at risk.

But she did have one escape. She just needed the right opening.

"She is the Black Lily!" Liam continued yelling. "I found one of her flowers in my room just this evening! Check her person, I'm sure she has more weapons on her!"

The guards did as they were told, divesting her of her gown and stripping away her mask. The onlookers gasped as her face was revealed, and again as the guards found two daggers and a length of metal wire in holsters about her legs. She stood before them in nothing but her undergarments, one arm held by each guard, and together they dragged her into the ballroom.

"My Prince, what should we do with her now?" one of the guards holding her asked.

The crowd parted and Adrian stood gaping at Lily, at a loss for words. She did not miss that he was now flanked by his own guards, these for protection, and they eyed her warily, their swords drawn. Then they did not underestimate her — that was good, for Adrian's sake.

"I demand vengeance!" the duke-milite yelled, pointing at her. "She killed my betrothed! And she tried to kill me as well!"

She watched Adrian's eyes betray his emotions — disbelief, anger, disappointment, fear. That last one was perhaps the worst, because it mirrored her own fear, fear that had set her heart to pounding and made it hard to breathe. She tried to tell him she was sorry without words, but she did not know if he would believe her.

Regardless, while everyone waited for him to finally speak, a moment of relative calm descended.

This was likely the best chance she would get, she decided.

Lily twisted her body, her arms wrenching at an awkward angle in the grip of the guards behind her. She brought a leg up and, without cumbersome skirts to weigh her down, easily lifted it over her head, the other kicking up to follow close behind, flipping her body around after them and overtop of the men holding her. The guards lost their hold on her as she vaulted them and landed at their backs, then spun to face her as the partygoers gasped and shrieked anew. Before either man could react further, she punched the nearest in the nose, breaking it, then struck the other in the weak spot of his armor between his helm and his neck. He fell to the floor gasping for breath as she skipped back away from them and grabbed the vial from around her neck. She broke the chain with a sharp yank and put the vial to her lips, pulling the tiny glass stopper out with her teeth.

"Stop her!" Adrian yelled at last. "Don't let her drink that!"

She expected more guards to rush her as she spit the stopper to the ground. She'd incapacitated the ones holding her first so the nearest who might react would be too far away to stop her in time. But she hadn't expected the prince to throw *himself* at her; and when he did, and she stumbled back just out of his reach, she was stunned for a long enough moment that she lost her only window of opportunity. She brought the vial to her lips again, but before she could drink, Adrian's frantic hand smacked against her own. The poison was dashed to the marble floor, where the crystal vial shattered, spilling its deadly contents in a splash of amethyst.

Then a heavy weight crashed against the side of Lily's head—the pommel of a sword, it must have been—and she collapsed. This time the three nearest guards pinned her to the ground, lying their full weight on her to hold her down lest she attack any more.

As the cold marble pressed into her face and body, she heard Adrian above her command in a shaky voice, "Take her to the dungeons. Find an empty room to use as a holding cell. We must…question her. Make sure she is restrained. But do *nothing* to her beyond that without my orders, do you understand?"

"Yes, Your Highness" one of the men atop her answered. Lily felt herself lifted from the floor and the room spun in her vision, her head still ringing from the blow she'd been dealt. Masks blended together, some beautiful, some horrific, into a twirling, chaotic dance. She heard whispers and murmurs all around her that sounded as if they came from far away, from someplace where ghosts or demons dwelled. Then she was hauled out of the room and down a corridor, and the pounding in her head made her nauseous enough that she had to close her eyes as they dragged her down to the dungeons beneath the castle.

Time and her sense of bearing swam as she stumbled along with her escort. She only knew she had arrived when a heavy wooden door opened with a loud creak and she was tossed unceremoniously onto the floor, where she finally shut her eyes and succumbed to unconsciousness.

Eighteen

A short time later, Lily awoke to a pounding headache and a sick stomach. She sat up slowly, holding the side of her head, and assessed her surroundings. There wasn't much to take in; she was in a small stone cell scarcely bigger than a broom closet, the walls cool and slick with condensation, the air rank with mildew. From the circles in the dust on the floor, it appeared to have recently held casks of wine. A short, heavy chain ran from the back wall to a steel cuff around one of her ankles, another such chain shackled her wrists together. The guards must have bound her while she was knocked out. At least they had given her the comfort of shackling her wrists in front of her, so that her arms were not bent behind her at an awkward angle.

"I demand that you let me pass," a man's voice argued haughtily from down the corridor. It was the voice that had woken her, she realized.

"Sir, the prince said we were not to do anything with the prisoner until he gave the orders," another man replied. A prison guard, she guessed.

"I won't bloody touch her, but I have a right to see her after what she has done to me. Would you deny me this?" She recognized this first voice to be Liam's.

"I suppose it couldn't hurt," a third voice (another guard, she presumed) responded. "After all, the prince just wants her hale for questioning. Not that she will be for long, once the king gets hold of her."

"Fine, you can speak with the prisoner," said the other guard. "But briefly. I'll open the door." Footsteps sounded down the corridor, arriving outside the door that marked the only escape from her stone prison. There wasn't even a barred window on the back wall that held her; the room would have been pitch black had it not been for a tiny flicker of light from a carried torch that seeped in through the small window on her cell door. The key grated in the lock and the door opened, the light growing so that it nearly blinded her at first.

The duke-milite stood before her, an ugly scowl across his face. He pulled a few coins from his breast pocket that flashed gold in the torchlight and handed them to the guard. "For a few moments of privacy, if you will," he said.

The guard glanced at the coins and Lily with equal amounts of apathy, then took the money and turned to leave the tiny room, mounting the torch in a sconce outside the cell. Liam stayed where he was, well out of her reach thanks to her shackling chain. Lily leaned back against the wall, her arms resting on her bent knees. "Come to have a little fun with the prisoner before the king returns?" she asked.

He did not answer, but waited instead until the guards' retreating footsteps faded away and he knew no one could hear them. "Oh, I don't intend to touch a hair on your head, my dear," he said quietly. "I only wanted to see how you were doing, make sure you were comfortable. Nice accommodations, though they could have aired the place out a bit." He sniffed for emphasis, wrinkling his nose at the pungent odor of mold.

"So you've just come and paid bribe money to gloat," she said. "You've outsmarted the Black Lily. Now you can say you have two assassins that you've assisted in capturing. And won't that look good with the king and Prince Adrian? If I didn't know better, I'd think you were trying to win your way into their good graces, rather than plotting to kill them both."

"Yes, but I am a patient man. I have waited this long to cast the royal family from power. I can wait a bit longer." He ventured another step further into her cell. "I could not, however, risk you ruining my plans. The moment I knew you were in love with Adrian was the moment your risk outweighed your usefulness. I just wonder how the poor boy must feel, knowing that the courtesan he had fallen for was planning on killing him all along. Oh, how that must hurt..."

"And tell me, how do you feel, Treventre?" she asked. "Are you afraid?"

He shrugged, looking around the small cell. "I am free and a hero, and you are stuck in here and will be executed before the week is out. I don't see what I have to fear."

She leaned forward, smirking. "Because, once the Guild hears of this—and they will in due time—you'll wish you'd never crossed them. Whatever Alec might do to me, you can bet they've thought of something crueler and nastier. Every torture inflicted on me you will feel as well, until you will wish I'd died an easy death. *When* they strike is the question. It may be this month, it may not be until ten years from now. It all depends on how long they want you to suffer, constantly looking over your shoulder, living in fear, wondering when they will come for you. You'll never marry, never have children, knowing that my Guild will destroy all that you love. The higher you try to climb with your grasping little plans, the further you'll inevitably fall."

"I see," the duke-milite said, pursing his lips. "Well then. That *would* be truly frightening, if I didn't know better." He smiled, crossing his arms over his chest. "I have nothing to fear from your Guild. But I can see from the look on your face that you truly believe they will get vengeance for your death. So before I let you die, I'll clarify a few things for you, as a gentleman's courtesy. Tell me, did you ever wonder how it was that a nobleman, even a knighted one, alone in his study in the middle of the night, could have caught and bested a trained assassin from the most feared assassin's organization in the country?"

She didn't answer him. She had no answer; Lily had wondered the same thing herself for years. But wondering didn't bring him back, so she'd eventually let it go. She sat straight against her cell wall and glared at him in the dark.

"Don't you get it?" Liam pressed. "Are you really that in love with your Guild and your Master Gavriel that you would blind yourself to the truth? Robert was set up."

"By whom?" she growled.

"Gods above, woman, do you ever actually *listen*?" he asked. "What did I just say? He was betrayed by the Guild. By Gavriel himself, in fact."

"You lie!" Lily yelled, jumping up and rushing at him, her chain catching her ankles. She fell forward onto the hard stone on her hands and knees. "Gavriel loved him. He loves us all. He would never—"

"Your Guildmaster did then what I am doing now," the duke-milite continued. "He had Robert disposed of as soon as he lost his usefulness. As soon as he proposed to *you*. Gavriel could not risk you, his prodigy and best assassin, in the prime of your career, getting married, having a child even, and running off with your lover. You were too valuable an investment. He knew what you two were planning. He'd always known. And he had Robert taken out of the picture. Fortunately, I had just contacted the Guild with my own needs to get the Duke of Cragstaff off of my back, and Gavriel and I were able to come to a mutually beneficial arrangement. They told Robert that Cragstaff was his employer, they told me what to expect, and your fiancé walked right into our trap. Gavriel rid himself of a growing nuisance, Cragstaff's reputation and position were destroyed, my nephew Gareth inherited his forfeited duchy, and the eyes of all the realm turned my way in admiration." He chuckled, shaking his head at the memory. "But if it makes you feel any better, Robert didn't actually disclose much of anything during my interrogation. All of the info I'd claimed I'd been able to extract from him? Fed to me by Gavriel beforehand. Your man was the utmost professional through to the end, which is more than I can say for you, Black Lily. You ask me, the Guild let the wrong agent go that day."

She found she was shaking. Her fists were clenched so hard her nails bit into her hands, causing them to bleed. But it all fit together. It made too much sense to be a lie. There was no way this man, however great a soldier he had been, could have bested a trained expert like Robert. And there was no way he could have broken Robert enough to know all that he apparently knew now of the Guild and it's workings. She hated to admit it, but that last revelation did make her feel just a bit better on her dead lover's behalf. "You bastard," she hissed.

"Tsk. I'm not the one who made him question his career and the whole life he'd been living to that point, made him want to leave the Guild with his lover and run away from his responsibilities. He died for love of you." Liam sighed and shook his head. "And now you will die for your love of Adrian."

"They will still make you pay," she said, though without the vindictive pleasure she'd felt before. "You said it yourself; I'm their best assassin."

"I said *were*, my dear," he replied. "You *were* the best. But you too have outlived your usefulness. You've forgotten just how expendable you are, every one of your kind. You're tools. However effective it may have been at its job once, when a tool is no longer useful, you throw it away." He took another step toward her, until she could almost touch him. "You most of all, Black Lily. You were never intended to survive this mission. You were getting too cocky, drawing too much attention to yourself and your kills. You forgot that an effective assassin does not revel in infamy. Gavriel himself told me that when I asked why they'd throw their purported 'best' away. The more you stood out, the more you put the entire Guild in danger." He stepped back again, leaning against the doorway. "After you took out King Alec and Prince Adrian, I was to expose you, have you executed, become even more of a hero and be made the new regent. Once it was officially clear that no...suitable...members of the royal family remained elsewhere, the realm would seek to crown me king of a new dynasty for avenging the old one. That was the plan to cement my induction to leadership. But instead, you became too much of an unknown variable, and now we move to the backup plan: sacrifice you to remove a liability for the Guild and move me into Alec's right hand, closer to his crown. I will simply have to bide my time until I can take out both brothers separately, make it look like accidents. When matters not."

Lily felt the threatening sting of tears as all of her remaining, unanswered questions fell into place one by one. She managed to fight them back, though, and kept her voice steady and her eyes dry as she glared at the duke-milite. "So why come here and gloat about it?" she asked. "That's such a tired old cliché, Liam. If you've already won, why do you care what I know or don't know anymore?"

"I apologize," he said, and sounded as though he might even mean it. "I wasn't trying to deliver some villainous monologue, and even though your professional failure has cost me and annoyed my plans, I don't actually bear you any personal ill will. I simply came here to bid you goodbye, and to tell you that it was a good game while it lasted. It is too bad it did not work out as beautifully as Gavriel and I had planned it, but then, you know what they say: When we make plans, the gods laugh at us." He turned away, already closing the door as he went. "I suspect you have a few days before Alec arrives. I suggest you spend them making peace with your god of choice. Goodbye, Black Lily. May you find your Robert again after your death."

And then he was gone, and she was once more plunged into darkness. Only then did she let her tears quietly spill over.

Lily was not sure how long it was before she heard footsteps once more coming down the corridor and a man's voice asking, "Has she given you any more trouble?" Her pulse jumped at the sound of Adrian's voice, and she sat up quickly, straining to listen.

"No, Your Highness. That blow to the head seemed to have tamed her somewhat," one of the guards answered. One of the same ones from before, she noted.

"And how do your comrades fare? The ones she attacked?" Adrian asked. His voice was drawing closer, along with the faint torchlight.

"They will live, but the captain vows they'll be sacked on the morrow for failing to protect you," the guard replied.

"There is no need for that. I'm alive, am I not? Tell your captain to give them a couple days off to heal and reflect, then have them return to their duty. I suspect we're going to need all of the protection we can afford for the kingdom, given the current circumstances."

"As you wish, Your Highness. Here we are." Once more the key turned in the lock and the heavy door opened, but this time Lily was glad for the face she saw. Adrian looked healthy and unscathed, albeit a bit haggard. She was not sure how long it had been since her attack at the party, a few hours or half a day, but he did not look as if he'd stopped moving for a moment since. Coupled with the effects of his persistent insomnia, he looked as though the slightest breeze might knock him over; but having lived with him this long, she knew better. If Liam never got to him, Adrian would likely out-stand even the palace walls around him.

"Thank you for your help…Jeremy, correct?" the prince asked the man behind him. The guard nodded, pleased. "If you won't mind, I'd like to be alone to speak with her."

"But, Your Highness, she's the Black Lily," his escort argued. "She's too dangerous to—"

"I doubt she can do much like that," the prince interrupted. "And what I wish to speak to her of concerns the safety of the realm. It is only for my brother or I to hear."

"As you wish, Sire," the guard said after a hesitant moment. He turned and walked away, but Lily did not miss his grumbled, "Never known a prisoner who needed so much privacy."

Adrian opened his mouth to speak, but Lily held up a hand, silencing him. She waited until she was certain that the guard's footsteps had faded and that he did not wait around a corner to overhear anything before she lowered her hand.

Adrian stepped forward, but the look on his face was disheartening. She saw his distrust there, saw how he stopped just out of reach, and she was surprised by how much it hurt her. "Did you do it?" he asked.

"No," she replied simply.

He nodded, and she hated how her spirits lifted slightly at his implied trust in her; but he paused halfway through the gesture as if second-guessing it. "How do I know you're not lying?"

Lily opened her arms as wide as her chains would allow, indicating the room around her. "What benefit would it be to me to lie now?" She sighed, leaning her head back against the cold stone. "It doesn't matter. I will confess to it, and many crimes, regardless of my guilt in them, before your brother is done with me."

"I will not let that happen," he said vehemently, his hand chopping down through the air between them to punctuate his denial. Lily was startled, and a bit warmed, by his passion. "I will fix this somehow, I swear it. You are innocent — which means Liam is guilty and framing you. I simply have to find some way to prove it."

"No, you idiot!" she hissed. "You have to lie low and leave the castle before he tries to hurt you!"

"What? You want me to leave? To just run away?" He sounded offended at the idea.

"It doesn't matter that I did not kill Duchess Sidonie," she tried to explain. "I have killed many others, there is no question of that. I am the Black Lily, and I did plan to assassinate you and your brother, and they will make me pay for my crimes. What is most important is that you protect yourself, that you get to your brother, and that you both get to safety away from Liam."

"Alec is coming here," Adrian said. "I had the castle locked down and sent him word to stay away, but he will not. His reply came by messenger pigeon just a few minutes ago. He will be here in two days' time, and nobody will sway him otherwise."

"Then you must watch your back until he arrives. Listen to me, Adrian." She got to her feet and leaned in toward him, her tone deadly serious. "Eat nothing. Drink nothing but water, and even then, only that you have filled and poured yourself into a cup you know no one else has touched. Many poisons are tasteless and colorless. Trust no one. Speak to no one until your brother has returned. Keep two guards with you at all times, but do not trust them either, for anyone can be paid off with enough gold. Keep a sword on you at all times and do not hesitate to use it. Even if you've never been properly trained with it, a desperate amateur can still pose a threat even to a trained killer. And above all, stay the hell away from Liam."

"Lily, I will not abandon you to my brother's vengeance," he said, closing the distance between them. Not a smart move for a royal alone with an assassin, she noted, even a chained assassin. He really did still trust her after all, it seemed.

It was a small gesture, one he didn't even realize he had given, but it touched her deeper than she would have thought nonetheless.

"You are innocent in this," the prince continued, oblivious to her thoughts. "And you...you've changed. You are a good woman despite your misguidedness, despite what you may have done in the past. I know, I *know* this is true. You're no remorseless monster. You do not deserve this." He reached out and grabbed her shoulders. "I don't know why I care so much about...about an *assassin*, even one as relatively easy to get along with as you, but in the end, you tried to help me. You tried to redeem yourself. That has to count for something. And I can't stand the thought of what Alec might do to you. I saw his tower. Those devices he has to hurt his lovers..."

"Those were sexual, remember?" she said. "For pleasure as well as pain. When he gets ahold of me, it will be different. He will likely call in a professional from the Ergastulum, one who will care only about bringing me pain until I confess to everything and expose all of the Guild's secrets. If you really cared, you would bring me poison." His eyes widened at that, but she continued. "You ruined my preferred concoction, but any will do. Even if it is not quick, it will not be as bad as what I suspect I will have to bear at the hands of a torturer."

"No. No, I won't do that." The prince shook his head, his eyes casting about the dank, dark cell as if he might discover a solution on one of the walls. "I will find some way to fix this. I will think of something..."

"Adrian." Lily grabbed his face in her hands, staring into his eyes. She had never realized just how deep and lustrous they were. In the darkness of the cell, they shone like polished jasper. "All that matters is protecting yourself. You are a great man, and you will make a great king someday, no matter what you say. I truly believe that you are the best thing that could happen to this country. And I...I was stupid for not realizing it soon enough."

She couldn't bring herself to say it. Damn Liam to every version of hell, but he was right. Somewhere along the way, Lily had fallen for her mark. It didn't matter now, and she doubted he felt the same. His concern was due only to his pacifist nature and his misplaced feelings of guilt and responsibility for what might happen to her at his brother's hands.

It didn't matter. The footsteps were returning. They had run out of time. She leaned forward and quickly pressed her lips against his. He was too surprised to respond, but she noticed he didn't tense or gasp this time like he would have not too long ago; and as she pulled away she whispered one word. "Delilah."

"What?" Adrian asked.

"You asked me once, my real name," she whispered. "Lily is short for Delilah." She pushed Adrian away before the guard rounded the corner.

"My lord, your advisors are requesting your presence," the guard said as he appeared in the doorway. "They wish to speak to you regarding the lockdown of the castle."

"Yes, of course," Adrian replied hollowly, eyes wide as he looked at her. For a change, his expression was unreadable. He turned back toward the guard, sparing her one last glance before the two of them stepped through the doorway and disappeared from sight. The door swung shut and the lock clicked. There was a scrape as the torch outside her cell was removed, and then the light disappeared down the hall, leaving her in pitch blackness once more.

Lily dreaded her next and final visitor.

Nineteen

"Terrible," the Duke of Montflos kept muttering. "Just terrible, is what it is. My deepest condolences, my boy."

"Thank you, Henry," Duke-Milite Liam responded quietly. He waved off the bottle of brandy that the older duke tried to hand to him as they sat on the steps of the palace's entry stairway, staring out over the courtyard.

It had been three days since Sidonie's murder and the Black Lily's capture and imprisonment, and many of the palace residents still seemed to be in a state of shock. The prince had called off all meetings and court appearances for the time being, and guard duty had been doubled to ensure the safety of the remaining residents should another assassin be in their midst. It seemed all were biding their time, waiting for the king's return to set the world right and deal with the imposter.

Duke Henry shook his head and took another swig of brandy himself. It was an inexpensive vintage, Liam noticed; the Montflos duchy wasn't the wealthiest in the realm, but they could afford better drink than this, surely. Perhaps Henry was humbler than he first considered. The thought made Liam like the man a bit better, he had to admit.

"Such a young beauty, so full of promise," the Duke of Montflos continued, slouching on his step and

369

cradling the brandy bottle in his lap. "To be taken from us so suddenly, so violently…"

"Indeed," Liam said with a sigh. "The mind reels. At least I know I am not alone in my grief, that many of our peers grieve with me." It helped appearances that he *was* genuinely sad at Duchess Sidonie's death. Besides her wealth, her beauty, and the social allure that an alliance would have brought, she was a surprisingly warm woman in private, and kinder than her icy public front had let on. She would have made an exceptional wife, Liam thought. He would not have sacrificed that potential for anything less than the throne itself.

"It's the damnedest thing, though," the Duke of Montflos said after another swig of brandy. His brow furrowed as he turned his gaze on Liam. "Why in the world would an assassin, waiting for so long for the king to return, attack young Sidonie unprovoked? Right under our noses, so close to her goal, and she tips her hand at the last moment. Can't make any sense of it. I've wondered circles around the thought, and I just can't grasp it."

"Who can really grasp the mind of such a vicious killer?" the duke-milite asked, staring down at his fingers crossed in his lap. So Duke Henry was humbler *and* more aware than he appeared. Luckily, he'd planned for this reaction. "Perhaps my dear Sidonie overheard something she shouldn't have. Perhaps she caught the assassin in a compromising situation, saw her with her weapons unhidden or something." He took a deep breath, then sighed again. "Or perhaps the murderous bitch simply couldn't pass up the chance to take revenge on me for bringing one of her Guildmates to justice," he added, letting muted anger slip into his tone. "Insinuated as she was in palace affairs, she had to have known what the duchess meant to me. I shudder to think that Sidonie's death may be my fault, that her getting close to me is what doomed her."

Duke Henry reached out to pat Liam on the shoulder, letting his gloved hand rest on the duke-milite's coat. "It's not your fault, my boy," he said, his voice gruff and somber, like a concerned father consoling a son. "You couldn't have known what would happen. Nobody will blame you for having sought some measure of happiness, and you shouldn't blame yourself. Young Sidonie's blood is on her killer's hands, not yours."

Liam reached for the brandy bottle this time. "Thank you, Henry," he said, then took a deep drink.

As he passed the brandy back to the older man, he heard the shout from the far walls of the palace grounds. The main gate, which had been shut tight since the incident, began to slowly grind open, heavy chains in the palace ramparts hauling the massive portcullis up and the thick iron doors inward. "What the devil?" the Duke of Montflos muttered.

They didn't have long to wonder before King Alec rode through the gate even before it was fully open, a retinue of six members of his personal guard trying and failing to keep up behind him. The king's warhorse galloped clear up to the bottom steps of the palace before he reined the beast in and quickly dismounted, tossing the reins at a steward who had scurried over and storming up the staircase without a backward glance.

"Your Majesty!" Duke Henry sputtered, rising quickly to his feet, seemingly startled by the king's informal and abrupt appearance.

Not that it mattered. Alec was upon them even as Liam was still getting to his feet, and the king's face was a thundercloud. "Montflos," he said curtly to the older man as both dukes bowed their heads. When Liam raised his face once more, King Alec was gazing at him intently, and a ray of concern shone amidst the storm of his anger. "Liam," he said, his tone slightly softer. "Caught her yourself, I'm told?"

"Your palace guards apprehended the assassin, Sire," the duke-milite said. "I merely discovered her and raised the alarm. We were in the midst of a celebration, and it all happened so fast, I did not have time to draw steel myself."

"You're a damned marvel, man," the king said, then clapped a firm hand on the same shoulder that Duke Henry had been companionably holding only moments earlier. "And I know it's not worth much, but I'm sorry about the duchess. She was a fine woman."

"That she was, Sire," Liam said, then steeled his expression and clapped his own hand on Alec's shoulder as well. "And if you would do me the favor, Alec, I would have justice done in her name."

The king's lips twitched up momentarily at the corners as he squeezed Liam's shoulder. "Consider it done, friend," he said, then turned and strode toward the front door as his honor guard finally caught up to his side. "Where is she being held?" the king barked as the doors opened. "Take me to my would-be killer at once!"

Liam and Henry stood where they were on the stairs as the doors closed behind the king and his guards, their team of horses at the foot of the steps being led away by harried stewards. "He wasn't supposed to return until tomorrow at the earliest," the Duke of Montflos said after a moment. "Why in blazes would he be in such a rush? I'd have thought he'd be more mindful of the potential danger, myself."

"I believe this is how our king meets danger, Henry," the duke-milite answered. "Affronted, and as directly as possible. I almost worry for the Black Lily."

Duke Henry chuckled once without any real humor, then looked down at the bottle of brandy still in his hand as if sad that his time with it was over. "I suppose someone must inform the young prince," he said. "He'll want to know at once, and the king is likely too preoccupied at the moment."

"Let me," Liam said, stepping in front of the Duke of Montflos before he could head off. "Prince Adrian is a rather sensitive young man. I fear he may have developed something of a fancy for our treacherous assassin before he realized what she truly was. Even knowing now, he may take this news hard."

"Poor confused boy," Duke Henry said, stepping back and shaking his head again. "Blast this whole sordid business. Please, convey my sympathies to our young prince as well, duke-milite."

"I will," said Liam, nodding. "Thank you, Henry, for your sentiments and your company. I shall have to take you up on your brandy in earnest later." With a final rueful smile shared between the two, the duke-milite left his companion on the palace steps to follow the king's wake through the main doors.

Once they were closed and the Duke of Montflos was out of sight, Liam made for his own quarters. He had promised to tell Adrian the news of his brother's return — and of course he would have to before long or risk the prince finding out on his own anyway — but the more time Alec had alone with the Black Lily, the better the chance of this whole matter being brought finally to a close. Liam had no doubt that Adrian meant well, but the boy's overzealous compassion had a habit of complicating matters that should have had simple solutions to men like Alec and himself. And now that the plan had been botched so thoroughly, the duke-milite was not eager to see it draw out any longer than necessary. Better to cut his losses swiftly and cleanly and take the consolation prize of having his court status raised to just below the throne itself.

Once back in his room, Liam rang for his personal steward and had an early supper brought to him. He sat alone in his study and took his time with the meal, knowing that no one would fault him for wanting to be alone in his grief. It really was quite a convenient thing, to be known to be grieving, he had to admit. He would have to time his recovery very carefully to avoid seeming too crass on the one hand or too sensitive on the other.

After dinner, and after the plates had been cleared and his servants left him again, Liam sat catching up on his reading until evening began to draw in. Soon, he knew, dinner would be served in earnest, and it wouldn't do to let Duke Henry and Prince Adrian meet at the dinner table without Liam having interceded first. With a sigh, he marked his place in his book and set out toward the palace library, where he knew the young prince could often be found trying to escape from his responsibilities, if only for a moment. And if Adrian ever needed an escape, Liam thought, it would be now.

As expected, he entered the vaulted room to find it empty but for the prince, sitting at a table amid the tall, packed shelves with a thick, leather-bound volume open in front of him, his head in his hands. He didn't seem to notice Liam's approach until the duke-milite was nearly upon him, when he suddenly straightened. "Oh, Duke Liam," he said, sounding more harried and exhausted than the duke had ever remembered seeing him. "Something I can help you with?"

"I would ask the same, my lord," Liam answered, gesturing at an empty chair across the table. "May I sit?" He expected a quick and polite answer in return, but Adrian gave him a long, almost calculating look before he gestured his approval. The duke-milite made a note of this unusual behavior before he pulled the chair out and sat, then bent his head over the open book between them. "Rather ponderous looking reading, but you appear to be in a ponderous mood this evening. Something in particular you're searching for in there?"

Adrian sighed and flipped a page dismissively. "It's *The Hartford Tome of Historical Arestean Law, Litigation, and Sentencing, Volume Twelve*," he explained. "I've already scoured volumes thirteen through nineteen, which is as high as they go so far. I'm hoping

I can find the answer I'm looking for without having to work my way all the way back through volume one."

"Quite the research project, then," Liam said. "And no luck at all so far? What are you looking for, if you don't mind my asking?"

Again, rather than the casual answer he expected, the prince eyed him for just a moment and appeared to hesitate. "No, no luck," he said after the briefest of pauses, turning his eyes back to the columns of cramped writing on the open pages. "Or at least not the kind of luck I was hoping for. I'm reviewing cases of high treason, attempted regicide, that sort of thing. It seems the pertinent thing to do, given the situation and what will inevitably come next."

"I see," Liam answered, but what he saw was more going on in the prince's head than he had anticipated, and he couldn't tell what it was. That he was worried with the case at hand was only expected, even if his concern may have stemmed more from Lily's fate than it should have. That he had suddenly lost the candidness with which they had talked until now raised the barest hint of suspicion in Liam's mind, however — as did the fact that despite Adrian's well-known bleeding heart, he had yet to offer his condolences for or even mention Duchess Sidonie's death. "And you say you're disappointed with your findings?" the duke-milite pressed. "I take it your ancestors' judgments don't sit well with you, Sire?"

"They..." Adrian began, then stalled and flipped a few more pages. Fidgeting, Liam thought. "They are predictable," the prince continued slowly. "What one would expect given the situation. Execution for the convicted, exile for cases where a clear sentence couldn't be reached, quietly increased watchfulness on the exonerated lest it turn out that something was overlooked in court. I'm looking to see if the pattern breaks anywhere, and if so, why."

"You're looking for cases of mercy," Liam said matter-of-factly, which got Adrian's attention once again. "You're hoping to find somewhere in the annals of statecraft an instance where a guilty verdict didn't equate with a swift death, and how you might replicate that here."

The prince didn't even attempt to hide his suspicion this time, his eyes widening briefly at the accusation before narrowing. "Perhaps I am," he said cautiously. "Do you object, duke-milite?"

If he even thought to ask that question, then something worrisome was happening here. Did Adrian know more than the Liam realized? Had he underestimated their beleaguered prince or his role in this scheme? That Adrian may have played any role other than unwitting dupe was a frightening enough prospect in itself. After all, if even the Black Lily did not know the whole of the plan that she was involved in, could the duke-milite reasonably claim otherwise himself?

The Guild had some questions to answer later, Liam decided. At the moment, he turned his best affronted frown on the prince. "Seeing as how she's only the most heinous criminal and murderer in living memory and the one who butchered my dear Sidonie, yes, I can think of a reason to object," he said quietly. "Do you fault me for that, my prince?"

Adrian took a deep breath and turned his scowl away toward the distant shelves. "I am sorry for what happened to the duchess," he said just as quietly. "And yes, I would see her murderer brought to justice. But justice is rather more nebulous than I initially thought." His eyes, still without sympathy, turned back to Liam's. "Wouldn't you agree, duke-milite? You do have rather more experience with the justice of murder than I, I must admit."

He knows, Liam realized, and the bottom dropped out of his stomach. He struggled to maintain his façade even as his knuckles went white gripping his knees beneath the table. Somewhere, somehow, the prince had found him out.

The duke's mind raced. Adrian must not be able to prove anything conclusively, or else Liam would have been exposed to the court by now. Unless the prince was waiting to bring the issue discreetly to his brother. That still didn't change the fact that the Camilla which both royals knew was in reality the Black Lily, nor did it exonerate her for her past infamy or her intent to commit a double regicide. Had Lily confessed to the prince in secret to try and bring the duke down with her? Did the prince still care for her false persona enough, even after the truth came to light, to believe her if she did? Or was there some other clue, some missing piece that linked Liam to the crime which he had neglected to cover and which Adrian had somehow found? Would the duke be pitting his innocence against the word of the empire's most reviled killer, or against the unassailable moral character of the prince himself?

So frantic were his thoughts that the duke-milite didn't even realize how long he had let the conversation lapse until Adrian filled in the gap. "Still, the onus of judgment lies most firmly on the shoulders of the king now," said the prince, leaning back in his chair and gazing intently down at the open legal book. "Since he will be returning soon, and since this matter touches him as much as myself, all are in agreement that he should be the one to dispense this particular justice. I merely hope to bring my own insights effectively to his consideration. My brother and I will have much more to discuss when he arrives than I had initially reckoned, it seems."

And there was the duke's next card, and now possibly one of his last. Liam schooled his mind and attention enough to play it. "Oh, you mean you haven't heard yet?" he asked, frowning. "Strange. I would have thought…"

Again, the suspicion on Adrian's face was nearly palpable as he looked up. "Yes, Liam?" he asked. "Something I should know?"

"I'm not entirely sure that I should say, my prince," the Duke answered evenly.

The prince leaned forward. "And I am entirely sure that you should," he said, and the steel in his voice was much the same as the tone that Alec usually took, Liam noticed.

The duke-milite cleared his throat. "As you say, Sire. It's just that the king *has* arrived only earlier this afternoon. He—"

"What?" The prince rose so quickly from his seat that the chair upended, clattering to the ground with an echoing crash in the otherwise silent library. "Why was I not informed?"

"As I said, I thought you *were* informed," Liam argued, holding his hands up defensively. "I met him on the palace stairs, and he told me to keep his arrival hushed, but I figured he would have at least gone to see his own brother first, whatever he was about."

"Why would he—" Adrian began, then froze, staring ahead at nothing. "Lily." He turned a poisonous glare on the duke-milite, the first time that the older man could recall ever seeing the prince truly angry. "You bastard," he growled with quiet menace. "You were stalling me."

Duke Liam rose from his own seat, stepping around toward the prince. "Sire, I'm sorry, I don't know what—"

"Enough!" Adrian cried, then rushed past the duke with enough haste and force that their shoulders clashed. Liam staggered back, but the prince flew straight toward the library doors. He caught himself in the open doorway just long enough to turn and glare back over his shoulder. "Duke-Milite, you are not to leave palace grounds until I command otherwise," he ordered. "I'll deal with you later." And with that, the prince took off down the outer hall.

Liam simply stood by the now-vacant table and stared after the prince's wake. His sudden anger, and the haste in which he'd left, spoke clearly of a deep concern potentially realized. And Liam could guess at which tower Adrian was speaking of. Did the prince worry for his brother's safety, left alone in a confined space with such a killer?

Or, even more telling, was it the assassin herself he worried for, left to his brother's wrath?

The implications were enough to make the duke-milite fall backward into his chair in shocked disbelief. It wasn't just that the prince still trusted Lily over himself even once she was caught, he realized. No one's conviction in a person could spring back so quickly after such a turn of events, not even their naïve prince. Only one explanation made sense.

Adrian had known all along who the Black Lily really was. And he had kept her secret from everyone.

Even better, Liam suddenly realized, he had proof. When the guards had apprehended her, it was Prince Adrian who had called out the warning about her necklace of poison, even risking his life to dash it from her hands before she could use it. As if he knew he was in no danger from her when he rushed her. That he knew about the poison at all pointed directly to a link with the Guild—and that he didn't want her to utilize it, wanted to save her life, pointed toward a potential relationship that would scandalize the entire empire if it surfaced.

The prince was in this just as deep, if not deeper, than even Liam himself, and the subtle signs all pointed toward a co-conspiracy to eliminate Alec. His original plan to create such a rumor and spread it—of the innocent-seeming younger brother who'd gotten a taste for the throne and now desired it all at any cost and his murderous lover who would dare to try and become his queen—was more true than Liam had realized.

Despite the rocky terrain on which he now found himself and his careful planning, the duke-milite couldn't help but laugh quietly. No need to create a false story after all — the fool prince was going to ruin himself all on his own.

Twenty

Lily was awoken to freezing cold water splashing over her and sat up with a gasp, staring at the figures in the doorway. She'd known this moment was coming, but now that it was here, dread and a fear like she'd never known before filled her, chilling her more than the water currently drenching her ever could have. Did Robert feel this way after he was caught, she wondered, or was she truly as unprofessional as Liam had accused her of being?

Alec wrinkled his nose at her and snapped his fingers. "She's awake, but she still reeks. Again." Another bucket was dumped unceremoniously over her head by her current jailor. She managed to bite back a gasp this time, though it was no less cold. "That will do," the king said as she knelt dripping before him. "Unchain her from the wall, but keep her shackled. I don't want her attempting to attack me."

"Yes, sir," his guard replied, doing as he was bid. The chain that had held her to the wall was shackled to her other ankle, hobbling her, and then Lily was dragged to her feet. She barely had time to get her balance before she was yanked after the king's retreating back. She didn't bother to ask questions, as she knew they would not be answered.

Lily was pulled up a long staircase and found herself stepping into a corridor outside the great hall. She knew that there was a more direct route from the dungeons to Alec's tower, and wondered why they were going this way. But as faces of nobles and servants alike began to peer around corners, she realized the reason.

He wanted everyone to see her. He wanted them to see her humiliation, stripped down to nothing but her underclothes, having spent three days in a dank cell with no proper lavatory and barely enough food to keep her standing, her shift still covered in the duchess's dried blood despite Alec's dousing. He walked so quickly that she stumbled more than once over her chained ankles, and the cold tile of the palace floors made her bare feet numb. He wanted them to look upon her face, to whisper, to spread the news. King Alec had the Black Lily in his castle in chains. He was going to execute the most infamous assassin in the land, but not before he brought her to her knees. The country would both celebrate him and shiver in fear at his power.

Alec said nothing as he made his way through the halls of his palace and to his rooms, but she could feel the smug satisfaction emanating from him. She tried not to think of what he had in store for her. She tried not to dwell on how painful it would be, to the point that she would beg him to kill her, or of the secrets she would spill before she did. She hoped that she would not name Adrian as an accomplice when all was said and done, but she knew that under the right torture, she would swear the king was her mother if it would make him stop.

At last they arrived at the tower. Alec had her hung from a hook in the ceiling by the chains around her wrists. Lily took in the room, shivering at what she saw. The pleasure instruments were gone. In their places were actual torture devices, perhaps delivered from the Ergastulum. There were a select few that she especially feared, those that even the Guild would not use on her during her otherwise extensive training out of fear of breaking her body beyond usefulness. The thumbscrews, the slow bone crushers, tongs to pull out her nails or tongue. There were a variety of blades of different sizes and sharpness. The sharpest ones would slice through her skin at the slightest touch, like a paper cut. The duller ones would require more pressure and leave deeper scars—not that she would live long enough for them to scar. There were a few items still remaining from the last time she had been in this room, including the various whips. She eyed the one with metal tips.

"Leave us," Alec commanded his guard. They did so, and the king walked to a brazier in the corner of the room, holding his hands over it. Lily welcomed the heat from the fire, even as she feared what he may do with it. "You seem acquainted with this room," he said conversationally after a moment. "Especially considering I never brought you here. I would hazard a guess that it looks a bit different than before, however." He waited, but she offered no reply. "Nothing to say?" he asked then. "Well, don't worry. By the time this is over, you'll have talked. And screamed. So much so that you lose your voice. Among other things."

He turned, making his way to her, walking in a circle around her helpless form. A predator circling its prey. "I knew you got a sick satisfaction out of this," she said. "That's why I refused to succumb to you before."

"Hmm? Oh, yes, I remember that night well. What was it you said to me then? That you 'need make sure I have reason come back safe to you?' Well, you gave me quite the reason to hurry home, I must admit. And now here I am, safe and sound, like you'd hoped. Your Arestean has improved dramatically since then, I must say." He stopped in front of her and frowned. "I want to let you know, however, that I will gain no pleasure from what transpires tonight. I don't deny that I enjoy mixing some pain with my fun, but then, so do all of my lovers."

Lily snorted. "I'm sure," she said. "And you being the king had nothing to do with women not wanting to tell you no."

Alec sighed. "Despite what you may think," he said patiently, "and despite what I know some people say about me, no, I've never forced anyone into my bed. Never coerced anyone, either. Some people just don't seem to understand that women can be just as depraved as men in matters of lust, or have just as much agency when it comes to how they wish to slake it. I'm open-minded, you hypocritical filth, not a sexual predator. It's not always sinister just because whips and chains are involved." He opened his arms, looking around the small room. "I'm actually somewhat angry that your traitor blood will sully a room that is meant purely for pleasure. But we repurposed that room of the dungeon decades ago. As I have nowhere else adequate to torture information from you, I suppose this will have to do."

"I am so sorry to inconvenience you," she replied.

He sighed again. "Defiant even when you've lost. I admire that. Had you not made an enemy of the crown by targeting my brother and I, you and I might have actually made wonderful allies. I am almost sorry that I will have to break that spirit of yours tonight."

She glared at him as he stepped closer and ran his hands up her arms, until his fingers found hers, intertwining with them as if they were about to begin a waltz. In a swift motion, he took one of her fingers and yanked, breaking it. Her scream pierced the air before she could stop it.

"You see?" he asked as the last echoes died away. "What did I say?"

"I didn't work alone, you know," she gritted through teeth clenched tight against the lingering pain. "I had an accomplice on the inside."

"We've barely begun, and you're already giving in?" the king asked with raised brows. "You *are* afraid, aren't you? I'm almost disappointed in you. I thought you had a reputation to maintain."

"If I'm going to die anyway, I'm taking that bastard with me," she growled, then glared into the king's eyes. "Duke-Milite Liam was my accomplice, the one who ordered the job in the first place. He meant for me to take out you and your brother so he could fill the power vacuum on the authority of his reputation. But he set me up for a fall. And he still roams freely in your castle, planning your demise. He could be with your brother right now, poisoning him."

Alec smiled coldly. "Do you really think I'll believe you right now?" he asked. "Perhaps in a few hours, I'll believe what you say, the names you give. Until then, you'll say anything you can to try to make this easier on yourself. But it isn't going to be easy." His eyes narrowed, and she could see the cold hatred in them. Any smug satisfaction he was feeling was smothered by anger. "You planned to kill me, you disgusting viper," he snarled. "You planned on hurting my brother, destroying what's left of my family, wrecking the nation I've bled for to raise up. And for years, you have threatened the safety of my kingdom and its people with your sick killing spree. I love my country, murderer, whatever other flaws I may have, and you and your kind have been a cancer eating at it from within for too long. This will not be over quickly..."

Alec stepped away again, going back to the brazier and stoking the coals with a poker, stabbing them viciously as if to vent his frustration before giving her his careful attention once more. She knew where this was headed, and couldn't help a small shudder as she drew in a deep breath.

He noticed. "You're shivering," he said when he glanced back at her. "Are you cold? Where are my manners? Let me warm you up."

As he said the last word, he whipped the poker around and smacked it hard across her side, just below her ribcage. She bit down on another scream, smelling the acrid burning of her shift, then the sickly sweet smell of cooking flesh beneath before any feeling of agony actually seeped through. The poker stuck somewhat to her skin when he pulled it away a few seconds later. It didn't hurt as much as it should have, which didn't bode well. Lily didn't dare to look at it, knowing the pain would settle in soon enough.

Alec turned his back on her as he shoved the poker back into the coals, stirring them, and Lily took the only opportunity she had. She grabbed the chain threaded between her wrists and over the hook that held her, using it to leverage herself as she swung back, then hard forward, lifting her legs in the air and ignoring the pain of the metal biting into her arms. In one swift movement, she got her legs up and over the king's head, looping the chain around his neck before crossing her ankles behind his skull. The poker in his hand clattered to the floor, spilling hot coals across the flagstones, as he reached back and grabbed at her legs, trying to pry them apart.

Had she been stronger, and not half-starved for the past three days, she might have been able to choke him until he passed out. As it was, though, she was too weak, and he quickly broke out of her chokehold, spinning around to glare at her with a rage like she'd never seen in him before, panting for breath. The king rubbed his throat gently where a large welt was forming around his neck. "That wasn't very smart, assassin," he said in a low, quiet voice. "But points for trying."

The fist he slammed into her midsection made her vomit up what little there was in her stomach and left her swinging gently from the hook, gasping for breath.

"You know, in some countries like Ovinurland, they mark thieves with a letter T branded on their hand or face," Alec said, forcing his tone back to casual conversation. "Pirates with a P. Rapists with an R. You get the idea. It only seems fitting that an assassin earn the same treatment." He picked up one of the sharpest knives, walking back to her side. "I think the face is best. That way, when anyone looks upon what's left of your body hanging from the gallows, they will know beyond a shadow of a doubt how you got there."

He placed the knife edge against her cheek, beneath her eye, and brought it down slowly. Lily tried to focus on the stained-glass window before her, in the hopes that she could drown out the pain. The last time she had been in this room, it had been too dark to make out the details, but now she saw that it depicted a red dragon spreading its wings as it lifted in flight. She tried to count each individual colored pane. She didn't get past four before the knife overwhelmed her thoughts, and her cries filled the room. By the time he was done, the cut reached down at an angle all the way to her jawbone.

She tried not to grimace, knowing that would only make the muscles clench and the cut open more. She only half succeeded "There's the first part," said the king as he stepped back to view his handiwork. "Stings a bit, eh? Now hold still for the rest of it."

Adrian reached the west wing stairway leading to his brother's private suite winded and gasping for breath. The guard, who'd been sitting at the bottom of the steps, quickly stood at attention and saluted. "How may I help you, my lord?" he asked.

"Is my brother in his rooms?" Adrian panted.

"Yes, my Prince," said the guard, "but he wishes not to be disturbed. He is interrogating the criminal. If you will return to your suite, I will let him know that you wish to see him."

"I don't have time for that!" Adrian shouted, then raced past the guard and up the stairs.

The guard behind him followed, stammering objections, and finally caught up on the first landing. "Sire, on the king's orders, I must insist—"

As he placed a hand politely on Adrian's shoulder, the prince frantically lashed out, shoving the man back. The guard tripped backwards and tumbled down the stairs beneath them with a heavy clatter of armor.

Adrian barely noticed as he sprinted up the steps into his brother's sitting room and burst through the tower door with a shouted "Brother!"

A couple of seconds was all he needed to take in the scene. Lily hung from the ceiling by her chained wrists. She craned her neck to see him, and one side of her face was black and blue, while the other had a bleeding cut running diagonally down it across her cheek. Her thin shift, the only thing she had on, clung damp to her body except for where it had been scorched away on one side, leaving a black mark across her abdomen. She was crying, and his brother stood, holding a knife, dripping with her blood. Both were staring open-mouthed at the prince.

Later, Adrian would barely remember what happened next. It was as if the world became muted and fuzzy, like he had jumped into a pool and the water submerged over his head. All sights and sounds came at him from far away. All he could do was feel: rage, terror, helplessness, guilt. He rushed his brother, shoved at him, yelling, shouting, screaming, unintelligible, trying to stop the barbaric scene before him, trying to somehow convince the king that if she wasn't exactly innocent, still she didn't deserve this, no one deserved this.

He only meant to separate Alec and Lily, to get his brother away from her. To make his brother stop and listen. He never meant for it to happen the way it did. He didn't realize his own strength. And he hadn't thought of the stained-glass window behind them when he'd rushed in, or how low it sat on the wall, or that no bars supported the decorative pane.

The window shattered under the force of Alec's weight crashing into it. Suddenly he was falling backward, fear and disbelief in his eyes as he toppled over the windowsill, not even enough time to scream. It took too long for Adrian to realize what was happening. When he did, he reached out a hand to his brother, tried to grab him, to pull him back. But Alec was already gone, and falling fast.

There was a sickening crunch a moment later, somewhere far below them. Lily stared at the broken window, frozen where she hung, trying to piece together what had just happened. Adrian stood above it, framed in the suddenly bright light shining in around the jagged shards of red and yellow glass still clinging to the stonework. He was braced against the empty windowsill, staring down. Alec was gone.

Alec was gone. Lily closed her eyes briefly, taking in a shuddering breath of relief. And then it hit her.

Alec was gone. The king was dead.

And Prince Adrian had killed him.

Her eyes shot open, and she looked at Adrian. He still stared out the window, down at the ground. His hands were on the broken glass, and there was blood dripping from them. The weight of her realization set in, and she quickly began to plan as only someone with a lifetime of practice in surprise murder could.

There was screaming, then shouting from outside and far below. Someone had heard the window break and saw Alec's plummet, saw the prince leaning out of the window he'd fallen from. They would find his body soon, if they hadn't already. She and Adrian didn't have much time.

"Adrian," Lily rasped once she'd found her voice. "Adrian," she said louder a moment later when he didn't respond.

"...Alec?" His voice was small. Broken.

"Adrian, I need you to come away from the window now," she said slowly, talking to the prince as if he were a skittish child. He ignored her. "Adrian...I'm hurt," she said, trying to hold back her rising panic. "I'm in pain. Please, I need your help."

Those last words caught his attention at last. He turned slowly, staring at her. His eyes were wide, unfocused, and confused. Lost. If she gave him time to process what had happened, what he'd done, he would break down and be useless.

"Adrian, I need you to focus," she said. "You have to help me down."

He came to her like a man walking in a dream, grabbing her sides gently to lift her; but she cried out in pain as his hand rested across the burn, making him flinch. "Your waist..." he said as his eyes found the burn mark. His voice was quiet and tremulous, just on this edge of panic.

"Don't worry about that," she said as calmly as she could. "Just get me down from here."

He lifted her gently, so that the chain came off of the hook above her, and as he lowered her back down, she collapsed against him. She wanted nothing more than to lay there in his arms, to cry and scream until she couldn't cry anymore. The fear of her impending death, the pain in her body, the elation at her freedom, the dread at what it all meant. It threatened to overwhelm her. Lily took a deep, shuddering breath and straightened up, calling on years of training and experience to put the pain and panic aside, to keep her thoughts focused on the task at hand.

"There are keys to these shackles on the table, next to the knives," she told him with a nod in their direction. Adrian grabbed them, then unlocked one of her wrists with a trembling hand. She had to the take the keys from him to undo the other three locks on her ankles and other wrist. "Okay, now my finger," she said half to herself. Lily took a few seconds to examine it, the angle it had been forced to, and sighed in relief when she realized that it wasn't actually broken but only dislocated. "Adrian," she said, focusing his attention once again, "I need you to take my finger and put it back where it goes. See what I mean? It's going to hurt like hell, but I can't do it myself, so you have to. Just grab it and all at once, in one quick motion, push it back in the right direction. It should pop back in on its own. Can you do that for me?" He swallowed and nodded, and she took a shuddering breath to prepare herself. "I'm going to count to five, but don't wait until I get to five. Just do it on any number, okay?"

He nodded again, gingerly taking her skewed finger between his own. "But what if I hurt you?" he asked quietly, a tinge of hysteria creeping into his voice. "What if I make it worse?"

She laid her good hand on his shoulder in reassurance, and to brace herself. "Listen," she said, "it couldn't hurt worse than it does right now. Just do it, alright? One, two—"

The prince winced himself as he suddenly jerked her finger back into position. Lily's vision went white as the pain radiated from her hand up her arm. She crumpled to the floor as Adrian stooped to catch her again, but after a few moments she could bend her finger, even if it hurt like a bitch. "Okay, that's the easy part," she said when she could speak again. "Now...we have to get out of here."

"What...what do you mean?" Adrian asked.

Lily took his face in her hands, staring into his eyes. "Adrian, we have to leave," she said urgently. "I'm the Black Lily. Everyone is hunting me. And now, everyone is going to be hunting you too."

"What? But...but I'll tell them they were wrong!" he argued, panic rising visibly on his face. "You didn't kill the duchess, you aren't plotting treason anymore, you aren't as bad as everyone thinks! I'll tell them, and...and Alec..." His voice broke, and she watched as his eyes widened in realization. The tears began to stream down his face. "Alec..."

She didn't let him get any further. "Adrian, listen to me!" she barked, grabbing his shoulders and shaking him. "Alec is gone. It was an accident. I know that and you know that. But nobody else will believe it." His eyes wandered from her toward the window again, but she grabbed his face and forced him to keep looking at her. "Adrian, the guards have probably already found his body. You were leaning out the window when it happened. People saw you, and they saw where you are. They're coming. We need to leave, now!"

She didn't wait for him to answer, but grabbed his hand as she stood and rushed for the door on still-trembling legs, pulling him along behind her. When they reached the bottom of the stairs, they found the guard's body, crumpled in a metallic heap in the open doorway. Lily kicked him in one armored shoulder, and he moaned. "He's still alive," she said, then knelt down beside him. She grabbed his helm and yanked it off, then took his head between her hands.

"What are you doing?" Adrian whispered.

"We can't have him telling everyone what happened," she explained. "There may still be hope to—"

"No!" Adrian grabbed her from behind, pulling her off of the guard, and she was too weak to resist. "No, he's a good man," he said, voice rising. "I know him! He has a wife and children!"

"Adrian, he's a witness—"

"I won't let you!" he screamed, voice ragged with a mania that threatened to overtake him at any moment.

She froze, staring hard at him. "You know what this means?" she asked. "If I don't kill him? When he wakes up, everyone will know what happened tonight. That you knocked him out and trespassed on his post. That you...killed the king." She saw him flinch, as if she'd struck him. "If you do this, you'll lose any hope you may have had at explaining your innocence. You will have to leave the palace with me tonight. You cannot stay here."

"I..." Adrian stared at the man's unconscious form next to her, then looked back at her and squared his shoulders. He seemed sure of himself for the first time since he'd burst into the king's torture chamber, despite the tears staining his cheeks. "I won't let anyone else be hurt. No more killing."

Lily hesitated a moment, then nodded, taking his hand and pulling him along once more. They made it out of the king's chambers and into an empty servants' hallway just before the first signs of guard activity erupted. The two managed to duck around a corner out of sight as a trio of armed soldiers rushed by the way they had come, stirring up the palace staff in their wake as doorways cracked open and heads peeked out. With a muffled expletive, Lily changed their direction and improvised a new escape route.

They alternated sprinting down empty corridors and tiptoeing past occupied ones, ducking into nearby rooms and alcoves as necessary, skirting more rushing guards and curious servants. Somehow, they managed to make it down a floor and to the prince's private suite of rooms without anyone taking notice of their flight. Once inside Adrian's personal sitting room, Lily bolted the door and quickly barred it with a chair for good measure. Only then did she allow herself to take a deep breath in relief.

"That won't hold up for long if they come looking here," she said as she strode through the room with the prince at her heels. "We have to pack quickly." She didn't go to her room but to Adrian's, kneeling down next to the wall beside his bed.

"What are you doing?" he asked.

She pushed against the hidden wooden panel, which slid away easily, revealing the small cubby hole between the rest of the wall's paneling and the stone interior. Lily pulled out a large bundle wrapped in dark brown velvet and raced back into the sitting room, Adrian following.

"That was in my room the whole time?" he asked. "If someone had found it there—"

"They would have thought you were conspiring with me, yes," she finished for him, dumping the contents of the velvet bag on the floor. Her armor, two daggers, a mini crossbow and a handful of bolts, a lockpick set, and an assortment of maps of the layout of the castle. Her myriad outfits and disguises were still in the armoire back in her own room. There were no correspondences, for she always burned those after coding them and sending them to the Guild, but the bag did contain a handful of black lilies, preserved by the ink they had been dipped in, as well as a small bottle of clear poison. She tossed the lilies and maps into the fireplace, then quickly began stripping off the now-ragged underclothes that were all she'd had to wear for the past three days.

Despite the urgency of the situation and his lingering shock at what had happened, Adrian still turned his back to her. She wasn't sure if this meant that he was getting control of himself or if the action was a mere habit by this point.

"I need to make a bandage out of something clean," she told him. "Bring me a sheet off of your bed."

He did so, still keeping his eyes averted from her when he returned with the sheet and held it out for her to take. She picked up one of the daggers from her stash and made quick work of cutting the silk sheets into long strips, then bound one around her midsection haphazardly. She was worried that the burn the king had given her still didn't hurt much. That meant that it ran deep and would likely fester, but she would have to worry about that later. The cut on her face *did* hurt with every shift of her expression, but there was no way to wrap it without looking even more conspicuous. Luckily the wound didn't seem too severe, cutting only into the skin and not the muscle beneath, and the bleeding had by now stopped. "Go and change your clothes," she said to the prince behind her. "Put on something dark, brown or black if you have it."

He disappeared again into his room without a word, and she pulled on her skintight bodysuit. It was made of a deep blue silken hose that covered her arms and legs completely. Over it she strapped on her black leather armor, making quick work of it, her hands moving from memory. It was a bit harder with her sore finger, but she bit her lip through the pain, donning her boots, bracers, cuisses, and chest piece. The leather was unhardened, protecting her from most fatal blows but allowing her full range of movement. Lily strapped the daggers to her thighs and slung the crossbow, which was attached to a long looped rope, over her shoulder. Everything else went into specially designed pockets and pouches on her armor.

She was ready as Adrian emerged from his room in his most somber clothing, a dark blue velvet vest over a black tunic and nut brown breeches. It was too rich, silk and velvet instead of the wool or cotton most people on the streets would wear, but it would do for now. At least the embroidering on it was minimal by nobility standards. "Get by the door," she said, and he did as she bade. Lily tossed what was left of his sheets into the fireplace. They quickly lit, and she grabbed a trailing corner before running around the room, dragging the fire behind her. The curtains went up first, then his bedspread as she tossed the burning sheet onto it.

"What are you doing?" Adrian demanded, panic creeping once more through the dull confusion in his tone.

"Creating a distraction," she explained as she ran past the now flaming windows. Hopefully, the fire would burn long enough to catch the wooden furniture as well. Then it would be most effective.

"You'll burn down the whole palace!" he said, voice rising over the low crackle as the flames fed.

"If that's what it takes to get out of here alive," she bit back more quietly. "Stone and marble won't catch, just the trappings. Now we have to figure out how we're going to escape. I know a few passages, but the only way out of the palace is through the gates, and we'll never —"

"No, it's not," he interrupted. "Come with me." He turned and headed back into the sitting room, the issue of the fire apparently no longer a concern for him.

Adrian took the lead this time as they darted through the halls, though Lily had to repeatedly pull him behind a tapestry or around a corner to avoid being seen. It didn't take long for news to spread of the fire, forcing them to repeatedly hide and backtrack to avoid being seen by the servants running up and down the halls with buckets of water and the guards who were now massing in greater numbers as chaos slowly overtook the palace. The two of them huddled for a minute in a particularly deep alcove behind a stone statue of one of Adrian's distant ancestors as a contingency of guards rushed past them toward Adrian's rooms, all security attention diverted to dealing with the blaze. When they finally stepped out from their hiding place, the corridors before them were nearly empty once more.

Adrian led her down a flight of stairs to the unused ground floor beneath his suite, where more relatives of the king would have lived if he'd had any left. Thankfully, this floor was dark and completely devoid of people, most of the rooms closed up to conserve the palace's heat. Adrian took her through a nondescript door, and once inside, it took a few moments for her eyes to adjust to the darkness.

"Adrian, there are no windows in here. How are we going to get out?" she asked.

"You thought you knew everything about this castle? There are some secrets that nobody knows but me and my brother. Only the king is ever told that this passage exists, in case he is ever betrayed by…by his closest allies." She couldn't see the prince's face in the darkness, but she knew what he was thinking. Adrian went to the bare room's empty fireplace, kneeling down. It was clean of soot, having been unused for so long. "You notice that this fireplace is deeper than most?" he asked. "Most people would attribute it to this just being an older section of the palace." He crawled into the fireplace, then stood up. "It's a bit tighter than I remember," his voice echoed from within. "We'll have to do this one at a time."

Lily watched as the shadow of Adrian's legs began to inch their way up the fireplace, and she wondered if he was planning on crawling out through the chimney. But then his feet disappeared, and after a few minutes of grunting and scraping, she heard a thud, like he had hit a solid floor. "Your turn," his muffled voice said through the stone.

She crawled into the fireplace as she had seen him do and stood up, using her hands to see in the pitch blackness. In front of her face, where she expected there to be a wall, was a small open space. The partial wall went up to her neck, though, and it took a good bit of maneuvering in the tight space to get up and over it, her body aching in protest all the way. Lily landed beside Adrian in what she guessed was a tiny room, too small for her to lay down in without her head and feet touching the wall at the same time. As it was, she found she was pressed tight against Adrian's body.

"Anyone stoking the fire would never notice that the back wall didn't extend all the way up unless they stuck their whole face in the fireplace," he said, his voice echoing slightly in the confined space. "From the outside of the castle, this room just looks like an extension of the chimney."

"And how do we get out of it?" she asked.

Adrian turned from her and felt around in the dark for a few seconds before he apparently found what he was looking for. "Here it is. And the flint is still here, where mother and father left it." There were a few moments of scraping noises, and the darkness of the room receded as the prince lit a single lantern that had been left in the corner of the small room. In the meager light, he knelt down as best as he could given the tight fit.

She stepped back against the half wall as his fingers searched around the floor, hooking under a loose flagstone. When he lifted, a whole square of the floor came up in his hands, revealing a ladder leading down a tight tunnel that was, fittingly, about the size of a chimney chute.

"I'll go down first," he said, then carefully maneuvered himself onto the ladder and descended through the vertical tunnel while Lily held the lantern above the opening, giving him a little more light to see by. When he reached the bottom, she passed the light down to him before following, silently closing the flagstone door over her head as she went. At the bottom of the descent, she found herself facing a narrow passage that sloped downward into darkness. Her breath came out in white puffs in the chill air, and the stone walls were wet with condensation, indicating that they were now underground.

Lily looked at Adrian, studying his face in the light. He had so far held up much better than she would have thought, especially if he had the foresight to think of this escape tunnel and lead her here. Still, his features were strained, his eyes still lost. He turned to look at her but only looked through her, and she knew he saw only his brother's face as he fell, again and again. She knew what it was to see a loved one die, how the image haunted the living. She could still see Robert's body hanging by the noose in perfect clarity if she closed her eyes. "Adrian," Lily whispered, unsure what to say.

"Let's go," he said curtly, relieving her of the need.

He led the way once more, though the tunnel went in only one direction and did not branch off as she would have expected. It also climbed steadily downward, twisting and turning, until she wondered how far under the ground they must be. "Who built this?" she asked, as much to distract him as for her own curiosity.

For a long time he was silent, and she thought he hadn't heard her, or was simply ignoring her. Then he spoke. "Three hundred years ago, there was a plague," he said quietly. "It wiped out a quarter of Arestea's population."

"The Crying Death," she said. "I've heard of it. People would get sick and vomit blood. They would bleed from their eyes and nose. Even after they died, their bodies would keep bleeding from the eyes, so that it looked like their corpses were crying."

"Yes, that one," he said, and she caught his shudder in the gloom. "It hit Luceran the worst. The city was overpopulated and unsanitary. The royal family and their subjects locked themselves inside the castle, barring the townspeople out. They had hoped to wait out the plague until the sickness was over. They had enough food to last them for months as their people died in the streets. But then months passed, and they ran out of food, and the plague was still running rampant. They had this tunnel roughly excavated by their guards and servants before their strength could wane too much, shoring it up inexpertly with stone statues and pillars and wood from broken furniture. At the time, it reached outside the city walls, and they could send their most loyal servants out to get food and bring it back. But the person would always be sent away after delivering the food, and if he or she refused to leave, they'd be killed and tossed over the palace walls. They knew that the plague was carried from person to person, and they went to great lengths not to let it be carried into the castle with their meals."

He shuddered again at his family's bloody history, then continued. "After this happened a few times, and servants and guardsmen kept getting cast out into the streets for their loyalty, one retainer decided he'd had enough. He contaminated some of the food he brought back, mixing blood from the diseased into the wine that only the nobles were allowed to drink. Soon, those in the palace became sick as well and began to die, one by one. The royal family reopened the gates, begging for aid from the neighboring kingdoms, but it was too late. They all grew ill. So as not to cause even worse of a panic among those still living in the city, the remaining palace servants carried the dead bodies of nobles and royalty through this tunnel to their graves." He took a deep breath and exhaled slowly, blowing a stream of white mist in the chilled air. "Eventually, the plague died down. Some say it was because the new king who took the throne was so pious that the gods finally took mercy on Arestea. He was a distant cousin of the reigning monarchs before him, and had never expected to inherit the throne himself, but every other heir ahead of him was wiped out when the plague hit the palace. He and his family only survived because they lived on a small estate far away in the northeastern forests and almost never visited the capital. When he learned of this passageway, he had it carved and shored up properly into this long stone hallway from the rough and sagging dirt tunnel it had been at the time. Those who worked it were sworn to secrecy, and when they and the king died, the only one left who knew about it was his daughter, who became queen after him."

His story ended, Adrian fell silent once more. Lily had never been the superstitious sort, but as they continued through the eerily quiet tunnel, she felt as if she were being watched, as if hands reached out from the darkness to brush against the back of her neck. Knowing the sordid and bloody history of the tunnel they traversed now didn't help ease the sensation. She kept her eyes straight ahead, never daring to look back into the darkness behind her.

"We've reached the end," Adrian said eventually. The wall before them was stone and dirt, impassible, and for a moment, Lily feared that the end of the tunnel had been found and closed up since its last use. "Up there," the prince said, and she looked up. There was a large rectangular block above them, made of solid granite by the look and feel of it. It took the both of them shoving and straining to shift it enough that they could squeeze through. Lily braced one foot against the dead end wall and pushed up to grab the edge of the hole, then pulled herself through, emerging from the ground to find herself standing inside a mausoleum.

The stone they had shifted out of their way was the lid of a sarcophagus, and more were laid evenly about the room, each with a name and date carved on the front. She realized that they all bore the d'Arestes surname, presumably those that had been wiped out when the plague took the castle.

Lily reached down into the false grave and took Adrian's hand, helping to pull him up through the opening. Once both were out, they pushed the lid back over the hole, and Lily paused to crouch down and read the name written on it.

"'Marianna, age eight.' Where is she buried, then, if not here?" she asked.

"I don't know," Adrian replied. "Perhaps she never existed at all. It was some time after the plague that the mausoleum was built here to conceal the passage's exit. Many of the events surrounding the Crying Death never made it to the history books, such was the chaos."

It was a wonder that it hadn't been forgotten by even the royal family, she thought, what with the life expectancy of some kings. "Where are we now?" Lily asked.

"In the Old City, in the south end of the Low Quarter," he said. "This tunnel once extended outside the city walls, but not anymore. We will still have to get beyond the walls before news of what's happening at the palace spreads."

"Well then," said Lily, standing and dusting off her hands, "we'd best get started."

Twenty-One

Duke-Milite Liam paced the halls with a faraway look on his face, staring at the floor in front of him as he walked, and making sure that everyone he passed saw a man lost in his own grief at the sudden and violent death of his beloved.

Inwardly, he wondered how long he should give King Alec his solitude with the assassin before seeking him out and demanding a chance to interrogate her. After all, he'd made his name on his experience as the only man in living memory to have thwarted the Guild and extracted any amount of information from one of their agents. He was also the clearly injured party in Lily's crime — or at least, he was the most recently injured party in her latest crime.

The fact that he already knew even more than Lily herself did about the plot she was involved in would make things easier, of course, and the more that Alec interrogated the woman and got nothing that he liked to hear, as Liam was sure would happen, the more impressive it would look when the duke-milite emerged with full details, succeeding where the king would undoubtedly fail.

The duke was nearing the throne room when he first noticed the commotion and looked up to see two of the palace guards and one of their officers marching purposefully down the hall toward him. It was only then that Liam noticed the corridor was empty except for them and himself. "Gentlemen?" he asked as they approached.

The officer leading them paused long enough to bow his head. "Duke-Milite," he said somberly, "I think it would be best if you returned to your quarters for now. There's been trouble. We need to halt movement throughout the palace and account for every individual as soon as possible, sir."

"Trouble?" Liam asked, but the trio of guards was already marching onward, the heavy clank of their armored feet echoing on the marble floor down the too-empty halls.

There was only one type of trouble that he could think of which might elicit such a concerted reaction from the guards. But if Lily had somehow escaped, he would be the first one she came for before she attempted to leave the palace. If this had happened, and the guards were already on alert, then too much time had passed, and he should be dead already. Confused and nervous, Liam quickened his pace into the palace's main hall.

Where he should have met a crowd of visiting courtiers and dignitaries engaged in perpetual gossip, he instead found the room empty except for a dozen more armed men, some of them members of the king's own honor guard, judging by the purple tabards draped over their polished silver plate. All of them stood in a tight knot at the foot of the dais that housed the throne, with the captain of the honor guard addressing them in a hushed tone.

Liam recalled the man's name as he closed on the group. "Captain Lucan," he called, and the easy tone of

410

command in his voice drew all of the men's attention as he reached them. "What is going on here, soldier?"

The captain bowed his head briefly to the duke, his plumed helm held under one arm, his exposed face flush with either exertion or anger. Perhaps both. "Duke-Milite Liam," he said, "I'm sorry, but this is a delicate matter of utmost urgency. If you would please find your way back to your quarters—"

"Captain, with all due respect, I am not simply another overcurious courtier to be herded aside," the duke-milite cut in. "In fact, I believe I hold the highest military rank in this room at present. If there is indeed such a dire matter at hand that concerns the entire palace, I should like to be informed."

Captain Lucan hesitated a moment, eyeing the duke-milite up and down and visibly wavering in how to respond. "A fair point, m'lord," he said at last. "The assassin, the Black Lily, has vanished from his majesty's custody. We've ordered an emergency lockdown of the entire palace as we seek both her and the crown prince, hopefully before they escape palace grounds."

"Prince Adrian as well?" Liam asked, careful to sound incredulous rather than merely surprised.

"Yes, sir," Lucan responded, gaze shifting nervously to his men. "On…on suspicion of conspiring to murder the king, sir."

This time, Liam didn't have to fake his incredulity. "Adrian tried to murder Alec?" he asked, voice pitched carefully low.

"No, sir," Captain Lucan answered, his expression suddenly solemn. "Not tried. Succeeded." He took a deep, steadying breath and let it out slowly. "King Alec is dead, sir. His body was seen tumbling from the window of his private tower. He didn't survive the impact. And several witnesses reported seeing the crown prince leaning over the windowsill when it happened." He shook his head, then ran a hand over the stubble of his close-shaved scalp. "It's not my place to say what exactly happened, sir, but we need to get the situation under control before word spreads too far and panic descends. While the rest of the palace focuses on getting the fire in the royal suites under control, we need to figure out where the prince may be now, and—"

"Check the king's official study," the duke-milite interrupted, half-turning to address both Captain Lucan and his men. "Beneath the coat of arms tapestry hanging behind the desk, there's an alcove with a false back that swings open if you press hard enough. Lodestones embedded into the stone of the door and the frame of the alcove. It takes a second to give, but it will. Beyond the door is a narrow corridor that leads through the palace within the very walls, exiting at strategic points into the courtyard. There may even be subterranean paths that lead beyond palace grounds."

"Sir?" Captain Lucan asked, brow furrowed. His men all wore the same expression. "Sorry, but how could you know of all this?"

"Alec told me himself," the duke-milite lied, striding past the guard captain and up to the nearby dais. "He is…was a pragmatic man. He knew it was conceivable something like this may happen one day, though I doubt he ever suspected his own brother would be the one to bring it about. He needed someone

412

he could trust to know the palace's secrets if the worst came to pass. And evidently, it has."

When Liam reached the throne, he turned back to the gathered royal guards, looking down at Captain Lucan. "I'm sure the prince knows of the passages as well, which means so will the Black Lily if they are truly in collusion. Send in your best men in staggered pairs. One man alone may be picked off by the assassin if he stumbles upon her, but a second shadowing him could escape and spread the word. They'd likely head down and toward the perimeter of the building to escape, but it's also possible they're holing up somewhere deep within the palace infrastructure to wait out the initial panic." He turned then to the man at Captain Lucan's right hand, which he took at a guess to be his second-in-command. "You, get word to the city guard as quickly as possible. We need the walls sealed, the gates locked, so no one gets out easily. Tell them to start their sweep in the Low Quarter—the assassin will likely have more contacts in the poorer districts, and fewer there will recognize the prince on sight."

The man at the guard captain's side blinked rapidly, looking between the duke-milite and his commander, before saluting and hurrying away. Captain Lucan turned to watch him go, then looked back to the duke-milite as if unsure whether the man had the authority to command him.

Liam did not give him time to question further. "Now, Captain!" he snapped, pointing toward the corridor leading to the west wing and the royal family's private quarters. "The security of the entire empire right now depends on quick, decisive action! If you can't see that, find me someone who can!"

An indignant look flashed across the captain's face, but it was fleeting. In the next moment, he'd clapped his fist over his chest in a military salute, donned his helmet, and led the rest of his men off to carry out the duke-milite's orders.

Liam waited several long seconds after everyone else had left the throne room, then took a deep breath and closed his eyes. When he exhaled, he couldn't help but chuckle quietly to himself.

No consolation prize, this. Somehow, fate or luck or both had seen fit to deal him a winning hand right at the end.

He couldn't imagine Adrian actually murdering anybody, let alone his own brother. Whatever had really happened, though, one thing was clear: with Alec dead and Adrian apparently complicit in the murder, the palace, Luceran, and the entire Arestean Empire were rudderless. Somebody needed to step up and take charge of their immediate course, and no one was better situated at the moment than Liam himself.

By the time the nobility would be in any position to call for a consensus on a new regent with the remaining royal line all but gone, he would have proven himself too invaluable and competent for his peers to make any other choice. No distant and uninvolved uncle of Alec's would have a chance of taking the throne from the man who'd held the largest empire in the world together during its darkest hours.

The Guild's plan had succeeded. *He* had succeeded. And best of all, there would be no need to get his hands dirty after all, no final act of betrayal for him to perpetrate. Lily and Adrian had kindly taken care of that for him, it seemed.

The duke-milite allowed himself a small, private smile as he sat back and settled into the empty throne, running his fingers over the smooth grooves that countless kings and queens had worn into the arms over the years. Alec had had a vision of crafting a greater nation, but he'd lost sight of what was most important years earlier in his reign. The new Lord Regent Liam would not make the same mistake.

It was past dusk when Lily and Adrian emerged from the graveyard where the old mausoleum was situated and found themselves in the Low Quarter proper. The cemetery itself was ill-tended, if it was tended at all, with ankle-high weeds choking the ground between cracking, weathered headstones and obscuring what little path there may have been. The gate that wrapped around the cemetery's perimeter was also rusted and falling in on itself in several places, and the roughly cobbled streets beyond were only dimly lit with the naked torchlight of simple lamps spaced few and far between, casting deep shadows across the street at regular intervals.

As Lily stood by the decrepit graveyard gate, checking the sky and the surrounding rooftops to get her bearings, Adrian simply gazed around at the ramshackle dwellings that stretched, cramped and uneven, down the road on both sides. There was no one out on this particular street at the moment, it seemed, but the signs of thick crowds littered his view — discarded bits of spoiled food and the odd stained rag were strewn about the broken and uneven cobblestones, and the gutters were so thick with dirt and other refuse that weeds had even begun to grow here as well. He was momentarily surprised to find the street free of any horse droppings until he realized that this was most likely due the fact that nobody who lived here was able to afford a horse.

"I know where we are," Lily announced, pointing down the street. "The main road should be a few blocks that way, which leads for about half a mile to the southern gate. But we'll want to avoid that and keep to the back ways. I think if we duck down through there…" She turned to point down a nearby alley, then paused when she caught him staring blankly around the street. "Adrian?" she asked. "You alright?"

"People live like this?" the prince asked, though whether he was talking more to her or himself, even he didn't know. "I knew we had poverty even here in Luceran, I knew we had rough spots, but this…Does the entire Low Quarter look like this?"

She glanced around briefly, then frowned. "Much, but not all," she said. "It's nicer by the river. This actually isn't that bad for a poor district — I've seen some in a few of the outlying cities that make this look like an upscale neighborhood."

"But the Low Quarter is huge," Adrian said quietly. "A third of the city's area, nearly half its population. I've seen the statistics on paper, but I've never actually been here myself outside that night we ended up in the tavern. Was I too distracted at the time to notice, or...?" He turned to her, guilt and realization dawning in him in equal measure, as if he needed any more of either. "Lily... *this* is why the riot happened. We've spent so much time looking at and worrying about our neighbors that we've neglected the people here at home. I thought at first it was just his callousness, but now, I think I finally see why so many hated Alec so much...enough even to want him dead..."

"Adrian, listen to me," Lily said, stepping up to him and grabbing his arm. She squeezed it through his sleeve until he looked down at her, then shook her head. "Yes, life is hard here, and those stuck in it resent it. But this isn't news, and Alec didn't cause it on his own. Maybe he didn't give it the attention it deserved, but no one person can take all the blame for the hardships of an entire city, let alone the entire nation — and no one person can fix them in one broad stroke, no matter how much you want to. Especially not right now."

She tugged him out into the middle of the street, then turned to look down a narrow side street that was little more than an alley, lacking even a simple lamp to illuminate it. "Right now, we need to focus on getting out of the capital without anyone recognizing us before word of what's happened gets out of the palace and the entire city is put on lockdown. Adrian," she added, taking his face in both her hands, "I *need* you to focus right now. You've done good so far, all things considered. Just a little further. I promise, I'll let you sulk and doubt yourself and wonder what might have been all you want once we're free and clear, okay?"

The prince swallowed the tide of emotion rising in him, staring down at her earnest gaze. He wasn't sure if it was panic, fear, guilt, or hopelessness threatening to overwhelm him, but he saw none of these in Lily's face—only determination and concern. He raised his trembling hands to place them on hers, steady and firm as they were on his face as if to ground him in the here and now.

And he realized with sudden, sick clarity that with Alec dead, the only person left in his life whom he could trust and who really cared what might happen to him was the woman standing before him, who'd been plotting to kill him since the day they met.

"Okay," he said, then took a deep breath and released it slowly, his fingers tightening against her own. "Lead the way."

They heard the bells ringing out an alarm across the city before they could reach the outer walls. The gates, which usually stood open at all times to allow for free and easy movement and trade, came down quickly once the news spread of the king's death. Couriers rode horses from gate to gate around the city, crying the news to citizens and delivering instructions to patrolling guards. Soon the whole of Luceran was shut tight and people were coming out of their homes and taverns into the night, wondering what was going on and adding to the confusion.

Lily and Adrian took advantage of that confusion to move about the city unnoticed. But there was no getting out through the gates right now, that was for certain. And come daybreak, a more organized guard force would be combing the capital looking for them, and they wouldn't be able to hide for long in the light.

She considered scaling the wall where it was darkest and least manned. Had she had her full arsenal of tools, her ropes and grappling hook and shoes made for climbing, she might have been able to manage it. But she didn't, and even then, Adrian would never make it. There had to be another way.

Lily was suddenly assaulted by the smell of rotting fish as they rounded a corner into the docks area. Adrian groaned in disgust and covered his nose, but Lily stopped in her tracks, staring out at the dark water that separated the Low Quarter from the Merchant District. "Of course," she whispered to herself.

"What?" Adrian asked.

"The Petrichor River," she said. "It runs through the city, it must go through the walls. We can escape there."

"There are gates across the river as well," the prince argued. "The Petrichor is deep enough that smaller seafaring ships can make the journey all the way upriver to the Luceran docks, which means the river gates are secure enough to withstand a naval attack from a small enemy fleet. And they're probably down by now already. There's no way we can slip through that."

"Yes, but those gates are designed to stop river traffic. Ships. They only go just below the surface of the water. Maybe ten feet down at most, so closing them doesn't dam the whole river. We can swim under them." She grinned, pulling him along once more, this time with a purpose in mind besides to keep moving.

"Are you insane?" Adrian hissed. "I just said, the water's deep enough to float whole ships down. And at the bottom of the hill where the gates are, it runs swift as well. It's not like taking a dip in a stream. We could drown."

"You're not telling me anything new, Adrian." She paused just long enough to turn and let him see the seriousness in her eyes. "We just have to stick to the shore as much as possible. We'll travel along the docks until we near the walls or can't go any further by foot, then we'll swim the rest of the way. Adrian, it's our only option."

While she tried to make herself sound confident, when they actually reached the water's edge and began wading out, she felt less so herself. The river was so vast and deep that its surface appeared deceptively slow and calm, but once the water had reached their waists, it became apparent just how swiftly it was flowing. As soon as she was in deep enough that her feet no longer touched the bottom, she was sucked up by the current and swept away at a speed that only a horse at full gallop would be able to overtake. Adrian was right behind her, splashing to keep his head above water, wide-eyed and gasping as the river carried him. "It will be easier if you lay back and relax, let the current take you," she shouted as loudly as she dared over the rushing water. "I suppose it's too late to ask if you can swim with any skill?"

"Passably," he grunted out, then clamped his lips shut to avoid swallowing a mouthful of river water.

"Either way, lift your feet," she called. "We're still in the shallows, so you can get snagged on a high rock or tree branch and drown if you're not careful."

He did as she commanded with some hesitation, and for a few minutes they floated like detritus on the current, until the gate loomed dark before them, a half-submerged wall of thick iron bars too tight to allow a person to slip through and which broke the river's progress into a churning foam. She forced her feet below her in the water, calling to Adrian to follow suit, so that they were upright when they were flung into the gates with the force of the river's speed, each clinging tightly to the bars as the water pressed them forward against the gates. They took a few moments to get their breath back.

"I'll go first, see how deep it is," Lily called to him. She didn't wait for him to answer, but took a deep breath and dived down. She didn't bother opening her eyes—even if it wasn't night, the river was too deep and clouded with silt and the refuse of the city for her to see anything underwater. She felt her way down along the bars of the gate, going deeper and deeper in the frigid water, until she began to fear that she was wrong about how deep it went. Before panic sent her back to the surface, though, her hands found the bottom edge of the gate at last. Lily kicked herself under it, rolling against the rusting iron edge, then hauled herself back up the bars to the surface, knowing that the current would take her too quickly downstream otherwise.

She surfaced with a gasp of air in front of Adrian, the gate between them. On this side of it, she had to hold tight to the bars with all her strength to keep from being swept away from him. "You're turn," she said, shaking wet hair from her face. "Hold onto the gate as you go, it will make it easier to guide yourself. The gap is about ten feet down. If you have to try a few times, that's fine."

He nodded, his teeth chattering with cold, and looked nervously at the water churning around him for a few moments before taking a gulp of air and diving down.

He vanished in the murkiness of the churning water almost instantly, and Lily waited for him to surface. When he didn't after a few moments, she called out his name before realizing the folly of it, as if he would hear her underwater. "You damn idiot prince," she muttered, then dived down once more.

She did open her eyes this time, what little help it did for her, and tried to ignore the stinging of the water against them. It took too long to find him—he had been nearer to the center of the river than she'd thought, away from the shore. She felt him before she saw him and realized why he hadn't resurfaced yet. His shirt was caught on the rusty edge of the gate's bottom, and he was flailing at the water and iron in panic, his air bubbling away from him. Lily tried to yank the cloth free, but when it wouldn't give, she pulled a knife from her belt and cut through it as quickly as the water allowed. She was nearly out of breath herself when the cloth finally gave—and Adrian had stopped flailing. Terrified for his life, she dropped the knife and hooked an arm under him, her other hand grabbing the bars. In this way, she half-swam and half-dragged him to the surface.

When they broke the water again, he was limp and not gasping for breath as he should have been. His head lolled in the water, eyes shut, his whole body dead weight in her arms.

Cursing as she went, Lily let go of the gate and kicked as hard as she could toward the bank, the current swiftly washing them away from the city. The first piece of solid land she could grab was a rocky outcropping, not the sloping bank she'd hoped for, but it would have to do. With a grunt and a strained heave, she pulled them both out of the grasp of the current, then shoved Adrian's limp body up onto land before crawling after it herself.

She remembered a time back when she had first begun her training. Master Gavriel had laid a dead body on a table in front of her and handed her a knife. He made her cut away the flesh and bone, identifying the major body parts as she went. Here was the stomach, here was the heart, there the pancreas, etc. In this way, she'd learned where on the body were the most effective spots to stab to kill, or to strike to debilitate, or where she might cause the most pain without hitting anything vital. She remembered now where the lungs had been, how much force she'd needed to get to them through the ribcage. She remembered how, when she accidentally leaned over the corpse's bloody ribs, she heard its last breath whoosh out of its lungs days after its death.

She ripped open the prince's sodden vest and splayed her hands against his chest over his soaked shirt. Scrawny, yes, just like she'd thought, but not quite skin and bones yet. There was potential here if he could get some more meat on his frame and actually put his muscles to use now and then—and if he didn't choke to death on the Petrichor before then, of course.

Straddling his waist, she put her full weight into her hands as she shoved them against his chest with all of her remaining strength. Once, twice, a third time. "Dammit, Adrian, I didn't save you just to watch you drown," she rasped, near breathless herself. "I swear to all the gods, if you don't come back to me…"

And with the fourth push, water spewed from his mouth, nearly splashing against her own face bent over his. The prince's eyes shot open and he rolled over, throwing her off of him as he braced himself against his elbows, vomiting river. Lily sat back on her haunches with a sigh of relief and waited until the water he was spewing gave way to a fit of hoarse coughing. Her hair was still plastered to her face, dripping water down her cheeks, but she wasn't sure that was the only reason they were wet anymore.

"Good," she said once he was only gasping and shivering in the dirt. She stood on wavering legs and held out her hand, hauling him to his feet. "I hope you enjoyed that little dip, prince. Now we just have to cross the river, because it turns out I hauled you onto the wrong bank."

His resulting groan, pitiful as it was, was still music to her ears.

As it turned out, they found a stone bridge half a mile down the river bank that was thankfully empty. It would have been too conspicuous if someone had seen two soaking wet people, a man and a woman, crossing it in the middle of the night from the direction of the city shortly after the king's death.

They kept off the road after crossing the bridge, following its path from a distance and trusting to the darkness and the high grass to keep them hidden in the open fields beside the main highway. It was after midnight, and the moon was high in the sky by the time they reached a roadside inn with a stable.

Lily headed quickly up to the side wall of the main building, crouching low and keeping away from the windows, motioning for the prince to follow her lead. "We're stopping?" Adrian asked quietly once he'd joined her.

"Of course not," she said. "I'll be back in a few minutes. Stay here and don't attract attention." She waited for him to nod, then snuck around the back of the building. It was a relatively small establishment, fairly empty tonight judging by the lack of sound coming through the closed windows. A light glow leaked out through the shutters, probably from a fireplace, and she was careful to avoid the spots of soft light as she sneaked by. The lack of business here tonight could be a blessing or a curse, she thought; but her worries were eased when she finally reached the stables and ducked inside.

The horses whinnied in their sleep — a stallion, two geldings, and a mare, she saw at a glance. Peering into the dark corners, Lily found what she was looking for. A stable boy slept on a pile of hay, likely there to prevent thieves from doing exactly what she was planning on doing. She couldn't risk him waking up to sound an alarm, but she also didn't want to kill the poor boy. By his scruffy face and the lankiness of his sprawled limbs, she judged him to be an adolescent, near to manhood in a few years. There was no bottle near him, either, which meant he wasn't drunk, just tired. It also meant he'd likely be easy to wake, so she couldn't just do her business quickly and be done with it. That made this harder.

She crept past the horses as quietly as she could, and the nervousness her passing caused in them sent a couple to snorting and stamping. By the time she reached the boy, he was already stirring in his straw. He threatened to rise, but she put a hand on his chest to stop him, crawling up beside him in his makeshift bedding.

"Hm?" he mumbled, cracking his eyes. When he saw her climbing over him, her smiling face inches from his own, he quickly blinked away his sleep and tried once more to rise. "What...who...?"

"Shh." She placed a finger to his lips, then slipped her arm over his scrawny chest, bringing one long leg up his own to hold them to the straw. "Relax. It's just a dream."

"I..." He swallowed but did as she commanded, lying back in the straw, his body rigid but still as she wrapped her arms around his neck and snuggled closer. "A dream?" he asked.

"That's right." She pressed her forehead to his, his nervous eyes darting between her own half-lidded eyes and her parted lips. "And you're really quite lucky," she whispered, her breath hot against his face. "Normally, there are a lot more unpleasant ways I might use to do this."

The stable boy was so focused on her hovering face and the press of her body against his that he reacted too late when she tightened her arms around his neck. Before he could think to call out, she'd clamped a hand over his mouth and rolled to the side, her forearm pressing against his neck, her legs clamping tight around his to minimize his thrashing. He bucked and flailed for only a few moments beneath her before slowing, then falling back into a deeper unconsciousness.

As soon as he fell limp beneath her once more, she rolled off of him, then quickly checked his pulse and breathing. It was a dangerous technique, to be sure—there was a fine line between knocking her victim out and choking them to death, or at least to permanent damage. Still, it was a safer and surer method than beating him in the back of the head and hoping for the best. The boy would live and likely wake in an hour or so with only a sore throat and confusing memories.

Her problem now was the horses, who had been spooked by the scuffle and whinnied nervously at the smell of a stranger in the stable. Lily walked slowly from stall to stall, holding out her hand to see which beast was least skittish of her. When the mare not only didn't back away but instead came right up to her and leaned her head into Lily's hand to demand a good scratch behind the ears, she knew she'd found the right one.

It took Lily a good ten minutes to saddle the horse—she'd ridden horses before but never done stable work and thus had little experience with such things—but she finally got the saddle to stay on without twisting around. It took another few minutes to figure out the right way to slip the bridle over the mare's muzzle. The horse bit down on the metal and shook her head in defiance, but after Lily fed her a handful of oats from a bag hanging nearby, she was consoled, and followed the woman out of the stable and into the night. There was no crouching and sneaking with a horse in tow, so she'd just have to be quick now.

"That's what you've been doing?" Adrian asked when she appeared at the inn's side wall again with the mare. He didn't sound happy. "I thought maybe you were just going to steal us a few provisions. Lily, do you have any idea the punishment for horse theft?"

"Do you have any idea the punishment for regicide?" she snapped back. That shut him up, but she immediately regretted it. She could see the pain and sorrow flash across his face, and knew he was only holding it together because his drive to survive and keep them both safe was still slightly stronger than his grief. The first moment they got to relax, she'd let him break down properly. "I'm sorry," she said more softly as she passed the reins to the prince. "Stay here with her while I get another one."

"Another? Are you out of your mind?" He took a step after her as she turned away, causing the mare to huff and both of them to freeze. When no one came running to spot them, he continued in a harsh whisper. "Horses are pretty noticeable, especially ones that have been stolen."

"Yes, but they're also fast, and right now we need to get as far away from the city as we can before daybreak," Lily responded.

"It's not just that. Lily, this is a family's livelihood," Adrian argued, laying a hand against the mare's back. "When they wake up in the morning and find one of their guest's horses is gone, they will have to pay for not keeping it safer. We can't do that to them twice over. Here." He dug through his breeches pocket and pulled out a small coin purse, still damp from the river but drawn and knotted tight regardless. "I grabbed this from my rooms before we left," he said, holding the purse out to her. "There's not a whole lot in here, but enough to pay for a horse, at least. Leave this in the stable and let's just go."

"Now you're the one being insane," Lily argued, ignoring the proffered money. "A stolen horse would get reported but go largely unnoticed. A horse stolen tonight will be noted as suspicious, but a horse stolen with its value left in gold coins where it used to be? That'll make it beyond obvious who the thieves are."

"All the more reason to only take the one," Adrian replied, but at least he put his coin purse away as he did so.

"Fine," Lily ceded with a sigh. She indicated a saddle bag she had secured to the mare's saddle. "I took a few old apples and some oats from the stable. It would be too risky to try to break into the inn for more. That may be all we find for a while, so we'll have to ration it."

Adrian nodded and gave Lily a boost onto the horse, then gracelessly pulled himself up behind her. The mare pranced and snorted in irritation at having the weight of two people on her, but was otherwise surprisingly complacent through it all.

Under normal circumstances, Lily thought briefly, she would tease him about the intimate proximity, and he would likely flush and argue the necessity of holding her so close, even for his own safety. But now was not the time — if there ever would be such a time again. She found herself unexpectedly sad at the prospect of losing that awkward connection with him, possibly forever.

And then the thought passed as she focused again on simply putting as much distance as she could between themselves and the capital. As much as everything had gone to hell, she still had one mission left to finish, albeit one she'd given herself and which was the exact opposite of the one she'd entered the city with. Disgraced though she may be, she was still a professional. Sentiment could wait until the job was over.

Within the hour, they had reached a bluff overlooking the surrounding farmland, staring out over the open fields with the edge of the forest beginning just behind them. Adrian dismounted and walked to the bluff's edge, looking back at the capital city sprawling over the distant hill, the moonlight spilling over it accentuated by the manmade lights shining all throughout it. Lily slipped down to join him at his side, ready to grab for him if he tried to step off the cliff in a fit of sudden guilt.

But he only stood and stared, and what little she could see of his expression in the dim light of the moon was blank. She didn't think he was thinking of suicide. She didn't think he was thinking of anything at the moment.

"Adrian," she said softly, and slipped her hand into his. He took it and held it tight without hesitation, clutching it as if he were still drowning in the river and needed her to keep him afloat.

"We lost, didn't we, Lily?" he asked, his voice distant and barely above a whisper. "The king is dead. Liam likely already commands the palace. You and I are both wanted for murder. We have no allies, no plans, no…" He trailed off, but not before she heard his voice threaten to crack. "This isn't how it was supposed to end…" he added, quieter still.

"This isn't the end," she said, forcing more resolution into her tone than she felt. "We'll figure something out. Come back and fix this somehow." She squeezed his hand tightly, as much for her own reassurance as his. "I'm not letting Liam win."

"How?" he asked, though he never took his eyes off the distant city. Luceran was bright in the darkness, lit by the torches and candles of hundreds of people living within its walls, wondering what was going on, if they didn't know by now. Soon, she knew, royal soldiers would ride out in all directions looking for them. They were safe, but only for the moment.

"I don't know how," she admitted. "Not yet. But we will. I've spent my whole life getting into places I shouldn't be in to kill people that others couldn't touch. I've made a lot of intentional messes that way." She took a deep, slow breath, steadying herself. "This time, I'm going to clean one up."

"Your Guild," Adrian said, and she felt his hand begin to tremble in hers. "They'll know you betrayed them. They'll come after us too. Oh, gods…" He raised his free hand to cover his mouth, his breathing quickening beneath it. "Guards, soldiers, assassins…We can't show our faces in any towns in the realm. We can't go *anywhere*."

"We can," she said, then released his hand to step behind him. He seemed reluctant to let her go until she wrapped her arms around him from behind, pressing her cheek against his back. "Adrian, I'm going to keep you safe. I promise. You're the last thing I have worth protecting, and I swear by any god listening, I *will* protect you."

Her hands clutched at his shirt front, her fingers digging into the fabric over his chest. She didn't realize that her tears were falling silently until she felt one drip off of her chin. From the beginning, ever since she'd arrived at the palace, everything had gone wrong. Terribly, terribly wrong.

But one thing, at last, had gone right. Whatever else happened, she would not see that undone.

"We have to trust in each other from now on," she whispered. "We're all we have left."

He was silent for so long she thought he had no reply, until he whispered, "That's not true. We might have someone."

"Who?" Lily asked.

"My uncle, Julien. He was…well, not exactly banished from the capital, but asked to leave. I think he was considered an embarrassment to the family because of his…preferred company."

"Preferred company?" she repeated.

"Men," Adrian answered. "When he made it clear that he would not take a wife, mother and father were disappointed. When he openly introduced his lover to the court, they were mortified. I haven't seen him in years, since I was a child, but he *is* my family. And he is the last of the royal line besides myself." His voice, still quiet, nonetheless held a small edge of slowly growing optimism as he continued. "Perhaps… perhaps I can speak with him, convince him to return, to get rid of Liam and take over as the new ruler. He has a stronger claim than the duke-milite. Even if he is eccentric, at least he's not a murderer. That has to count for something."

"That's a lot of 'ifs'" Lily told him gently. "He may not even see you. He may just have you arrested."

"I know. But…I can't leave my country like this. I can't just abandon all of its people now." He began to laugh nervously, and Lily wondered if his composure was finally breaking as the weight of what he'd done bore down on him. "Funny, I never wanted to rule, never wanted to be next in line for the throne, never wanted any of it. And now that it's been taken away..." Once again, he wrapped one of his hands over her own, clutching it to his chest. "I'm scared, Lily," he breathed.

"I know," she whispered back. "I am too. But we're alive, and we still have each other." She released him, then spun him about in her arms, and he turned willingly toward her. "It's enough for now."

And then, before she could think twice and possibly stop herself, she rose up onto her toes and kissed him, wrapping her arms around his neck and pulling his mouth down against hers. He went tense with surprise for only a moment before surrendering to it and pulling her in to hold her tight.

It lasted only for a moment, and when they separated, she saw the same silent tear tracks on his own face. Perhaps she had just complicated an already stressful situation even further, but right now, at least, she didn't care, and she wasn't sorry.

Adrian swallowed audibly, then turned his gaze toward the trees behind them, his eyes much less vacant now. "We should keep going," he said, his voice no longer wavering. "Uncle Julien lives on a small estate to the northeast. Perhaps we can reach him before the news does."

She turned to follow his gaze as if she could see this distant goal through the immediate forest. "Worth a shot," she said, then turned back to him and smiled despite herself. "Is that your will, princeling?"

"I…" He sighed, then returned her weary smile. "Yes, I suppose it is. For now." He turned to cast one last glance over his shoulder at the city and the life he was leaving behind. "We will come back," he said. "We'll fix this."

"As you command, my Prince," she answered.

They mounted their stolen horse once more, then turned toward the trees and headed into the forest. A million doubts assailed her again, and likely would for many, many nights to come. She was a traitor to the realm and the Guild, on the run from nearly all of society, and now they had to make their way through a kingdom that was already close to chaos and was likely about to spill over into outright anarchy. All of it was her doing, and she only had a relatively short amount of time to make things right again. And her only ally was a young prince who'd never known hardship or want but was now suddenly the most wanted man in the country. And maybe an eccentric old man living in a forest somewhere far away, if they could reach him.

The odds were stacked heavily against them, no doubt. It would be a miracle if they survived the month, much less managed to fix the nation they had inadvertently broken. But she was the Black Lily, and she'd built her reputation, misguided or not, on being able to do the seemingly impossible.

As the forest swallowed them up and darkness enveloped them once more, she repeated Adrian's words in her head like a mantra to give her strength:

We will come back.
We'll fix this.
Somehow…

About the Authors

Mandy French and G.D. Burkhead (who goes by either Gary or Dan, take your pick) met in high school in a writing chatroom, where they began working on their first story together and quickly fell in love. At the time, Mandy lived near Atlanta and Dan resided outside St. Louis, so the first few years of their relationship was long distance. They don't recommend it, if avoidable.

After high school, they attended Lindenwood University in St. Charles, Missouri, where they began writing *The Black Lily*. They both graduated with BA's in English with a creative writing emphasis and married shortly afterward. They then moved to Atlanta for a few years, where Mandy received her MLIS.

They now live in Tennessee with their cats, Luna and Phantom, and their dog, Zoe. When they aren't working or writing, they enjoy reading, playing video games, cosplaying, attending conventions, and generally nerding out.

You can find them on Facebook, Twitter, and Instagram @Burkshelf or visit their website, www.burkshelf.com. You can also check out their Goodreads pages. If you are so inclined, they humbly ask that you leave an honest rating or review on Goodreads or the website of your choice.

Printed in the USA
CPSIA information can be obtained
at www.ICGtesting.com
JSHW021551240924
70152JS00005B/13